BLUSHING BRIDES

You're invited to a wedding given by three beloved Zebra authors as each shares a wonderfully romantic tale of love and marriage during the month of June.

Each of these talented authors will introduce us to a special couple who have discovered the magic of love and surrendered to a passion that can't be denied! Join Dana Ransom as she takes us to the Civil War; accompany Sylvie Sommerfield to the James River; and travel back with Linda Windsor to medieval times with three unforgettable novellas that will touch your heart and make you believe in the magic of love!

A BRIDE'S PASSION

DANA RANSOM'S RED-HOT HEARTFIRES!

ALEXANDRA'S ECSTASY (2773, $3.75)
Alexandra had known Tucker for all her seventeen years, but all at once she realized her childhood friend was the man capable of tempting her to leave innocence behind!

LIAR'S PROMISE (2881, $4.25)
Kathryn Mallory's sincere questions about her father's ship to the disreputable Captain Brady Rogan were met with mocking indifference. Then he noticed her trim waist, angelic face and Kathryn won the wrong kind of attention!

LOVE'S GLORIOUS GAMBLE (2497, $3.75)
Nothing could match the true thrill that coursed through Gloria Daniels when she first spotted the gambler, Sterling Caulder. Experiencing his embrace, feeling his lips against hers would be a risk, but she was willing to chance it all!

WILD, SAVAGE LOVE (3055, $4.25)
Evangeline, set free from Indians, discovered liberty had its price to pay when her uncle sold her into marriage to Royce Tanner. Dreaming of her return to the people she loved, she vowed never to submit to her husband's caress.

WILD WYOMING LOVE (3427, $4.25)
Lucille Blessing had no time for the new marshal Sam Zachary. His mocking and arrogant manner grated her nerves, yet she longed to ease the tension she knew he held inside. She knew that if he wanted her, she could never say no!

Available wherever paperbacks are sold, or order direct from the Publisher. Send cover price plus 50¢ per copy for mailing and handling to Zebra Books, Dept. 4198, 475 Park Avenue South, New York, N.Y. 10016. Residents of New York and Tennessee must include sales tax. DO NOT SEND CASH. For a free Zebra/Pinnacle catalog please write to the above address.

A BRIDE'S PASSION

**DANA RANSOM
SYLVIE SOMMERFIELD
LINDA WINDSOR**

ZEBRA BOOKS
KENSINGTON PUBLISHING CORP.

ZEBRA BOOKS are published by

Kensington Publishing Corp.
475 Park Avenue South
New York, NY 10016

Copyright © 1993 by Kensington Publishing Corp.
"Charade of Love" Copyright © 1993 by Dana Ransom
"The 'Right' Bride" Copyright © 1993 by Sylvie Sommerfield
"Ransom My Heart" Copyright © 1993 by Linda Windsor

All rights reserved. No part of this book may be reproduced in any form or by any means without the prior written consent of the Publisher, excepting brief quotes used in reviews.

If you purchased this book without a cover you should be aware that this book is stolen property. It was reported as "unsold and destroyed" to the Publisher and neither the Author nor the Publisher has received any payment for this "stripped book."

Zebra and the Z logo are trademarks of Kensington Publishing Corp.

First Printing: June, 1993

Printed in the United States of America

Contents

CHARADE OF LOVE
by Dana Ransom 7

THE "RIGHT" BRIDE
by Sylvie Sommerfield 129

RANSOM MY HEART
by Linda Windsor 237

Charade of Love
by
Dana Ransom

Chapter One

She wore white.

Reflected in the mirror was the image of Southern female purity: all shimmering pristine silk overlaid with Brussels lace and satin ribbon. Never mind that she was standing in the private rooms of one of Memphis's most successful whorehouses. Cherice Parnell looked like an angel. Or so the woman adjusting the yards of sumptuous fabric over stiff hoops thought as she looked on with tears in her eyes.

"Oh, sugar, if only your mama could see you now."

The young woman turned to embrace the elder. "I'd like to think she can, Aunt Mimi. I know she'd be happy. And I know she'd be ever so grateful for all the things you've done. You've been like a mother to me for these last six years. I wish there was some way I could repay you."

"Repay me?" Miriam Leslie stepped back and dabbed at her face before her artfully applied cosmetics began to smudge. "Don't you talk nonsense to me, Cherice. There's nothing I would not do for my sister or her only child. All I've ever wanted was to see you got the best. I promised your mama and there's no paying back that kind of vow. Except to make it come true. I'm seeing to that promise now."

Cherice was turning back toward the mirror and missed the hard edge of determination that stole over her aunt's features. But then Mimi smiled and was again fussing with the off-the-shoulder flounces of her niece's gown.

"What's he like, this Tom you're fixing to marry?"

"His family's from Albany. They have a shoe manufacturing business there. Tom has plans to go into a partnership with his brother after we're married. Filling all the orders from the War Department has left them in a good position to expand. We'll be living with his parents, just for a while. They're good people. Honest, hard-working people. Papa would have liked them, aside from them being from New York and all."

"That's all well and good but what about Tom? What's *he* like?"

"Tom will be a good provider, Aunt Mimi. He's very business smart. He'll make a good home for us."

Mimi stopped arranging lace and watched her niece's reflection, searching for signs there in the young woman's expression that would betray what was in her heart. Finding none, she prodded deeper. "The man can make shoes but can he make you happy?"

Cherice answered with just the slightest hesitation. "Of course. Why else would I be marrying him? Tom loves me. And he's very kind and thoughtful."

"Do you love him, Cherice?"

The girl's dark eyes evaded in the glass just as her reply evaded with its vagueness. "He's very good to me."

"That's not what I asked, child," Mimi said gently. Her hands rubbed the soft white shoulders, feeling them square beneath her light touch. Again, she asked, "Do you love the man you're going to marry?"

"I care for him," Cherice replied staunchly. "I enjoy his company. I trust him. I believe he wants the best for us."

Mimi smiled a small smile. She recognized a rehearsed response when she heard one. Who was the girl trying to convince with such a grim recitation? It had the oft-repeated tone of someone who'd needed a great deal of convincing. But did Cherice believe it? That was what Mimi had to know.

"Those are fine reasons to marry, practical reasons, and you are an intelligent girl, Cheri. But there is more to life with a man than simple fondness and good footwear."

Cherice drew a breath, looking as if she was about to protest with more pat arguments.

"Cherice, does your Tom make your heart race when he looks at you? Do his kisses make you eager for his bed? Does the thought of being apart from him fill you with an ache like death?"

Cherice avoided her aunt's pointed stare, looking down at her expensive Worth gown as a hot flush of color stained her cheeks. She spoke with a forced calm. "I put aside those things long ago, Aunt. They were the fancies of youth. I have found that a prudent man of sound judgment is far better than one who makes the heart palpitate with his smiles and break with his lies. If ours is not a great love match, it will be founded upon respect and trust. And that's what I want."

Mimi pursed her rouged lips. "How very sensible of you. And how very deadly dull."

Cherice smiled indulgently at her outspoken aunt. "Don't mock me because I choose to wed a man who would not frequent your rooms."

"What's wrong with the men who come here? At least they're alive. And what's wrong with wanting more in marriage than a contract of security? It's my opinion that if the good women of the South had been more energetic as bed partners, their men would not have been so eager to go off to war."

Cherice laughed at her aunt's suggestion. She was used to the woman's bold opinions and her graphic notions that all things could be settled lustily between the sheets. She herself had spent formative years in Mimi's parlor house and had seen for herself where such free-thinking attitudes got a woman. Flat on her back for a fee. That wasn't love. And that was not where she wished to be. Nor would her aunt allow it. Cherice may have lived in such surroundings after the death of her parents but Mimi was careful to shelter her from its effects.

"I'm sorry you don't approve of my boring choices, Aunt Mimi, but I'll be content with them."

Mimi made a noncommittal noise. "If you say so, sugar. And it's not that I don't approve. I approve of anything that's in your best interest. And if you think a tepid arrangement with your shoemaker better than a robust romance, I won't argue. But I hope you'll allow me to send you back to him with some rather scandalous pieces of lingerie. Nothing wrong with a little healthy stimulation within the bounds of matrimony."

Cherice had to smile when she imagined her somber fiancé's reaction to the costumes of Mimi's working girls. He would probably be stimulated into an early grave. "I'm sure Tom will appreciate your thoughtfulness."

"If he doesn't, he has water instead of red blood in his veins. Now stop your fidgeting and let me see how you look with the veil." Almost reverently, Mimi lifted the circlet of white silk roses with its heavy trailing net and secured it upon the coronet of dark hair. And she sighed. "Oh, darlin', you are a sight to behold. So like your mama. I'm so glad you came home, even if it's just for a visit. I wouldn't have missed seeing you like this for all the world."

Then they were hugging each other, all dewy-eyed

with emotion, as close as any mother and daughter could be. Mimi stepped back and brushed at the bell of silk and lace. "Here now. We'll be crumpling your dress."

"I don't care. I wouldn't have any of this if it weren't for you, Aunt Mimi."

"Pooh. I just want you to be happy, sugar. I just want you to have all the things your mama wanted for you. Are you sure?"

"About what?"

"This Tom. Is he the one?"

"Yes, of course."

"There's no other that holds to the corners of your heart?"

Cherice stiffened slightly. Her reply was equally brittle. "No. No other."

Mimi smiled with bittersweet affection. "I've tried to do my best for you, child. What I've done, I've done for you. I hope you can understand and not think badly of me for the choices I've made. I thought they were the right ones at the time."

"Now you're talking nonsense, Aunt Mimi. How could I think badly of you? Everything's turned out just perfectly. I'm going to be married in three weeks. The only thing that could make it better is if you'd decide to come back with me."

"Oh now, honey, what would you want with a gaudy ol' harlot like me at your wedding?"

Cherice seized her hands up and squeezed them fiercely. "You're my aunt, my only family. What you do isn't who you are. I'm not ashamed of you and what you had to do to provide for us. Don't you ever think that. Where would I be if you hadn't taken me in? Living in some squalid home for orphans in Nashville? You loved me, you clothed me, gave me a roof over my head and an education that's the envy of any planter's daughter. I dare anyone to criticize you in front of me."

"Now you hush, Cheri, before you get me to crying. I didn't ask you to act ashamed and I certainly don't expect you getting your feathers ruffled at anyone who speaks the truth. I made my way off what I knew best: men and money. I don't apologize for anything I've done in my life and I'm not sorry for any of it. If you have to apologize for doing something, it's not worth the doing. I hope I raised you to believe that. All I ask is that you take your time and you make the decisions that are right for you, ones you won't be sorry for down the road. And honey, it's a long road to walk hand in hand with your regrets."

"Yes, ma'am," Cherice murmured respectfully.

Mimi took a deep breath, expanding her ample bosom to the extremes of her low neckline. "Now, I didn't invite you down here to lecture you, so enough said." She patted the young woman's cheek, then her expression grew serious. "I asked you here to settle with the past before you go starting a new future. I wanted you to remember where you came from and what you were leaving behind."

Cherice smiled, somewhat perplexed. "I haven't forgotten anything."

Mimi smiled back, hers hinting at a secret sadness. Then she gave herself a mental shake. "Let me go and get those slippers and see how they fit under that new petticoat."

Cherice turned back to the study of her dress. "All right."

The older woman gave her niece one last loving look and stepped out of the dressing room into her private parlor. She regarded the figure waiting there with a cool intensity.

"It's up to you to convince her. I can't make any promises."

"I'll convince her," came the quiet drawl.

Alone in the room, Cherice gave a sigh of relief. She was sure she hadn't fooled her shrewd Aunt Mimi for even a minute. Slowly she unpinned her veil and carefully laid it aside. It was a beautiful confection, obviously costly, just like the gown her aunt had ordered all the way from Paris. Wearing it, she looked every inch the lucky bride. Why didn't she feel like one? Was it Tom? She didn't think so. He was all the things she'd told Mimi he was. And he was also all the things her aunt feared he was not. It wasn't Tom. He was a good man. He couldn't be blamed for who he was not.

Stop, Cherice told herself sternly. She'd vowed to herself not to take this punishing trail of thought. Mimi was right. She had to put the past behind or its shadow would haunt her future. She just hadn't expected it to be so . . . hard. Everything here in her aunt's establishment made her think of what she'd lost. Even the loamy scent of the Tennessee soil made her remember. Why had she ever left New York? There, all seemed like such a distant dream. Here, it was a painful reality.

She was marrying the wrong man for the wrong reasons.

Cherice let her eyes close to the mocking reflection of the lovely bride-to-be. She wasn't going to do this to herself. She had too much of her Aunt Mimi in her veins. She would do what had to be done and she would hold no regrets.

If only she could believe that was true.

She heard the door open and close softly behind her. Afraid to be caught with so much of her vulnerability showing, she reached for a convenient excuse for her teary appearance.

"Could you hand me a hankie? I think I've got something in my eye."

And the moisture just kept welling up and spilling over, out of control.

"Here."

The low masculine rumble brought her eyes snapping open. First, she saw the large linen square proffered by strong brown fingers. Then she looked wildly to the man extending the courtesy. And the way her heart raced would have made her aunt proud.

"Ruben." His name escaped, a mere whisper of disbelief.

"Hello, Cherice."

Instead of reacting chivalrously to her impending collapse, Ruben Amory took a slow sweeping survey from head to toe, his expression inscrutable. Almost frantically she did the same. Her first thought was that he hadn't changed and the second registered how much was different. He was still the tall, elegant planter's son in his light tan broadcloth suit, his blond head bared of its usual wide-brimmed hat. But rather than assuming a pose of lounging ease, he was leaning upon a silver-headed cane. He was regarding her with the same small smile, through the same sultry eyes that always reminded her of the dusky gray skies that gathered at the end of a sweltering Southern summer. His look held that same hot promise of relief. Yet beyond the arrogant confidence of his gaze, she noted lines etched deep and indelibly, bearing witness to the things he'd done, to the things he'd seen away from the sheltered boundaries of his father's cotton empire. Those lines read like a road map of Confederate suffering. And after traveling those byways, he would never be the same. But oh, how seeing him made her think of the man he'd been, of the way things had been between them. And the remembering had her all but helpless.

He spoke first because she'd lost the power of speech.

"I hope you don't mind me coming here like this. Your aunt told me you were paying her a visit and I thought—I thought I'd just stop on by to pay my respects."

Had anything ever sounded as inviting as his low Tennessee drawl? The words flowed slow and strong, like the current of the nearby Mississippi, all muddy and rich and soothing on the ears. A sound that spoke so eloquently of home and of all the things she'd turned from when she'd gone north. His voice alone had her near tears.

"You look mighty fine, Cherice."

He reached for her hand and her breathing faltered as he lifted it for a gallant kiss. His courtly manners had always devastated her. As a girl of fifteen, his deference held her spellbound. As a woman of twenty, it wasn't his gentility as much as the rough warmth of his grasp that reduced her to a nervous trembling. That, and the way his lips moved in a lingering caress along the row of her knuckles. He hadn't done that five years ago. If he had, she might not have left. Her fingers tightened around his in a convulsive clutch. The solid feel of him brought her out of her daze. How could she have been so foolish to think she hadn't wanted to see him again? To believe she could come all the way from New York without hearing his voice or reliving the memories his smile brought rushing back? Ruben Amory was the past she had to put behind her.

And that was the last thing she wanted to do.

"You're looking well, Ruben." The steadiness of her own voice surprised her and gave her the strength to draw her hand from his. The sear of his mouth still burned upon her skin.

"A little worn around the edges but I can't complain." He held her gaze within his, the intensity of his stare swallowing her whole. She had to break from the mesmerizing power.

"I was sorry to hear about your father. I was going to write . . ." She let that trail off. She hadn't written because in that same letter carrying the news of John Amory's death, her aunt had mentioned casually that Ruben was home from the war nearly lamed from a mini-ball, but alive. Alive. Her nightmare of anxiety ended with that knowledge. Cherice had cried a river in relief and was beset by an impossible urge to run to his side. She hadn't, of course. If he'd wanted her to be waiting, he would have said so. And he never had.

Her expression of regret brought a solemnity to his features. He glanced away. "Thank you. It still feels funny going home and not having him there. A lot of things have been hard to get used to." And his gaze was back, both poignant and provoking with a host of hidden meaning. "I guess I ought to congratulate you. When's the happy day?" He smiled wryly at her blank response. "Your wedding day?"

"Oh." Seeing him had her so rattled that her fiancé had ceased to exist. Ruben's reminder made her flush guiltily. How could she so easily forget her whole reason for coming back to Tennessee? "In three weeks." It sounded so distant and so uncomfortably close all at once. Seeing Ruben had warped her sense of time. With the past crowding around her, the future was suddenly an unwelcome intrusion.

"He's a lucky man."

And up from the achiness of her heart, whispered the silent words, *It could have been you.*

To deny that wistful sentiment, she forced a smile.

"I'm the lucky one. Tom's a wonderful man. He'll make a fine husband."

"Good. That's what you deserve, Cheri."

Abruptly, he felt too close, the room too small. She'd forgotten how the humidity of late spring settled in a blanketing dampness of heat. It was hard to breathe. She'd allowed Mimi to lace her too tightly. Having never fainted in her life, she was unfamiliar with the rippling wave of wooziness. It was heat. It was the snug bodice.

It was Ruben.

Grasping for a distraction, she asked, "How are things at Stillwater?" That seemed safe enough. Mimi said the grand estate had survived the rending tides of war. And they needed to speak of something other than their connection which all the hurts and all the years hadn't been able to sever.

"Stillwater's fine. I'm building it back up. It's going to take some doing but I got nothing but time. A war doesn't stop the cotton from growing or the sun from shining. The land's rich as ever. I just don't remember the house as being quite so big and lonely."

He'd taken a step closer. He was rubbing the pucker of lace that eased off her shoulder, moving it between his fingers the same way he would sample the loamy earth; with appreciation and the anticipation of planting deep for a fertile yield. Cherice should have pushed his hand away. She didn't.

"How long are you staying?" His fingertips moved along the tiny gathers, grazing bare skin with a feather-like brush. She didn't object to that, either. In the back of her mind, rational thought was shouting, *What is wrong with you? Stop him. Stop this.* But she couldn't.

"A day or two," she murmured, looking up and losing herself in the stormy horizon of his stare.

"Then this will probably be the last time we'll see each other." His palm was circling the smooth slope of her shoulder.

"Probably," she agreed faintly.

"Think your Yankee'd mind if I kissed the bride?"

"No . . ."

She meant no, don't. He heard no, he won't. But then Ruben was leaning down and when she swayed up to meet him, she realized, somewhat belatedly, that they'd both meant the same thing. She wanted his kiss. She'd come all the way back to Tennessee to have it. One kiss wouldn't make any difference.

His eyes were open right up until the last possible second, then they drifted closed just as his lips touched to hers. It was a soft, sweet kiss, as stirring as the ones she remembered from five summers ago. Kisses that made her believe those summer days would last a lifetime. But they hadn't and all too soon, he was lifting away.

It never occurred to her that she was dressed in the gown she'd be wearing when she wedded another as her arms stretched up to circle his shoulders. Or when her fingers meshed deep in his hair to pull him back down to her. She only knew how much she needed that taste of long-ago summer again.

Only there was no May-June tenderness in his next kiss. It went right by the budding months to a full blaze of autumnal glory. His mouth moved on hers with a seasoned heat and hunger she'd never before experienced. When his tongue shocked through the last barrier of her innocence with a bold conquering charge, the idea of protest never arose. She parted her lips and let him in to plunder the bounty of her untouched passions with a merciless scorched-earth policy, demanding her surrender. Her cause was lost the instant his arms drew her tight against him. Surrender had never held such a sense of victory.

She was close to swooning when he pulled back far enough for her to gasp for air and for him to whisper, "Cheri, don't go. Stay with me."

"I can't."

"Yes, you can." And he was kissing her again with those same deep, foraging plunges that stole away all logic. The only retaliation she could muster was the feeble moan of his name. A token resistance and they both knew it.

"Ruben, please . . . I can't."

But she was offering up her face for the hot trail of his lips, over her cheekbones, across her temples, tugging at earlobes, sizzling down the vulnerable arch of her throat. He could feel her answer pounding there but he wanted to hear her speak it aloud.

"Come to Stillwater with me. I need you there."

Argument was slow to form and faint at best. "But I'm to be married . . ."

"To me. You're going to marry me. Right now. Say yes."

"Ruben, I—"

"Don't you want to be my wife? Don't you want to be the mistress of Stillwater? Isn't that what you've always wanted, right from the first?"

Her thoughts were whirling madly. Yes, yes, of course it was. But . . . but what? She couldn't seem to remember why she had to deny him. Tom . . . "I'm marrying Tom." It was a desperate plea for understanding. But Ruben didn't want to listen to reason.

"Mine was the prior claim."

He took up her left hand and wrenched the betrothal ring from it. She heard it strike the dressing table and roll in frantic circles. The same way her mind was moving in panicked revolutions. Ruben . . . married to Ruben. Oh, yes.

"Yes."

And the moment the truth escaped her, she was overcome with the relief of saying it. Yes, she wanted him, had always wanted him, was dying for the need of him.

"Yes."

And he was kissing her again, hard, soul-snatching kisses, that left her too numb to gather a coherent thought. "Now," he was saying, as he ravaged her damp lips until the bruise of desire was upon them. "Marry me now. Right now."

"But—"

"Haven't we waited long enough?"

"Yes," she panted wildly, hanging onto the front of his coat for balance within her reeling world. "Now."

Abruptly he gentled, and the change of passionate degree was like stepping off the high Memphis bluffs into the wide Mississippi below. Cherice sagged in his embrace, breathlessly, frightened by her sudden loss of control. But his touch was a tender anchor stroking along one flushed cheek.

"Cherice, it's what you deserve after making me endure those long five years."

He said that with an odd quiet and she was of a mind to protest how hard those years had been on her as well, but his mouth eased over hers again, sealing in the words, chasing away the need to claim her own distant anguish when the suffering was about to end.

"Might as well make use of that dress. You wait here. I'll grab onto a preacher and be right back."

"Here?" Images of a church all decked in flowers, of music swelling up to win the grace of God upon them, brought forth that faint objection. She hadn't planned to marry in the back rooms of a bawdy house.

But Ruben smiled somewhat thinly. "Can you think of a better place? 'Less you want to wait."

"No. No." If this crazy rush was madness, she didn't want to risk the return of her senses. Would it matter where they spoke the words once Ruben was hers? "Hurry."

He moved toward the door and she noticed his steps were slightly halting. And she noticed the absence of something else within his impromptu proposal.

"Ruben, do you love me?"

He drew up, his hand upon the doorknob, and he gave her a long, unreadable look. "What kind of question is that? My feelings for you haven't changed since that day I rode off to war."

Was that a yes?

Before she could ask him to state it clearly, he was gone and she was alone to face the enormity of what she'd just done. Her knees started shaking and finally gave way. It was there in a pool of hoops and silk and lace that Mimi found her. One look at the young woman's tragic expression brought her aunt down to embrace her.

"Oh, Aunt Mimi, am I insane? What am I doing? What about Tom? Our plans? I can't believe I've done such a thing!"

"Hush, now, sugar. Don't fret over that now. Are you happy? Do you love him?"

"Yes," she cried, wrenching back to regard her aunt with a certainty. "Yes, I love him. I've always loved him."

Mimi sighed. "I suspected as much."

"You arranged this?" Thoughts were just starting to assemble.

"I wanted to make sure you'd have no regrets. I wanted to make sure a wrong didn't need righting after all these years. It's what your mama wanted, Cheri. And it's the only way I could make it happen."

Mystified by her aunt's tone of remorse, Cherice hugged her tight. "I don't care how or why it happened, I'm just so glad it did. I'm going to be Mrs. Ruben Amory and I've never been so happy in my whole life."

"That's all I needed to hear, honey. That's all I needed to hear."

And cleared of conscience, Mimi held her back to smile excitedly. "Let's get that veil pinned on. We're going to have a wedding."

Chapter Two

They were married in Mimi Leslie's parlor an hour later, Cherice as flustered as a new bride should be and Ruben all silent dignity. If the parson thought anything of the setting or the hurried circumstance, he kept his opinions to himself, aided by the large sum Mimi pressed discreetly into his palm before his brief service.

To Cherice, it was more dream than reality. Ruben tall and elegant beside her, speaking the words *cherish* and *honor* and *for as long as we both shall live*. She never heard herself echo those sentiments. Her mind was a world away, reaching back to the time she'd first seen Ruben Amory almost six years ago. Perhaps this was the perfect spot for them to take their vows. They'd met in the main parlor one cool late August evening. She'd been playing the piano when the then seventeen-year-old came in with his father after a business trip in Memphis. She recognized John Amory as a frequent friend of her aunt's. At the time, Mimi was still working the upstairs rooms and Cherice stayed busy downstairs during profitable hours, dressed demurely and tucked away from the boisterous hub of entertainment. She remembered Ruben wore a white suit and his hair was bleached almost as pale by the summer sun. Against the tan of his skin, his eyes were luminous and his smile a flash of brightness as he caught her stare and obliged her with the tip of his hat. And he didn't look away. When Mimi came to cozy up to his father, Ruben said something to her. She struck at his arm playfully and shook her head. Later, Mimi told Cherice he'd asked about her and was told she was not available. Still, he continued to smile at the blushing fifteen-year-old, not in the leering way most men did but with a flirtatious charm just as if she was a young belle at a late summer barbecue. As if she wasn't sitting in a parlor house, surrounding by half-naked harlots and the sounds of lusty affections. And that impressed her the way nothing else could.

"The ring? Is there a ring?"

Cherice glanced up to meet Ruben's questing stare but it was Mimi who supplied a flashy band of colorful stones off her own right hand.

"Use this," she offered.

Ruben took it, his expression closing in around what might have been a frown, but then he was holding Cherice's small hand in his, repeating after the preacher, "With this ring, I thee wed," and Cherice forgot that she'd seen a hint of displeasure in her new husband's eyes as he pushed the circle of precious metal upon her finger.

His palm scooped beneath her chin, lifting her face so his kiss could settle firm and claiming upon her lips. He leaned back, his gaze penetrating, his tone oddly forceful when he spoke. "You're mine, Cherice, all that you are, all that you have."

Then, when she wanted to sway into his arms to offer all unconditionally, he stepped away. She hesitated, confused by the sudden distance in his manner and by the brusque way he dismissed the clergyman with his thanks. And as she waited, his bride of only a few minutes, hoping for some sign of his devotion whether it be in touch or communing look, her bewilderment deepened. Ruben Amory no longer acted the impatient swain. He was cool of eye and tone.

"I'll be back for you in about two hours. Be ready."

"Yes, of course."

Mimi shot a furtive glance between them, noting the tension. She placed a gentle hand on her niece's arm. "Come, sugar. Let me help you get out of your gown. Mr. Amory, help yourself to a glass of something soothing before you go." Then she was shooing Cherice from the room and closing the door behind them.

Mimi made quick work of the small buttons as if she wasn't of a mind to linger. When the gown was opened, she pressed a scented cheek to her niece's and bid her to take her time in changing. Then she slipped from the room without another word and, again, closed the door.

Cherice stepped out of the frothy gown and carefully laid it out across her aunt's bed. Her fingers were shaking as the impact of all she'd done sank in upon her. She'd have to wire Tom. What kind of explanation could she possibly give? That she'd run into her old beau and had been consumed by rekindled passions? Wasn't that exactly what had occurred? It had happened so fast. Even now she was unable to fully grasp the fact that she was a wedded woman. Married to Ruben

Amory and Stillwater. About to repack her bags and head off toward a surprising new chapter in her life, one she'd considered closed behind her years ago. And when she thought of what lay ahead with Ruben, she could form no lasting regret about leaving Tom with only a vague excuse and the return of his ring. If she'd truly loved him, it wouldn't have been that easy. It would have been as traumatic as the day she'd left Tennessee behind.

Enough, she told herself. She had to get ready. She was anxious to get to her new home. Try as she might, her unsteady fingers couldn't coax cooperation from the snarl of her corset lacings. Rather than struggle to the point of suffocation, she decided to relent and ask for her aunt's assistance. But as soon as she reached the door, the sound of voices drew her up short. Mimi and Ruben. And the topic of their converse held her as if paralyzed.

"Did you see to the transfer?"

"All the funds are in your account, Mr. Amory. Just as we agreed. And now you'll see to your part of the bargain?"

"I married her, didn't I? She'll be my wife, have my name and my home. What more did you want?"

"I want you to love her."

Ruben laughed, a soft, harsh sound. "Even if I were to put a price on my affections, you couldn't afford them, Miss Mimi. I'm quite satisfied with the sum you've supplied already. It's enough to get Stillwater working again and that's the only thing I care about at the moment."

"Then at least let me have your promise that you'll not make her unhappy."

"Miss Mimi, ours was a business arrangement, pure and simple. I bought my plantation a future and you bought your niece a name. She's nothing to me beyond that, except for the begetting of an heir. Other than that, she can do as she pleases. Discreetly, of course."

"How like your father you've become, Ruben."

"Don't talk to me about my father. You were nothing more than his concubine. My mama has his house and his lands and his name."

"Ask her someday if she would have traded those fine things for the love he gave to me."

"Madame, I think our dealings are through. Have her ready when I get back."

Mimi's features were still pulled with consternation when she entered the dressing room. She came up abruptly when she saw Cherice's face. "You heard." Her tone reflected the regret flooding her expression. "I'd hoped you wouldn't find out."

"You didn't think I'd discover my new husband only married me for money?" Cherice was surprised by how calm she sounded. She didn't think anything could hurt as badly as learning Ruben had left for the battlefield without even bothering to say goodbye. But this did. This went beyond hurt to a level she couldn't begin to describe in terms of pain. "How much did you have to pay him?"

"Now, sugar—"

"How much? I'll reimburse you every cent if it takes me the rest of my life."

"Now, Cheri, don't go on so."

"Don't go on? Merciful heavens, Aunt Mimi, whatever were you thinking? Did you truly believe I would go along with such a horrid scheme?"

"No need to make it sound ugly."

"Ugly? It's vile. It's a lie."

"It's business, honey. And I know about men and business. You said yourself that you loved the man."

"But I didn't ask you to buy him for me." Cherice whirled away, emotions thickening to the point of choking her. No wonder he hadn't said he loved her. He hadn't lied, not exactly. Some consolation. She squeezed her eyes shut against the burn of tears. She flinched away as gentle hands capped her shoulders.

"Cheri, I did it for your mama. Her last wish was for you to have yourself a fine name. You think about it. She'd be proud as all get out to see you as an Amory."

Cherice jerked away. "I don't want to be an Amory."

"That's not what you said a little bit ago."

"It wasn't the name. It was—"

"Ruben? Well, honey, you have him."

The distraught young woman spun on her heels. "What good is having him if he doesn't want me?"

Mimi chuckled. "Oh, sugar, that man wants you plenty or I don't know nothing about the species. He's just got himself a whole load full of his daddy's pride to get over. He'll come around. With the right kind of persuasion."

Cherice dropped down on the edge of the settee and mourned, "Oh, Aunt Mimi, how could you do this to me?"

"I did it for you, child. I owed you this chance for happiness with him. You were so very young and he was going off to fight with no guarantee of coming home. I did what I thought best for you."

Cherice sniffed miserably and peered up at her aunt through misty eyes. "What are you talking about?"

"I'm not so much paying him to wed you as I am returning what was paid me long ago. By his mama." Now she had her niece's full attention. "Sugar, you have to understand things the way they were. I was working a trade. I couldn't afford to house you somewhere respectable and I couldn't stand to see you blossoming in such a disreputable place. A whorehouse is no place for a young lady looking to better herself. When Miss Lilith offered me money to send you away, up north to where you'd be safe from the horrors of the war, where you could get yourself a fine education and become a fine lady, I had to take it."

"When did all this happen?" Cherice demanded in a constricted voice.

"When Ruben enlisted in the army. His mama was afraid he meant to offer for you before he left and she paid me well to see the two of you never got together. She said she couldn't allow the family's impeccable bloodlines to be tainted by such an alliance." Mimi made an uncharitable noise.

"You took her money."

"I had to, child. It was the only way I could get you away from this. You and Ruben were both so young. You didn't know nothing about life. He was all eager to go off and kill himself a passel of Yankees and you were so starry-eyed, you never would have survived it if he hadn't come back. I wanted you to have the chance to learn, to experience good things before you learned all there was to know about grief firsthand. Since the start of that damned war, all I ever saw was grief. And not a day went by that I wasn't thankful I took the money from Mrs. High-and-Mighty." Mimi spared a sly smile of speculation. "What I wouldn't give to see her face when her boy tells her who's coming home as his bride."

And just for a moment, Cherice put aside her hurt to imagine it. Lilith Amory was one of the society pure: the ultimate Southern hostess, all full of oozing charm and gentility. And the niece of a Memphis harlot hadn't been good enough in Ruben's mother's eyes. Cherice thought of all the anguish she'd suffered because of the woman's planter-class snobbery. It was fine that her husband frequented a brothel but heaven help their pristine image if her son brought one of the fallen creatures home to soil their honor.

Had Ruben been ready to offer for her in those final hours before the war? If so, Lilith Amory's pride had cost her five years and brought back the sweet man she'd loved in the guise of an indifferent schemer. Someone should pay for those losses. For all the dreadful sorrow she'd suffered thinking he hadn't cared for her at all. For making her face five years of loneliness away from all she knew and loved. For nearly causing her to throw away all hope of happiness with a man she didn't love. Lilith Amory had no monopoly on pride. However, as badly used as Cherice felt, it wasn't bad enough to goad her into relinquishing her chance to be Ruben Amory's bride. There had to be a way to make him regret having deceived her and to humble his haughty mother into paying for her interference. And Cherice was just beginning to realize how she was going to collect.

"So, she wanted to spare her family the disgrace of having me as a daughter-in-law."

Mimi gave her niece a close look. "Now, Cheri, what are you thinking?"

"I'm thinking that the Amorys must have taken a big step down to come knocking at our door for salvation."

"Pride goeth before a fall, they say," Mimi murmured. She watched a good healthy color return to the girl's face. And a glint of fire spark her eyes. Cherice began to smile.

"Well, if the Amorys have fallen far enough to take a whore's money to save themselves, I think they should get exactly what they've paid for."

"You what?"

His mother's shriek rang through the near-empty halls of Stillwater. Ruben could swear he saw the murky prisms on the tarnished chandelier shivering. Calmly he walked past the apoplectic woman. "I married Cherice Parnell." He was heading for the front sitting room, anxious to pour down some bourbon to ease the ache in his leg. Riding any distance was still hard on the healing wound. And the liquor would help him swallow down his mother's tirade, too. He was forced to halt when she grabbed onto his sleeve. There was nothing frail about her grip.

"Tell me you didn't! Ruben, you couldn't have done such a thing!"

"It's already done, Mama."

"Why? Why? Haven't I suffered enough? What have I done to deserve this final humiliation?"

Ruben covered her fingers with his own, patting gently, then firmly prying them off. "I've listened to nothing since I've been home but your complaints about having no money, no means to restore Stillwater. Now you do. My wife comes with a most generous dowry, enough to satisfy Stillwater's needs inside and out. All I'm asking is for you to make her feel welcome."

"Welcome? You bring a whore into my home and ask me to draw her to my bosom like family? Well, I won't!"

"Cherice is no whore," Ruben gritted out with a dangerous degree of quiet. His mother paid it no heed.

"You know where she's lived, and who knows what she's done while living up there amongst those Yankees. I'd rather invite Abe Lincoln's ghost into my parlor than have that woman defile my home. I won't have it, Ruben. I will not let her cross the threshold."

"You will and you'll do it with a smile."

Lilith Amory took a step back. Her son's sudden forcefulness startled her, but she was determined to stand her ground on this oh-so-important issue. "Think of the scandal. Ruben, your father—"

"Would applaud me for doing whatever necessary to

see we keep our lands and food on our table. My father isn't here. I wish he were but he's not. I'm the master of Stillwater now. I make the decisions regarding what goes on here and I expect you to abide by them."

She stared up at him and for the first time realized she'd lost all authority over him. He was no longer her boy, subject to her rule. He'd stepped into his father's place and as such demanded subservience of all who lived within his realm. That was what she was raised to believe. That was the way she'd raised her son. And so, she took a deep composing breath and muttered, "Very well, Ruben."

Sensing his victory in this first test of his power, Ruben was wise enough to be gracious. "Thank you, Mama." He leaned forward to lightly kiss her cheek and she endured it stoically. "It won't be so bad having her here. Cherice is very much a lady and none who meet her need know of her prior circumstance. She won't be an embarrassment to you. I promise."

Ruben Amory swallowed the promise he had made to his mother the moment he doffed his hat in Mimi's parlor and set eyes on his new bride.

"I'm ready, Ruben."

His mama was going to die. After she'd killed him first.

Cherice Parnell-Amory came down the bawdy house stairs wearing more fringe than most buggy tops. It shimmied and swayed over acres of the brightest orange satin he'd ever seen. She was painted up like a circus wagon. Wondering what the hell had happened to the serenely lovely bride he'd taken only hours ago, Ruben stood his ground as she minced up to him with coquettish little steps to send bare arms gliding over his shoulders.

"I thought you'd never get here," she scolded with a huskiness that tightened everything inside him. Lips the same glaring hue as her gown fastened over his for a long, sucking kiss as fringe wiggled suggestively against him. Instead of the 'Let's go upstairs' her actions intimated, she purred, 'Let's go home.'" And that was enough to douse his ardor quick. Because he was bringing this woman into his mama's house. There had to be some way of lessening the damage. He uncurled Cherice's arms and held her back. She was looking up at him through eyes weighted to a seductive half-mast by cosmetics. A healthy response rippled beneath his proper revulsion.

"Maybe you should change first," he suggested diplomatically.

She glanced down at the indecent amount of white bosom then back up to him in surprise. "This is the going-away dress I had made special for Tom. Of course, I won't be going away with him now, will I? It's all the rage where I worked in New York City."

Worked. Ruben went stiff at the connotation of that word. Had his new wife been plying her aunt's trade up north? His mother hinted at it. The garish gown all but screamed it. But he was hanging on rather desperately to the sweet way she'd melted in his arms beneath that first kiss. Or was Cherice Parnell as good at playacting as her manipulating aunt? Which was the real Cherice? The dainty innocent? Or the brazen creature rubbing against him? It shouldn't have mattered if the bold claims he'd made that day were true. But it did.

Cherice shifted her shoulders to send the fringe dancing wickedly. "This is one of my more modest gowns. For the solemness of the occasion, don't you know. I want everyone who sees us to be impressed by how fine we look together. I'm an Amory now and I want to look the part."

Ruben gritted his teeth. He wondered if he should throw a blanket over her. The color of her dress would scare horses on the main street.

"Cheri, honey, here are the rest of your things." Mimi swept down the stairs, leading an entourage of her fallen sisterhood who each carried a bulging bag. "Put them out in the carriage, girls."

As the harlots passed, they eyed him flirtatiously and murmured their congratulations. At his side, Cherice hugged his arm, beaming possessively.

"Good for you, Cheri."

"Treat her right, Mr. Ruben."

"At least you won't have to tell her what to do on your wedding night."

That brought gales of raucous laughter from the women.

"Think of all the money you'll be saving by staying home at night," came another crude observation. "You won't need to come to places like this anymore. Will he, Cheri?"

"Ladies," Mimi chastised mildly. "Don't embarrass Mr. Amory. I'm sure he's considered his good fortune."

He was considering a lot of things and he wasn't particularly pleased by any of them.

"Don't wear him out on the first night, Cherice," came a parting call as the women filed back up the stairs. "There won't be any more waiting in the parlor to take his place."

Laughter trailed down from the rooms above, and Cherice sidled up to her new husband with a flicker of her lashes. "Let's go, sugar. I want to get started on the honeymoon." Her hand stroked up his inner thigh. "I'm going to be the wife you deserve."

And Cherice carefully veiled a gleam of malicious promise with the droop of her lids.

Chapter Three

Lilith Amory greeted her new daughter-in-law with a smile as stiff as lockjaw.

She saw the dress as soon as they turned down the drive. It grew worse as they drew nearer. By the time Ruben pulled in the horses, Lilith was white with horror. But she was smiling. Her son had brought every gentlewoman's nightmare to her door. Cherice Parnell, oh, she couldn't bear to think of her as an Amory, was a vulgar creature of the most obvious sort with her teased hair and gaudy fringes. And that dress. She would die of shame if any of their friends had seen Ruben's new wife wrapped up in such a tasteless package. The sooner they got the bold hussy behind closed doors, the better. She kept reminding herself of the fortune that accompanied the travesty of a marriage. It would save their home but, she began to fear, at the cost of their family dignity.

She'd been right to drive the woman away all those years ago. If only Cherice had stayed gone.

Cherice didn't see Ruben's mother at first. She was too stunned by the condition of the house. When she'd first met Ruben, she used to sneak over to the edges of Stillwater and gaze dreamily at the big house. With its pale slave brick and soaring columns, it was the bastion of Southern success and she'd longed to live within its walls. But years of neglect and near abandonment had dulled that look of prosperity. Paint was peeling, weeds ran rampant, carefully trained hedges encroached upon the unkept lawn. All at once Cherice realized the desperation driving the Amory family and she was not unmoved by it.

Until she looked upon Lilith Amory's superior countenance and was thrust back into the role she played. She could afford no sympathies. These people hadn't asked for them. They hadn't asked for a helping hand. They'd tricked her into giving aid and she must be cautious in her compassion. And she vowed to make them work for every scrap of her charity.

Ruben reached up for her, his expression carefully masked. Cherice let her palms wander over the firm line of his shoulders just until he stiffened in awareness of what she was doing. Then she smiled and allowed him to swing her down. She wouldn't be put easily aside. Instead she leaned into him so that their bodies were flush as she slid along him all the way to the ground. So he didn't care about her. Then why did his eyes darken to that particular shade of slate and his fingers tighten ever so possessively at her waist? And Cherice could see the wisdom in her aunt's words. Ruben Amory wanted her plenty. He just wasn't ready to admit it. Until he did, she refused to show him mercy.

"Welcome to Stillwater," Lilith managed with a thin veneer of the polite if not the hospitable. Then she went rigid as Cherice cast her arms impulsively about her new mother-in-law and hugged.

"Oh, thank you. I can't tell you how much it means to me to hear you say that. Why, I'm sure we'll be as close as mother and daughter in no time."

Over the young woman's shoulder, Lilith fixed her

son with a felling glare. Ruben pretended not to see it as he went to see to his bride's mountain of luggage.

Cherice leaned back and cast a dismayed eye over the elder woman's gown. "Oh, dear me. I can see we'll have to get you some new things. It looks like you've been wearing that ol' dress since the occupation."

"I have," Lilith said stonily. "There was no money for things of a frivolous nature."

"But that's all going to change. All that I have is yours, right, Ruben?"

"I'll start taking these things upstairs." He had several of her bags shouldered and looked anxious for a reason to escape. When he passed her, Cherice patted his rump and warned playfully, "Don't strain anything useful, sugar. We've got to start working on providing you with heirs."

Mother and son winced simultaneously.

If the house was decrepit on the outside, the interior was even less inviting. It was almost stripped bare of its haughty elegance, more a shell than a showplace. Were things so bad they'd had to sell off the furniture? Cherice wondered. She thought of the heirlooms, the family mementoes, the imported knickknacks that must have graced the faded walls. How sad a documentation of the times. Lilith was watching her warily as if expecting her to make for the silver, if there was any left.

Cherice summed it all up in a sentence. "How ironic that my aunt and I should come to such good fortune while yours has gone into decline. T'would seem you have little more than pride to cling to."

"It's more than some can claim."

Cherice smiled at the stiff-backed woman as she marched ahead into the parlor. Plenty of pride left beneath this roof. She stopped and examined the room. "I can't wait to get started."

Lilith eyed her suspiciously. "Started doing what?"

"Redecorating, of course. This old place could use a little color and warmth. Orange is my favorite color. Maybe orange—"

"No!"

Cherice pursed her lips. "Perhaps you're right. Red for the front rooms. I like a room to make a striking first impression, don't you? My Aunt Mimi has a way with decorating. I'll ask her opinion. Red." She nodded, pretending not to hear the crack of Lilith Amory's molars. "And while I was up north I grew particularly fond of artwork. There were these life-sized cupids all gilt-covered and, shall we say, in a natural state. Cupids on either side of the arch." She sighed expressively. "Oh, this is going to be such fun."

"Ruben, I am going to murder that creature!"

"Now, Mama—"

"Don't 'now, Mama' me! She wants to have naked cupids fornicating in the front room!" When the suggestion of a smile started on her son's lips, she lost all patience. "What are you going to do about it? I will not have my home made over into a bordello!"

"And when have you ever seen the inside of a bordello to make such a comparison, madame?"

"Do not mock me, Ruben. This is not at all amusing."

"Perhaps all she needs is some guidance in the proper direction."

"How about to the front door?"

"The inside of a bordello is preferable to the outside of the poor house. Remember that when you think you've reached the end of your endurance."

"I'm not so sure."

"Then you have my blessing if you'd like to see for yourself."

Lilith stood fuming across the desk from her son. He

wasn't taking it seriously. Worse, he wasn't the least bit concerned. "Ruben, why are you taking her side against me?" She sighed dramatically and conceived a convenient well of tears. He wasn't sufficiently impressed.

"Mama, I have a warehouse full of cotton to sell. I've got fields lying fallow and no one to work them. I've got a roof leaking over our very heads. Forgive me if I can't get all worked up over a few cavorting cupids. You and Cherice will just have to work this out between the two of you. It is her money, after all. It's up to you to see she spends it wisely."

Lilith's eyes narrowed fiercely. "You wouldn't be half so smug if she said she was planning to sell off half our acres to carpetbaggers."

All traces of humor were gone in an instant. "I suspect she is a bit too wise to interfere in my business. Now if there is nothing else—"

"Forgive me for bothering you with my complaints."

The pain of her bruised dignity finally reached him and he leaned back in his chair. "Mama, I wish it didn't have to be this way. I'm sorry if you find her a trial. I'm doing everything I can to get us back on our feet. Can't you support me in this? It'll get better."

"And if it doesn't?" Their wills held in a silent challenge, then Lilith backed down with a massive moan. "Oh, very well, I shall try. At least I have good breeding to fall back on."

Ruben smiled, but she wasn't at all certain he wasn't making fun of her when he should have been nodding in agreement. With all her considerable poise, she withdrew from the room. Time would convince him that she was right. That she'd been right all along.

Ruben closed his eyes and let his head fall back against the poorly padded chair cushion. This was not going well. When Miriam Leslie had come to him with her offer, it had sounded so simple. A merger to their mutual benefit. How difficult could it be to take Cherice as a wife if it meant restoring his beloved home? It had been his own intention at one time. If only she'd answered his note those many years ago. Even if it were to reject his offer. That he could have stood with better grace than the humiliation of waiting in the rain for three hours only to learn she'd left for New York on the morning train. How could she have cared so little to have hurt him so badly? He never got his answer to that. He'd ridden out with his unit the next morning. And the losses sustained by the South were nothing compared to the loss he felt for the woman he'd loved. At least the Confederacy could rebuild. He hadn't that hope until Mimi had come with her outrageous proposal.

He'd been crazy to listen to it. He'd been foolish to think it might succeed. And he'd been an idiot to believe what his heart told him when he saw Cherice standing there in that pious gown—that she was everything he'd ever wanted and now could have and hold. That she was still that sweet girl he remembered who'd shared his ideals and his passions—all very chastely, of course. That he could overlook the past and take up where they'd been five years before. He'd been ready to cast off all he'd been raised to hold sacred by taking a woman of lowered circumstance for his bride. He would have endured his parents' horror and the disdain of his peers to have her. He hadn't cared then; he'd been wildly, impetuously in love. And now he'd wanted to believe that by some miracle they could go back to that time of innocence, that the passing of years hadn't changed her. They couldn't and she had. But he could still have her. He could make her his wife and use the bounty of her circumstance to build them a good home. Did it matter if she loved him?

Yes.

It mattered.

Now what was he going to do with a wife who was more whore than housekeeper and a mother who was determined to make his daily existence hell?

"I hope I didn't keep you waiting. I wanted to dress for dinner, this being my first night at my new table."

Cherice breezed into the dining room in a cloud of potent scent and a blinding shimmer of gold sequins.

"You shouldn't have gone to the trouble," Lilith murmured, glancing away as her daughter-in-law bent to nuzzle her son's neck with an improper degree of affection. The front of the girl's tawdry gown pulled away from a great deal of pale bosom shoved into prominence by a snug corset. Ruben had no comment, too distracted by the swelling softness dropped unceremoniously over his shoulder. And when his new wife turned, his face was thrust between those milky globes for just a fraction of a second before she straightened and went to assume her own seat. Long enough to send a bolt of red hot lust streaking to his loins.

Cherice slurped at her soup. "This is quite tasty. Did you make it yourself, Mother Amory?"

Lilith gripped her tableware, praying for control. "We were able to retain several of our house servants. We have an excellent cook. She's been with the family for almost a generation."

"Oh, how nice. We'll need to engage more, of course. So we can entertain. Aunt Mimi and the girls are just dying to visit."

Lilith went white. She turned to her soup with a savage gusto.

"I mean, what's the use of having money if it can't be used to make the lives of those who care about you more comfortable?" Cherice met Ruben's stare and he had the decency to glance away. "And what can I do for you, Ruben? Surely you must have given some thought as to how to spend my fortune."

"Don't concern yourself over it, Cherice. I've everything under control."

"But I want to help. I've so much to give. You mustn't feel shy about asking. There's no need for you to feel humble about applying to your own wife for funds. What's mine is yours."

"That's very kind." How good of you to rub my nose in it, he thought to himself. He was beginning to feel the chafe of his mother's discontent. He couldn't remember Cherice's voice having such a strident quality. As the meal dragged on, it took on the sound of an unoiled wheel, wearing on his nerves as much as the generous display of her breasts wore on his composure. She never stopped talking, even as she chewed, and he could see his mother's alarm increasing as she discussed her plans to refurbish their home. The cupids were one of her more modest ideas. He found it difficult to transpose this brassy, uncouth female over the sensitive young woman he remembered. Could five years make that much difference or had he been that willing to overlook her flaws in favor of her more pleasing attributes?

Thinking of her attributes made the rest easier to tolerate. Five years was a long time to dream about what he had waiting for him on this night. He'd wanted Cherice since the first time he'd seen her playing the piano in that Memphis whorehouse. Only then he'd been foolish enough to think she required careful courting. Now, he knew better. And there was something to be said for not having a virgin bride.

He'd always expected his wedding night to be one of awkward trepidation, coaxing a frail and modest female into the necessary crudeness of procreation. From what he knew of Southern ladies, their mothers had saved them from their sinful natures by convincing them that pleasure was immoral. He'd expected a virtuous bride who would submit out of a religious and familial duty. His father told him their were only two classes of women: ladies and whores. The ladies were chaste—delicate as lilies, spotless as doves, fragile as porcelain, and, of course, pure as the driven snow. Ladies were marrying stock. Whores were all females of color and white women who'd fallen from grace. Wives were to be living examples of Christian virtue, above reproach and treated with an exaggerated gallantry. A gentleman laid with them to beget an heir. When he wanted to enjoy it, he went to a whore.

There was something to be said for marrying a whore. At least she would know what to expect when the lights turned down low.

Except Cherice didn't.

As she gabbed on and on, baiting her horrified mother-in-law into near hysteria, Cherice was all too aware of her approaching wedding night. And she continued talking to stall the inevitable: when Ruben would expect her to act the harlot she pretended to be. In his bed.

It was one thing to tease him with kisses and bold caresses. She'd seen Mimi's girls carrying on with men as a prelude to the actual upstairs dalliances, but her experience went only as far as the bedroom door. She had no great difficulty pretending to enjoy the amorous exchanges. She enjoyed them very much. There was something wildly pleasurable in initiating love play. She'd desired Ruben Amory as a fifteen-year-old girl checked only by the rigid notions of what was proper behavior. Now she could throw away those guidelines and act the pure wanton. And she liked it. But what was she going to do when he called her on those seductive overtures? How was she going to convince him that his shocking kiss was not the extent of her knowledge?

She nearly jumped out of her seat when Ruben set down his glass to exclaim, "It's late. Cherice, you go on up. I'll be there directly."

Her heart beating madly, she held to her charade, grazing her fingertips along his waistcoat with a coo of, "Don't be too long." Then she headed for the stairs.

It was a beautiful staircase, all hand-carved freestanding elegance as it wound its way up to the second story. This is what she'd dreamed of: climbing the stairs in his ancestral home to share his bed of passion. But what if he discovered her sham along with her maidenly status? She'd taunted mother and son with insinuations that she was no stranger to her aunt's trade. Now, if she meant to hold to that bluff, she would have to fool Ruben into thinking her worldly in all ways. It was that or let him know that she was a vulnerable innocent he'd devastated with his deception. He'd made a mockery of the feelings she held for him and to display them now was too humbling to consider. She would go for the bluff. If she provoked him to a desperate state, he might never notice he was the first to claim her. And she knew just the provocation.

The bedroom was so dark, at first Ruben feared she must have retired. A growl of annoyance and disappointment swept him at the thought of postponing their first night together. Delay was not what he had in mind. Not when he could still smell the perfume on her skin. If it were some coy game she was playing, he'd have her know right quick he meant for her to be his wife in every way starting tonight. He'd waited five years and though the circumstances left much to be desired, Cherice didn't. He'd done the dutiful wedding and now it was time to get to the anticipated bedding. He reached for his tie, pulling it loose as he approached the bed.

All the lights weren't off. Cherice had drawn the curtains about the bed and he could see the faint flickers of a lamp on the other side. Curious and growing impossibly aroused, he parted the drapery and froze. Cherice was stretched out atop the bedcovers, awaiting him. Muted lamplight glazed the pale sheen of her skin and teased wickedly along the garment she was wearing. He'd no experience in such things but he was certain it wasn't the usual attire brought by a chaste bride to the wedding night.

He'd expected a swaddling of linen buttoned up to the chin. Cherice wore a corset cover that skimmed her lithe torso and circled to the outside of her arms leaving her creamy shoulders bare. Long legs were clad in pantalets trimmed in eyelet and lace. Neither piece was made as an everyday undergarment. They were black and they were completely transparent. The languid shift of her knees provided him with a glimpse of dark down. There was no crotch in the pantalets. She lifted graceful arms to him and the invitation sent desire spiking hotly.

"Come to bed, husband."

Cherice waited, growing unsettled beneath the searing caress of his stare. What was wrong? Why was he hesitating? Blanche, the working woman who'd lent her the scanty attire swore it would provoke a man to draw quick and shoot straight. Whatever that meant. She hoped it meant it would hurry the final act to its conclusion before she lost her nerve. But Ruben appeared to be in no rush as he took in every intimate curve of her body until she was ready to writhe in embarrassment.

"Come here, Cherice." It was a low command and she was quick to obey. Anything to get this awkward moment beyond them. She came up on her knees, facing him, assuming a posture she hoped would fracture his control. Contrarily, he reached out to cup her jaw in one palm, cradling her upturned face as he lowered to her lips. The taste of his slow kiss wrung a shuddering response. She forgot that she was angry with him for his trickery, that he'd hurt her with his scheming. His kiss was sheer rapture. The now-familiar warmth it stirred was comforting and exciting all at once. And she'd just begun to relax when his other hand curved around her breast. The stroke of his thumb across its center brought a quick pucker and a jolt of sensation.

Cherice gasped and stiffened in surprise. She'd expected him to drop her down and get right to the purpose of matrimony—the passionless joining needed to produce an heir. She'd seen livestock engaged in such mating ritual on her family's small Nashville farm. She just assumed it would be much the same between man and wife. It never occurred to her that he would want to touch her. She drew back in confusion and alarm, for a moment forgetting her role of skilled courtesan. Until she saw the puzzlement in Ruben's eyes. She wasn't going to fool him for a minute.

"Let me turn off the light," she said rather breathlessly. But when she reached for it, Ruben caught her hand and brought it up to rest against the sleek heat of his waistcoat.

"Leave it on."

Panic was pounding within her chest. She tried to smile. "I thought you'd be in a hurry."

"Cheri, I've waited five years too long to want it over in five minutes."

She swallowed convulsively.

"Just 'cause I'm your husband doesn't mean you have to get all missish."

"What would you like me to do?" she crooned seductively, hoping desperately he would tell her so she wouldn't have to guess.

"You can start by undressing me."

That sounded simple enough. She straightened to ease

the coat from his broad shoulders, letting it fall to the floor behind his heels. The buttons of his vest were next. She was purposefully slow, thinking maybe he'd get so impatient, he'd become the aggressor and relieve her of the burden. He didn't seem to mind waiting. Collar and cuffs came next, then his crisp white shirt. When she tugged it over his head, she came up flush against the heavy mat of hair covering his chest. There was something faintly sinister about all that thick furring, as if it made the link between man and beast all that much closer. Her fingers were trembling as they reached for the flap of his trousers. He helped her by levering out of his boots then stepping out of his pants after they, too, fell.

Confronted by the thin cotton of his drawers, Cherice kept her head down so he wouldn't see the mortification flaming in her face. She unfastened the suspender buttons, and the narrow straps gave across his wide chest. Then, there were those last few buttons. Her courage faltered.

"Cherice?"

Her eyes flashed up, all wild and grateful for the distraction. And Ruben was struck once again by the impossible notion that this was the first time she'd gone so far with a man. That, by her own admission, was not true. Was it? He'd felt her shiver in his embrace, and not with anticipation. He'd seen panic in her gaze instead of wanton expectation. Then he recalled her reaction to his kiss at Mimi's and he couldn't dismiss the possibility that the woman in his bed was a virgin. For some reason, she was playing an elaborate game with him and he wanted to know why. But first, he had to be sure before they came to the point of intimacy.

He drew her up for another kiss and she opened for it willingly enough. Her hands rode over the hard line of his bare shoulders, sliding in an encouraging rhythm, but when his hand splayed wide upon the center of her back to compel her against him there was no mistaking that jerk of shock as she came in contact with the evidence of his need. He took one of her small hands and fit it over the rigid contour, guiding her through a pleasing motion. Her touch was timid but not reluctant. If she didn't know, she wasn't unwilling to learn. What kind of wife did he have, whore or maiden?

He let his hand stroke easily along her thigh, shifting the wispy material over smooth skin, moving upward. Cherice tucked her head into his shoulder. He could feel the quick little pants of her breath. When he reached the juncture of her femininity and rubbed across those tender folds, her breathing stopped altogether. With one gentle thrust he determined the truth. Even before he encountered the slight barrier of her innocence, her gasp and uncertain whimper told him he was the first to cross this sacred ground. And that suddenly pleased the hell out of him. A great wave of possessive tenderness filled him. And a provoking bewilderment. If she was pure, why the pretense? Had she no idea how he could have unknowingly hurt her in thinking her experienced? Why goad him by flaunting such a lie? Unless it was by design. Was her intent to shame him, to make him squirm at the thought of having a sluttish wife? If so, how far was she willing to carry this bold charade? And at what cost to her own humility?

Ruben leaned back to study his deceiving wife. He watched her gather her composure to present him with the illusion of wantonness. Her lips pouted ripely; her lashes lowered into a sultry veil. And he almost smiled in amazement. She was a spirited piece of work. He was as amused as he was aggravated that she would go to such lengths to annoy him. Time to make her squirm a little.

He plucked at the small buttons holding her camisole

together, and her tension increased as each one released until, finally, he was sliding the brief concealment aside. She controlled her inward tremblings as he filled his hands with her soft white breasts, plying them with a gentle appreciation. His head lowered and she bit her lip. She fought the need to arch and moan with the wonder of sensations he stirred, reminding herself that she was not supposed to find them so exciting and new. That grew almost impossible as hot kisses became a vigorous suckling. Her fingers clenched in his fair hair, kneading convulsively as shocks of pleasure rode through her. She'd never dreamed . . . Surely, it wasn't always so between man and wife or mothers wouldn't have to gird their daughters with commands to endure and obey. She needed no stern warning to suffer for the sake of duty. She saw no need to play the martyr when engulfed by searing pleasure. And suddenly she was eager to give all to this man who evoked them.

Ruben lifted up and rubbed his thumb over one tightly budded breast. "How is it that such a tender fruit can be handled by many and yet remain unbruised?"

His words called her back to her role and she reluctantly complied. "Would it please you, husband, if I were to pretend you were the first to pluck me from the tree?" That would hardly be difficult for her.

Ruben's smile was one of goading. "I would prefer you showed me all that you've learned. Unless such tricks require payment up front."

Her gaze narrowed at that challenge. Her tone was thick as syrup and sour as vinegar. "Sugar, you already bought and paid for me."

"Then I'd like my money's worth."

Chapter Four

Ruben sprawled out full length, all bold and bare upon the bedcovers to prompt her with his expectant gaze. He enjoyed watching alarm darken into a murderous intensity before his wife's features became all seductive and insincere. She was no whore. A whore would have taken no nonsense from him. She would have climbed aboard and ridden to a quick economical conclusion. But Cherice felt cornered into showing her creativity and, oh, he meant to enjoy a first-rate performance.

Slowly she came down to him, touching his mouth with just the briefest brush of her own. She trailed nibbling kisses along his jaw while her hand rumpled through the crisp mat on his chest. Clever fingers plucked his flat male nipples into a surprising state of arousal, then she lowered to torment them with the feathering of her tongue and exquisite tugs between sharp teeth much as he had hers. And her hand slid lower, down the firm terrain of his abdomen to where his passions beat hard and hot. Her touch was maddeningly light, and soon his amusement was forgotten beneath her teasing curiosity. He suddenly lacked the patience to continue their game of wills.

With a powerful move, Ruben pinned Cherice beneath him. Immediately she was all stiff and angular in fright. He took a moment to ease her tension with deep, plunging kisses. When she began to respond, he moved against her, pushing slightly at the guarded entrance of her womanhood until her body greeted him with an increasing moisture. Her mind, however, was resistant. She wiggled under him, bracing her palms against his chest. "Ruben . . ."

He was still. Lifting up, he could see the pretense crumble. She looked plainly scared and his heart melted. This was what he'd wanted since the first time he'd seen her: to calm and claim as his own. And all was as it should be. The particulars of how they got there no longer mattered.

"Trust me, Cheri," he whispered as his fingertips caressed the taut column of her throat. He felt her nervous swallowing, but she managed a faint smile of sweet surrender. That was his complete undoing. He said her name again, his voice fracturing with emotion before he crushed her lips under his own. Hers parted for him and he thrust inside the warmth of her mouth. At the same time, her slight form relaxed beneath him and he was quick to breech her innocence with one sure stroke. He swallowed up her cry of pain and protest with his demanding kisses until the pinch of her fingers eased on his upper arms, until the movement of her hips ceased to be denying struggles and became a subtle shift of acceptance.

His kiss gentled into a sharing of breath then he looked down upon her. Her features were flushed; her eyes glittered. And then she had the audacity to smile with a smug pleasure. "I didn't mean to cry out." Her apology was a husky purr. "It's just that you're so much . . . more than I'm used to."

He almost laughed aloud in relief at her brazen bluff.

But his reply was equally raspy. "I shall always try to be . . . more."

He began to move within her and Cherice was surprised by how quickly the burn of invasion left her. It was replaced by a crowding fullness that chafed sensation to a shivery intensity. And it occurred to her to wonder why on earth something so delightful was so feared by the virtuous. Perhaps for that very reason. *Lie still and endure,* was the advice given at her prestigious school. *A lady does not display any undo passions.* She was frustrated by that command for the last thing she wanted was to accept him placidly while her blood sang and her body pulsed with urgent desires. Those same strictures had held her back from knowing the wonders of his embrace five years ago. Then she remembered. She was not supposed to be a lady. Why, then, be forced into the role of one?

With a deep, gusty moan, Cherice let go of the restrictions of propriety, responding instead with womanly instinct and a greedy want to experience that "more" her husband promised. She twined her legs around his, arching to meet him, gratified by his lusty groan of appreciation. She encouraged both their passions with the restless stroke of her hands along his taut shoulders, through his dampening hair, down the sleek curve of his back to the hard flex of his buttocks, clutching there to pull him closer, deeper, nearer to the distracting center of sensation she discovered within her. She breathed his name in wonder and he was kissing her. She answered wildly, with an abandon that had her soaring. Once that spiral of pleasure began, it was a whirlpool, sucking up her senses until they spun and expanded at a furious rate. She clung to Ruben as her anchor in that maelstrom of emotion, suddenly fearful of the pull that would snatch away her grip on reason. The tighter she hung on, the fiercer the pull until Ruben whispered raggedly, "Let go, Cheri. Let go."

She did, trusting him, and she was instantly swept up and away in a whirlwind of explosive feeling. Never had she imagined such a place existed, where the body responded separate from the mind, responded with tumultuous quakes of passion and deeper tremors that shook to the soul. No schooling was needed here, and she didn't have to wonder if she'd pleased him when Ruben moaned her name as his final thrust sowed his satisfaction deep and sure.

It seemed to take forever to gather up her scattered senses. A heavy lethargy was determined to claim her in sleep, yet she resisted. She felt her husband withdraw and was vaguely aware that he was cradling her close to the hard thunder of his heart. She smiled lazily to herself, smug and sated and sure she'd fooled him into believing her pretense. For certainly no frail Southern bride would act so shamelessly. Silly females, she mused as her fingertips grazed the powerful swell of Ruben's arm.

Feeling her stir, Ruben stroked the tangled luxury of her hair and said her name softly. She looked up at him through eyes dark-centered and dazed with sensual awareness. A stunning sense of accomplishment overcame him that he should be the one to awaken her with the bliss of union. But she would deny him even that honest expression with her games. What motivated his lovely, treacherous wife?

"Ruben," she began softly with the words "I love you" at ready. But then she saw the way his smoky eyes cleared and hardened to an impenetrable barrier of distrust. And tender feeling died within her. He wasn't the loving husband she longed for, who would share this precious moment in sweet communion. Their marriage was founded upon a lie, their act of consummation one of desire not devotion. She couldn't afford to forget those cruel facts when her spirit was so vulnerable. Theirs was not a match of love but rather one of financial and social security, and so she couldn't speak the words straining against the walls of her heart for fear only sorrow would answer.

Instead Cherice tucked her head, resting it within the warm lea of his shoulder. She squeezed her eyes shut as she felt his arms encircle her and his lips move softly against her hair. And she tried not to weep for the loss of their innocent years when they might have lain together as lovers untouched by bitter schemes and forced pretenses. When she might have shared his loving with the added ecstasy of knowing she was loved and let her heart speak without the fear that he would break it.

To wake as the sole occupant of her marriage bed was the loneliest feeling Cherice had ever experienced. Light was streaming in through louvered windows telling her the hour was early, yet her husband hadn't cared to linger beside her. Ruben hadn't bothered to wake her with a kiss or even a civil good morning, and now she was faced with confronting a hostile household from an uncertain stand. If he'd chosen to appear with her at breakfast, her status as mistress of the house would be guaranteed. As it was, she'd be forced to slink downstairs alone in search of her reluctant family.

And that she would not do!

Cherice heard their voices as she approached the dining room; mother and son discussing the unwelcomed intruder who brought them both salvation and humiliation.

"What are you going to do about her, Ruben? You can't let that creature run loose as your wife. The family would never survive the gossip. Annul this travesty of a marriage."

"Too late, Mama. She could already be carrying an Amory heir."

Cherice heard the other woman's harsh intake of breath. "Oh, Ruben, how could you?"

"She's my wife. Why shouldn't I?"

"But to join with such a female, risking disgrace and disease—"

"Enough." He didn't sound outraged by this attack on his wife, only annoyed by his mother's harping. Cherice noticed he made no attempt to defend her against the slanderous words. Perhaps because he believed them.

"Ruben, you know even a good marriage cannot reduce the stain of impropriety from a woman's character. The world will never forget what she is, nor will you escape the slights and jibes of your peers for having taken in a creature of fallen virtue. I will not have you come to a point of nonexistent honor."

"I have no plans to duel over imagined insults. During the last five years, I've shed enough blood for one lifetime."

Though Cherice applauded his sensibility, she couldn't help being hurt by his callous dismissal of her. She was his wife, after all, and deserving of some degree of protection.

"You needn't worry, Mama. I've no intention of allowing Cherice to leave Stillwater. She's one asset I've no desire to lose."

"And just what is she good for, pray tell?" Lilith's sneer cut Cherice to the bone. "A whore in charge of a household? What can she possibly know about the way decent folks live? Why she's probably not even used to seeing daylight hours. The only thing she knows how to do is dress badly, behave worse, and lie on her back for pay."

"Mother—"

"Good morning!" Cherice sailed into the room, fearing if she listened to more she'd be unable to ever face them again. "I must have been sleeping so hard, I never even heard the call to come join you for breakfast."

Neither had the good grace to look the least bit ashamed by the oversight. It could be that they were too stunned by her appearance. After washing, Cherice had let her hair remain down in a wild dark mane. She'd taken elaborate care to apply a heavy mask of face paint and surround herself in a cloud of intensely floral scent. She looked exactly like what they expected to see and she swallowed down her modesty to act the part as well. Sauntering over to Ruben's chair, she slid around in front of him, climbing up on his lap to face him with her knees straddling his thighs. She was wearing a red satin robe and it was obvious to him from what his shocked eyes could see when the cloth parted that she wore nothing else.

Before he could say anything, she simpered naughtily, "Of course, I wouldn't have heard ol' Sherman himself marching downstairs after the way you wore me out last night. I missed you this morning. I'd have thought you'd want to take another shot at begetting yourself an heir."

She was watching his eyes, the way they darkened first with unbridled want, then chilled in objection. He started to frown and scold, "Really, Cherice, this is hardly the place for such—"

Cherice grabbed him by either ear and hauled him up to meet her vigorous kiss. Since her grip prevented him from pulling away, he endured her open-mouthed onslaught with a stiff decorum; however, he was breathing with difficulty when she eased back. He looked angry at her boldness and even angrier because it aroused him. He stood, nearly dumping her to the floor. She clutched at the overlap of her robe to keep it closed as she was bumped back against a table that was dressed much better than she.

"I'll be back sometime this afternoon," Ruben told both women tersely.

Cherice caught at his shirt front. "Where are you going?"

"I have a plantation to run. So if you'll excuse me." He removed her from his clothing with a firm hand, then strode away, almost too furious to think about favoring his bad leg.

Then it was just Cherice and Lilith Amory. And neither was happy with the situation. Cherice bestowed a dazzling smile upon the pinch-faced woman. "I guess it'll be just you and I."

Lilith stood, tossing her wadded napkin to the tabletop. "I feel a splitting headache coming on. I think I shall lie down in my room until my son's return."

She marched from the dining room with a dignity Cherice couldn't mock. Alone, the young woman dropped into a chair to solemnly regard the other empty seats. She couldn't bring herself to make peace with Lilith Amory after what she'd done to destroy her chances for happiness, yet she couldn't help but mourn the lack of a tranquil home. Playing harlot had seemed such wicked revenge at the time of conception, but now Cherice realized the strain of maintaining such a pose. How on earth would she ever be able to ease from it to win the love of the man she'd wed? Or the respect of the woman who swore to bar her from her home? Pride had pushed Cherice into an uncomfortable corner. How to get out? How to make it known to these two suspicious and inflexible people that she meant them no harm, that she only wanted the opportunity to fit in? She brooded for some time before she was aware of anyone else in the room. First, she heard a disparaging cluck, then a low muttering. "Comes in here acting like trash, then wonders why folks loses their appetites. And after ol' Maddy done worked so hard in the kitchen."

Cherice glanced up glumly to observe a thin old black woman gathering up the soiled tableware. The woman never spared her a look. Or the cut of her tongue. "Thinks marrying quality makes quality. Sheeoot. Like calling a crow a dove makes him anything but a crow. Cain't change a bird's feathers, I always says."

That was the final blow that battered through Cherice's pride. Her shoulders slumped. A soft, hitching sob escaped her. She tried to contain her emotions beneath the scrutinizing black-eyed stare but it was impossible. It was too humiliating to face the fact that even the servants thought her a peg below them. But once her charade crumpled and her true misery was exposed, the black woman was kneeling at the side of her chair, patting her arm and making soothing noises. "Now, now, child, doan go taking anything ol' Maddy says to heart. I didn't mean to hurt your feelings. Guess I ain't used to folks round here ever listening to what I gots to say." She supplied a linen napkin and Cherice blew her nose gustily. "There. Better now?"

Cherice managed a feeble affirmative.

"I'm Maddy, child. I been cook for the Amorys since Mr. Ruben was in swaddling. He's a good boy and a proud man. Why you want to go shaming him so?"

"It's—complicated."

"It's foolishness. And why you pretending you was some kinda cheap woman?" When Cherice looked surprised, Maddy chuckled wisely. "Honey, I know you ain't no easy piece. I seen them fine clothes way in the back of your closet and I seen the way you looks at Mr. Ruben when he ain't watching. And I seen them bedsheets you stripped off this morning. You're the one the mister was in love with before the war, ain't you?

My boy, Jeremiah, he heard plenty about you while he was tending young Mr. Amory. I know you ain't one of them town girls. Now, it ain't none a' my business, but I'd think you'd be proud being wedded to a man like the mister."

Cherice gave a wavering sigh, compelled to trust the grizzle-haired cook when there was no other in which to confide. "He doesn't love me anymore. He took me for a wife because I brought him enough money to restore Stillwater."

"And you loves him."

"It's that obvious?"

"To everyone but him and his mama. So you planning to shame him outta spite. One thing about that ol' demon revenge: it ain't as sweet as some folks be thinking. Not that it's any a' my business, but was I you, I'd be acting like I was the master's wife instead of his doxy."

"You're right. It's none of your affair." Cherice said it kindly but Maddy wouldn't have taken offense in any case. Nor would she listen.

"So, missus, you want me to bring you some laudanum like his mama so's you can waste the day away or you gonna do something useful for your man?"

Cherice sat up slowly, thoughtfully. She was the mistress of Stillwater. Maybe not under ideal circumstances, but she was. And as such, she had certain responsibilities. It wasn't her way to be pushed aside and ignored. She wanted her presence felt at the once-grand plantation and she knew just where to start.

He couldn't believe it.

Ruben had to look twice but then he realized there was no mistake. It was Cherice there in the middle of the Memphis boardwalk arm in arm with another man.

She was looking up into the well-dressed gentleman's eyes, laughing gaily over something he'd said. And Ruben's sense of reason snapped in a second.

He went storming down the sidewalk, gripping his cane the way he would his saber. Cherice glanced his way and her dark eyes rounded with surprise and pleasure. That last didn't register in the midst of his rage.

"Ruben, I—"

Her mouth snapped shut when he grabbed her arm to jerk her up against his side. The older gentleman was still holding her by the other elbow.

"Sir, take your hands from my wife."

"Ruben!" The gladness was gone from her gaze. Instead, there was a deepening upset. He ignored it.

As the dapper gentleman stepped aside, murmuring placating sentiments in his tart Northern tongue and quickly relinquishing Cherice's arm, Ruben ground out, "Seek her out again and I will look to you for satisfaction." The proud planter felt a slight punch to his ribs but he refused to acknowledge it as he continued his furious warning. "I can see you're a Yankee and probably know little about treating a woman with respect, but down here, we value our women and—"

This time, Cherice struck him hard enough to make him wince in surprise. He scowled down at her and found her glaring up fiercely. A fine way to show her appreciation . . . unless she hadn't wanted the interruption. His features grew rigid.

"Ruben, you owe Mr. Pettibone an apology."

"What?"

"Mr. Pettibone has been kind enough to help me make drapery selections for Stillwater and was assisting me from his store to the carriage."

Ruben went very still, understanding hitting him like cannon shot. "I didn't—"

"Apologize," she hissed.

Manners conquering embarrassment and confusion, Ruben doffed his hat. "I seem to have been in error, sir. I do hope you will forgive me if I impugned your name or your intentions. The lady and I were only married yesterday and—"

The transplanted Northern merchant laughed good-naturedly. "Say no more, sir. That says it all. And Mrs. Amory, your order will be brought to you when it's completed. It's been a pleasure working with a lady of your refined tastes." He bowed and Cherice responded with a neat curtsy. Then when the merchant turned back toward his shop, she shot her husband a killing glance that set him back on his heels. She started for the buggy.

"Cherice—"

"You humiliated me, Ruben."

"What was I to think?"

She spun to face him, fuming and so beautiful his heart was staggering wildly. "I don't know. What did you think? That he was accosting me or that I was propositioning him right out in the open? That I'd grown so bored with your bed after one night that I couldn't wait to find another to leap into?"

"Cherice, lower your voice. People are staring."

"Let them stare! I'm sure we're all the talk anyway— Ruben Amory and his slattern wife."

He was no longer looking at her but toward the buggy and all around them. "Who came into town with you?"

Her chin angled up defiantly. "I came alone."

His expression was thunderous when he turned to her. His words were low and labored. "Get in the buggy."

"I have some more shopping to—"

"Get in the buggy, now!"

Stiff-backed, she allowed him to hand her up but when she started to gather the reins, he jerked them from her.

"Just sit there."

She sat, a pillar of displeasure as he went to fetch his horse and tied the animal in back. She never so much as glanced at him when he climbed up beside her and took up the reins himself. It was a long, tense ride back to Stillwater with silence speaking louder than any of the strong words they'd exchanged in town. As soon as he drew up, Cherice jumped carelessly out and with skirts hiked up out of the way, ran for the front steps. Cursing his own awkwardness, Ruben followed, managing to catch up to her as she started up the staircase. He grabbed her wrist and tugged her around so that they faced one another. His pulse was racing all out of control, fueled by crazy fear and crazier jealousies. And deeper, by his own knowledge that he'd hurt and offended her without cause. Those impassioned feelings collided and the turmoil came out as an irrational fury.

"You are not to go into town like that again. Do you hear me?"

"Afraid you can't trust me, sugar?" she snarled back at him, equally incensed.

"Not when your judgment allows you to do stupid things like you did today! You will stay here at Stillwater where you belong."

"Belong? Oh, please! I won't be kept prisoner here. I go when and where I please. I am not like your acres of land and scores of former slaves that will allow you rule without rebellion. You don't own me, Ruben Amory!"

"Yes, I do. In the eyes of the law and in the sight of God, I do. I married you and that makes you mine. And as your husband, it's my duty to see you safe even from your own carelessness."

"I am perfectly capable of driving my own buggy."

"And are you perfectly capable of defending yourself against whatever you might find out there off these lands? These are dangerous times, Cherice. There are men who roam those roads who would kill you for your horse . . . or do worse."

Cherice was panting unevenly, frightened by his savage words, angered because she wanted to believe he was concerned for her safety, but couldn't. Because of those things, she reacted with a brash rebuttal. "Don't you dare pretend you care what happens to me. I'd think you'd be glad to see me go and would sit back with your mama hoping for the worst! Except you'd probably regret the loss of the horse."

Ruben froze as she jerked free and fled for their room. She made it up a half-dozen steps before he snagged onto her again, this time spinning her into the wall, where he pinned her with the leverage of his weight. And he kissed her until there wasn't an ounce of breath in her lungs, until there wasn't a coherent thought in her head. Until her arms were wound so tightly about him, he didn't ever want to think of letting her go.

So he didn't.

Cherice gasped as her feet swung up off the steps and Ruben bore her, bunched hoops, yards of fabric, and all up the stairs.

"Ruben, your leg—"

"It'll hold us." His teeth gritted. *Hold, dammit.*

And it did, even though he was hobbling badly by the time he eased her down at the edge of their big bed. She didn't mention his leg again. She was too busy returning his kisses.

There was no time for any pretending and he didn't have to ask Cherice to undress him. Her fingers were hurrying down the buttons of his vest, eager to push inside next to the heat of his body. He was working her fastenings just as rapidly until there were no more barriers between them, at least not that they'd admit to at this particular point. He took her down upon the fluffy coverlet, and this time he didn't have to show her what he expected or what he wanted. It was what they both wanted. Her arms lifted to twine eagerly about his neck, drawing him down to drink from the sweet wet heat of her mouth. Her shoulders flexed, inviting him lower, and she gasped softly as his lips played hotly about each taut peak until she was trembling with anticipation. His touch was magic, leading her down a path of exquisite discovery, lifting her desires upon a sea of liquid sensation. And when he brought her to a crest, she cried out his name and let pleasure burst beyond all physical boundary.

Even as she drifted down upon that hot current of completion, he was filling her, carrying her aloft again with a need more powerful than the first. Driving her with his urgent desire, feeding her starving lungs with his greedy kisses. And as she was caught once more in the thrall of a soul-dissolving release, Cherice heard her husband claim, "You are mine, Cheri. And I will never lose you again."

Chapter Five

Daylight was gone when Cherice awoke. Evening had settled in with its own special rhythm of night birds and cicadas. Sound and soft breezes carried in from where the windows opened onto the upper gallery. Out in those deep shadows, she saw her husband's silhouette. He was seated in a big wicker chair, staring outward. It was a pensive pose, a lonely pose, and for a moment she just watched him, wondering if he would welcome her intrusion into his private thoughts. She had yet to establish where he did want her, other than between his sheets. And as glorious as that treasured spot might be, she wanted more from the man she'd married.

He'd been angry because he cared. Cherice couldn't convince herself otherwise. He cared and that was the first step toward what she desired. She wanted to be mistress of his household, mistress of his heart. And he would learn to value her more than the money she brought to their union. This, she vowed silently as she listened to the lazy resonance of the Tennessee night and breathed deep of its black river-bottom earth and sweet spring honeysuckle. Those things, like Ruben himself, were a part of her now and she would cherish them forever.

Ruben glanced up as her shadow passed over him. She'd forgone the flashy satin robe in favor of his linen shirt, and it swaddled her slender figure while leaving a provocative expanse of pale leg bare. And from the way her husband caressed her with his gaze, it would seem he preferred the simple covering of his shirt to the obvious charms of her wispy costumes. Cherice liked the fact that he did. He himself was wearing only his cotton drawers and his bad leg was stretched out on a stool before him. She couldn't keep her eyes from admiring the way twilight played all golden upon the form she was both familiar with and fascinated by.

"Can't sleep?" She came up beside his chair, too timid in this quiet setting to reach out to him and unwilling to spoil the beauty of the moment with any bawdy games. It was just she and Ruben, with defenses down, almost like strangers to one another.

Absently he rubbed his thigh. "My leg gets to aching sometimes. It'll ease in a while. I decided keeping it would be worth any amount of suffering. Haven't changed my mind yet."

Cherice knelt and began a gentle kneading just above his knee. She'd seen the scars, dreadful reminders both front and back where the bullet had passed clear through. He'd been so lucky to survive it. At her first touch, she could feel all his sinews tense, then gradually, when he realized her purpose was comfort not seduction, he relaxed.

"Better?"

He nodded wordlessly, the edge of wariness slow to dim in his watchful gaze. Her touch held healing properties that went far beyond poorly mended flesh and bone. It gave ease to his mood and to his troubled heart, and he found himself looking outward once more, speaking of what played upon both things.

"My daddy settled this land in '35. Mama was only sixteen. He put up a house with a leaky roof and they worked the fields themselves. He hauled his crops forty miles in a wagon, sleeping under it at night to protect his profits. And this good earth rewarded him. Before the war, we owned three thousand acres and two hundred slaves. His people would bring in five hundred pounds of cotton a day when three hundred and fifty was considered good. He filled this house with the finest Philadelphia, New York, and Europe had to offer. He wanted the best for me and Mama."

Cherice remembered John Amory as a proud man who dressed in good broadcloth with plated buttons. He'd liked his drink and her Aunt Mimi. He'd bragged on two things when whiskey warmed his mood and loosened his tongue: he talked of Stillwater, the showpiece of his fertile acres with its spacious receiving hall, library, music room, dining rooms, and parlors with fireplaces in every one of them, of the handsome front staircase for family and friends and narrow rear steps for servants. And he talked of his son, as if Ruben was the most valuable cash crop he'd ever raised.

"They called it a rich man's war and a poor man's fight but my daddy was one of the first to enlist. Daddy taught me that a man wasn't a man without his pride and his land. He believed in the gun, the Bible, and in his own rights to control what he had. And that no man could take his pride from him. So did I when I rode out after him. That pride carried me through till Shiloh. Like shooting squirrels, we were told, only these squirrels had guns. We were at a place called Peach Orchard, and the bullets were so thick they cut the petals from the trees until they were falling on the dying like a pink rain. When we marched from Missionary Ridge to Knoxville to winter in the eastern valleys, it was after a bitter cold night of freezing sleet, and I was so tired it was all I could do to follow the footprints of the men walking ahead of me. It was easy 'cause their feet were bare and all I had to do was follow the bloodstains. What the hell kind of pride is there in that, Cheri?

"We crossed and recrossed Tennessee, laying woodlands to waste, tearing up fence rows for our fires, stealing crops to survive, and everywhere I looked, all I could see was Stillwater suffering the way all the land was suffering. They had a special name for a disease that struck us soldiers from Tennessee. They called it nostalgia. Troops would get to missing their homes and lands and families so much it was like a sickness. I got real sick, sick of the killing and the loneliness. And I wanted to go home so bad there were nights I would have just up and run if the pickets wouldn't have shot me down for it."

Cherice had laid her head atop his thigh, and he could see trails of dampness glimmering on her lovely face. A face he'd carried into battle within his memory like protective armor. He'd refused to believe he would die without seeing her again and that faith had brought him home. To what? A ravaged plantation? A marriage made upon restitution and revenge? After what had happened today in Memphis, could he deny to himself the uncomfortable truth? That thinking of Cherice with another man had catapulted him into momentary madness? That hearing she'd made the trip alone had scared him so badly his knees had shaken all the way back to Stillwater?

His fingertips rested lightly on the curve of one moist cheek. He spoke softly, with gruff emotion. "Worse than seeing the railroads wrenched from their beds, the farms burned or abandoned, and the crops destroyed was coming upon the helpless women of Tennessee, left alone to defend themselves against the ugliness of what war does to men." He closed his eyes to shut out the horrifying memory, his voice breaking painfully. "Cheri, you promise me you won't ever make that trip to Memphis alone again. I don't want to have to find you like that. You promise me."

"I promise," she whispered, pressing a tear-wetted kiss to his palm.

He should have just broken down and said it. He loved her. But pride held the words back, and he suffered just as the Cause had suffered because its men didn't know how to humble head before heart. He wanted to cry out, "How could you have left me? How could you have hurt me so?" but those questions remained in agonizing silence to torment his soul.

She rose up to kiss him briefly and to encircle his neck with her slender arms. He grabbed her close, crushing her to the confusion of his heart, burying his face in her hair the way he wished he could bury the anguish of the past. And the bitterness of the present. The woman he'd wed had spurned him, had lied to him, had betrayed him. Yet he couldn't stop loving her. He couldn't stop wanting her. He couldn't help believing that if he held her long enough, strong enough, she'd love him back. And if that was a bad bargain, he didn't care. All he knew was when she was in his arms, when he felt her near, he had a reason to go on. And to a spirit worn raw by four years of continued horror and a heart as laid to waste as the once-prime fields, it was enough to just absorb her softness, to lose himself in her sensual abandon. To know she belonged to him at last.

And when he was able to sell the bales of cotton concealed in a Memphis warehouse, he'd be able to buy his way out of Mimi Leslie's bargain. Then he'd have back his pride and he'd know if he had himself a marriage.

"What do we do first?"

Maddy turned from the scouring of the day's pots to regard the new mistress of Stillwater. And her dark eyes widened.

Cherice stood at the doorway to the kitchen dressed in faded calico. Her hair was bound back in a bandanna much like the one the old cook wore. Noting the black woman's surprise, Cherice explained, "I'm from a small farm outside of Nashville. I can still remember how much work went into keeping that place running. I figured it's time I started doing something for my man."

"That what you figured?" Maddy was grinning. "Well, you come to the right place if it's work you be wanting. Gots plenty of jobs and no hands to fill 'em. Ready to get dirty?"

They started by scalding the bedding from all the upstairs rooms. It was hot, heavy work, and the only thing that made it tolerable was listening to Maddy's endless stories. She was opinionated for a woman of color in a

Southern setting but fiercely loyal to the Amorys. When asked why she'd stayed on at Stillwater after the start of the war, she laughed as if Cherice's question was naive.

"Honey, it'd take more than some white man's words to make me free. Did the North's winning of the war change the color of my skin? Did it make folks look at me any different than I was before? The Amorys, they done always treated me like family. I gots this fine house to tend. I gets to watch my children grow. What'd I want to go North for and live like trash outta white folks garbage? I got me free rein in the kitchen. I got a good life here. They can call me slave or servant, it don't much matter, 'cause Miss Lilith and Mr. Ruben they always treated me with respect. That's more than my kind gets where they be crowding in on the southside of Memphis, living in pestholes and off promises. Them fools'd rather starve than work and here be Mr. Ruben's lands a crying for the lack of hands to tend them."

"He can't find any labor for the fields?"

"Not from them what thinks taking orders makes 'em someone's slave again."

Cherice flung a sodden comforter over the washline, then rubbed her shoulders to ease the strain. Her expression was thoughtful. "You'd think they could come to some sort of compromise, with Stillwater desperate for workers and all these men who know nothing but the fields preferring to see their families suffer for the sake of pride."

"That's how things be, missus. It's just me and a handful here to do the work of two hundred."

"What about Mrs. Amory?" She glanced toward the house where she knew Ruben's mother lingered, preferring to keep to her rooms since Cherice was in residence. Apparently the strain of being polite had grown too much for her.,

"Miss Lilith, she be the strongest woman I ever seen. When the men folks was gone, she took up the running of this place like she was born wearing britches. Then word came about Master John, and then the Yankees came into Memphis. She met 'em at the front door, holding the mister's saber, saying if they was to torch the house, they'd be burning her up with it. She let 'em take everything in the barns and smokehouse, let 'em strip the house right to walls. Told me every house in New England would be filled with her stolen plates, pictures, books, and clothes. But she said it didn't matter as long as she held to the house and the lands for Mr. Ruben."

Cherice hated to admit to a stirring of admiration for the austere Lilith Amory.

"The first notice said Mr. Ruben had been killed, and Miss Lilith took to her bed like the heart'd been cut outta her. I was spooning her full of laudanum, just trying to get her talked into living through the day. She weren't never right again after that, even when the mister came home, more dead than alive. She just sorta lost that sass for living. I seen it spark in her since you been here. And in Mr. Ruben, too. You shook up this household plenty, and I thinks it needed it mighty bad."

Cherice looked out toward the fields, her clever mind turning as her tender heart ached for mother and son. There had to be something she could do. Something that would ease their loss and at the same time ease her into the family. She could think of several ideas but they required going against a promise she'd made to the man she loved. She hesitated, loyalties torn.

"Did Ruben say when he'd be home?"

"He's gone to the Chesterfields to see about leasing off some of the land. 'Bout to break his heart, too."

Then he wouldn't be back until late. And he need never know where she'd been.

"Maddy, let's finish up. We're going into Memphis."

* * *

The first thing Cherice saw when she pulled up before the porch at Stillwater was Ruben, waiting there at the edge of the steps. One look into his eyes spoke of the crippling anxiety he'd endured in her absence, and the stark relief upon his face would haunt her conscience forever. Then the vulnerability was gone.

"Where have you been, Cherice?" The lower registers of his voice rumbled like a cannon volley. His gaze darkened to match the ferocity of slated storm clouds. The firm set of his jaw warned he would not be fooled by any casually spun lie.

"I had some things to attend to in town. Maddy went with me."

"Things?" he questioned shortly. "What sort of things? Increasing your fine wardrobe, perhaps? Or was it just to see if you could have me down on my knees by the time you decided to come back?" He didn't wait for a reply. As she started to gather her skirts to climb down from the buggy, he turned and stalked down the length of the veranda, his steps quick and painfully uneven.

"Ruben," she called after him. "I didn't mean for you to worry . . ."

He stiffened at that, then favored her with the slash of his cold glare. "Don't apologize, Cherice. It's my own damned fault for thinking I could believe your promises now anymore than I could five years ago. Do whatever you want, madame, but don't expect to find me waitin' upon your return."

He closeted himself in his library, and Cherice had the dining-room table to herself. After pretending to enjoy the meal, she finally gave up hoping that her husband would appear and went to help Maddy scrub what was left of Stillwater's copper pots until she was sagging with exhaustion. There was little relief to be found upon climbing into an empty bed. Or in waiting unhappily until the early hours of morning only to wake and find Ruben had never joined her.

Nor was he about the house when she came down to breakfast. She had only a hard-eyed Lilith for company. And Cherice was too miserable to even bait her with improper behavior. She ate in silence, then went to seek out Maddy.

They spent the day at hog killing. Grimly the two women went about it, stunning the creature with an ax, slitting their throats, and dipping them in scalding water before scraping off their bristles. The carcasses were then hung head down from trees, disemboweled, and halved. Small intestines were emptied and scraped for use with sausage. Fat was processed into lard. Back meat was chopped, seasoned, and funneled into skins for smoking. Ham shoulders and bacon flanks went into barrels of brine to be corned. Nothing went to waste from the bristles saved to make brushes to the intestines for chitlings. It was grueling, repetitive work, and after hours of salting meat, nearly all the skin felt burned off Cherice's hands. But she had the satisfaction of seeing the storeroom beams hung with hams and loaded with rows of corned and pickled pork. She remembered her mother saying that keeping a house in order began at the pantry, and now she held those keys to Stillwater. It was up to her to see the larders filled, and the responsibility felt good.

By the time she finished inventorying the storeroom and smokehouse, Cherice was startled by the lateness of the hour. Lilith was a stickler for dinner to begin not a minute after the appointed hour and that left Cherice with no time to clean up. Disheveled by the day's work and not quite as fresh as she'd like to be, she hurried into the dining room to find the other two already seated. Ruben rose wordlessly, his gaze curious while his mother's was plainly dismayed as they both took in her soiled gown and untidy appearance.

Noting the way Lilith's nose wrinkled up, Cherice paused behind the chair Ruben held out for her. "Perhaps I should go change first."

Through her linen napkin, Lilith drawled, "Why should you worry about offending our sensibilities at this late date?"

Her barb both wounded and provoked. Cherice straightened with a cool hauteur. "Perhaps, madame, if you were more interested in earning a little honest sweat to preserve your home than in sleeping the days away, I should hold more value to your opinion."

She'd started to flounce away from the table when Ruben caught her hand. The gentle pressure made her wince, and he was quick to examine the source of her distress: fair flesh scalded to the point of rawness. He frowned slightly as his thumb rubbed over the reddened skin.

"What have you been doing?"

"Tending your larder, husband. Don't look so surprised. Did you think me incapable of domestic endeavors or just indifferent to them?"

He didn't answer. An odd expression moved upon his features as he continued to study her poor ravaged palm. She tried to reclaim her hand but was unsuccessful. A flutter of confusion stirred within her breast and it caused her tone to sharpen. "For heaven's sake, I was raised on a farm. Do you think these are the first blisters I've ever worked for?"

He lifted one sore hand and touched his lips gently to its back. His voice was a husky rumbling. "They're the first you've ever raised for me." Then he turned her hand to kiss its tender valley in appreciation, his eyes closing briefly as her fingertips sketched his cheek. Then he released her. "I'll ask Maddy to hold dinner until you return."

Pleased to the point of tears, Cherice swept from the room and made the necessary reparations to face and form. Much of her spirit returned with the reviving process, and she began to think of Lilith's sneering judgment. And when she hurried back into the dining room, it was upon a cloud of potent scent and within a dress that in no uncertain terms stunned the senses. It was canary yellow and black stripe with a bodice that barely covered what it was meant to in clear defiance of gravity. Lilith dragged in a strangled breath but Ruben was smiling wryly as he rose to greet her.

Instead of graciously taking her seat, Cherice stepped up flush to her husband, entangling her arms around his neck and her tongue about his in a deep, descriptive kiss while her breasts threatened to pop from their confines. Lilith was grinding her teeth and Ruben had broken a sweat by the time Cherice leaned away. She stroked the lapels of his coat and murmured, "Thank you for holding dinner for me, sugar. I thought I'd best make it worth the wait."

As he seated her, she was aware of his lingering touch along her bared arms, along the slope of her shoulders and the graceful column of her throat, and she was content with the knowledge that she wouldn't have the big bed to herself on this night. Smiling brightly, she tucked her napkin into the plunging vee of her neckline and mentioned casually, "Oh, I've some furnishing arriving for the house tomorrow—draperies and the like. I can't wait to see how the colors look in this stuffy ol' place."

And Lilith was hard pressed to choke down even a mouthful of Maddy's ham and red-eye gravy while imagining cupids and chartreuse curtains.

As Maddy served up coffee, the three of them heard a commotion outside. Ruben bade the women to remain while he went to the front door. The moment he was out of sight, both Amory women rushed to peer out the parlor window and were astounded by the sight of a gathering of black men, most of whom Lilith recognized as former field hands for Stillwater's vast acres. She gasped in alarm as her son stepped down amongst their number but Cherice placed a bolstering arm about her shoulders. Unaware of their supportive stance, they waited anxiously as Ruben talked and listened for a good hour. Then as orderly as they'd arrived, the group disappeared.

When Ruben failed to come in right away, Cherice carried his cup of coffee out onto the front porch, approaching cautiously. He was looking toward the far fields, his expression hard to decipher in the fading evening light.

"Ruben? What did they want?"

"They offered to put in my crop if I'd share out a portion of my lands for them and their families."

"And you said?"

"I told them we'd plot out some acres tomorrow . . ."

"And?"

He looked at her then, animation coming into his eyes like a bright Tennessee dawn. "Stillwater's going to be all right. We're going to make it, Cheri."

His hand rubbed over the curve of her shoulder. That inclusive touch and the way he said "we" brought a wonderful fullness about Cherice's heart. Yes, they were going to make it.

Then his forefinger hooked beneath her chin to lift it. "And what part did you play in all this, Cherice?"

Her eyes widened in feigned innocence. "Me? Why, sugar, what do I know about cotton fields?" When his brows rose to demand the truth of her, she smiled saucily. "Only that they need men to work them. And Maddy just so happened to know some men who were willing to work. She visited them while I—increased my fine wardrobe."

As he thought about that, she gave him a flirtatious smile.

"I'm going up to bed. Shall I warm your side of the sheets or have you other plans?"

"No plans that can't wait until morning." And he followed the sassy twitch of her skirts up the wide curve of Stillwater's stairs.

Chapter Six

Throughout the following weeks, while Ruben readied the fields for planting, the things Cherice ordered began arriving for the house. She was so busy, she scarcely had time to miss him during the daylight hours. It was when his seat stood empty at the table at night that she wished for his company and when their big bed held her as sole occupant till late into the night that she longed for his presence. But she didn't complain, knowing how hard he was working to bring his dream to rights and because he never failed to wake her with his slow kisses and passionate caresses. After he'd loved her thoroughly, he'd fall fast to sleep. Then she'd lie awake wondering if he'd ever come to her for conversation and council instead of just for physical comfort alone.

Several of his workers's wives came to help her in the house, stripping yellowed wallpaper, scraping and painting moldings and trim, oiling hardwoods to a glossy sheen as furnishings filled the rooms. During all this activity, Lilith stood warily in the wings, ready to pounce upon a gaudy choice of papering or the first sign of tasteless accessorizing. And it galled her that she found no reason for her worries. Cherice's decorating touches were all ones of subtle elegance but Lilith was ever reminded that her home was being restored by ill-gotten gains. That kept her from any words of thanks as the great rooms went from ruin to returned beauty. Even as Lilith came to a slow appreciation of her daughter-in-law's tireless efforts, she couldn't lower herself to be gracious or grateful to the inferior creature who'd taken over her position of control within the Amory household.

Cherice didn't expect thanks but she did resent the other woman's constant petty criticisms. Shouldn't the pictures be hung higher? Wouldn't that vase look better there? Isn't that rug just a tad too green? Their former drapes had been fuller, didn't these let in too much light? And all those little jibes were concluded with the haughty statement that of course a woman like Cherice couldn't be expected to know any better. But far be it for the former lady of the house to offer a hand of assistance.

Cherice tried her best to ignore the woman. When they were in the same room, tension cracked like a stormy spring sky. Lilith was quick with the slurs upon her character and Cherice was just as quick to reinforce them with some new vulgarity designed to shock the older woman.

Ruben had no patience with his mother's lists of social offenses committed by his bride. He had no time for it and advised her to school her daughter-in-law in proper behavior if that was her intention but not to bother him with the details of it. From Cherice, he heard no ill will, and he was grateful to seek out the soothing silence and sensuality of her company.

Stillwater filled up like an April pond, swelling with the bounty of Mimi Leslie's generosity. Both essentials and luxuries stocked the big house: perfumed soaps, fine tapers, pillowcases, blankets, dimity counterpanes, feather mattresses, preserves for the breakfast table, a sideboard, several settees, necessary chairs with their chamber pots discreetly hidden beneath the seats, silver, crystal, and lamps that shed light upon the returning glory of the Amory home. Each night, Ruben took a moment to assess the improvements but somehow, his intention to compliment his bride was always lost when he saw her curled within his bedcovers and other intensely personal priorities took over.

On one particularly gloomy day, Cherice decided to tackle the fireplace cleaning in her oldest clothes. She was elbow deep in ash when she heard Lilith drawl, "Now there's a fitting picture."

"It's good someone is not above such humility or we'd find the house burning down around our ears."

"Why concern yourself?" the older woman asked spitefully. "It's not as though it's your house, after all."

Cherice felt a fury grip her jaws but she struggled to be civil. "Perhaps not by blood, but by bond. As Ruben's wife, he's entrusted me with the demands of his household."

"Ruben doesn't trust you with anything. If he did, he would have given you my mother's ring instead of that flashy harlot's piece you wear. I would not get too comfortable at Stillwater, were I you."

Normally Cherice refused to be provoked by Lilith's

taunts, but today she was unusually susceptible to them. "What do you mean by that?" she demanded.

"Once Stillwater is rebuilt, he'll have no use for an embarrassment like you. He'll be ready to start a family, and bringing the taint of your blood into our family line is hardly acceptable. When we're ready to open up the doors to entertain, do you honestly think he'll want you receiving at his side?"

"I'm his wife," she stated flatly. "And even your meddling intentions couldn't keep that from happening." She felt a sense of vindication when the older woman paled at the reference. But a terrible fear began to gnaw through her as she listened to the next hateful words.

"For the present, for as long as he needs the money you bring in. And that, my dear, will not be for much longer. The planting is going well. Ruben is negotiating for the sale of the cotton he has stored. With the profit it brings, he won't need the coin your aunt earned upon her back or trading with the Yankees during wartime."

"My aunt was not a traitor."

"No? Ask her whom she entertained in her house. Ask her how she came to such a vast fortune while the rest of the patriotic South suffered. How dare you think we'd welcome the vile evidence of her duplicity upon our walls or beneath our feet! It will be my great pleasure to put you and every bit of your trash out on the front steps when my son is done with you."

With that, Lilith whirled away. She'd reached the doorway when she paused and drew a letter from her skirt pocket.

"Oh. This came for you from New York." She tossed the letter across the room. "I hope, for your sake, it's a train ticket. One way."

Barely able to control the tremors of upset Lilith caused with her insinuations, Cherice broke the seal of

Tom's letter and began to read. She should have waited until her outlook was better. Reading her former fiancé's wounded and embittered prose was hardly the remedy for her blue mood.

Ruben paused at the doorway, bemused by the sight of his wife sitting on the hearth all covered in soot. He'd come in from the fields early with the intention of working on the plantation ledgers but the closer to the house he rode, the more his thoughts strayed to the woman waiting there. He had to smile because her filthy exterior was not exactly conducive to his idea of rolling her on the parlor floor in a bout of impassioned lovemaking. Not after she'd spent days cleaning the rugs. Unless, of course, she didn't mind about the rugs, then he wouldn't mind being soiled in the process of rolling.

Then she heard him and glanced up, and thoughts of ardor dissolved. Her smudged cheeks were lined in white, definitely the tracks of weeping.

"Cheri, what's wrong?" As he approached her, he noticed her crumpling a sheet of paper within her hands and shoving it deep into her pocket.

"Nothing." Her denial wavered pathetically. "Why would you think—"

He bent to touch his fingertips to her damp and dirty cheek, and she realized the folly of her lie. And all at once, her melancholy was more than she could stand.

"Ruben, I have to see my Aunt Mimi. Could you take me to her?"

"Now?" He'd begun to frown, wondering what her tears had to do with the sudden request.

"Please. Please, Ruben."

He was helpless to resist the beseeching dark eyes. "Go get yourself cleaned up. I suppose I can tend to business while you do your visiting."

Her eyes brimmed with a gratitude all out of proportion with his deed. In fact, his wife's very meekness was enough to alarm him. Something to do with his mother? Cherice never mentioned it but he was well-aware of the persecution she endured. But unless asked, he was loath to step in between the two women. He wasn't insensitive to the isolation of Cherice's life at Stillwater, so he couldn't deny her this trip no matter how uneasy he felt about its purpose.

Especially when she hurried from the room to change and he noticed the envelope lying forgotten on the hearth. And saw that its return read New York.

Mimi Leslie took one look at her niece and rushed to embrace her with a coo of "Oh, sugar, what is it? What's wrong?"

"Everything," Cherice wept in unrestricted sorrow. "Oh, Aunt Mimi, I've made an awful mistake."

"You hush now. Sit a spell and I'll fix you up some nice cold lemonade. Then you can tell me what the trouble is. I'm sure it's not as bad as it seems."

Cherice wasn't convinced but she did as her aunt suggested. The cool drink did soothe her, and the company of a sympathetic female worked wonders upon her ravaged emotions.

"Now, darlin', you tell me what's got your eyes all red."

Cherice sniffed miserably. "I should never have gone through with it."

"With what, honey?"

"Marrying Ruben."

"Isn't that what you wanted? Doesn't he make you happy?" Silently Mimi was already considering what methods she might employ to gain a better treatment of her niece. She couldn't bear the thought of her only family in such woeful straits. "What's he done to make you cry?"

"He hasn't exactly done anything," the young woman confessed mournfully. "It's just that he doesn't love me and I'm not sure he wants to keep me as his wife. I'm more a mistress in his bed than of his household."

Mimi chuckled. "Now, sugar, that's nothing to complain about. I'd say you got the best part of that bargain." When Cherice's chin began a contrary quivering, she made her tone more serious. "Perhaps you'd better tell me everything."

So she did. She poured it out, the hurt that provoked her into playing the role of wanton, the pride that held her to it even when she cringed beneath its consequence, the maliciousness she suffered at Lilith Amory's hands. That last had Mimi gritting her teeth.

"And she dares call you a harlot," the indignant madame huffed. "That woman has the stone cold heart of a whore with none of the benefits of the profession."

"But she's right, don't you see," Cherice cried out in anguish.

"No, sugar, I don't see. You tell me."

"I'm not good enough for them. I never will be. No matter what I do, no matter how hard I try, I'll never fit in as an Amory. It was wrong of you to buy my way in and wrong of me to allow it. As soon as he can afford to, Ruben means to set me aside."

Mimi gasped. "He's told you that?"

Cherice shook her head. "Not in so many words. Not in any words. He never talks to me. I might as well not exist except to warm his sheets at night. I might as well be his whore. It's the only role I'm suited to, the only one they'll allow me." With that, she began to cry, great gusty sobs that saw her wrapped up in her aunt's cushiony embrace.

"There, there, sugar. Damn those arrogant Amorys, anyway. You come on home to me, honey, and give them what for. They'll not be treating us like we was dirt."

"I can't." Cherice took several deep, composing breaths and sat back with a show of courage. "I belong at Stillwater, with Ruben. Especially now. I'm sorry I'm behaving so badly. All I can seem to do lately is cry and carry on."

Mimi inhaled sharply and gently took up her niece's hand. "Does he know yet?" she asked quietly.

Cherice shook her head, renewed tears beginning to gather on the tips of her dark lashes like heavy jewels.

"Oh, darlin', you've got to tell him. It could make all the difference."

"But I wanted him to want me to stay because he loves me, not because he's honor-bound to provide."

"Cheri," her aunt said in her no-nonsense tone, "that may be the best you're gonna get so stop your sniveling right now and think about what you're gonna do. Do you still love the man?"

"Yes."

"Then you fight to keep him. No Leslie has ever been a quitter. We do what we have to do to get what we want and what we deserve. You deserve to be happy. You deserve to live in that big ol' house with the man you love. You told me you wouldn't apologize for me being who and what I was. Well, honey, you stop apologizing for yourself. There ain't nothing in this world wrong with who you are. And if that man of yours can't see that, well, then maybe he's just not worth having!"

Cherice tried to hang onto those staunch sentiments when Ruben settled beside her on the buggy seat, but somehow all she could see was the handsome planter's son with his halo of blond hair and his birthright of privilege smiling at her across the parlor of a bawdy house. And there was no way to shake the consequence of that first meeting. She was the niece of a brothel owner and he was landed gentry with bloodlines as pure as a Tennessee walking horse. Money had exchanged hands to bribe her from threatening that lineage five years ago, and again, it was money that bought her way in. Were she and her aunt any better than the Northern carpetbaggers who swarmed down to capitalize on a broken and desperate populace? If it hadn't been for Mimi's offer, would Ruben have bothered with her at all? His house, his lands seemed to be all that mattered to him. It didn't help her confidence when the first thing he began to talk about was the sale of Stillwater cotton.

"I figure with the combined profits of what we managed to hoard during the war and what we're in the process of putting in the ground, we'll be making a tidy sum." He glanced at the silent figure beside him and frowned. She was listening but she showed no enthusiasm for his news. "In no time we'll be out of debt and heading in a forward direction. Then I can get on with my plans for the future." He slipped another look at the woman sharing the seat and the unsettling sensation returned. She was too quiet, too inward in her mood.

"Cheri—"

"Ruben, my aunt suggested I see a doctor."

The sudden words slapped the breath from him. "What? Why? What's wrong? Are you sick? Why the hell didn't you say something?" His mind was racing, imagining life-consuming fever, lingering consumptive ailments—

"I'm saying it now, Ruben. I'm with child."

His whole thought process blanked as he stared at her. The first thing that registered was his mammoth sense of excitement. The second was how very distressed she seemed about the entire matter. As if she was far from thrilled with the idea of his child.

"Are you sure?" he couched carefully.

"Of course, I'm sure," she snapped back. Tears began to glisten as she focused on the road ahead instead of upon the cautious confusion of his expression. "I'm sorry you're not pleased."

"I'm—surprised, is all." And deeply, mortally wounded by her lack of anticipation. He sat stiff and stunned as the horse started for Stillwater. So much so that Cherice canted a resentful look his way.

"Worried that it's not yours?"

No, he wasn't. He knew it was, but because she would throw up the suspicion in his face, he found himself thinking of her earlier tears and the letter from New York, and heartache made for a brittle tone. "Wishing it wasn't?"

When she said nothing to deny it, his mood fell deeper into blinding despair. Had the letter from New York included a plea for her return? One that she would have considered if not for her present condition? Had she been planning another disappearance from his life once she tired of playing games with his pride? The sudden thought that she might do so, not only abandoning him but depriving him of his child, started a flood of panic rising. And a frightening line of questions. Why had Cherice married him? For his name? For his lands? It certainly wasn't for his wealth. Or had it been some cold scheme of her aunt's to humiliate his mother? He'd been so anxious to have her, he hadn't stopped to consider Cherice's motives before he wed her. It hadn't mattered then. It hadn't mattered until he realized how much he still loved her. Over the last weeks as he'd watched his wife pour her efforts into Stillwater, he'd begun to hope it was because she was eager to make it her home. Why would she bother if she didn't care? But now he wasn't sure. He wasn't sure of her. He wasn't sure of anything except that he couldn't let her go. But other than shackling her within the boundaries of his plantation, what could he do?

What could he do when she offered no reassurances and he was too scarred by past betrayals to rally behind any degree of trust?

When they reached Stillwater, Cherice allowed him to lift her down but she didn't linger teasingly in his arms as he'd grown used to expecting. She stepped quickly away, pleading fatigue, and bade them not to wait supper for her. She wanted to lie down. He let her go because she did seem genuinely weary and because she never once looked back at him as she mounted the stairs. If she had, she would have seen his heart in his eyes.

But standing across the foyer as yet unnoticed, Lilith Amory did, and the sight horrified her. Almost as much as the one in the parlor.

"Ruben, where have you been? Come look at this at once. I am nearly prostrate with distress. How could you allow her to do such a thing?"

Ruben shifted his attention to his mother with a dragging reluctance. One she was not unaware of and that knowledge made her tone more desperate.

"You simply must take my side in this. She's gone too far."

He followed her to the front parlor, then drew up short at the amazing sight just within the arched entry. Two monstrous gilt cupids on marble pedestals flanked either side, wearing wings and nothing else. They were the most tasteless pieces of statuary he'd ever seen and the thought of Cherice's malicious enjoyment in picking them out brought a sketchy smile to his lips.

"Well?" his mother demanded in full-blown indignation. Then her haughty expression fell at his response.

"I like them. Adds a certain—color to the place." He hung his hat over the modestly proportioned anatomy of one of them and walked toward his library. Lilith gaped after him.

"Ruben ... Ruben, you can't mean that you'll do nothing!"

He turned to give her a stern look of warning. "I mean I am sick of all this bickering. Cherice is my wife. She is mistress of this house."

Those truths stung Lilith Amory. "Maybe you don't care that she's turning our home into a whorehouse, but I care. I care! And if you had any respect for me, you would demand she put aside her whorish ways while beneath the roof of decent folk. I won't have that slut making a laughing stock of your father's fine memory."

Ruben's gaze narrowed dangerously and his voice was a cool drawl. "I don't know that we're all that decent, Mama. And as for my father, I seem to recall Daddy had a distinct fondness for whorehouses, so why should I be any different?"

He didn't consider the consequences of his harsh words until he watched his mother's features pale. Abruptly she turned and would have fled the room if he hadn't caught her up in a tight embrace.

"Mama, I'm sorry. That was a thoughtless thing to say and I truly didn't mean it."

Lilith clutched his forearms, choosing to blame another instead. "It's that woman, Ruben. Can't you see it? She's going to ruin our lives. How can I ever hold my head up amongst my friends with her living in my house? I'll never be able to invite anyone to visit me again."

He covered her hands briefly with his own, then released himself from her grasp. He spoke very concisely so she wouldn't misunderstand. "It's my life, Mama. It's my house. She's my wife. Invite your friends if you want to. Throw a blanket over the cupids if they offend you. But don't ask me to be ashamed of the woman I married because I'm not. I love Cherice." He heard his mother gasp in dismay but continued strongly. "I have always loved her. I wouldn't have anyone else. Not ever. You criticize her, you criticize me, and I won't have it. You hear me, Mama?"

She stood stiff and proud. "Yes. I hear you. But don't expect me to forgive you for it. You're weak, just like your father was weak when it came to wicked women. Neither of you could see past your lusts. Well, don't think that I'm going to show you the slightest sympathy when she tears your heart in two. It's your house, your life, your heart. Destroy them all if you want." And with that, she, too, climbed the stairs without looking back.

Cherice clenched the edge of the bedcovers as she heard the door open before her husband's uneven step. She closed her eyes to pretend sleep. The last thing she wanted was more words with Ruben. Or worse, more silences. She listened to him move about the room, disrobing and washing up, then he approached the bed. His side dipped beneath his weight and she heard him sigh as he lay back. Then, nothing. He made no move to press his usual good-night kiss upon her brow or gather her up to him for the first of many ardent caresses. Tonight, they shared the bed but they slept alone. Could Lilith be right? Considering his lack of reaction to her news, it seemed to make too much sense. If he wanted to share a child with her, wouldn't he display some sort of gladness? Instead, Ruben was grimly silent. Was he cursing the fertility of their union because it bound her to him with a debt of honor? Or because now he had to rid himself not only of an unwanted wife but an unworthy heir, as well? Or, if Lilith was wrong, was he no longer interested in her now that she was breeding the next in the Amory line? Both choices were so cruel to consider, but consider them she must because now she had more than just herself to think of.

She was carrying the Amory heir.

Chapter Seven

As more weeks passed, the impersonal impasse only deepened between husband and wife. Ruben rose early and came home late. If Cherice were still awake, he managed a civil good night before rolling away from her. It was easier for him to pretend she wasn't there than to acknowledge her and be forced to face the fact that she didn't want him. She no longer played the tempting little games he'd come to enjoy. She didn't prance around in skimpy little nothings to drive his passions wild. She stopped taunting him with her naughty behavior and tormenting kisses. He even found he missed his mother's ceaseless complaints over her faults. Cherice became a quiet shadow in the big house, almost more servant than mistress of its halls. She slept little and ate less, and Ruben fretted over her increasing pallor.

The one thing she did seem to care about was Stillwater. She was always with Maddy, busy with some element of running the plantation's household. Floors and windows gleamed, and rooms were revived to their former sumptuous glory. Under her attentions, the storerooms filled, as the quality and quantity of their meals attested. She spent days in the steaming kitchen preserving spring fruits, then put in her own ambitious garden, telling him softly when asked that she liked the feel of the earth in her hands. Those quiet words planted a seed of emotion in his heart that just kept growing. Putting things into the ground meant planning on a future.

Hope burst into full bloom the day he found a new shirt and socks fashioned in an unfamiliar pattern of precise stitches placed in amongst his other things. Something about those handmade items ... He stood for the longest time, overwhelmed by the ridiculous desire to just break down and bawl. He couldn't remember the last time anyone had done something of a personal nature for him. Why would she bother if she didn't care for him—just a little. That throat-clogging tenderness stayed with him all day, and every time he put his hands in the dark, loamy Tennessee soil, he thought of the woman he'd married feeling that same attachment to the land he loved.

That well of caring was filled to overflowing by the time the sun trailed scarlet slashes across the sky above Memphis. He rode in from the newly sown fields, dazed by a wondering sense of devotion and frustrated by his inability to display it. The fact that he'd wed her for her resources and his want for a bitter revenge had somehow evolved into something he didn't understand. It was no longer the trip out to work the land that motivated his days but rather the journey back to the home she'd made for him. A home that would be nothing more than empty rooms and an empty life if she were not there waiting. Cherice had become the anchoring point for his entire world, and he had to think of some way to show his wife how much she'd come to mean to him.

It came to him as they dined that evening in their usual silence. As he looked around him and saw the return of elegance and comfort, he felt pride rise up to surround him with an engulfing satisfaction. He wanted everyone in Shelby County to know of the rebirth of Stillwater and who was responsible, not so much because she brought the needed capital but because she supplied the driving force to see it done. She'd pulled all of them up from the sinkhole of devastation left by the war. She'd given Stillwater a chance for revival. She'd given him a renewed purpose. She'd even infused his mother with the will to go on. He'd found Lilith polishing silver that afternoon. It was the first time she'd stirred from her lethargy since he'd come home. There seemed no end to what he owed Cherice Parnell, and he would see her paid back if it took him a lifetime. And he meant to start right away.

"The cotton's in," he announced over dinner. "I was thinking we have a reason to celebrate. Why not toss open the doors and invite all our friends over to share in our good fortune?"

He'd directed that to Cherice but as she lifted her gaze, it was Lilith who jumped in to snap up the idea. "Oh, how grand it will be to entertain at Stillwater again. It's been so long since I've arranged a party. I never thought I'd care to after your father . . . He'd be so proud of you, Ruben. You deserve this chance to show off all your hard work. He would have approved."

What could he say after that? That he'd meant for Cherice to take charge of the planning? That his reason was to show off his wife and announce the impending birth of his heir? He watched his mother's face positively glow with anticipation, and he knew right then that it was better to say nothing than to destroy her pleasure. She'd had so little to look forward to since his father's death. But then, what to do about Cherice? Her eyes lowered quickly to her untouched plate, and even from across the table, he could feel her withdrawal. Cursing his inept handling of the situation, he sat listening to his mother go on and on about how she was going to make their party the social event of the season, a sort of testimony to the reviving South. And he wondered how he was going to make it up to Cherice.

She excused herself from the table as soon as politely possible, and Ruben followed her out onto the front veranda. She'd gone to stand at its far corner and was looking out toward the rich cotton fields. She stiffened in her awareness of him but he forced himself to overlook that defensive posture as he approached to lean against the rail beside her.

"She's going to need your help in putting it all together," he broached casually. Cherice only laughed, a soft, cynical sound.

"She doesn't want my help, Ruben. The only thing she'd appreciate from me is my promise to lock myself in the storeroom until everyone is gone."

That he couldn't argue it was a source of irritation. Ruben let his knuckles graze along the line of her jaw. He felt her flinch. "You could change her mind, Cheri." She could, he realized. In the last few weeks, he'd been seeing the real Cherice; the strong, independent and capable woman hidden behind the playacting. She'd begun to wear sedate clothing and the abrasiveness was absent from her manner. There was nothing in the least bit offensive in the figure she presented. All it would take was a nudge for his mother to notice.

But Cherice smiled sadly. "Your mother made up her mind about me a long time ago. She doesn't want to change it. The best thing I could do to make your party a success is stay out of the way. Perhaps the guests would think I was a servant."

His fingers curled around her determined jaw and angled her face up toward him. "I don't want them to think that. You're my wife, Cherice."

She reached up and gently drew his hand down so she could look away from him. Her voice was soft and emotionless. "I know what I am to you, Ruben."

"No," he corrected with a quiet intensity. "I don't think you do."

She glanced around, and he heard her snatch a quick breath as he lowered down to possess her sweet mouth with his. It was a light kiss, just a brushing of his lips over hers before he straightened. He had her attention then. She was staring up at him warily, wantingly.

"Do you remember that first summer we met, that Fourth of July party at Mimi's?" He watched her eyes soften and knew she did. "She wouldn't let you mingle with the others so I had to follow you outside so we could have a minute or two together. Your Aunt Mimi was one strict watchdog." Cherice smiled faintly but her gaze never left his. "You were wearing a white dress with green bows and with all that moonlight shining on you, I thought you were the most beautiful thing I'd ever seen. I still think so."

He saw her skepticism and in that moment he knew. He'd made the mistake of courting her passions first. She'd reacted to him on a purely physical plane but elsewhere, they were still unused to one another. Now it was time to gently court her cautious heart the way he had one long-ago summer.

"I can still hear the music playing and feel you in my arms as we danced out in the shadows. I was so in love with you, I don't think my feet were touching the ground."

"Neither were mine," she answered in the fragile hush.

"I knew right then that you were the woman I wanted to marry."

He leaned down to kiss her again, with slow, sensual sweeps that tasted the tender offering of her lips, the seducing curve of her throat, and the unexpected dampness of her cheek. That stopped him.

"Cheri?"

"Ruben, please," she whispered raggedly. "Please don't do this to me if it means nothing to you."

His fingertips framed her face so she couldn't escape the sincerity of his gaze. "It means everything to me, Cherice."

His earnest words made her tremble. The kiss that followed made her sigh. Then her arms were about his neck, squeezing tight with the fierceness of her need to believe.

Gradually he began to move, just a slight shuffle at first that evolved into the steps of a waltz. He wasn't as graceful as he'd been all those years ago but Cherice experienced the same emotions within the strong circle of his arms. She felt protected, cherished. Loved. She rested her head upon his shoulder, shutting her eyes as the tears threatened to flow. Oh, if only it were true. If only he loved her still.

For several minutes, they glided along the veranda to the music of memory then Ruben came to a stop. When Cherice lifted her head, he kissed once, very sweetly, then straightened away with one last caress of her cheek.

"I'm going to turn in," he told her, then went back inside, leaving her to interpret what had occurred between them beneath the dazzling Tennessee stars. Leaving it up to her as to whether she followed.

Cherice was shaken. She knew how to respond to his

desire but this quiet courtship had her flustered. She trusted his passion for her; she couldn't be sure, however, his tender words were as honest. And she wanted so desperately to believe they were. The only way she could find out was by taking a risk at disappointment. Could she be hurt any worse than she already had been? And then, when she thought of the benefits ...

The only light in their bedroom came from the open gallery doors. Cherice began a slow disrobing, keeping an uncertain eye upon the motionless figure already beneath the covers. She started to reach for the modest lawn nightdress she'd been wearing then hesitated. Then decided to forgo its discouraging concealment. She slipped, instead, between the sheets wearing no more than her delicate perfume. There she lay a safe distance away from her husband as she searched for some means to convey a request for closeness that he wouldn't confuse with a simple seduction. The only way he wouldn't was for her to tell him.

"Ruben?"

"Ummm?"

"Ruben, would you—" Her courage faltered. They'd shared next to nothing for almost three weeks. She didn't know if closeness was even possible.

"Would I what?" he prompted when the silence stretched out between them.

"Nothing."

"Would I what?"

She took a timid little breath and muttered uncomfortably, "Would you just hold me?"

He didn't say anything right away. His arm came up to slip beneath her shoulders, crooking to bring her up against the hard line of his side. He shifted slightly so she fit in snug harmony to his every contour. Then he asked, "Like this?"

She nodded, settling in contentedly.

"That it?"

She nodded again and she felt his tension ease into acceptance. His hand rose to brush her hair away from her face and his mouth touched lightly to her brow. Then he just held her, afraid if he did more he would push the moment beyond what she'd requested.

But Cherice felt no such restrictions. She nestled her cheek into the hollow of his collarbone and let her fingers thread through the crisp mat covering his chest. She'd meant for it to be a soothing gesture but soon, despite her best intentions, the movement grew restless. Finally she fit her palm to his cheek, turning his head so she could stretch up for his lips. Finding his mouth warm and parted in welcome, she lingered and lavished him with her kisses, with her roving caresses, with all the yearning in her heart. Breathless and with heart racing, she pulled away. He was staring down at her through deep, fathomless eyes, waiting upon her will. Her pride crumbled in an instant when pitting the loneliness of those wretched nights against this intimate reunion.

"Ruben, would you love me, please?" When he didn't respond right away, she added humbly, "That is, if you want to."

"If I want to?" He repeated that with a small half smile. "If I want to, Cheri? I haven't wanted anything else for as long as I can remember."

And he was up and over her in an instant, consuming her with the fiery tenderness of his kiss until she was panting urgently, with the unhurried thoroughness of his hands until she was writhing wildly, and finally, with the slow, searing strokes that had her whimpering and keening his name right up to the breath-stealing point of completion.

Body lax and senses wonderfully worn, she curled against him with a contented little murmur and the totally unplanned words, "Oh, Ruben, how very much I love you," just before she surrendered to sleep.

It was a long while before Ruben could find a restful slumber. *How very much I love you.* Never had one phrase so pleased and terrified him. Because he wasn't sure it was true.

Cherice stirred from a heavenly lethargy into a surprising and deeply satisfying reality. Ruben was still beside her. He looked as though he'd been awake for some time, and she wondered how long he'd been lying there, content to hold her when he was usually off to the fields at the first pink of dawn.

"Good morning," she ventured somewhat shyly.

His answer was a long, explicit kiss and the rasp of his chin against her cheek as he hugged her close. "'Morning," came his husky rumble. "Thought I'd see you to breakfast to make sure you ate something." He leaned back to frown at her sternly. "You're going to eat if I have to spoon it down you every morning. It's not good for you or the baby to go without."

He put his big hand over her still-flat belly and rubbed soothingly. Everything in Cherice dissolved into a pool of liquid emotion. It was the fist time he'd spoken of the child since the day she'd told him and now, to do so with such a tone of concern—she was positively radiant.

"I'll eat," she promised. Then her lids lowered provokingly. "But I rather like the idea of you spoon-feeding me every morning." And because she followed those words with a pouty, wet-lipped smile and a suggestive shift of one silky bared leg, it took them twice as long to get down to the breakfast table.

Lilith looked between them suspiciously, displeased with their obvious reconciliation. She'd begun to have hopes of an irreparable fracture within their marriage bonds. But this morning those bonds were solid, and the kiss Cherice sent him off with was steamy enough to wilt the pleats in the parlor drapes.

Floating on the afterglow of their time together, Cherice waited until Ruben was out of sight before turning to smile at her dour-faced mother-in-law. She didn't even care if the woman glowered back. It didn't matter what Lilith Amory thought. Ruben had made her the unquestionable mistress of his house, and she was well on to working her way through the barriers around his heart.

Cherice took another sip of her coffee and pretended not to see Lilith craning over her shoulder at the pattern book of new Eastern styles. If one thing held universally true, it was that neither war or class lines could destroy a woman's need to know the latest fashion news. While the plates were dated by the time Mimi got them from her connections in New York, they were still far and away more current than the recent parlor gossip. And it had been a long time since Lilith had enjoyed any of that. Purposefully Cherice angled the book so her mother-in-law was teased by the closer silhouette of modern skirts. She then shut the book. She smiled to herself at the muffled sound of disappointment.

"Oh, forgive me, Mother Amory. Were you looking at these?"

"Just curious, is all," the other woman snapped. "I'm perfectly content with what I have."

"Oh, but don't you think the drape of these gowns would look divine on someone with your grace and height?"

Lilith hesitated, wary but wavering.

"Especially this one." Cherice flipped through the

pages, then enticed Lilith to lean forward for a closer look. The older woman sighed in appreciation.

"That is lovely."

"And wouldn't you be the envy of all if you were to greet them in this dress in, say, a silvery blue moire?" Cherice began to close the book again. "But then you're content with what you have."

Lilith's hand shot out to stay the pages. Her gaze hungrily detailed the elegant, closer-cut bell skirt. "I haven't had a new dress since . . ." Her voice trailed off wistfully.

"Maddy," Cherice called as the old black woman passed in the hall. "Could you bring me that bolt of fabric we got in Memphis?"

All Lilith's staunch objections fell away as soon as Cherice rolled a length of the shimmering material across the table top. The older woman's hands lingered lovingly along the icy ripple of silk. Watching her, Cherice experienced an unexpected surge of compassion for this woman who'd only wished her ill for as long as she could remember. But it had to start somewhere, that laying down of the arms. If Lee and Davis could do so with dignity in an effort to establish a lasting peace, so could she.

"I think this would be much better suited to you than me." When the other woman's gaze leapt up in surprise, Cherice pretended not to notice. She planned to make the terms of surrender as face-saving as possible. "It's too pale for my complexion. But with your fairness, it should be quite stunning. If we took some measurements this morning and cut a pattern, it would be done in time for you to wear at the party."

Through a subtle cant of her eyes, she watched Lilith try to muster a protest but the older woman's hands couldn't relinquish the feel of the fabric, the glossiness, the richness, the return to the security it represented.

And when Ruben came in from the fields, he could have been felled with a puff of smoke at the sight of the two women bent industriously over their stitching in camaraderie. Both looked up to greet him with smiles, and the double-barreled welcome was like a punch of squirrel shot to the midsection.

Lilith went back to her seam while Cherice rose and came to meet him in the foyer. Paying no mind to his soiled and strongly scented state, her arms went about him and her face lifted for his kiss. What could he do but comply? When she came down from her toes, he whispered, "What have you done to my mother? Spiked her tea with laudanum?"

She chuckled warmly and the sound twisted around his senses seductively. "We found a common ground, is all."

"Sewing?" His brow arched. "I was not a common ground?"

"You were a common battlefield, husband. Don't question. Just be glad for the state of truce."

Seeing the wisdom of that, he said no more and enjoyed the harmony that settled over his home. Just as he enjoyed the attentions of his wife after the lights turned down low and the evening played its own sultry songs. The only thing that could have made it better was hearing her say again that she loved him, but she was stingy with those precious words. It never occurred to him that she was waiting for him to speak them first.

Replies began to pour in to Lilith's invitations. A hum of excitement filled the big house as preparations neared completion. Cherice was busy, and she kept her thoughts purposefully turned from questioning her place in the revelry to come. It was one thing for Lilith to lower the barriers when it was just the two of them working a common seam. It was another for the woman to stand arm-in-arm with her while greeting guests at the front door. That would be the real test of her status within the Amory household. The fast-approaching trial by fire had her nerves strung to a fine tension. The last thing she needed was a last-minute complication.

The strange men arrived at the door in the sweltry late morning hours the day before the Amorys' ball. Cherice greeted them with a loaded shotgun.

"What can I do for you gentlemen?"

The tallest of the three doffed his hat. "Ma'am, my name's Keller. I represent the Treasury Department of our United States government."

His tone set Cherice's stomach to quivering but she forced her words to exude a haughty calm. "To the best of my knowledge, all our taxes are paid up, sir."

"This ain't about taxes, ma'am. It's about the cotton you folks have stored in a warehouse down on the river front."

The cold terror just kept mounting. "What about it?"

"The government has entitled us to seize it as Confederate goods."

"Th-there must be some mistake."

"You can't do that," came Lilith's fierce protest from behind her. "That cotton belongs to Stillwater. It's my son's. It's robbery, that's what it is! Shoot them off the steps, Cherice!"

The men assumed an aggressive pose, and Cherice was quick to discard her rifle lest they need more of a prompt to open fire. She had no faith in the integrity of such men whom she'd heard were swarming the countryside, possessing abandoned properties and seizing up its cotton bales in the name of the Federal Reserve. Her first duty was to Stillwater and the preservation of Ruben's family. All else was inconsequential. As the men scowled warily, she adopted her most congenial smile.

"Why, what has come over me? You poor boys must be drooping out there in that heat. Where are my manners? Please, come in to the parlor and let me fetch you a cool libation." She turned and sashayed inside, gripping Lilith's arm in passing. To her, she whispered urgently, "Send someone for Ruben. Hurry. I'll stall them as long as I can. And Lilith, I don't want him alarmed. We can't risk having him hurt."

Her mother-in-law paused, assessing her with a cautious stare.

"Hurry!"

Then Lilith swept down the hall as Cherice turned into the parlor with her three uninvited guests. Each of the men lifted an eyebrow as they passed the unique statuary.

"Gentlemen, please seat yourselves. Now, what is all this nonsense about cotton? Surely you can't be referring to what we just put in the fields? My husband may have fought on the side of the Confederacy but he took an oath of allegiance and as a citizen of our great country, I don't believe you have any rights to what's taking root on our land."

"We're not interested in what you've got growing, just in what you've got stored away in Memphis. Them there bales were harvested to further the cause of treason and, as such, are to be confiscated."

Lilith was right, Cherice figured furiously. It was robbery under the guise of Reconstruction. Confederate cotton, indeed. They were looking for a way to steal from a submissive and broken South. And she was not about to let them snatch anything from Stillwater.

She gave a giddy laugh and placed a hand upon her bosom, drawing attention there with the fluttery gesture. The distraction couldn't hurt. "Silly me. Forgive me for appearing so foolish but I honestly did not know what you were talking about. You're speaking of the bales my husband *sold.*"

"Sold?" The speaker's gaze narrowed suspiciously. "To whom?"

"Why, to my aunt, Mimi Leslie. Have you heard of her?"

The men exchanged smirking glances, so she assumed they had.

"Well, then. If you know of my Aunt Mimi, then you know you cannot consider this contraband. She was a neutral during the unfortunate altercation between our North and South, so you can't call her property Confederate cotton."

"A convenient sale of goods, wouldn't you say?" the tall one muttered, and the others looked equally doubtful.

"Oh, I don't expect you gentlemen to believe me, what with me being married to a Southern officer and all. I surely don't know where my husband put his bill of sale. I don't confuse my head over matters of business." She flickered her lashes helplessly and the men smiled with more tolerance. "But if you can be patient, I'm sure he can find it for you. Perhaps he could bring you the paperwork, say, tomorrow?"

"Ma'am, we'd like to get this matter resolved. If you can't produce proof, we'll have to proceed."

Cherice cursed silently but held to her insipid smile. "Well, then, I guess we'll just have to go right to the source, then, won't we? Would you gentlemen care to accompany me to my aunt's? I'm sure she can clear up this little misunderstanding."

The Treasury men exchanged looks and sly smiles, then the speaker relented. "All right, Mrs. Amory. Hitch up your buggy and we'll see you into town."

Lilith was standing sentinel at the doorway. Her expression had objection etched in every strong line.

"Cherice, you can't mean to go with them," she hissed as her son's wife paused on the way to get her wrap.

"I have no choice. We can't let them take what's ours without a fight. Keep Ruben here if you have to hold that gun on him. Now's not the time for temper. It's a time for a little diplomacy. And if that doesn't work, a few outright lies."

Then Cherice swept by, oblivious to her mother-in-law's look of respect.

Chapter Eight

"You just let her go?!"

Lilith wrung her hands in the face of her son's rage. "What could I do, Ruben? She was right. We couldn't do nothing."

"You should have waited for me. Damn! If anything's happened to her . . ." He let that hang threateningly as he strode back toward the front door.

"Ruben, where are you going?"

"After her."

"No!" Lilith grabbed onto his arm and hung on tight. "No, you can't. Ruben, you can't." But he kept walking, dragging her until she had no alternative but to let go. When he paused to pull his heavy Navy Colt from a drawer in the foyer table, her protests began anew. "Why are you taking that?"

"Just in case," he told her with a grimness that had her blood chilling.

She put herself in front of him to bar the door, and it was stop or plow right over her. He stopped.

"Mama, get outta my way."

"Not until you put that gun back. I buried my husband. I will not bury my son. This isn't a time for temper." Cherice's words came back to her and she wielded them with authority. "Go after her if you have to, but be smart about it. Their kind looks for any excuse. Don't give them one. Ruben, I don't know what I'd do if the two of you didn't come back."

Her tears were what finally broke through the madness. Slowly he replaced the pistol in the drawer, letting four years of fury drain from him. He wasn't going to Memphis in search of confrontation. He was going to bring his wife home. The only way he would go forward was by putting the days of violence behind him.

"Ruben, be careful." His mother embraced him, trembling more fitfully than she had the day she'd sent him off to war. Of course, then there had been the illusion of immortality. She leaned back and her next words bemused him. "Trust Cherice. She's doing this for all of us."

He rode hard and fast. The roads were in terrible shape, having hosted the flow and ebb of two warring armies, so he raced cross-country to save both time and his mount. By the time he reached Memphis, he was almost as lathered as his animal. If anything had happened to Cherice . . . He couldn't play out the rest of that phrase, nor could he ignore it. He'd seen too much not to worry about her safety, so it was in a frantic anxiety that he reined in before Mimi's house of ill-repute. And it was in a heightened state of panic that he strode into Mimi's private parlor to find the madame casually hostessing his wife and the three government men to tea and amiable conversation. Tension released in a huge wave of relief and responsive anger that they should all appear so cozy when he was shaking right down to his boot soles with dread.

"Ruben, how good of you to join us," Mimi cooed with her infallible charm. "Would you like some tea?"

"I'd like to know what the hell's going on."

"Come sit by me, sugar," Cherice simpered prettily. But behind her vapid smile came the piercing signal of her dark gaze. Warily he complied, and instantly she was snuggled up against him like an old hound on a cold night. For all her coquettish behavior, he could feel her tension, and remembering his mother's advice, he relaxed and followed her lead. "Honey, I was just telling these fine gentlemen about our arrangement with Aunt Mimi."

"You did bring the bill of sale, didn't you, Mr. Amory?" one of the men prompted.

Cherice was nuzzling at his neck and nibbling on his ear. He heard her whisper, "Play along, Ruben. Please." He slipped his arm around her shoulders easily and smiled in affable ignorance.

"I'm sorry, but my mama was so scattered she didn't tell me a thing. She hasn't been herself since the occupation. Now, what's all this about?" He directed himself to the men with typical planter arrogance, ignoring the women as if they were meant for nothing but decoration.

"Your lovely wife was explaining that you'd sold your cotton to Miss Mimi before the fighting."

Ruben never so much as blinked. "Yes, I did. Is there some problem? I needed money to provide for my mama and our property so I contracted with Miss Mimi for—"

"For seventy-five dollars a bale," Mimi supplied smoothly.

Cherice felt his every sinew snap taut and was quick to rub her palm up and down his inner thigh, hoping to cap the explosion until the government men were gone. But she needn't have worried.

"That's right," he drawled. "Seventy-five a bale."

Mimi regarded the Yankees with a sultry smile. "So you see, gentlemen, just like I told you, the cotton's mine and you could hardly call me a Southern sympathizer, now could you? I'm for free enterprise and not the least bit of a threat to the United States government. Unless you consider having yourselves a good time a danger to morale."

They chuckled and the mood of suspicion eased. "Mr. Amory, you'd have no trouble producing a bill of sale if we were to stop over tomorrow morning, would you?"

"None whatsoever," Ruben assured them.

"Then we don't need to take up any more of your time." The three of them stood and Mimi rose with them.

"Why don't you boys come on back this evening? Consider it a professional courtesy. On the house."

The men were grinning, and their spokesman murmured, "Thank you kindly, Miss Mimi. We just might take you up on that. Good day to you all."

A strained silence settled until the men were shown the door and Mimi returned. Then all Ruben's pretense fell away.

"Seventy-five dollars a bale?" he ground out. "Surely you know they're worth two hundred each."

Mimi met his challenging gaze head on. "Of course I do, sugar. And so do they. But they also know I wouldn't have paid you top dollar. I'm a businesswoman, honey. I tend my own interests first. Shall we get to that bill of sale?"

"You don't seriously think I'm going to let you have that cotton for that price."

"Why, darlin', I don't think you have much choice. It's not like you could go selling it to anyone else with them breathing down your neck, now could you?"

"Ruben, I'm sorry," Cherice said softly as she studied the savage play of emotion on his face. "I didn't know what else to do. I couldn't just let them take it."

"No," he drawled out frigidly. "You just thought you'd let your aunt steal it from me." Frustration slowed his reasonings. All he could comprehend was that all his plans were gone. His plan to buy himself out from under Mimi's bargain, to begin fresh with Cherice with a sincere proposal and a solid start to their marriage. Now all he recognized was a deeper hole sucking him down into Mimi's debt. And in his irrational mind, he drew another unpleasant parallel.

"Why, Miss Mimi, you seem to be thriving off my family's misfortune. You buy your niece a name off our financial desperation, then you jerk the only means of getting back on our feet right out from under us. Quite a clever plan, wouldn't you agree, Cherice?"

Cherice went very still, not liking the assumptions she could see forming in his slated glare. Then he rose up and the lethal thrust of his question speared right through the heart of all they'd begun to build between them.

"How long have you been a part of it, Cherice?"

When she was too stunned to respond, he presumed her silence implied guilt. All the unanswered questions surfaced again, forming a pattern of lies and hurt that none of the past few months of pleasure could overcome. She'd used him then. She was using him now. Why had he ever thought they could build something lasting upon a foundation of mistrust when the slightest jar sent them spinning back into doubt?

"Was this some new game the two of you concocted? A way to strip Stillwater of its chance to survive without you? A way to keep your dainty little foot on the back of my neck? Did you send the Treasury Department knocking on my door so you'd have a way to cripple me? Well, the Union Army couldn't do it, and I'll be damned if you're going to. Wasn't humiliating us enough? How far are you willing to go? And to think I wouldn't let my mama call you a whore."

Mimi's slap sent him staggering back. Her voice was razor-sharp. "I think you'd better go. You go home to your high-and-mighty house and you tell your mama I paid her back in full. We're even now. She'll understand. Maybe she'll even explain it to you. Give her this and ask her if she still thinks it was worth the price she paid."

Ruben looked at the sealed envelope she extended then at Cherice. Cherice was staring up at him through an impenetrable gaze. Without remorse. Without apology. Without shame. He snatched the letter and strode out of the room.

"Fool," Mimi spat. "Arrogant fool. Just like his father. That damned land, his damned pride. That's all that matters to an Amory." Then her tone softened as she put her arms about the rigid form of her niece. "Good riddance, I say. We don't need the likes of him." Then she regarded her stoic ward with a touch of worry. The girl was too calm. "At least it's over now, sugar, and you can get on with your life."

"No," Cherice answered with a quiet certainty. "It's not over and he has no idea how far I'm willing to go."

Lilith was waiting on the front porch, but Ruben had no patience with her inquiring look. He came down off the back of his sweaty stallion and stormed past her, heading straight for the whiskey in his study. The first swallow served to steady the tremor in his hands. It would take the whole bottle to ease the pain blazing up from his leg. But he suspected there wasn't enough liquor south of the old Mason-Dixon line to soothe the agony in his heart.

"Ruben?"

"Go away, Mama."

"What's wrong?"

"It must please you to no end to hear me say you were right and I was wrong." He poured himself another tumbler full. The neck of the decanter clattered against the glass.

"Ruben, where's Cherice?"

"I don't know. Probably with her aunt."

"When is she coming home?"

"Home?" He gave a short laugh and bolted down the amber liquid. It seared all the way down. "I can't say I know if she is. Or if I even care."

"Ruben—"

"Mama, leave me alone," he cried out in torment, then added with a low moan of despair, "please. Just leave me alone. Go plan for your party. Enjoy it while you can 'cause as soon as it's done, we're selling everything inside this house and all the land it takes to pay that woman off. I don't want to be beholden to her for one more second than I have to. It was a stupid thing to do and a stupider thing to wish for. Go on, Mama. Go."

And when she did with an obvious reluctance, he settled in for some heavy-duty drinking, the kind he'd seen his father indulge in when the crops were bad. A soul-swallowing, mind-numbing drunk that was supposed to drown all his troubles. Except it didn't. He sat for hours, hunched over his glass, his thoughts reeling with the uncoordinated effects of alcohol, trying to piece together things that were far beyond his feeble reckoning. Why had she married him? How could she love him so well and yet not at all? Why had she left him with a broken heart only to come back years later to buy her way back into it? She was having his child even as she was destroying his name. It made no sense. Nothing did in that fog of bourbon except how much he loved her. Dear God, how was he going to get through the days and nights without her?

Where was she?

It was late. He wobbled out onto the porch to stare blearily down the drive. Where was she? He shut his mind to the images of the poor ravaged women he'd seen along the road to Knoxville. He prayed for her safety in the same breath that he cursed her. He shouldn't have left her in Memphis. He never should have married her. Cherice . . .

Oh, Ruben, how very much I love you.

"Liar. You liar. You never loved me. Not ever. Not ever." With that, he sank down on the steps and finally into a hazy oblivion.

With daybreak came the painfully cruel reminder that he'd survived the night. Light pierced through even the tightest seam of his eyelids. When he tried to stand, his leg buckled, swamping him with exquisite agony rivaled only by what pulsed between his temples. Never had he felt quite so wretched. Nor had he ever deserved it more.

Cherice hadn't come back.

Slowly, with awkward care, he hobbled inside where it was blissfully dim and cool. Where was she? Surely she couldn't mean to stay gone. Didn't she know how much he loved her? Needed her? Then he stopped his graceless advance. No. No, she probably didn't. Because in all his haughty arrogance, he'd never told her. Not once.

Would it matter? Would it have changed anything? Perhaps he'd never know. Or perhaps there was a merciful God because at that moment, he heard the sound of an approaching carriage over the dull roar in his ears. And he heard the brisk sound of Cherice's footsteps in the hall. He paused long enough to murmur a brief, "Thank you, Lord," before turning to face his errant bride.

She drew up outside the door with a drawling exclamation of "Why, Ruben, how awful you look!"

"Where have you been?" he demanded.

Her dark eyes slitted. Her tone was a syrupy slash. "As if you cared, sugar. Why, we've got guests coming this afternoon. I had to get a proper dress. I couldn't be less than expected at the social event of the season, could I?" She hoisted the garment bag she carried and smiled ferociously. "And I brought you your bill of sale. Paid in full. We both got what we wanted. Now we don't owe each other anything."

With that, she started up the stairs. He would have followed; he wanted to follow but his leg wouldn't support his decision. So he hung onto the back of the settee and stared sightless at the slip of paper she'd let drop to the foyer floor.

Their future.

Paid in full.

Cherice dressed with care. She tried to divorce her mind from any thoughts other than the hours that lay ahead. She refused to look toward the big bed where Ruben had taught her about rapture, where their child had been conceived. She denied herself the chance to think out the details of what her life would be like once this evening ended. It didn't matter. Nothing mattered except this last point of honor. The Amorys had taught her about honor. About how only pride mattered when all else was said and done. That's why she knew she could never overcome what they believed her to be.

She took extra time with her appearance, wanting everything to be just right. She owed them that. After tonight, she would never have to worry about the Amorys and their impossible standards again. And she'd leave no doubt in the least of what she thought of them and their like: snobs and hypocrites all. The women caged by their rigid pattern of manners while their men behaved immorally without rebuke. She had no more patience with that myth. It should have died with the Cause but like that failed patriotic frenzy, they clung to past glories instead of moving on toward new horizons. And Ruben was just as bad in his refusal to let go. He would never love her. The system he cherished would not allow it.

"Cherice?"

She stiffened at his low call of her name, denying the eddies of longing that even now assailed her. With a deep breath and a bold tip of her head, she turned to face her husband.

"I'm ready. What do you think?"

Ruben stared. When he didn't speak, she answered for him.

"Is this *whore* enough for you?"

His eyes took in the dazzling display of spangles, the expanse of soft white bosom smashed up almost over the edge of immodesty, at the scarlet lips, the kohled eyes, the splotches of rouge. His senses recoiled from the reek of perfume. But it was the hard glint of defiance in her dark eyes that pushed him beyond the brink.

"Take it off," came his rumbling growl.

"You don't like it?" She arched her brows and struck a blatantly seductive pose. "Isn't this how you want all your fine friends to see your wife? To see the whore you bartered for in order to save your lands. You liked the money well enough. What's the matter? Can't own up to where it came from? Who's the prostitute, Ruben?"

He drew a soft, seething breath. "Wash that stuff from your face and soak off that stench."

"Why? Afraid I might offend someone? One of your good neighbors who'll cheerfully romp with a paid companion yet won't acknowledge her in the light of day? Someone in the proud tradition of your daddy?"

She gave a startled gasp as his arm swept across the top of her bureau, sending her paints and powders flying. "No more, Cherice."

Anger and hurt fed her courage. Her shoulders squared as she snapped, "Don't you like what you see? Aren't I everything your mama warned you about? Maybe you should have listened. Isn't this everything you ever wanted?"

"No," he snarled. Then his hand closed about the back of her neck to propel her to the wash basin, forcing her to meet her own garish reflection in the mirror hung above it. "That's not what I wanted." He sponged up the cold water in her washrag and applied it vigorously to her face, ignoring her muffled protests, holding her firm when she would wiggle away. When her own delicate features began to emerge, he turned her toward the glass again. "There. That's what I wanted. Not the paint. Not the games. Not the lies. Just you, Cherice. The woman I love."

"You love?" She fairly shrieked it. "Where was that love when you married me? Where was that love when I was working my fingers to the bone to please you? Where was that love when I told you I was going to have your child? Don't you talk to me about love. Not now. It's too late."

To disprove that, he seized her chin, holding her in place for his masterful claim of her lips. She pushed against him, squirming, fighting then finally surrendering to the passion she couldn't suppress. Her arms came up to encircle him; her fingers lost themselves in the fairness of his hair. And her mouth opened beneath his, accepting and returning with a like desire until they were both panting with frustration. She gave a whimpering cry and shoved away from him. Panic and pain gleamed in her wild gaze.

"That isn't love, Ruben," she argued fiercely. "If you loved me, you would have believed in me, just a little. But you couldn't, could you? After all I did for you, you still couldn't believe in me. It was always easier to think the worst. It was easier to believe the lies your mother told you. You couldn't look beyond this." She gestured to her vulgar dress with shaking hands. "Was it so hard to believe that I could have made you a good wife?"

"You are my wife, Cherice. And I'm not the one who is ashamed of who you are."

She opened her mouth to fire a harsh retort and found she had none. Taking advantage of her silence, he leaned down to kiss her again, this time softly, slowly, until he could taste her tears.

"Cheri, it didn't matter who you were five years ago. It doesn't matter now. If you thought it did, why did you marry me? Just to get a name you abhor? Just to hurt me all over again with what you wouldn't allow me to have? If you couldn't love me, why—" He broke off in anguish, unable to go on. The pain was too great, the sense of loss too devastating. In a quiet reflective tone, he murmured, "How different things might have been if you'd said yes that first time. Maybe it is too late."

She stood there with mute tears coursing down her face. Her eyes squeezed shut at the caress of his fingertips and when she opened them, he was gone. Then it struck her all at once. What first time?

* * *

Ruben took the stairs one at a time, clutching at the rail to keep his balance. He wouldn't think about the long climb back up them when it was time to change for his mother's party. He was obligated to be there, and he'd endure with the dignity befitting his station. Or what? he wondered suddenly. Would the world end if he wasn't there with a false smile and rote welcome? Would he be cast out of society if he chose to spend the evening with his foot propped up on a stool, mourning the lost love of his life? He'd been torn from all that was civilized for over four years and he'd returned no less a man for it. Were those pretenses all he was led to believe? Or, as Cherice pointed out, was he just another of the shallow elite, dancing attendance upon a bunch of unfair rules? Rules that would exclude the woman he loved from being in his circle. If they did, why was he paying attention to them?

He paused at the bottom of the staircase, rubbing the knotting pain from his thigh and trying desperately to think of something profound that could yet save his marriage. It was then he remembered the letter Mimi gave him. While he couldn't think of the woman with any degree of fondness, he was curious about her parting words.

Give her this and see if she still thinks it worth the price she paid for it.

He pulled the yellowed envelope from his coat pocket, noting its seal was intact before turning it over in his hands. Then he saw the name on the front and there was no doubting the pen it was written in. A single name. *Cherice.*

Lilith was fussing with an arrangement of spring flowers on their new buffet table. She turned to ask her son's opinion, then froze at the sight of his features. He looked as if lightning had struck him. Slowly he extended a letter. His words were raw.

"Madame, please explain this to me."

Chapter Nine

Lilith stared, aghast that this particular ghost had come back to haunt her. A ghost that could yet destroy the relationship she had with her son. Face very pale, she whispered, "Where did you get that?"

"More importantly, what do you know about it?"

She fumbled for a chair and sank down strengthlessly. "Oh, Ruben, I should have told you. I should have told you the moment I realized I was wrong."

"Wrong about what?"

"About Cherice."

"Mama, I need to know. I have to know. Has Cherice ever seen this letter?"

Lilith swallowed hard and shook her head.

"And the ring?"

"It was never delivered."

Ruben took a shaky breath. He wished his head was clearer. He wished his heart wasn't beating quite so madly. "Tell me, Mama. Tell me everything."

She looked away from him then. She couldn't bear to watch disgust alter his expression when the truth was known. But she was not such a coward at this late date as to hold anything back. It was time he knew the whole tale.

"I won't make any excuses for what I did. I thought it was the right thing then. I know I was wrong. I can't even say I did it for you. I was thinking of myself, of our family name, of our pride. A false pride. I knew you were going to offer for Cherice before you left. Ruben, I was so sure she was out to ruin you, to take advantage of you. I thought it was just youthful passion. I was sure you were caught up in the romance of going off to war and I didn't want you to suffer that mistake for the rest of your life. I didn't want our family to suffer for it." She paused to take several shallow breaths, feeling that same desperation, that same panic she'd experienced then. That same hollow terror of losing her only son.

"I ordered Jeremiah to come to me with any message you might send her. I was deathly afraid you meant to elope before I could stop you. He brought me the ring and this letter. I never opened it. I could guess what it said. Ruben, I never stopped to think that you might actually have loved her. I'm so sorry."

"What did you do, Mama?"

She focused on the old letter, worrying it in her hands. "I went to Mimi Leslie. Oh, you don't know how hard that was. I knew, you see, I knew that your father was—fond of her. I couldn't stand the idea of her blood kin with you. I just couldn't. So I went to her and I applied to her greed."

"You bought her off?" That surprised him. Somehow he'd thought better of Mimi.

"No. At least not with an outright bribe. She laughed at my offer of money. She said love was worth more than anything I could pay her. It was Cherice. She wanted the best for Cherice and she didn't think it was marrying a boy about to go off to battle. I gave her the money to send Cherice away to school, and she demanded I give her the letter to hold should I be late in making my payment. I wanted to make certain the two of you didn't meet before you left, and I wanted to be just as sure she wouldn't be here when you came home. I'd decided she wasn't good enough for you. Without ever having met her, I judged her an inferior."

Quietly, almost fearfully, Ruben got right to the crux of it. "Did Cherice know?"

Lilith shook her head. "No. Not about any of it. Not then. I'm not sure what she knows now. Enough to have ruined me with a malicious word in your ear. But she never said anything . . ." Lilith let that trail off, marveling at the compassion of a woman she'd seen as her enemy. Had she the same information when Ruben brought the girl home, she wouldn't have hesitated to use it. She should have known right then the true character of Cherice Parnell, but she hadn't wanted to recognize it. Because of her husband John and Mimi. Because their illicit relationship had wounded her to the point of vicious spite. To the point of blindness in the face of true love. And she'd known that was the case the moment she saw her son and his new bride together. The years hadn't dimmed that passion they held for one another. The separation made it burn all the brighter. She put her hand on Ruben's arm and knew a fleeting hope when he didn't pull away.

"I don't expect forgiveness," she told him somberly. "Not from you or Cherice. But I would do anything within my power if I thought I could undo what was done. I could do no better for a daughter-in-law. She is just the sort I would pick for you, Ruben: brave, loving, spirited. And stubborn. Outrageous, too. My, but I chuckle to think of the things she's done to upset this household. Not that I was chuckling then."

Ruben smiled faintly in response.

"She loves you, Ruben," Lilith told him in all sincerity. "And she has the strength to hold to you, a strength to flaunt convention that I didn't have or perhaps your father wouldn't have strayed. She's the one for you, I'm certain of it."

He didn't doubt that. Not anymore. "She's carrying my child, Mama."

"Oh!" She stood and hugged him happily. "A child. That's wonderful. These pompous old rooms could use the laughter of a child." When he didn't relax from his unyielding stance, she stepped back in alarm. "What is it?"

A brief expression of terrible grief spasmed across his face. His tone was hushed with misery. "I think I lost her, Mama."

Lilith was silent for a long, anxious moment. Then she patted his arm firmly. "Well, we won't let her go, will we?"

They'd gotten as far as the base of the stairs when Lilith gave a little gasp, her eyes riveted upward. Ruben sucked a slow, stabilizing breath, vowing that no matter what his wife's appearance, he would not be shocked or display his disappointment. He looked up, readying for the worst, then stared in rapt appreciation.

Cherice came down slowly, a shimmering vision in pale antique gold moire with a pattern of raised velvet roses in a slightly richer hue clustering along the hem and vining gracefully up the flattened front of her skirt. Yards of fabric bunched in the back in the newest fashion silhouette. Creamy shoulders were bared above the dramatic neckline that was both elegant and enticing. All of her was elegant and enticing. She lifted her hand languidly when she reached the bottom and Ruben took it gently in his own.

His touch initiated a faint trembling within her. Cherice quelled her uncertainty with a boost of brash confidence.

"Is this lady enough for you, husband?"

He brought her hand up for the light stroke of his lips. "Beautiful as always, wife."

As always. As if he'd have welcomed her just as graciously if she'd been wearing that spangled atrocity. But then, she thought in some surprise, perhaps he would have. She began to suspect she'd never fooled him in the least. And as she'd stared long and hard at her reflection in the upstairs glass, she'd come to recognize the truth of his words to her. Had she hidden behind the smears of paint and gaudy gowns because she was afraid he would not accept her for whom she truly was? It was easier to think he could not love the brazen image she projected then to fear he didn't love the woman she was inside. Despite that fear, she couldn't force herself to go downstairs in the harlot's dress. She couldn't humiliate the man she loved or the woman she'd come to respect. It was time she acted the mistress of Stillwater and take her chances.

Her smile grew saucy. "Then lest you want to embarrass us, you'd best go change your own clothes. We have guests arriving soon."

When he retained her hand for another long moment as his gaze delved into hers, Cherice's fingers curled tightly through his. Her eyes took on a like intensity, posing questions, offering answers that time and circumstance had denied them. No more lies, no more games. She let her love shine through and was rewarded by his ease of tension. Then, as she watched him make his awkward way up the stairs, she made herself a promise that once their guests had gone, she would sit down with her husband and they would talk: about the child she carried, about the lush acres of Stillwater, about the complications that had pushed them apart but couldn't keep them away from where they longed to be. Ruben loved her. That was all the bolster she needed to get through the evening ahead with pride. She would give them no reason to be ashamed of the new Amory bride.

Realizing Ruben was only half the battle, she turned to Lilith and found herself taken up in an unexpected embrace. When the older woman stepped back, Cherice saw her mother-in-law all shiny-eyed and was perplexed. Before she could ask what was wrong, Lilith pressed an envelope into her hand with a fragile whisper of "Forgive me, Cherice," then was gone in a rustle of icy blue silk.

When the guests began to arrive, they were taken by the lovely woman proudly displayed upon her husband's arm. Cherice Parnell of Nashville. Some thought she had a familiar look about her but none could quite place her. Obviously she was of some well-bred stock for her manner was impeccable and Lilith Amory was positively smug with pleasure. More than one eyebrow lifted in reaction to the huge gold cupids framing the parlor entry. But Lilith simply smiled as she adjusted the length of silk swaddling one statue's hips and said she'd grown quite fond of them. Added color, didn't they agree?

From her place at Ruben's side, Cherice had never known such happiness, not because of the station she'd attained but because of what they'd accomplished together: the rebuilding of Stillwater and the creation of life within her. Standing on those front steps, talking with the cream of Memphis society while bathed in the loving gaze of her husband's eyes, she realized her every dream. Until she witnessed the approach of a fancy carriage and, recognizing it, saw ruin.

"Mimi," she whispered hoarsely.

Seeing her daughter-in-law's distress, Lilith was quick to band her shoulders with a supportive arm. "What is it, Cherice?"

"Oh, no. I'd forgotten. I invited my aunt and her parlor girls to shame you. What will we do? The party will be ruined and we'll be disgraced in front of all your friends." Tears of horror brimmed in her eyes. "Oh, I'm so sorry. Ruben—"

But he didn't look at all upset. In fact, he was nonchalant as he suggested, "Let's invite them to stay for supper."

"But Ruben—What will people think?"

"Oh, who cares what they think?" Lilith put in brusquely. "I'll extend the invitation myself."

As Cherice stared at her agog, the carriage made a turn, traveling around the side of the great house, out of the view of the guests before discreetly stopping. No one got out. The three of them walked to where it sat in early summer shadow. Ruben opened the door and Mimi smiled out at him. She was alone.

Lilith stepped forward, seeing her chance to set things right. "Miss Leslie, won't you come up to the house? As Cherice's family, you are more than welcome."

Mimi settled back in her plush seat with a wry expression. "How gracious of you, Mrs. Amory, but it's not my intention to disrupt your party. I only stopped by to see if my niece came to her senses." Her shrewd gaze took in the possessive bend of Ruben's arm about her ward's waist, and her features softened. "I can see she did. And I wanted to tell you that the cotton sold for two hundred a piece. I plan to invest the profits in trust for your first child. If that's all right."

Cherice looked up at her husband, beaming when he nodded. "Thank you, Aunt Mimi."

"My pleasure, sugar. I'd better be off and let you get back to your guests."

Ruben reached out to capture a bejeweled hand, bringing it up for a courtly kiss. "I owe you much more than a simple apology, Miss Mimi."

"Nonsense. You take care of my girl and you steer clear of my upstairs rooms."

He grinned. "Yes, ma'am."

Then she opened her arms to Cherice and the younger woman filled them with an emotional sob as she whispered, "Your mama'd be so pleased. Goodbye, sugar. You be happy, you hear?"

"I will."

As the carriage pulled away, Lilith regarded the handsome couple with an approving smile. "I'll go see to our company," she offered, pressing a soft cheek to her daughter-in-law's. Then she took up her son's hand to curl his fingers around the object she placed within his palm. "Give her this, Ruben. Rather late but well-deserved."

The two of them stood in the quiet shadows of the side yard as the first strains of music filtered down from the house. Silence deepened around them until Ruben's hand nudged Cherice's and their fingers were quick to lace together.

"I love you, Cherice."

The time to strip bare all deception had come. She held up the letter she'd never received until almost five years too late—opened and finally read. Its words poured out all the tender emotion from the heart of a man deeply in love. "I didn't know, Ruben," she began in a whisper. "I always thought you'd left without a goodbye. Aunt Mimi told me you were already gone, that you'd ridden out that morning, and it broke my heart. After that, it didn't matter where she sent me. I had no reason to stay, no reason to think you felt the same way I felt about you. I vowed to put you out of my mind and out of my heart."

"Then why did you marry me?"

"Because I couldn't do it. I couldn't stop loving you."

"Would you have come to meet me if you'd gotten that letter?"

"Yes." Strongly said.

"And would you have worn this?" He held up the ring his mother returned to him, the ring he'd thought meant so little to the woman he loved that she'd refused to wear it even after he'd honestly wed her.

"Yes." Stronger.

"Will you wear it now?"

"Yes." Without hesitation.

He took up her hand, slipping off Mimi's gaudy ring to replace it with his family's heirloom. The fit was perfect. He kissed her knuckles then the back of her hand, working his way up the delicate turn of her arm to her shoulder, her graceful throat, and finally to the inviting part of her lips where he was met with unbridled enthusiasm. Her palm came to rest on his vested front, rubbing restlessly, stroking impatiently until, with a rumble of needy desire, Ruben jerked her up tight against his chest. There was nothing subtle about Cherice's surrender. Her arms wrapped around him as her mouth returned his greedy plundering.

"I love you, Cheri."

"I want to make love to you, Ruben." And she began to push at his coat.

Thinking she meant to disrobe him in full view of all their guests and fiercely aroused because he had no real objection to it, he muttered huskily, "Let's go upstairs. We can take the back steps."

Cherice laughed wickedly, teasing, "Why, Ruben Amory, where are your fine manners? You have guests, remember?"

"*We* have guests," he corrected. "Let Mama take care of them. I have other things to see to, my shameless bride. Right after this dance."

He moved her gently within the cherishing circle of his arms, guiding her slowly, unerringly toward the rear of the house where they paused to share a kiss . . . and began to share a lifetime.

The "Right" Bride
by
Sylvie Sommerfield

Chapter One
London - April 1, 1859

The chimes of Big Ben tolled the hour of eleven, and the streets of London were filled with carriages and pedestrians all deeply involved in their own daily routines.

On the fringe of this bustle of activity, before a massive three-story house surrounded by an iron fence, a young woman was just closing the gate behind her and setting her baggage on the curb so the driver of a hansom cab could place them inside.

Julie Mackentire stood by the cab while the last of her baggage was being loaded. She stood with her back to it and gazed up at the house that had been the only home she'd ever known.

For twenty-three years she had raced up and down the polished wood staircase, had met her father when he had returned from the bank, and had shed tears and laughter in the warmth within these walls.

Now the rooms were mostly empty; what furniture was left was covered by white sheets. Pictures had been removed and all salable things had been auctioned several days before. The money she had received from the auction had been enough to buy her passage to America with a bit left over . . . a very small bit. She had, at first, decided to make do on it before common sense took over. Within a few months she would have been on the streets, and she shivered to think about it. What few valuables she still owned were contained in the two trunks and three smaller pieces of baggage.

Julie fought the tears. She felt she had already cried every tear she had. She was an orphan and, worse, a very poor one. The fact that it was April Fools' Day seemed more than appropriate.

What was even more miserable was that she was being forced by circumstances to be, as she put it, a charity case.

Her mother's sister, Aunt Barbara, whom she hadn't seen since she was ten, was the only family she had left. As such she had insisted, as soon as the word of Julie's situation was revealed, that she should come as soon as possible. That letter was followed, almost at once, by a letter from her cousin, Amilee, who had practically begged her to be part of her wedding.

She remembered Amilee as a timid child, afraid of her own shadow, and excruciatingly disciplined to the point that whatever her father said was law. She could only picture the man Amilee was to marry as an equally timid, bespectacled, and bookish man who would expect the same discipline from his wife. As far as Julie was concerned Amilee was going from one prison to another.

Julie wondered what this Wide Oaks plantation was like. To her the James River estate seemed to be on the other side of the world. She didn't want to go ... but the choice was no longer hers. She had the ticket for the ship, and what money was left would never be enough to live long on should she decide, as she secretly desired, to run away and find a life of her own choice.

With obvious reluctance she turned and entered the

cab. All the way to the dock she fought to keep from dashing back to the only security she'd known.

Of course it was possible to stay in London. All she had to do was agree to marry Lord Jeffrey Lowden. The thought made her clutch her hands together in her lap. He had proposed a number of times, but the thought of Jeffrey, with the wandering eye and even more wandering hands, made her skin crawl. No, the unknown was a better choice than Jeffrey would ever be.

At the dock she was held spellbound by the tall masted ships that rocked gently in the harbor. When the cab pulled to a halt before one particularly beautiful one, she disembarked and stood looking at it. Her adventurous spirit, sparked by any opportunity to escape the mundane, was lifted, and her heart felt a bit lighter. At least she would have the pleasure of a sea voyage before she was locked either into spinsterhood or unwanted marriage. She laughed to herself. Perhaps she would be stolen by pirates and never have to face either fate.

But the voyage yielded no other adventure except the sheer pleasure she found in the freedom of being at sea and away from civilization.

The captain was a polite seaman of nearly fifty, and he kept her amused with tales of maritime adventure. Still, she hated to see the mouth of the James River come into view.

She stood on deck and watched land grow closer and closer. When the captain came and stood beside her, she turned to smile at him. He was a tall man with a weathered face and eyes as blue as the sea he loved. His white hair was startling against the deep tan of his face. Julie liked the way his eyes crinkled at the corners when he smiled and the warmth and companionship he had given her throughout her lonely journey.

"It be a pretty place you're on your way to, lass. I

been stoppin' at the dock of Wide Oaks nigh onto nine years now. It gets prettier every time. The Sheridans, they be a right fine family. In fact, you must be about the same age as that pretty daughter of theirs, Miss Amilee."

"No, Amilee is two years younger, but I am to be in her wedding."

"Oh, aye, the lass is going to marry Craig Miles. Nice family. One of the richest along the river."

For a minute Julie thought she heard a note of disapproval.

"I'm sure the marriage will be a very good one. They must love each other."

The captain cast her a quick, almost surprised look. "I think the marriage was settled by the parents. I don't think either party has much to say about it. Only thing is, Miles is a man who's sowed his wild oats, you might say. I can't see him going along with marrying a lass lessen he's a mind to."

"Then he must care," Julie said, "or he just wouldn't agree."

"I'm thinking he's just decided to settle down and give Wind Haven an heir."

"But—But that's terrible! It sounds like Amilee is some kind of a . . . a brood mare!"

"I never meant to imply no such thing." He looked at her in shock. "That's just the way things is done here. Ladies along the James have a reputation for making the right kind of marriages. Real disciplined and good ladies."

Julie thought she might say something drastic if she heard any more of this. She had a sudden sympathy for her cousin and an unprecedented anger at a man who would "sow his wild oats," then choose a woman like he would choose horseflesh, and for the sake of breeding heirs for his plantation!

Julie walked down the gangplank to be greeted by her aunt, uncle, and cousin, whom she hugged fiercely.

Amilee Sheridan was fascinated by her cousin from England. Compared to Amilee's petite figure, pale blond hair, and her wide sky blue eyes, Julie was all brilliant color.

Her eyes were as green as fresh spring grass and her hair was burnished flame. Cream skin and an open smile created an aura of rare beauty.

Amilee's parents were almost exactly as Julie had remembered. Amos was a tall, broad-shouldered man with an easy smile. His hair was brown as was his moustache. Barbara, Amilee's mother, was Amilee with a few years added. Since Julie had never seen her mother, she had no way to compare the sisters.

Within minutes Julie was more than certain Barbara was her daughter's role model. Barbara looked to Amos for the answer to every question, smiled when he spoke, and seemed to wait to know his will before she spoke or moved.

"Julie, my dear, welcome to Virginia. I hope you will consider Wide Oaks your home," Amos said.

"Thank you," she said breathlessly after being embraced by all three newfound relatives.

"I'm so glad you could come for my wedding," Amilee said in a gentle voice. "We'll be sharing my room for a while, while yours are renovated. Mama insisted on doing them over special. I'm looking forward to having a chance to get to know you better."

"I'm looking forward to it, too. We've not seen each other since we were children. You must tell me all about the man you're going to marry."

It seemed to Julie that Amilee's face grew a bit paler, but she nodded and smiled under her parents' watchful eyes.

"Of course, I'm sure you'll like Mr. Miles. You'll meet him tonight at dinner."

"I'm looking forward to it." Mr. Miles indeed! Amilee was no more in love with her future husband than she was with one of the dockworkers. Where was the enthusiasm a young bride should have? Where was the glow of romance and adventure that usually surrounded a happy fiancée? Of course, whatever blame there was Julie was quite ready to heap on the missing Mr. Miles. She was already beginning to dislike the groom. A man who would force a woman into a marriage without asking if she wanted it or not.

The trip back to Wide Oaks was inspiring. Julie didn't know when she had seen any place as beautiful. The hills rolled away from them in a gentle flow, all coated with the same fresh April green brought by the season's rain. The sun literally bounced from the gleaming leaves of the trees. As they passed the well-tended, white-fenced pastures, she could see beautiful horses, some with foals at their side, racing with the exuberance of spring.

As they went on, flocks of birds would occasionally swing upward from a tree almost as one, then settle back into the trees that bordered the road. From there they would sing their love of the day and their annoyance at those who cared to disturb it.

Julie breathed in the beauty around her and thought she would never see anything to match it, until she saw Wide Oaks.

She gazed at it as they approached. It was a large two-story house with four white pillars that supported a roof over a wide front porch. From the back one could look out over a smooth lawn that extended down to the river. Four huge oak trees bordered a stone path that led to the private dock, the same oaks which gave the plantation its name.

The house itself contained twelve rooms, all spacious with gleaming hardwood floors. In the formal dining room floor-to-ceiling windows faced the morning sun. To Julie it was wonderful.

Amilee brought her cousin directly to their room. Even though she knew a room could have been prepared for Julie, she wanted to share some time with her relative. To Amilee, Julie was the bravest, most adventurous person she had ever met. To have the courage to cross the ocean all by herself was overwhelming. Amilee had hardly ever been out of her parents' sight, much less free to travel. She had a million questions she wanted to ask.

They had time before dinner for Julie to unpack and for Amilee to get a chance to ask all the questions that spun in her mind. Julie realized that to her cousin she was a heroine of sorts, and this amused her. She had already begun to like her new cousin.

"Weren't you frightened?"

"Of what?"

"Goodness. I've heard so many stories. Pirates and men who'll ... take your ... virtue." She half-whispered the last words, and Julie had to restrain her laughter.

"Oh, Amilee, the ship's captain was like a father and there was no sign of a pirate anywhere."

"You sound disappointed."

"Actually," she laughed softly, "I was."

"Oh," Amilee giggled. "I would never be able to do that."

"I had no choice. It was stay in London and go hungry, or brave the ocean. The ocean seemed an easier way, pirates or no."

"I almost envy you." Amilee said softly. Julie turned to look at her cousin closely.

"Amilee, tell me about the preparations for your wedding."

"Preparations? Oh, Mama will take care of all that."

"Well, what about your plans for a honeymoon? What kind of a romantic place do you plan on visiting?"

"I . . . I don't know. I think Papa has arranged that." Amilee had gotten to her feet and nervously moved about the room as if she didn't want to meet her cousin's gaze directly. "But you should see my wedding gown, Julie. It's ever so pretty. And just everyone in the county has begun to send gifts. There are so many lovely things."

"Well," Julie tried again, "are you building a new home? Where are you planning to live?"

"I . . . I guess we will live at Wind Haven. I'm . . . I'm not sure Mama thinks I can run a household on my own yet."

"Well, what does your future husband think about that? Have you talked about your ideas and what you would like to do?"

"No. Mr. Miles and I have never had such an opportunity. Besides, I'm sure that whatever he decides will be quite appropriate."

Julie was aghast and angry, and tried her best not to show it. Her disgust at the prospective groom was growing by leaps and bounds.

To take an unwilling, innocent bride and never consult her on her feelings and thoughts was unbelievable. It seemed to her that Amilee was only a bystander at her own wedding.

"I see." Julie realized she was going to have to control her wayward temper. She had to continually remind herself that this was not her home and she could not cause a problem. But, oh, how she would like to give the arrogant Mr. Miles a piece of her mind!

She made herself a promise that no matter what she

had to do, her aunt and uncle would not be allowed to maneuver her life and choose her a husband.

Finished with most of her unpacking, both girls began to choose what they would wear to dinner. Julie was inundated with questions about her life and was glad for the time to talk about her father and how much she had loved him.

She told Amilee how they had taken walks and ridden together. How her father had insisted she have an education that was usually reserved for rich young men.

"How much fun you must have had. I've never been to school, I've always had tutors."

"Oh really?"

Yes. Mr. Phillip Gallierd is the most recent. He's been here a little over a year. I'm so slow at French, and arithmetic just horrifies me. I suppose when I marry he'll have to find other employment."

"I should think you wouldn't want a tutor underfoot once you marry. Unless you expect to have children soon."

"Mr. Gallierd is a wonderful and educated man." Amilee said, obviously trying to ignore the last statement.

"I suppose he is or your father would never have hired him. Do you want a family soon?"

"I suppose."

Julie wanted to grip Amilee's shoulders and shake her. It seemed she didn't have one passionate desire in her whole makeup.

She was about to throw caution to the wind and say something to shake Amilee out of her little girl fancies and indecisiveness, when a light rap sounded on their door.

"Amilee? Julie?"

"Come in, Mother."

Barbara entered the room with a smile for each girl.

"My, you girls have been chatting for quite a while. I'm glad to see you are unpacked and comfortable, Julie. And how nice you look. The green matches your eyes. Amilee, change into your gray silk."

"Yes, Mama."

Julie felt rebellion growing and had to bite her lip. She was a newcomer in this household, and she didn't intend to alienate them her first day here. She reserved her opinion that Amilee would look much nicer in a bright color, like blue, to match her eyes.

It was obvious Amilee would be a matron before she was a mother. Again, her animosity having no outlet, she turned it against the now infamous Mr. Miles. Still, she considered the fact that Amilee's parents were as much to blame as he. They had, in reality, put Amilee on the auction block almost as if she were a slave.

Julie found it difficult to blame Amos as much as she did Barbara. Of course, Barbara seemed content to do what society demanded, but did she ever question what Amilee might want? Julie found herself wanting to do or say something truly scandalous, just to see if it would wake them up.

It also made her very curious about the conditions under which Barbara and Amos were married.

"I was just telling Amilee how flattered I am to be asked to participate in her wedding."

"My dear, you're family. The gowns have been chosen. Tomorrow you will go for a fitting."

Julie could hear the velvet-gloved demand; she was expected to say, Yes, Aunt Barbara. But her rebellious nature would put up with no more.

"I'm afraid I shall have to put that off until the day after. I must write some letters and see to the disposal of what money I've brought along."

"Yes . . . of course. The day after will be fine." Barbara smiled, but her eyes held surprise. She made both girls promise to be down soon for dinner, then left.

If Barbara was surprised, Amilee was awed. No one had refused either of her parents before, especially not her. She said nothing, but she took the gray silk from her wardrobe and put it on.

"Will your future husband be here tonight?"

"Yes. He comes every other night. We'll have dinner, take a walk in the garden, and then he'll go home."

"At a reasonable hour I'm sure."

"Of course. What would people say if he remained here too late?"

"I can't imagine." Julie replied dryly.

"Your hair is so beautiful. Let me finish it for you."

"How kind you are. Thank you, Amilee." She handed her the brush she had been using to remove the tangle from her waist-length hair. Amilee brushed it smooth then twisted it intricately to pin on top of her head.

"Now let me do yours."

Amilee smiled with pleasure and sat before the mirror while Julie brushed her hair.

"Amilee?"

"What?"

"Do you really want to get married?"

"Of course." She met Julie's gaze in the mirror. "Whatever else would I do? I mean, every woman wants to get married."

"I don't."

"But what else can a woman do? You're teasing me, aren't you?"

"No, I'm not. I doubt very much if I will ever find a man I would choose to marry. All they want are mothers for their heirs and an overseer for their household."

"What do you want?"

"To travel, meet interesting people. To do as I please,

I guess. My father must have made a drastic mistake. I should have been a man."

"Oh, no," Amilee laughed. "You're much too pretty to be a man. I think it's time we went downstairs."

"You're very sweet, Amilee. I'd just like to see you happy."

"Truly, Julie, Mr. Miles is a very nice man. He'll be good to me. Besides, he's very handsome."

"Come on, let's go eat," Julie laughed. She wondered what Amilee thought of as handsome.

They walked down the stairs together, but Julie paused halfway down.

A tall, broad-shouldered man with the devil's smile and wicked promises behind his eyes stood just a few feet below them looking up with as much surprise on his face as Julie's. Handsome, Amilee had said. Julie's heart began to beat heavily. He wasn't handsome, he was beautiful. As beautiful as Lucifer before he was ejected from heaven.

"Oh my," she whispered to herself. It seemed she was coming face-to-face with the infamous Mr. Miles.

Chapter Two

Craig Miles was bored, but he certainly had no intention of mentioning that to his father who was already angry enough at him.

He thought of the exciting lady he'd been with last night and wished fervently the need for an heir to Wind Haven hadn't brought his father around to dire threats.

He had known too many women and too much about them to seek the state of matrimony. He'd expertly dodged it for quite some time, dallying with ladies who weren't looking for permanence or had their own secrets to keep—and shying from the women who threw themselves at him with church and children in mind.

To the women in his social circle, Craig Miles was the material of dreams. At twenty-nine he was tall, two inches over six feet, fatally handsome, with hair the color of ebony and eyes as gray as a summer storm. He was a man of breeding, elegance, and style ... and could be as polished and hard as the most brilliant diamond.

When he walked into a room, his uniqueness was fully displayed in his tanned skin, for he loved the outdoors and riding, his tall, rugged, and muscular body, and his air of power and authority. He had a smile that could devastate a woman with its warmth or freeze an adversary in his tracks with its chill.

He was well-educated and well-traveled, which was the thing that had filled his life with most of its real pleasures.

But, as Joseph Miles expounded, where you found your pleasure and where you found a wife and a possible heir were two different things.

He knew his father was right. Wind Haven did need an heir, and his wife had to be chosen among the "acceptable ladies." One night he'd arrogantly and angrily left the choice up to his father, who had smiled in satisfaction and told him the lady was already selected. He'd regretted the action when his temper cooled, but it was already too late by then. The arrangements had been made. So he gave himself over to enjoying what was left of his freedom and put off any thought of the wedding to come.

"Good heavens, boy," Joseph had smiled, "marry and produce an heir. Then if you choose to dally elsewhere," he shrugged, "you need only be cautious."

"Sneak around back doors?" Craig said scathingly. "Hardly." He had breathed a ragged sigh. "I guess you've chosen the right bride for Wind Haven."

When his father had told him, Craig had winced. He knew and liked Amilee Sheridan. She was sweet, docile, and wifely. Just the kind of woman his father would expect to be mistress of Wind Haven—but not who Craig would have picked. In fact, he'd wondered lately just what kind of bride he would have chosen.

Someone, he thought, who was spirited, who liked to read and discuss world affairs. Who liked to ride and be a bit adventurous . . . definitely he wanted a companion in bed who would not do her duty and let him make love to her, but would make love with him, matching his passion.

He thought of his and Amilee's formal engagement. Of the "every other night" visits and their walks in the garden where he always searched desperately for something to say.

Actually he meant to be an absentee husband. Amilee would be mistress of Wind Haven, and once an heir had been produced he would leave her to her child and her home, which is all society demanded of him anyway and most likely all Amilee herself would demand.

He dressed as carefully as usual for his dinner with his promised bride and their tedious walk, wondering how a man could bear interminable years of this.

As he rode toward Wide Oaks, he searched his thoughts to come up with something that could put him and Amilee on common ground and perhaps get her to really talk to him, tell him what she felt, what she expected, what she dreamed.

Greeted warmly by Amos and Barbara, he realized again that Amilee would be her mother in another few years. He looked at Amos and saw a satisfied man, and the wicked thought came to him that Amos' mistress must be a delectable tart.

"Craig, my boy, you're a bit early," Amos said. "The ladies have not come down yet."

Since Barbara was already in the room, Craig began to wonder who the other lady might be.

"My niece is here from England." Barbara solved the problem. "Poor child."

"Poor child?" Craig inquired politely.

"She was left orphaned recently by the untimely death of her father. Her mother, my sister, died giving birth to Julie. We insisted she come and live with us. I'm afraid the poor dear was nearly destitute."

"What a shame," Craig agreed sympathetically.

"She will be maid of honor in your wedding."

"Oh, then she isn't a child."

"Hardly," Barbara smiled. "I'm afraid she is destined to spinsterhood. Why, the girl is twenty-three. I don't know what her father was thinking, not to have had her married. Look at where his negligence has gotten her. No home, no husband, no children."

"Poor thing," Craig replied solemnly, trying to contain his smile. Clever thing, was his first thought. At least she wasn't under pressure to produce another branch of an old family tree.

The sound of laughter coming from the top of the stairs drew everyone's attention. Trying to be the attentive groom, Craig walked to the bottom of the steps. He looked up with a half smile and a gentle word on his lips, but no words came.

What he saw before him was a vision that had

stepped from a man's wildest dreams. She stood beside Amilee and looked down at him.

Where Amilee was all moonlight and delicate texture, this woman was like the first morning sun. He caught his breath for a moment.

Then he realized her look was not in the least bit friendly. Curiosity drew him to her like a magnet as both women reached the bottom of the steps.

"Mr. Miles," Amilee smiled timidly up at him. How he hated being called Mr. Miles by a woman who planned on sharing his bed in the not-too-distant future. He was certain Amilee would never change customs as long as her parents were there to supervise. She would probably be calling him Mr. Miles in public when they celebrated their fiftieth wedding anniversary! But tradition could not be shaken. "I want you to meet my cousin, Julie. She's from London and will be my maid of honor."

"I'm very pleased to meet you, Julie."

"Mr. Miles," Julie acknowledged him with the accent on the "Mr." and the tightest smile on the most delectable lips he'd ever seen.

Julie could feel Amilee trembling a little and realized this tall, powerful man frightened her cousin to death. It only added fuel to the anger already burning within her.

Craig could see the smoldering flame in her eyes and it puzzled him. Why on earth should she be angry with him? He'd never met the little chit before. One thing was certain, he meant to find the answer to that and a few other questions that lingered in the back of his mind.

Through dinner he half-listened to Amos and Barbara's conversation and Amilee's shy replies. His mind couldn't seem to let go of the lovely creature who sat opposite him and why she seemed to be getting angrier by the minute.

Julie had listened to enough random conversation. She had watched the handsome and, she thought, very conceited Mr. Miles practically ignore Amilee's few soft words. He seemed to be interested more in Amos' discussion on planting and markets than he was the woman he was to marry. Julie had had about enough.

"Tell me, Mr. Miles," she said sweetly. "Have you made plans on where you mean to spend you honeymoon? Amilee seems unable to make up her mind."

Craig was truly puzzled now. Amilee, until now, had not suggested any particular place she would like to go. "No," he said casually as he sat back in his chair to study her. "I'm sure Amilee will make a decision soon."

Amilee looked startled. Her mother had told her to allow major decisions to be made by her future husband.

Craig smiled a particularly fetching smile. "Do you have any suggestions, Julie? Perhaps there are places you dream of going."

"Me?" Julie smiled. "There are many places I would like to see."

"Oh? Such as?"

"France, Germany, all of this vast country ... just about every place I've ever read about."

"You read a great deal?"

"When money is not always accessible, reading is the only form of travel left. Besides, a woman cannot travel just as she chooses."

"That convention annoys you?"

"Exceedingly. I cannot, for the life of me, understand why a man may do exactly as he pleases—'sow his wild oats' is the euphemism I believe—and a woman is so constricted she dares not breathe unless it's socially decreed."

"Julie!" Barbara gasped. "It is not seemly for a young woman to speak so."

Amos tried to smother both his interest and his laughter, and Craig was not far behind. He was fascinated and longed to talk to Julie more.

But before he could speak again, there was a bustle of activity at the door, and another man entered. Julie studied him for a minute.

He was tall, but not nearly as tall as Craig. His hair was honey brown, and he looked about the table through spectacles that made his eyes seem larger and bluer than they were.

He was a nice-looking man, but hardly the forceful presence of Craig Miles. His face was pale, and Julie guessed at once he spent very little time out-of-doors. She liked his smile: it was warm and shy as a boy who'd been caught with his hand in the cookie jar.

"I'm so sorry I'm late," he proclaimed at once. "I had to acquire some new books and I'm afraid I was diverted."

"We've only just begun dinner," Barbara calmed him. "Please, join us. Julie, this is Mr. Phillip Gallierd. He is Amilee's French tutor." Julie was surprised. He was young, she guessed not too many years older than herself. "Phillip, this is our niece, Julie Mackentire, from London. She will be making her home with us from now on."

Julie smiled at Phillip, who smiled in return. "Pleased to make your acquaintance, Miss Mackentire."

He sat down, and Amos questioned him about something, but Julie's attention was riveted on Barbara, whose eyes flickered from Phillip to Julie in the most calculating way.

Oh no, Julie thought, don't get any ideas. I will not be thrust into a marriage. I'll run away before I fall into the trap Amilee is in.

She would have been quite surprised at the same surge of resistance in Craig, who had accurately read the look as well.

Julie Mackentire was not the kind of woman meant for the bookish and shy Phillip Gallierd. She was a thunderstorm with lightning; she was self-opinionated, and not in the least intimidated. In short, he thought in shock, the kind of woman that could intrigue a man year after year.

Since Julie was a recent visitor, Craig and Amilee decided to forgo their walk in the garden, about which both were intensely relieved.

Instead Barbara insisted Amilee play the piano for them and with alacrity that was a bit surprising with his length of leg, Phillip rose to stand by the piano to turn the pages of the music for her.

This gave Craig the opportunity for which he had been looking. He took the seat on a small settee beside Julie, leaving Barbara and Amos to find places a short distance away.

They sat in silence for several minutes, and Julie was more than annoyed with the fact that she was intensely aware of him, from the large strong hand that lay relaxed against a muscular thigh to his clean scent.

She refused to look at him, but all her senses told her he was watching her. She felt her cheeks grow warm, and a strange and unwelcome heat uncoiled deep within her. She fought to retain her composure and her concentration.

Awareness was a mild term for what Craig was feeling. No other woman had ever affected him this way. He saw the blush on her cheek and he wanted to reach out and touch the silky smooth skin, to plow his fingers through the thick mass of her hair.

She wore a delicate and elusive perfume that made him fight the urgent desire to pull her into his arms and press his lips to the pulse that beat rapidly at her throat.

A slow burning rage built in Julie. How dare he look at her like this, sit beside her . . . be so damned attentive that he strummed her nerves like the strings of a guitar—he was to be married to Amilee, for goodness sake!

But, to Julie's further annoyance, Amilee was playing the piano and smiling up at Phillip, totally oblivious to her fiancé's actions.

Julie's anger was directed as much to herself as it was him. She had no business feeling this way about a man who was to be married to a girl as sweet and trusting as Amilee. She was simply tired from her trip and needed to find her bed as soon as possible.

When the music ended, Julie was the first one on her feet. She went to Amilee's side at once.

"Amilee, you play so beautifully. I have never been able to master the piano, despite all the lessons."

"Thank you. Mr. Gallierd has helped me so much. He plays so well. You should hear him some time."

"You do play very well, Amilee," Craig said. "I'm sorry I never heard you play before."

Julie turned to glance at him. He was impossible. He knew so little about Amilee and yet would marry her. To Julie this was a travesty. She would never marry a man unless he knew all there was to know about her and she all there was to know about him.

"I'm very tired, Aunt Barbara. The trip was more arduous than I thought. If you all don't mind, I think I shall retire now."

She could see Craig, who gave her a very knowledgeable half smile and a look that told her she might be fooling everyone but not him.

Again she felt the heat on her cheeks and had to fight to keep from lashing out at him. After all he had done nothing, and her imagination might be overreacting since she was annoyed with him before she even met him.

"I'm afraid I must be going as well. We had a hard

day in the fields today and have an early start tomorrow." Craig reached to take Julie's hand. "Good night, Julie, pleasant dreams . . . and welcome to Virginia."

She nearly snatched her hand away and then said a hasty good night to everyone else. Once she left the living room, she lifted her skirts and ran up the steps.

Amilee walked to Craig's horse with him and for the first time in a long while, Craig truly considered her feelings.

In the moonlight she seemed even more delicate than usual, and a pang of conscience made him realize that he could embarrass her, hurt her with so little effort. He knew the gossips of the area. Hadn't he been the topic of their whispers enough times?

Everyone who was someone for a two-hundred-mile radius had been invited to the wedding. He wanted to ask her if this marriage was just a family convenience or if she could love a man she hardly knew. But he guessed, as sensitive as she was, she would only be confused and hurt. Family, convenience, convention, and obedience were what she was raised with.

No, he blamed himself. How could he have let his guard down long enough to be convinced to take part in this? To marry a woman who would come to him assured she was doing the "right thing"?

He bent to kiss her cheek. It felt to him as if he were kissing a child.

"You're a very lovely person, Amilee. You have a right to every bit of happiness you can find."

He mounted his horse and rode away. Amilee stood quietly and watched him leave. She could not understand herself. Craig Miles was the handsomest man in the county, was, in fact, considered the catch of the season! She did not doubt for a minute that her parents had chosen well for her and had her best interest at heart.

Still, some of the things Julie had said clung like cobwebs to her memory.

She sighed. Well, as her mother explained, it was the duty of an obedient daughter to make a marriage that would bring respect and honor to the family name. Perhaps she needed to concentrate on that instead of trying to understand the look she had seen in Craig's eyes.

Chapter Three

Julie woke very early the next morning, washing and dressing quietly so as not to awaken Amilee. While she ate breakfast, she was surprised to learn that Amilee often slept until after eleven.

The cook was one of the few people among the workers of Wide Oaks that was not a slave but an indentured servant. A motherly woman, she was surprised when Julie said she would just take a quick breakfast in the kitchen. In this house no one ate in the kitchen but the servants.

"The biscuits are delicious, Hannah, and last night's dinner was fabulous. I'm going to have to have a lot of exercise or living here will make me fat."

"Well, what a nice young lady you are, thank you."

"Tell me, does anyone else ride in the family?"

"Yes, miss. Mr. Sheridan, he rides pretty often. Has a

string of real nice horses. Miss Amilee is kind of afraid of them, and Mrs. Sheridan, she don't ride at all."

"Do you think he would mind if I borrowed a horse and rode for a while? It's so beautiful here, I'd love to look around."

"Oh, I'm sure he wouldn't mind. You go on out to the stable and tell my husband Henry to get you what you want. But you be careful."

"Why? Is there danger around here?"

"Lands no, my dear. I mean be careful you don't fall."

"Don't worry, I've been riding since I was a little girl. I'll be perfectly safe."

Julie crossed the wide stretch of lawn to the stable where she found Henry already at work.

"Henry?"

"Yes, ma'am." Henry fairly beamed. He was a scarecrow of a man with unruly blond hair and a smile that seemed to divide his face. His friendly brown eyes elicited a smile from Julie. "You be the young miss just come fresh from England."

"Yes, I am. I'd love to go for a ride this morning, if you would be so kind as to saddle me a horse."

"My pleasure."

While he saddled a snow white mare, he kept up a steady stream of conversation which amused Julie, who felt, when she rode out, that she knew a lot more about the James River plantation than she'd ever bargained on.

She cantered away from the house and eventually came to a shallow stream, which she crossed to enter a stand of trees. She was already falling in love with this green and verdant place. The English countryside through which she and her father had ridden had been beautiful, but this was just as rich in comparison.

After over an hour of riding, she decided to stop to

rest both the horse and herself. In the distance she could hear the rushing water of the river, so she rode toward it.

When Craig had returned home so early the night before and in a foul mood, both his parents were surprised. His father, with a secretive smile, shrugged it off as pre-wedding jitters.

His mother soon retired, then Joseph watched his son pour himself a hefty glass of brandy, gulp it down in two swigs and pour another.

"Craig?"

"What?"

"Is something wrong?"

"No, why?"

"You seem . . . tense."

Craig laughed and took another drink of brandy. Then he carried the bottle and glass with him and sank into a chair opposite his father.

"Why did you choose Amilee Sheridan?" he asked abruptly.

"Because you gave us carte blanche to do so. Are you having second thoughts?" Joseph scowled. "If so, I hope you will stop them right now. Amilee suits perfectly. Besides, have you any idea what kind of a scandal you would cause? You would disgrace that poor child, make her the laughingstock of the county. I've put up with your renegade ways far too long. It's time you turned into the man it will take to run Wind Haven."

"I could run Wind Haven quite well with or without a wife," Craig laughed, but his voice was tight.

Joseph twisted in his chair, tossing aside the newspaper he had been reading, and bent toward his son. "Now see here, Craig. I don't know what has caused this problem of yours, but I cannot tolerate this. You must marry.

Trust me to say it is important, not only to the reputation of our family, but to so many others as well."

"I don't understand."

"I . . . I didn't want to embarrass Amilee's family, but it seems Amos has had some . . . ah . . . severe financial setbacks. He is afraid and wants his daughter safely married where she will be comfortable."

"Why not just lend him money?"

"He is too proud a man for that."

"But not too proud to give away his daughter to a man who is—"

"He's giving his daughter to a man of integrity and honor. Or am I mistaken? Are you scoundrel enough to break that girl's heart and damage her family's reputation, all because she's not exactly like some of the 'ladies' you have known recently?"

"You know I won't hurt her," Craig said.

"Good. Then there is no need to discuss this any further. Trust me that once you're settled into marriage you'll learn to be content."

Craig knew he had boxed his own self in when he had agreed to this. What had he been thinking? Just as his father had said, a comfortable wife who would "tolerate" both him and his roaming, provided it was done discreetly.

But he had looked into Amilee's eyes and had seen her delicate spirit. He couldn't hurt her. He was disgusted with himself. He had created his own problem by his own jaded attitude. He'd been certain that there was no woman alive who could waken in him what Julie Mackentire had.

When he had sat beside her on the settee and watched her, he had felt something stir to life. He was not ignorant of women. He could see the rise and fall of her breasts as her breathing deepened, the rose in her cheeks and the rapid pulse. She had been as aware of him as he had been of her.

He had carried the bottle with him to bed and gotten pleasantly drunk. He was hoist by his own petard and he didn't like the situation one bit.

The morning greeted him with a brilliant sun and a splitting headache. No matter how he had tossed and turned all night, there was no answer.

He decided that an early ride might clear his head, so after several cups of very strong black coffee he had his horse saddled.

Few people knew the area between Wind Haven and Wide Oaks the way Craig did. He had roamed them as a boy and ridden over their lush acres as a man. Soon, the two would be joined.

He spotted Julie long before she even had a thought that anyone was near.

He watched her ride and could see she was an expert horsewoman. He thought of the lingering anger in her eyes, considered it, then decided it was at least one answer he could have.

Julie had stopped on the edge of the woods that marked the border between Wide Oaks and Wind Haven, but she didn't know that. She sat on a fallen tree and admired the view, a view that was breathlessly beautiful, and for the first time she felt as if she had come home.

She looked across a broad expanse of meadow that was dotted here and there with mature trees: a pine, a pair of mighty oaks, several chestnuts, and a willow swaying like a ballerina. The sun was climbing in an azure sky making the trees cast dark, cool shadows. The birds were silent, but a hum of contented bees came from random pockets of wildflowers.

The spring rains were nearly over, except for an occasional shower, and everything was a lush green, so lush one could feel it as well as see it. She inhaled a breath of fresh, scented air and soaked up the beauty, feeling a sense of rejuvenation and pleasure. She had sat so for some time before she reluctantly faced the fact that she had to leave the Eden and go back to the house.

She was about to return to her horse, which was grazing contentedly nearby, when she saw the rider approaching.

Although she couldn't see him clearly, some deep sense within her knew him. For an instant she wanted to mount up and ride away, but common sense prevailed. Once Amilee and Craig were married, she would see a great deal of him. She had to get used to the fact and to realize that she had no control over events. She was acting like a child, pretending Prince Charming was still in existence. Men were as they were, and she would not allow him to alter her life ... or to hurt Amilee.

So he took the idea of marriage vows very casually, well, she did not. Nor could she put aside the gratitude she felt not only to her aunt and uncle, but to Amilee who had accepted her more as a sister than a stranger.

Perhaps Amilee was not in love with Craig, but if he put forth every effort, was gentle and considerate, maybe her cousin could learn to love him.

Julie refused to recognize the fact that her every sense had come alive, that her heart was beating rapidly and she felt a bit breathless. She wasn't frightened, she told herself, but some teasing inner voice questioned whether she might be afraid of Craig ... or of herself.

When Craig brought his horse to a stop beside her, she looked up at him and managed the friendliest smile she could.

"Good morning."

"Good morning, Julie. You're alone?"

"Yes, I'm afraid I'm an early riser. Besides, I've been told that neither Amilee or Aunt Barbara ride."

"I've been watching you from that hill over there," he said as he dismounted and stood alarmingly close. "You ride well."

"Thank you. Father and I rode quite often."

"It must have been very difficult for you. Losing your father then tearing up roots like you have."

"One has to do what necessity dictates," she replied with a half smile. "Besides, when Amilee asked me to be part of her wedding, I could hardly refuse."

"No . . . I suppose not." Amilee had come between them like a vaporous ghost.

Craig walked to the fallen tree and sat down, trying to encourage Julie not to ride away. "Will you ride every day?"

"Well, at least as often as I can."

"Has Amilee told you about the Parkersons' party next week?"

"No, she hasn't."

"It should be one of the best parties of the season." Craig was aggravated at his inability to say the things he wanted to say but was forbidden to. All this polite conversation was guaranteeing only one thing: Julie would be riding back to Wide Oaks sooner than he would like. "Do you know you were trespassing?"

"You mean I'm on Wind Haven property? Then we are not only going to be related, we're neighbors. Your marriage will . . ." she paused, suddenly understanding why Amilee was marrying Craig. It was to join the plantations. If she were horrified before, it was worse now.

"Join our two plantations together," Craig finished for her, unaware of her thoughts.

"How . . . how very convenient," she managed. "I'd best go." She started to pass him, but he rose quickly and reached out to grip her arm and turn her to face him.

"Don't go."

"I have to. Both my aunt and uncle—not to mention Amilee—would be upset if they discovered we were here alone. We must keep up propriety."

"Julie, why are you angry with me?"

"Angry? I'm not—"

"You're angry with me now and you were angry last night. It seems you were angry before you ever met me. I wish you could at least tell me why."

"It's nothing. Last night I was tired, and you know how things can get out of perspective when you're exhausted."

"Exhausted? Maybe. Although when I look at you, I wonder if you were ever really tired. You're so vital, so—"

"Please." Julie was breathless with a sudden emotion she refused to identify. "You must not talk to me like this."

"Then you must tell me why you were angry."

"Must?"

"Yes, must. I don't want to see anger in your eyes when you look at me."

"I shall be careful not to appear angry," she said cautiously. But he was standing so close and his aura of intense masculinity was overpowering.

"You mean you'll pretend?" he said softly. His gaze held hers until she could not stand it.

"What is it you want me to say!"

"Nothing," he replied. Before Julie could even consider the tone of his voice or move away, his arm snaked about her waist and drew her against him. She could feel the hard strength of him and could not pull her shocked gaze from his.

He bent his head and his mouth caught hers in a

fierce, yet sensitive kiss. Expertly his mouth tasted her sweetness.

Julie was held in a grip more powerful than she could ever hope to break. For one moment she gave in to the kiss and enjoyed his hard strength.

But reality followed. This was Amilee's future husband! What was she thinking? What was she allowing herself to feel?

Craig felt her momentary surrender, felt her soft, slim body mold to his as if they were two parts of one whole. He was caught in the magic of an emotion he had never felt before. Lust he could handle, but this was more than lust. He wanted Julie Mackentire in a way that he'd never given a thought to. Wanted her completely, wanted her to belong to him.

She pushed herself away from him, gasping for breath. Without thought she struck him across the face. But Craig could see tears glisten in her eyes before she turned from him, ran to her horse, and rode away.

He watched her go, realizing he didn't regret the kiss at all. What he did regret was that he no longer had choices. He felt caught, engaged to marry the wrong bride, while the right bride was riding out of his life. The horrible thing was, for Amilee's benefit, her father's benefit, there was nothing he could do about it . . . or was there?

Julie rode as fast as the horse beneath her would go, but she could not outrun the feelings Craig's seductive kiss had wakened within her.

She had never felt so disloyal or unappreciative in her life, for she had to face the truth that welled within her. She had wanted his kiss, in fact, had wanted him to make love to her, and for that she was ashamed.

She thought of Amilee, who trusted both her and the

man to whom she was promised. Amilee had, most likely, never considered the fact that she was being used as a way to blend two families, two plantations, and two vast fortunes into one. Used to breed an heir who would one day own it all.

When she finally arrived at the stable, Julie had regained a semblance of control. She walked from the stable to the house and had to pass through the garden, for she wanted to come into the house as quietly as possible.

But as she passed through the garden, she saw Amilee seated on a bench with a book in her lap and Phillip standing close beside her. The tutor looked up. "Good morning, Miss Mackentire," he said.

Amilee rose to her feet, and Julie could see the book she carried was one of poetry. It surprised her a bit, but she presumed Amilee, as gentle as she was, would respond to poetry as an educational tool.

"Good morning, Julie. My, you must have been up very early. And you've been riding one of Father's horrible beasts."

"It was such a pretty day, and I enjoy riding. Especially first thing in the morning."

"Phillip was just having me translate poetry from English to French. It's beautiful verse," Amilee laughed, "but absolutely atrocious French."

"Miss Amilee," Phillip denied, "you are doing so much better."

"Well," she said, amused, "I guess in comparison, I'm better at that than I am at riding a horse." She linked her arm through Julie's, who felt even guiltier than before. "Come along, Julie. I want to show you some gifts that have arrived from some distant relatives. I swear that table of gifts is growing bigger each day. I don't have any idea how many thank-you cards I'm going to have to write after the wedding."

Julie swallowed heavily at the scene that flashed before her eyes. Amilee, walking down the aisle to a man who would deceive her when the mood struck him. And herself ... walking down the aisle toward a man who had awakened something so volatile it frightened her.

Chapter Four

The next few days were spent in a flurry of activity for Julie and Amilee: they fitted gowns, shopped, and in general got to know each other better.

But Craig knew quite well Julie was dodging him when he came to dinner and found her missing. He still did not have the answer to why she had been angry at him before, but he knew why she was angry now.

He needed to find a way to force her to face him. It would not do to continue this until everyone noticed.

Though he wanted to talk to her, he was certain she wouldn't afford him the opportunity.

The Parkersons' party was, at least, a chance to talk, to apologize—yet he wondered how to apologize for something for which he wasn't the least bit sorry.

Julie tried her best to wiggle out of the party but neither Barbara or Amilee were having any of that.

"Just everybody will be there," Amilee said. "And I want you to meet all our friends. They'll be yours, too, Julie; they'll love you."

"Well, if just everybody is there," she laughed, "no one will miss me."

"Oh, Julie," Amilee giggled, "you know Mother and Father by now. They won't tolerate shirking our duty."

"Duty," Julie repeated softly.

The two women were in Amilee's bedroom lying about amidst masses of petticoats, dresses, stockings, and other sundry items.

Julie was quiet for a minute, studying Amilee closely.

"And it's the duty of a woman to become a good wife."

"Of course. Oh, Julie, I know about men and women. Mother and I have had a long talk. I shall do what is expected of me."

"Isn't there more to it than that?"

"What?"

"Oh, I don't know, like, getting to know each other ... what each other likes ... learning to trust and to ... well, just enjoy being together."

"We'll have lots of time for that."

"Amilee, sometimes I worry if you're going to be happy. You really don't know Craig Miles at all. I've heard he has a rather wild reputation."

"I know. But Father says people just like to whisper. And besides, it kind of makes him exciting."

"And you're really sure he loves you?"

"You sound just like Phillip. He's always saying I have some kind of illusion about love that I've been getting out of poetry books."

"Phillip is a very good friend, isn't he?"

"Yes. He's very nice. We can find ever so much to talk about. Do you know he once taught at one of the finest schools in France?"

"I don't doubt it." Julie had begun to believe Amilee was not only being obedient but that she was falling in love with the idea of a wedding. A beautiful gown and flowers and people to pamper her.

Again she thought of Craig and the day of the wedding, and didn't think she would be able to stand it.

The day of the Parkersons' ball arrived whether Julie wanted it or not.

Her gown was beautiful, a deep wine with lace adorning the elbow and the neckline, which Julie felt was cut a bit too low. But both Amilee, who wore a demure pink, and Barbara assured her she looked beautiful.

When the four of them arrived at the Parkersons', the sound of music drifted through open windows, accompanied by laughter and murmurs of conversation.

They were greeted at the door by Charlotte and Daniel Parkerson, where Julie was introduced. It took very little time for the young bachelors to begin hovering around her.

Craig and his parents arrived a few minutes after them, and Julie was acutely aware of the buzz of whispered conversation, predatory and envious looks, and female sighs that followed when, as she knew was socially proper, he danced with Amilee first.

Though Julie tried to keep out of his way and refused to look in his direction any more than she had to, she could feel his eyes on her and her nerves were strung tighter. Despite the fact that she danced nearly every dance, she wished for the evening to go by faster so that she could be safely home and not face the possibility of Craig asking her to dance.

Sometime later she slipped outside for a bit of air. The night was scented with the fresh sweet scent of new blossomed trees and wildflowers. The air just cool enough to be comfortable after the heat of the ballroom. There was a moon so large and golden that it touched the patio with mellow light, and the stars were like a host of diamonds scattered across black velvet.

She strolled across the patio and stood in a shadowed corner, wishing to enjoy the scene in solitude. Just as she began to relax, though, she heard the soft laughter of two women deep in conversation who were walking slowly out onto the patio.

She stepped back into the shadows, not wanting to be noticed or join their conversation. But she could not help but overhear.

"I'm telling you, Matilda," one woman said, "that marriage will be an unhappy one. Why, it's like mating a wolf and a lamb."

"Sophia! What a terrible thing to say!"

"Terrible, maybe, but true. Have you heard that he's still 'involved' with that Emery woman? And her husband traveling like he does."

"No one knows that's true, Sophia."

"Where there's smoke there's fire. Why, the way she was looking at him tonight when they danced should have told everyone. That boy is a roamer and that sweet Miss Amilee is not the one to keep him at home."

"Marriage might settle him down. Besides, they really are socially suited. Both wealthy and look at what their children would own. Why, Wind Haven and Wide Oaks together would be the most prosperous place on the river."

"And I wouldn't put the idea out of your head that that's the real reason. Both Amos Sheridan and Joseph Miles are pretty shrewd. It would be just like them."

"He'd be better off married to that pretty cousin of hers. She's stunning and from what I've heard a bit independent. Their cook told mine that she rides out alone every morning and pretty much does as she pleases. And can you imagine, traveling from England to Virginia with no chaperone? I've heard she came with practically nothing but the clothes she had and a few dollars. They'll probably marry her off to someone soon. But I suspect it won't be to one of the wealthier planters sons."

"Maybe she wants to make such choices on her own."

Julie could have hugged Matilda for her defense.

The voices of the two women faded as they walked back into the ballroom, and the young Englishwoman was left with tumultuous thoughts. This marriage was not wise, but neither she nor anyone else would be able to turn Amilee away from "duty," especially when her parents' displeasure or society's censure was the punishment.

Julie drifted back to the balcony where she could look out over the garden and consider what she wanted for her life.

As she mused, her last meeting with Craig flashed before her eyes. The kiss had been so electric that she could still feel the insistence of his mouth on hers and her momentary desire to surrender to it.

Julie was not one to lie to herself or to others. Craig Miles was a danger to her and she knew it. His kiss had questioned her and she was more than scared of her answer.

If it were a game to him, she could not afford to play it.

Slowly she wandered down the flagstone steps to the garden. It was nice to be alone on this starlit night. She sat on a white stone bench and listened to the strains of music in the distance.

Craig had known quite well Julie was expertly avoiding him. But he was grimly determined she wasn't going to get away with it.

He knew this just as he knew unless he could find a way to change fate it would come to little avail. He'd considered one plan after another, rejecting them all.

He'd silently prayed for someone to come along and sweep Amilee off her feet. He didn't mind one bit being jilted nearly at the altar. He could manage the supposed scandal, but he could imagine it in Julie's arms. Then, of course, he would have to convince Julie she had never been second and he was not the jilted groom feeling sorry for himself or longing for what he couldn't have.

It was some time before he missed her in the ballroom and had set out to find her, hoping she'd be alone.

He walked out onto the balcony at the same moment that Julie reached the bottom of the steps and walked down the garden path.

So that escape back into the ballroom would not be easy, he gave her a few minutes, then followed her.

He found her seated on a bench, resting back on her hands, her face lifted and her eyes closed. Obviously she was listening to the music.

He walked carefully, not really wanting to disturb the beautiful scene she created. The moonlight touched her flawless skin and glowed across her bare shoulders and the soft rise of her breasts. He felt the blood race through his veins, and the need to speak, to touch her, destroyed whatever caution he might have had.

"Julie."

Startled, Julie blinked her eyes open and nearly leapt to her feet. Before she could regain enough control to flee he was close beside her.

"You've not given me one dance tonight," he said with a smile. "That's not fair since you've danced with every other man here."

Julie could feel his warmth surrounding her, and his gaze held hers until she was swimming in a gray mist.

The night's magic was an overwhelming force that gripped her until Craig moved even closer.

"I shall be glad to dance with you," she said, as she started past him. Surely the ballroom was much safer than this starlit garden. But Craig took hold of her arm in a strong but gentle hold.

"The music has begun," he said softly, "why not share the dance here?"

She wanted to shout no, but she considered his amusement and the fact that she really would look frightened of him. Before she could speak, his arm came around her and very slowly he drew her closer and closer.

For one moment she thought he was going to kiss her, then he began to move with the music.

Neither spoke. Craig surrendered to the delightful feeling of holding her, of the way she seemed to fit against him.

Julie felt as if every bone within her was melting, remolding to fit around him. It leaving her without strength and conscious of the heavy beat of her heart that seemed to be blending with his.

He inhaled the scent of her perfume and touched his cheek to the soft burnished glow of her hair. If he could have had his way, the music would have gone on forever.

But too soon the music came to an end. Craig did not release her but stood looking down into her moon-touched green eyes.

"I'm falling love with you, Julie Mackentire," he said in a voice so soft that it caressed her spirit. But after a second the depth of his words struck her. She tried to move out of his arms but he refused to let her go. "Don't run from the truth."

"Craig, stop," she cried. "This can't be true. It can't happen."

"But it has," he continued to hold her in a relentless embrace. "Julie—"

"No," she gasped, "No! You can't be so unfeeling. What of Amilee? What of her family?"

He continued to hold her, fighting just to make her see. "I'm not now, nor have I ever been in love with Amilee."

"Then what they say of you is true," Julie said fiercely. "You are a thief of hearts. You are careless of a woman's feelings. Have others come under your spell as easily as you thought I would?" She struggled in earnest now and finally broke his hold. Backing a few steps from him, she continued to look at him in shock. Her eyes seemed to widen in her anger, glistening like emeralds. "I will not betray Amilee, and if you don't love her, perhaps you should go away."

"If I could go away, I would have a long time ago. There is more to this arranged marriage than you know."

"Then you must be honest with her. She should not be hurt." Her voice was chilly. "Did you think to marry her and continue to have a liaison with me when it was convenient? You do not know the meaning of love!"

With these last words she turned and ran back toward the house.

"Oh yes, Julie, I do. And I don't mean to let it leave my life now that I've finally found it," Craig said to the now-still garden.

When Craig walked back into the ballroom, Julie was nowhere to be seen. He knew she would keep even more distance between them from now on.

But he was far from giving up. There had to be a god of fortune who would not allow this travesty to continue, and it was this god he questioned. Why did he meet Julie too late? Why were there barriers between them?

So preoccupied was he that he didn't realize someone was standing right beside him until Phillip spoke.

"It is a delightful ball," the tutor said.

"Yes, delightful."

"Amilee is having such a wonderful time. She is the belle of the ball and the envy of just about every woman present, so I've heard."

"You shouldn't listen to the busybodies."

"Oh, I'm not," Phillip laughed. "I've been watching Amilee all evening. She is really the most beautiful girl here."

Craig turned to look at him, then followed his gaze to Amilee who was dancing and laughing at something her partner had said.

"Yes," he concurred, "Amilee is very pretty."

"And you, sir, are a very lucky man. As the women are envious, I find it hard not to believe every man here envies your good fortune as well."

"Yes, I suppose," Craig replied noncommittally. His mind certainly wasn't on Phillip and his admiration of Amilee. "If you will excuse me, I must say good night to Amilee and her family."

"Of course."

Craig bid adieu to his fiancée and her parents. His own parents were surprised that he chose not to stay until the end of the ball, but they raised little protests when he left.

It was when he went outside to find the family carriage that he discovered Julie had gone home as well.

He would send the carriage back for his parents, but for now he needed a ride in the cool evening air to clear his mind.

It was after several minutes that the words Phillip had said to him returned full force. "You, sir, are a very lucky man.... She really is the most beautiful woman here.... I've been watching Amilee all evening..."

"Good Lord," Craig breathed softly, "the boy is smitten. Well, well. Perhaps young Phillip needs a bit of encouragement."

Chapter Five

The very next day Craig began to carry out a plan he had lain awake most of the night considering.

Seldom had he been a regular daytime visitor at Wide Oaks, but now he appeared just after lunch, when he knew Amilee and Phillip would be together working on the language Amos insisted she learn.

He was pleased to find them and even more pleased at their shocked faces when he appeared, especially Phillip's.

"Good afternoon." Craig smiled warmly on the two. "I've come to collect you, Amilee. My dear Aunt Beth hasn't seen much of us and she is complaining. I've told her I'd bring you by today." Aunt Beth was not Craig's favorite person but she would do for an excuse.

"But ... her lessons," Phillip said as he slowly stood up, the book of poetry in his hand. "Her father wants her to master French, and she is a long way from doing so."

"Well, you needn't worry about that, Phil, old boy,"

Craig laughed, a bit too arrogantly to suit Phillip. But his next words were more of a shock. "When Amilee and I are married she will be much too busy for French lessons. You won't need to be hanging around and can get on with your life. I'm sure you have places you'd rather be and things you'd rather be doing."

Amilee and Phillip exchanged a look of helpless disbelief. But Phillip fell into the trap first. "Oh, no, there is no place I'd rather be. Miss Amilee has a feel for . . ." he paused.

"Well, when Amilee is my wife there will be no need for your services. This is April, and our wedding will be in June. Perhaps two months' notice will give you ample time to find another position." He was delighted with Amilee's response. Her lips parted in the face of a reality she hadn't considered, and her wide eyes turned to Phillip as a subtle new emotion began to waken.

Yes, my dear Amilee, Craig thought, look at a man who truly loves you and one who would be more suited for you. Look at him and realize your own emotions and not those of your father's. Think for yourself, Amilee, think!

"So, get your cloak and let us be on our way." He spoke to Amilee without looking at her as if she were just a servant. He saw the flush of indignation on Phillip's cheeks.

"Yes . . . of course." Amilee struggled against the first surge of disobedience she'd ever felt. But she left the two men alone. Craig prepared his first frontal attack on Phillip's masculinity.

"Biddable little chit," he said with smug self-satisfaction. "That is the way it should be. I don't think I could tolerate a wife who crossed me." He winked at Phillip and nudged him with an elbow. "Keep 'em obedient and docile, I always say. That way you'll get no arguments about your other . . . ah . . . interests."

He watched Phillip's shocked gaze turn angry, and was more than pleased that he had stirred the Frenchman into considering Amilee's life with a brutish husband.

Craig was certain Phillip had chosen poetry to teach with because he had a romanticist's heart and Craig meant to play on it as hard as he could.

"Won't need this poetry either," he laughed. "I'll take Amilee to France. Give her a few lessons on how the bohemians live. Why," he leaned toward Phillip conspiratorially, "they say that the ladies over there can teach us a thing or two. I've heard—"

"Really, Mr. Miles." Phillip could hear no more. This man would treat Amilee as if she were a—He couldn't think of gentle, precious Amilee, sweet Amilee, being exposed to such prurient matters. "I don't think this is a subject for us to discuss. I—I hesitate to make a suggestion, sir . . ."

Don't hesitate, Craig thought, get angry enough to fight for what you want. "A suggestion?"

"I've found Miss Amilee to be a delicate young lady. Not one to be treated . . . ah . . . strenuously. She is of a gentle spirit."

"That's for little girls and romantics. A woman is a woman, and she should know her place." Good Lord, Craig thought with malicious humor, I hope Julie never hears about this. "One has to wake them up sometime, doesn't one?"

Phillip had never struck another person with anger in his life, but at this moment he could happily have committed mayhem, and Craig was more than satisfied for now. He turned as he heard Amilee approach.

"Let's be on our way," he said to her and started to walk away as if he'd never considered that she wouldn't follow.

Turning to glance back, he was rewarded by a burning glare from Phillip that would have burnt him to a cinder.

If Craig had been ruthless with Phillip, he was more so with Amilee. As he handed her into the carriage and sat beside her, he laughed. "I do suppose you would like to thank me."

"Thank you?"

"Why, for rescuing you."

"Rescuing me?"

"From that tedious bore Phillip. Always spouting poetry or some such. Teaching you French. As if it will be of any use. You won't have to deal with any of that once we're married and have children. You'll be too busy with me to worry about that spineless creature."

"Cra—Mr. Miles!"

"Well, Amilee, you can't possibly consider telling me that you are amused by him. Why, all he does is talk about faraway places. Poetry, romance, and all that foolishness." He turned to look at her as if he were appraising a piece of beef. "Once we're married, I do not want him around. He'll be filling your head with God knows what."

He'd stung Amilee, and he silently prayed one day she would be able to forgive him, preferably once she'd jilted him, married Phillip, and left him free to pursue Julie. He wondered what Julie's reaction would be if she could hear him now.

For the rest of their outing, their more-than-uncomfortable visit with his aunt, and the ride home, Craig kept up his scathing remarks about Phillip, love, romance, and marriage until he could feel Amilee's desire to get away from him palpably.

He had one more card to play this day. As the carriage moved away and before they entered the house, he caught Amilee in his arms with a forceful embrace that nearly took her breath away. He kissed her until he felt her struggle and heard a soft sound of protest. Then he smiled down into her stricken eyes. "We'll be married in two months, Amilee, then we can conclude this more to my satisfaction."

He heard her gasp as he left her there and walked down the drive where he had instructed his carriage to wait. Once inside he closed his eyes and considered how Amilee would react. He could imagine what his parents, her parents, and especially how Julie would react if they knew what he was about. The only thing that frightened him was the fact that it might not work and he would go into a marriage with a wife who thought him a heartless, unfeeling monster.

Grimly determined, Craig followed his plan by interrupting and separating Phillip and Amilee every day. He watched Phillip's incensed feelings grow stronger and wondered how long he was going to be pushed before he took matters into his own hands. Was Phillip going to allow Amilee, his sweet gentle Amilee, to marry this cold and forceful man? Craig prayed he wouldn't.

Every other evening he saw Julie, who tried her best not to make eye contact. He drank in her beauty like a ravenous man at a feast.

Any other time Phillip might not have noticed, but he had become very aware of Craig and his eccentricities. He saw him looking at Julie, but his fear was for Amilee. This man was a lecher who would deceive Amilee at his first opportunity. Phillip's rage began to grow into a force that surprised even him.

Two weeks of this was driving Craig to distraction as well. He wanted a moment alone with Julie. Though he knew it was not a wise idea, the desire would not go away.

Remembering that she liked to ride early in the morning, he rose almost before dawn and rode toward Wide Oaks.

From a discreet distance he watched the stable and was rewarded in less than half an hour when he saw the groom emerge with Julie's horse, saw her walk from the house, mount up, and ride away.

Satisfied that he knew which direction she was going and where it would undoubtedly lead, he rode to a place where their paths would cross.

Julie trotted along, deep in thought. She, more than anyone else, was aware of the subtle change in Amilee. Lately her cousin had been less her smiling self. She had grown withdrawn and thoughtful.

Then the night before while the two had been walking in the garden, Amilee questioned her.

"Julie?"

"Yes?"

"How is it in England? I mean, if you were there would you marry the person your family chose?"

"No, I think not. I never knew my mother, but I know Father talked of her often. He loved her fiercely and swore to me I would never have to marry anyone not of my own choice. But," Julie smiled, "he knew me quite well. I have a stubborn streak that I inherited from him. I should have done anything in my power to thwart such plans."

"But you're so brave."

"Amilee, I am no braver than any other woman. Father always said I should follow where my own heart led and not along the path others chose for me."

"Then how do you know if you love someone?"

"I . . . I don't know, truly I don't. You must, I think, be able to look at him and honestly say, 'This is the man with whom I would like to spend the rest of my life.

The man whose dreams and ambitions I share, and the man I would like to be the father of my children.' "

"But Mother says that a woman, to be a good wife, must simply understand that a man has to choose a wife best suited for his place in society. She is his reflection."

"Good heavens, Amilee." Julie was losing her patience and that was the last thing she wanted to do. "You are no one's reflection. You are you, Amilee Sheridan. You have likes and dislikes. You have a mind as well as a body. A man can't spend every waking hour in bed."

"Julie!" Amilee's cheeks grew pink.

"Amilee, consider what you like, what you truly are. Then consider all the years ahead. You have to be happy, too. Perhaps you should discuss such things with . . . Mr. Miles. It should make your marriage so much easier on both of you."

"Do . . . do you think he considers me—I mean—"

"I know what you mean and I'm sure he does. You are really a very pretty girl, and I know you want to be a good wife. You must demand more from your husband, yes, your future husband, than just to be the mother of his heir. Let him know you intend to be a wife in all ways." And heaven help him if he hurts you, Julie thought angrily. And heaven help me if I hurt you, too.

Julie had thought of Craig constantly since the ball, and to her distress, she had even dreamed of him. No matter how hard she tried to push it from her mind, she could still feel his strong arms about her and taste the warmth of his hard demanding lips on hers.

The words he had said lingered in the back of her mind. Julie would not lie to herself. She was vulnerable where Craig Miles was concerned, and she knew she had to do something about it.

She had retreated from him, but that only made her

thoughts more tumultuous and her dreams harder to face. No, she had to do something—but what?"

Amilee, too, was considering all that her cousin had to say in a most unusual way.

Now Julie rode slowly through the early morning light. Not one to run from situations, she decided she must face Craig, but only after she had solidified other matters.

Although she didn't think she had any other relations, she questioned her aunt, anyway.

"Relatives? Why, of course, my dear. Your father's distant cousin, Sir Claude Sommerville, lives in South Carolina. Then ... let me see, your Aunt Stephanie and Uncle Walter died, but you have several cousins in Philadelphia."

"I should very much like to write to them, Aunt Barbara. If you would be so kind as to supply me with their addresses."

"Of course, my dear, but I'm sure a few, if not most of them, will come for the wedding."

"I know, but I would like to correspond with them before that."

"Well, I'll give you the addresses."

"Thank you."

Julie had written long and involved letters, shortly receiving her first answer. Sommerville had told her in no uncertain terms that he and his wife would welcome her under their roof anytime she chose to honor them with a visit. He and her father had shared many years of their boyhood together, and he would love to exchange old memories of her father and gain new ones from her.

She kept his letter a secret, planning on writing to him again very soon to strengthen their family ties.

Julie was not sure if her conversation with Amilee had helped or not. She just wished for her young cousin to find happiness, and she was not sure Craig Miles was the man to make Amilee happy.

He was too ... too ... uncontrollable, too aware of the effect his damnably sensual magnetism had on women. Too comfortable using women, enjoying them for a fleeting moment, then leaving them to pursue other interests. In Craig's case she was sure it would be the first pretty face or neat ankle that could lead him away.

Hadn't he told her he was falling in love with her? To how many women had he told the same thing? Well, she was not going to have her heart broken. This was one butterfly who would escape his net.

Julie found a secluded meadow, surrounded by trees. She dismounted and let her horse graze while she walked slowly about, gathering an armful of wildflowers.

Their scent filled the air, and in the stillness she could hear the hum of bees and the song of birds nesting in the nearby trees.

Finding a spot where the grass was thick and soft, she sat down, laying the flowers next to her. The day was growing a bit warmer, but it glowed with a rosy mist.

Unconsciously she reached to unbind her waist-length hair, running her fingers through it to cool herself.

She unbuttoned the top two buttons of her blouse, then rested back on her elbows, lifting her face to the sun.

Never considering that interested eyes may have been watching her, she was much too caught up in a kind of glorious hazy lassitude.

She was still unaware when a shadow fell across her and only opened her eyes at the sound of a deep familiar voice.

Chapter Six

Craig had stood motionless beneath the limbs of a huge tree where he had tied his horse after following Julie to the meadow. He had watched her with growing fascination and building desire.

He watched her loosen her hair and run her fingers through it, and his hands quivered with the need to do the same. Then she lay back, lifting her face, and the need flamed to a brilliant conflagration. He walked toward her.

The grass was full and soft, and he knew she did not hear him approach, for she remained still, a half smile on her lips. She had unbuttoned the buttons on her blouse for the touch of the air, but they revealed to his hungry gaze a bit of lace and the soft swell of creamy skin.

He stood beside her for a long moment, simply soaking up her beauty, wanting her with every fiber of his being. Finally he could not resist one touch, even if it meant the reappearance of the resistance he'd seen in her eyes. He knelt close and watched her eyes open with shock when he said her name.

When their gazes locked, time stopped for a brilliant moment. With both hands he cupped her face, then bent to touch her mouth. Gently he savored the soft warmth.

The kiss deepened and still Julie could not seem to find the will to resist the flow of heat that made her feel boneless. Slowly they lay back on the sweet-scented grass. Her arms came about him, and she became lost in the magic he was weaving about her.

It was wrong and she knew it was wrong, but the sheer pleasure of this stolen moment might have to last her for a long, long time.

When the kiss ended, neither seemed to be able to speak. Julie gazed up into Craig's smoldering gray eyes and realized how easy it would be to love this man. How lucky Amilee was to share the rest of his life with him. All her anger seemed to melt before the realization that no matter what kind of scoundrel he was, she had come to love him.

"How did you know I was here?"

"I followed you. Julie, we have to talk. I have so much I would like to say and, in time, will say. For now, can you not trust me?"

She rose to her feet and walked a few steps from him, searching for control before she said things she might regret. "Craig, why did you propose marriage to Amilee in the first place, if you didn't love her?"

He rose quickly and came to stand behind her, taking her shoulders in both hands and drawing her back against him. Her question had sent a premonitional fear through him, and he knew he would have to be cautious.

"Julie, how could I know someone like you would walk into my life? I was . . . I was certain love was only a dream that didn't exist. I allowed a decision to be made for me the same way Amilee did. It was a mistake. But it's not fair either. I don't want to hurt Amilee and if you just give me time, I promise you I'll work this out."

She turned to face him, and he cursed himself for the tears he saw in her eyes.

How could he explain to her that he was playing a deceptive and drastic trick on both Amilee and Phillip without having her believe everything he thought and did was deceptive.

"Oh, Craig, don't believe your little 'games' for which you have an amazing reputation can be played even as you marry. To you, and it seems to most men, women are nothing but a possession that carries the only thing of worth, their name. Wives are selected for their ability to breed heirs of suitable position. Then they're turned out to pasture, left to their own devices or to die of boredom. I know Amilee was 'chosen' because she brings Wide Oaks with her, and you because Wind Haven needs an heir. If Amilee can go along with that—Well, that is her business. But I will not settle into the position you would like. I will play second to no one, and I will be no rich man's mistress. I would rather die poor and alone."

"Now you're being unfair. You have your mind set on something and you're jumping to conclusions. Whatever made you think I want you as my mistress?"

"Because," she held his gaze relentlessly, "you cannot break your engagement without crushing Amilee and making her the topic of gossip for the rest of the summer. Not to mention what would happen to your reputation."

"To hell with my reputation!" He gripped her shoulders and jerked her against him. "You think I lied to you when I told you I loved you? Deny what you want, I know what I felt. You tell me, is this a lie?"

He crushed her to him in a relentless embrace that nearly took the breath from her. Then he took her mouth in a kiss that fairly exploded.

Julie was rocked to her soul, set on fire by the kiss

that seemed to draw her into him. She knew then she must either put a great distance between her and this overpowering man or succumb to whatever he wished. She also knew she could lose herself in him and forget everyone and everything.

It was a sharp noise that made Craig lift his head, and Julie's surprised gaze followed his. Just within the trees that bordered the meadow, Amos sat on his horse and regarded them with a frozen look. They had no way of knowing how long he had been there or what he had seen. But when, without a word or a sign, he turned his horse and disappeared into the woods, both Julie and Craig knew he had seen everything.

She gasped in dismay, then turned to look up into Craig's face, which seemed to have become a mask. Her heart felt as if he had gripped it in his hands and crushed it. Of course he was angry. He had no plans on being found like this, with her. No, he intended this little liaison to be his secret.

With a sob she tore herself from his arms and ran to her horse.

"Julie! Wait!" he called after her, but her horse was already disappearing. "Damnation!" he growled. Now he would have to encourage Amilee and Phillip a little stronger, then find a way to get Julie to listen to the explanation he'd been about to give her.

He walked to his horse and rode home, angry at himself for not explaining first and enjoying the kisses they might have shared later.

Amilee and Phillip noticed Julie's quietness at dinner but made no mention of it. Amos, too, was more silent than usual. When dinner was finished, he came to Julie's side and spoke softly so that the others would not hear.

"Julie, I would like to talk to you in my study later tonight. Preferably after the others have retired."

"Yes, Uncle Amos." Julie felt defeated, and she only hoped Amos would let her carry out her plan and be gone before anyone noticed.

The evening seemed interminably long, and Julie gritted her teeth at Amilee and Phillip's laughter as they sat by the fire talking. She prayed for the hours to go by quickly, so she could escape her nightmare. At this moment she hated Craig Miles.

The time finally came to retire, and Julie did not have to worry about slipping away unnoticed, for her cousin seemed preoccupied, changing for bed with very little conversation.

"I believe I'll go and warm some milk," Julie said. "I'm too tense to sleep. Good night, Amilee."

"Good night." Amilee's voice was soft, as if her mind were elsewhere.

Grateful that it was this easy, Julie went downstairs. When she reached the study door, she rapped softly.

"Come in."

Once inside, Julie crossed the room and stood near her uncle, who was standing by the window sipping a brandy. To her surprise he did not appear angry.

"You wanted to talk to me, Uncle Amos?" Julie felt strangely calm.

"Julie, this is a very difficult situation. I hope you understand what I am about to say."

"Of course I will. You are protecting Amilee's future, as any father would. I'm . . . I'm sorry about this afternoon. It was a dreadful mistake on my part."

"I would not like this to reach Amilee's ears. Were the two of you planning on—"

"No . . . No, as I told you, it was a terrible mistake on my part. Craig is not to blame. I know he loves Amilee and wants to marry her. Uncle, you must help me."

If Amos looked at her strangely, Julie didn't notice. She was too intent on seeing he understood her plan and would help her. Slowly and very firmly she told him what she was going to do.

Craig was to come to dinner that night, but he appeared again in the late morning to make sure all the pointed remarks he meant to make to Phillip and Amilee had time to brew.

They sat in the garden again, and Craig was well-aware of Phillip's frigid look as he approached them. He sat in a nearby chair and stretched his long legs before him, drawing a deep breath and expelling it as if he were already bored.

"Confound it, I shall be glad when we're married. These lessons are devilishly boring. We will be able to find much better ways to while away our days later." He smiled slowly, watching Amilee register poorly contained shock and Phillip's face grow crimson with the rage he was trying to contain. Craig was much too good with pistols for Phillip to think of challenging him. But to Craig's satisfaction he could see he wanted to.

"It must be boring for you, Mr. Miles," Phillip said coldly, "but one has to be as sensitive as Miss Amilee to understand poetry the way she does and translate it into French."

"Hmm, I suppose so. But then," he grinned again, "I can't see the use for it when Amilee will have her hands full, what with children and a home. I suspect the female mind was not meant to harbor much education anyway." Lord, he was really putting it on.

"I—I do believe I will fetch some lemonade," Amilee said as she rose to her feet and nearly fled.

"You shouldn't speak to Amilee that way," Phillip finally choked out. "You speak as if she is one of the loose women in town. She is a lady of breeding and quality."

"Are you teaching me manners?" Craig asked with dangerous mildness.

"It seems someone ought," Phillip said, setting his chin stubbornly. "You can call me out if you choose, but I will not tolerate your terrible treatment of her while I'm near."

Craig laughed, rose to his feet, and looked down at Phillip. "What then," he said quietly, "do you think you can do about it? It's time Amilee learned what a man is. I do so get bored with sweet innocence." He tapped Phillip lightly on the shoulder with his riding crop and walked away. Be a hero, Phillip, he thought. Pull yourself together and do something about it.

Julie had remained in her room most of the day, professing a headache and asking to be left alone. Neither Amilee or Barbara considered disturbing her. Julie had assured them she would be down for dinner.

She sat before her mirror, searching her eyes for strength. She knew what she had planned would break her own heart, but she was determined. She packed her clothes carefully, then slid her bags under the bed. These she would take with her. The rest her uncle would send once she was settled . . . and the wedding was over.

She considered her decision. She did not want to hurt Amilee, but if her plans were carried out, it would be a secret that would be hers alone.

She sat down and wrote a note, putting it in the pocket of her dress. Then she went down to join her uncle and aunt, Amilee and Phillip . . . and Craig, for dinner.

Again it was a quiet affair. Amilee didn't seem to

know what to say to Craig, and she barely looked at him. Phillip had to keep his eyes from Craig or he would have attacked him, and Craig was overjoyed with the situation. They both hated him. Now all he had to do was push them toward each other a little harder and the game would be his.

As for Julie, Craig was delighted that she smiled and kept up the conversation and even included him, as if she had forgiven and forgotten what had happened. In time he meant to remind her of the events in that secluded meadow. Perhaps, he thought, with intense pleasure, he would take her there again to conclude what had begun. The thought did things to his body that might have frightened Amilee half out of her wits.

"Julie, my dear," Amos said. "I have a client in town who knew your father. He would like to meet you. Would you like to ride into town with me tomorrow?"

"Why, yes, I'd like that very much."

"Would you mind if I ride with you?" Amilee asked.

There was a moment of silence then Julie laughed. "She has caught us out, Uncle. Amilee, if you must know, I asked Uncle to take me to town to buy your wedding gift. You don't want to spoil it, do you?"

"Oh, no, I didn't know. Don't be too extravagant."

"I shan't." Julie smiled warmly at Amilee. "What I'm going to give you is something special, and I want you to have it with all my heart."

Amilee was pleased, Amos looked satisfied, Barbara looked puzzled, and Craig fought the strangest feeling he'd ever known.

The conversation moved to other subjects and soon the dinner was over. Amilee refused to walk in the garden with Craig ... politely but firmly. Craig couldn't have been more pleased.

Again Amilee chose the piano and again Craig conveniently allowed Phillip to stand by, turn the pages of music, and look down into Amilee's blue eyes.

Amos and Barbara were engrossed in the music and didn't notice Julie slide closer to a more-than-surprised Craig. The surprise grew when he felt the folded piece of paper being pressed into his hand. He slipped it in his pocket and looked with a silent question at Julie who simply smiled the sweetest, most innocent smile he had ever seen, which abruptly gave him cause to wonder just what she was up to.

The note seemed to burn through the cloth of his shirt where he had thrust it. He wanted to read it, and the anticipation made time crawl by.

But eventually it was over, and he said his goodnights and left. But he'd hardly heard the door close before he stepped into a patch of moonlight, unfolded the note, and read.

> Meet me in the meadow at midnight. There is something of utmost importance I must share with you. Don't be late; it is a frightening place to be alone.
>
> Julie

"Lord," he said aloud. "Late?" He laughed. Hardly. Perhaps she remembered what he said, had felt what he had felt, and had understood. No, he would not be late. In fact, he took his watch from his pocket and glanced at it. A quarter to eleven. From there to midnight was not long to wait, not for Julie . . . not for the woman he loved and wanted with every fiber of his being. He mounted and rode away.

From an upstairs window Julie watched and prayed his thoughts were what she had planned them to be.

Chapter Seven

Craig sat on the soft grass in the moon-touched meadow, more than amused at himself. He had never been in the position he was now. Always he had taken women where he found them, never wanting any kind of permanent relationship, and certainly never needing one of them.

But this time was so different. He knew he needed and wanted Julie, loved her as he had never loved before.

Soon she would come, and he could take her in his arms and tell her how much he loved her. He could explain his entire plan, knowing she would understand and comply.

In time they could marry, and although others might think it just a rebounding romance, he and Julie would know differently.

Impatience bit deeply, and he rose to pace. He had looked at his watch only minutes ago, but still he dragged it from his pocket. Ten past twelve. She was late. Was it—He paused in mid-stride.

At the edge of the meadow, a misty white cloud was slowly forming into horse and woman. When she drew closer, the moonlight defined her.

When she was just a few feet from him, she drew the

horse to a halt. She hadn't bothered to saddle it and now slid down from the sleek back and stood for a moment regarding him.

She wore something filmy and white, and he could have sworn there was little beneath it, for the moonbeams seemed to drift between its folds and caress a shadowy form. Her hair was loose and fell about her shoulders. Touched by the glow of moonlight, it seemed as if the fire of starlight danced there.

Craig couldn't seem to move as Julie drifted slowly toward him.

Now, as she stopped beside him, he could see the inviting warmth in her eyes and the teasing half smile on her lips, and he felt a profound sense of relief. Of course she knew and understood. Why else would she come to him like this? Without words she was agreeing to trust him as he had begged her to do.

The gift of her total faith and trust overwhelmed him, and he could not speak. He only stretched out his arms and she walked into them, circling his neck with hers and raising her face so their lips could meet.

His arms circled her, drawing her against him until she could feel the thunder of his heart matching hers. His parted lips touched hers, and for Julie all thoughts passed into oblivion but for him and this magic moment.

He took her face between his hands, tangling his fingers in her thick hair. He held her a willing captive while he kissed her with a devouring hunger that spiraled him to a hot and welcome place where nothing else mattered but her and this tender and complete surrender.

Julie leaned into him, because her legs were too weak to hold her and because she was savoring and returning his endless drugging kiss. He heard her moan softly and flame raged through him. It was a kiss like no other either had ever known. She offered no resistance to its depth and gave him her parted lips, moving them against his, kissing him as erotically as he was kissing her.

She felt as if she were melting, as if part of him was flowing around her, surrounding her, becoming part of her until she did not know where she ended and he began.

When she took her lips from his, he felt the sudden emptiness, the void in which he would live the rest of his life if not for her. He groaned in disappointment but couldn't let her go.

She looked up into his eyes, seeing the smoldering heat and glorying in it. Then she reached up and cupped her hands around his face, caressing the hard jaw, then drifting to his shoulder and chest, surprised at the hard muscle and the warmth that pulsed beneath it.

"Julie." He said her name softly. "Julie." He spoke from his heart where she was a live flame.

She knew that only a few hours were left to her, and she was desperate to make him a part of her, a part she could hold forever when there was nothing else left, for she had already made her vow that no other man would take his place, that she would keep his memory for the rest of her life . . . alone.

When he drew her down to the soft grass, she did not resist, and when they lay side by side, she came against him, her body searching for his, her mouth seeking his, and her love filling him with a feverish passion such as Craig had never felt before.

She closed her eyes and felt his fingers, gentle despite the need that was tearing at him. When the cool breeze touched her heated skin, it was followed by an even deeper warmth as his hands caressed her. Her hands, too, began to work the buttons on his shirt, continuing until they lay flesh to flesh.

When he gently cupped her breast in his hand and

bent to taste the rosy crest, she cried out his name softly and arched to meet his questing tongue.

It exploded within him, the fierce overwhelming magic. He wanted to be within her, to feel her take him and hold him, and ease this conflagration that was slowly disintegrating his control. He also knew he would hurt her and the pain this caused him was surprising.

His hands slid down the curve of her thigh and almost reflexively she pressed her legs closed. She wanted him but was fearful.

"Don't be afraid of me, Julie." His voice was as warm a caress as his hands and mouth had been, and she forced her body to relax feeling his hand slip gently between her legs to caress and stimulate her until he felt her moist arousal. He knew she was ready, but still he dreaded hurting her.

"I will hurt you, I know it and I hate it. But, Julie, I promise the hurt will go and I'll never hurt you again. Will you trust me?"

"Yes," she whispered, and his heart swelled with more pleasure than he had ever experienced.

Shivers of delight and fear raced through Julie's body, but neither her heart nor her passion could respond to those; she responded to the feeling his hands drew from her and the feel of his mouth on hers and the sound of his voice as he repeated her name over and over.

She felt as if her body was on fire, and she held onto him, waiting for the promised pain. Craig moved over her, his hands sliding beneath her to lift her to receive him. She felt the heat and the throbbing hardness as it probed the pulsing entrance. She closed her eyes and clung to him in ultimate trust.

He inched into her incredible warmth, and he felt the tight moist sheath. He withdrew then pressed in again, withdrew and pressed in, poising himself for the touch of the inevitable barrier and desperate to bury himself deep inside her.

"Julie," he whispered as he drove deeply, hearing her gasp of pain and feeling her clutch him.

He waited as long as his flame-touched, passion-filled body would allow and could have laughed at a restraint he'd never needed to practice before, but was of supreme importance now. Then he began to move slowly. Delicately he circled his hips against her and could have cried out his joy at her response.

He began to move in rhythmic thrusts and felt her body pick up the rhythm and move with him.

Sensation after sensation rippled through her, and she was without any thoughts but of him and the wild tumult that coursed through her.

The force of Craig's thrusts increased, and Julie felt the building of some vibrant violent thing. Still she was unprepared for its shattering effect as her body reached a furious climax.

Craig had sensed how close she was and restrained himself until he heard her gasp. Then he drove fiercely until they reached that pinnacle together. Her cry of his name blended with his, and they clung to each other as they tumbled into the void.

Lying on his side, Craig drew her to him, and she rested her head on his chest, overcome with a weightless feeling and as she listened to the wild beat of his heart until it began to slow.

Julie raised herself to rest across his chest and look up into his eyes. She returned the warmth of his smile and sighed as he tangled his fingers in her hair and drew her to him to kiss her gently and leisurely.

"Julie," he whispered against her hair. "You're so beautiful, so perfect."

She felt the heat of tears in her eyes, and that was the last thing she wanted him to see.

"This night has been beautiful and perfect, and I'll cherish it always. Even when I'm a very old woman."

"There are many, many years between now and the time you're an old woman. Many nights I hope to enjoy with you. I have a feeling that even when I'm an old man, I shall still be chasing you about." He laughed softly at the thought of sharing years filled with nights like this one.

"You will need children . . . an heir to protect the Wind Haven legacy."

"You don't want children?" he asked quietly. She could feel his body tense as he waited for her answer.

"I should like to have children one day," she said wistfully, knowing it might never be so. If he had planted his seed in her tonight, it might be the only consolation for a lifetime spent without him. She would put distance between them, and one day perhaps he could forget her.

"Then we are agreed on that." His chuckle was warm as he hugged her to him. How calmly he accepted the fact that a mistress could give him as much pleasure having a child a his wife one day would.

For a minute Julie was choked with bitter tears, and she wanted to cry out against his unfairness. But she had come to him, she had forced the issue, and she had to take the consequences.

Not wanting to spoil this one and only night she would share with him, she had to keep his mind from questions until their hours had passed.

She ran her fingers lightly across his chest, and his arm grew tighter around her. Low, beneath his rib, a ragged scar marred the perfection of a body she thought beautiful. Her fingers lingered on it, and she looked up at him questioningly.

"Would you believe a knife wound?"

"Craig!" He was thrilled by the fear and worry in her voice.

"It's very old. I got it when I was with Nelson's Rangers in the Mohawk uprising."

Julie imagined the pain the knife must have caused and realized that she could not bear the thought of him being hurt, that she felt pain at the very idea. She bent forward and kissed the scar, then began to lightly trail kisses across his chest. She liked the warm taste of his flesh and his heady masculine scent.

He closed his eyes to more fully absorb the almost painful pleasure her touch brought. He could feel her to the center of his being. Deep inside he knew he would always feel so, that her touch would be able to waken him no matter how many times, hours, days, or years they were together.

But closing his eyes and allowing her touch soon was not enough. He could feel his body re-awaken and was a bit surprised. Still, he figured she could wake the dead, and he was far from dead, never feeling more vital and alive in his life.

He reached down to catch her chin between his thumb and finger, lifting her face. Then, looking down into her eyes, he smiled. He was warmed even more when he saw the look in her eyes. He could not name the emotion; it seemed a cross between a hot and hungry need and a gentle flow of unrestrained love.

He'd planned on talking the situation out, but words seemed to fail him in the face of the sweeping surge of love that filled him.

Turning slightly, he drew her against him and took her mouth in a soul-searing kiss that wiped everything else away. She responded by lacing her fingers in his hair and drawing him even more firmly to her.

Her response was less hesitant than the first time, and

he felt a new joy at the fact that she was as hungry for him as he was for her.

This time, when they had teased each other with sensitive hands and heart-melting kisses, this time she was as much the aggressor as he.

The thought of sharing the rest of his life with this creature of beauty and fire momentarily overwhelmed him. This time when he came into her, he left a part of him that was irretrievable. From this night on, both minds were filled with the same idea: each would not be whole without the other.

Craig knew this with joy. Julie, with a pain so devastating she wanted to scream. There would never be another night like this for her.

When he felt her body tremble on the verge of a shattering climax, he allowed himself to pour every ounce of his being into the pleasure of making Julie his.

Sated and quiet, they again lay together, and now Julie felt apprehension. She must be careful. Craig would want answers, answers she could not give. He would want to make plans, plans she could not bear to make.

She knew that coming to him like this would convince him that she was more than willing to be the shadowed part of his life. She would rather be without him completely.

"Julie," he said gently, long before she was ready to face the problem. She wanted to hold him a little longer, be in his arms, close to him. "There's so much I have to explain to you . . . so many things we have to plan."

Again she rose to look up at him. She put her fingers gently against his lips. "Not tonight. I don't want to talk about the future or make any plans. Not tonight. For this one night, can't we just share what we've found?"

"I'm glad you decided not to walk out of my life,

Julie. The years would have been empty if I didn't know you were there to be a comfort when I need you."

She sighed. Reality was there to tear at her whether she wanted to face it or not. Of course Craig had every right to jump to the conclusion that she had accepted the fact that he must marry one woman from necessity and want to make love to another out of need. She could no longer blame him. She had wanted to come to him, for this goodbye would be final, and she wanted to carry part of him away with her.

But now it was over, and she must do what needed to be done.

"This night has been perfect. But now I must go back before someone discovers I'm gone."

"Julie, you have to let me explain what I've planned."

"Craig, I promise, the next time you see me you can explain everything and I'll listen."

"Why not now?"

"Because I don't want to spoil this."

"But—"

"Please, Craig, for me? Leave the explanations later."

He hesitated, uncomfortable with the situation. Some deep instinctive voice was clamoring to be heard, but he didn't know what was wrong. He had asked her to trust him and she had, completely. So completely that he was still stunned by it. Yet somehow he felt he should force her to listen.

But now she was whispering that time was too short, that this night was special, seducing him with the touch of her hands and the warmth of her kisses until he let reason slip from his grasp. He would explain it all ... the next time he saw her.

It was not dawn, but the moon had set and the stars were disappearing when they reluctantly left each other's embrace. Craig knew he would never be satisfied until Julie was permanently his and they shared his bed and would not have to part.

Despite her assurance that she could go safely home, he insisted on riding with her until the house was in sight.

Then he leaned toward her and brushed her lips with a gentle kiss, holding the memory of her heavy-lidded eyes and tremulous look.

"Will I see you today?"

"No, I promised Uncle Amos I'd go to town with him."

"You also promised—"

"Yes, to let you explain. When next you see me."

"Until then," he whispered. She smiled as he brushed her cheek with gentle fingers. He then turned his horse and rode away. Only then did she allow the tears.

"Goodbye, Craig. . . . Goodbye my love." She watched him until he disappeared into the night.

Chapter Eight

The next morning Amos was helping Julie into his carriage by the time Amilee awoke. No one but Amos and Julie knew of the two satchels of clothes she carried or of the train ticket in her reticule.

No one but Amos saw her tears either, and the two rode in silence for a long while. Julie turned as they drove through the gates and looked back at Wide Oaks. Beyond it lay Wind Haven.

Was he awake? Was he thinking of her? Had his few hours of sleep been as filled with longing and dreams as her as had been? Would he be able to forgive her one day knowing the truth, that she could not live a shadowed life on the edge of his world?

She relaxed back into her seat and for a moment closed her eyes. Amos stared at her in silence. There was nothing he could say to lessen her hurt, but even if there had been, he would not have said it anyhow. Things were going according to his plans and that pleased him.

When they reached the station, he helped her board and stood watching until the train disappeared in the distance.

Satisfied that none of his schemes would be thwarted, he went back to his carriage and drove into town where he intended to stay until dinnertime.

Amilee, too, rose early, just a quarter-hour after her father and Julie had left. She was conscious of an inner struggle that had seemed to blossom after Julie's arrival.

She would have remained steadfast in her thoughts if it hadn't been for the lascivious way Craig had been acting. She was looking at him with different eyes lately, and not quite liking what she saw.

Not only afraid that she was making a mistake, she worried that she did not have the courage to change the situation. Worse than anything else, for the past few days she had been comparing Craig and Phillip. That alone surprised her. Where Craig was overpowering and so masculine that he frightened her silly, Phillip was gentle and kind, and not in the least bit aggressive.

Julie's words came back to her again and again ... A man with whom she had things in common, a man who liked the things she liked, and a man with whom she could talk. Had she ever really been able to talk to Craig? No, she could not seem to open her mouth when they were alone.

But with Phillip, she talked of poets and composers, of fine art and music, of faraway places and so many other things.

She sighed and turned to her only form of release, her piano. She sat down to play.

Phillip was having thoughts that might have shocked Amilee. He was coming to the end of his patience with Craig Miles, who was displaying what was to Phillip a dishonorable and disgusting side of his personality. Thinking of his sweet, gentle Amilee tied permanently to a man as callous as Craig Miles enraged him.

He had intended to say and do nothing, because he, above all others, knew his place. He had very little money saved, but he had confidence in his ability to earn a living. Of course it would be nothing compared to the luxury Amilee was used to.

There was no doubt in his mind that Amilee's parents would never permit their relationship, and Amilee's wedding was only a month away. Still, there was a nagging question in the back of his mind. Disregarding all else, what would Amilee say?

Could he tell her that he dreamed of her day and night, and found his greatest pleasure in the hours he spent with her? She was so intelligent, so aware of the fine and beautiful things in life. And they shared the same things.

He rose that morning determined that before it was too late he must say something. Craig Miles had made him aware that he could not let Amilee go to the brute without doing battle of some kind.

The idea of any confrontation between him and Craig

made him sweat. Still, Amilee's future was at stake and he was now desperate to do something.

Of course he did not remember that Craig's taunts were always directed at his seeming lack of courage, that every time he left, he was furious and wishing Amilee would not have to marry this man.

Now as he walked downstairs he realized another truth. In less than a month he would leave this house never to return, never to see Amilee again and always to carry the vision of her in another man's arms.

The sound of music came to him and he smiled. Amilee was playing. He followed the sound and stopped in the doorway to watch her. His smile faded when Amilee's hands paused on the keys, then dropped into her lap. She looked much like a lost little girl, and something within him was wrenched.

"Good morning, Amilee. You're up early."

Amilee turned at the sound of his voice and smiled. "Phillip. You are up very early as well." Perhaps, she thought, she had never really seen Phillip before. Had she noticed how warm and gentle his smile was or how his azure eyes seemed to touch her? Had she noticed how thick and wavy his brown hair was or how small strands of gold seemed to be woven through it? Had she really not noticed how handsome he was? She remained still, considering how improper her thoughts were.

"It's a lovely day," he said, wanting instead to say, Amilee, you're so lovely. Her blond hair picked up the sunlight and shimmered like spun gold. The blue cloudless sky could have been matched by her eyes. Her skin seemed to glow with vitality and a pulsing warmth.

Crossing the room to stand beside her, he looked down into her eyes and saw shadows there that upset him. He wanted to see her smile.... Of course he always wanted to see her smile. "You were playing Chopin again. Were you upset?"

"Upset? Why would you think that?"

"Because you always play Chopin when you're upset."

"I didn't realize you knew me so well," she said softly, looking at him as if it were the first time she had truly seen him.

"I have a secret."

"A secret?"

"Yes, I meant to show you before, but every time you play I forget about it." He sat down on the piano bench beside her. "Listen carefully." He struck middle C, and a tinkling hum filled the air. It sounded to Amilee as though someone had run a damp finger around the rim of a crystal glass.

"Beautiful," she smiled, and he watched her eyes warm with it. "But what is it and where does it come from?"

He struck C again, and she listened carefully to the sweet sound. It seemed to come from the center of the room.

"There must be one true and pure crystal in the chandelier. When the C is struck it vibrates and hums. Listen." He struck it again and watched Amilee's eyes brighten with pleasure and her quick smile.

"What a delightful thing."

"Yes ... delightful," Phillip repeated. Then he reached to take one of Amilee's delicate hands in his. "Amilee, there is something of supreme importance I must talk to you about."

"And there is something I wish to say to you also," she smiled. "But you tell me first."

"Amilee ... I have been here for quite some time and I've always found you to be a unique person."

"Thank you, Phillip.'"

"But I've always hesitated to say what is in my heart.

I ... I know you are promised to another and that I must soon leave, but I must say this before I go."

"Yes," she said softly, "say what you must."

"Amilee, you must not marry Craig Miles."

If she were startled, embarrassed, or angered by his words, she displayed no sign of it. Instead she retained her poise and her steady gaze.

"You know I have little choice in this matter."

"But you do! Don't you see? It's your life and it should be your decision. I would never have said anything, but I have seen a change in him that I do not like and I'm afraid for you. Amilee, you are so ... so fine and so sweet. You don't deserve a man who will bully you, who will demand with no return. Craig Miles will not give you all you deserve. He will simply take your love and leave you with nothing."

"Take my love," she breathed softly. She was just beginning to realize what Julie had said was the truth. She had been forced by tradition, obedience, and her parents to give what had been her right alone to give. She closed her eyes for a moment, trying to recall if Craig had ever said one word about love to her. No, he had not.

Once again the door was open, multitudes of thoughts forced their way into her consciousness. Years upon years of giving everything to a man who gave nothing in return. Would Craig give consideration to her music as Phillip did? Would Craig understand her love of poetry and books as Phillip did? Would Craig not demand from her ... as Phillip did? She blinked and her eyes grew wide as realization came to her ... as Phillip did ... as Phillip did. Had he always been her support and consolation?

She gazed closely at him. He regarded her with a gleam of near desperation in his eyes. They were kind eyes, warm eyes, revealing eyes. The truth came to her as easily as her next breath.

"Phillip?" She breathed his name softly and saw him pause.

"Amilee, I would never have spoken if I did not care about you. I have sat by and watched what has been happening because ... because I have nothing to offer you. I know that I will have nothing of you but what I carry in my dreams. Still I cannot bear to sit here and watch you crushed, and you will be. He is no match for you, but in the eyes of your parents, neither am I."

"I know you are speaking from your heart, Phillip," she said softly as she laid her hand atop the one that was still holding hers. She felt quite breathless and her cheeks were flushed, but she looked up at him. "Can you not speak all that is in your heart?"

"Can I tell you that I have loved you almost from the first day I came to this house? That the hours I have spent with you are the most perfect in my life? That I would give my soul if I could ask you to share the rest of your life with me?"

"Yes, you can."

"And what would it avail me?" he said bitterly. "You must still choose a man your parents would approve of."

"But have you not just come to persuade me not to do that very thing? You tell me, as Julie has so often told me, to know my own mind and heart, and to make my own choices. If I have the courage to refuse my parents' choice for a husband, should I not have the courage to choose the man I would like to marry?"

Phillip seemed frozen in awe. He gazed raptly into Amilee's eyes and prayed that what he was hearing was the truth. Then he lifted her hand and pressed a gentle kiss on it.

"I want you to be happy, Amilee. You deserve every bit of happiness you can get."

"That is surprising."

"What?"

"Craig said the same thing to me some time ago. I did not understand him then. But perhaps it is because I was not his choice for a wife either."

They looked at each other in shock. This thought had never occurred to either of them. But then Phillip shook his head.

"A man always has choices. He could simply say no. There would have to be a great reason for a man to be pushed into marriage. Craig Miles is not dependent on his family. He has amassed his own fortune. What force could compel a man like him to conform to someone else's will?"

"How would we know—unless I ask him?"

"Amilee!"

"Phillip, I must say to you the things I have never had the courage to say before. I do not want to marry Craig. He is a wonderful man, a beautiful man, but, oh, Phillip, he scares me to death. We have little in common and he is so ... so forceful that I am afraid he will drown me. But you, you are so different, so gentle and kind. You have been my source of strength so often that maybe I did not see or realize how important you have become in my life. But now that I know how you feel about me, I can speak the truth and not be afraid anymore."

"God, Amilee," he breathed her name like a prayer. Slowly he rose, both her hands clasped in his and drew her up to him. Their eyes locked and, as if he were touching a miracle, he drew her into his arms and their lips met in a tender kiss that spoke volumes more than words ever could.

"Amilee, you know I have so little to offer you."

"You're wrong," she said softly. "You offer me

peace, contentment, and companionship. You offer me all the love you possess. Can a woman ask more than that from a man?"

"My dear love," he said. This time he crushed her to him, and the kiss was deeper and more promising than the first. Amilee responded to his kiss with the awakening spirit of a woman in love for the first time.

Her arms came about his neck, and his about her seemed stronger and more possessive. Her lips parted and both were shaken to the core as this new and vibrant emotion nearly got beyond their control. When their lips parted, she smiled up at him.

"Now, for the first time, I know what Julie meant."

"We must do something. You cannot allow this marriage to go on. I would die if I had to lose you now. We must go to your parents and brave their displeasure."

"Wait! Maybe it would be better if I went to Craig first."

"Why?"

"Because if he did not want this marriage he would be an ally. It might make Father accept it easier."

"You are clever."

"But first, I must tell Julie. I know she went into town with Father. Do you mind if we wait for just a little while?"

"For me it has been weeks, months, and years," Phillip smiled. "I do not suppose a few hours makes much difference now."

"I do believe," Amilee laughed softly, "that I love you, Mr. Gallierd."

"And I know I love you." Phillip was so happy that he could hardly stand not shouting it to the world. He kissed her deeply and savored her response.

* * *

If Barbara had suspected their emotions while they sat in the garden together, she displayed no sign of it. They were studying as they usually did.

But the hours seemed to drift on and on, and there was no sign of Julie or Amos. By midafternoon both were nervous.

It was nearing four o'clock when the carriage arrived, arrived with Amos and no Julie. When Amilee questioned Julie's absence, Amos made a vague statement about her staying in town until the next day, that she had some business to which had to be attended to. But Amilee knew her father better than he thought. There was something very wrong.

Telling Phillip in a whisper to wait for her, she raced to the room Julie had shared with her. In less than fifteen minutes, she knew. Too many of Julie's things were missing. Julie was gone.

Amilee sat on the edge of the bed and worked out the puzzling situation in her mind. Then she leapt to her feet, furious for the first time in her life.

When she returned to Phillip, she asked if he would accompany her to Wind Haven. She had just a few more answers to get before she faced her parents.

Craig whistled softly under his breath as he dressed for breakfast. He'd never been happier in his life than he was at this moment. He grinned at himself in the mirror in utter satisfaction. If he felt this way now, how would he feel when Julie was his bride?

The idea only made his smile broaden. It might still take a while, but the right bride would be in his arms one day.

He was more than confident that both Amilee and Phillip were near the breaking point. Especially Phillip, in whose eyes he'd seen both the light of love for

Amilee and rage for him. A few more jibes, a little more push, and Craig would drive them into each other's arms. From that point on he need only be the noble, jilted suitor and wish them well. After that he would have Julie. The thought actually made his hands shake.

He planned to go to Amilee's today, another of his impromptu and unwelcome visits, and see if he could push Phillip into action.

He went downstairs to enjoy a hearty breakfast, his mind so entwined with the past night that the world looked very rosy. In his heart he was certain Julie understood—of course she would. He was overjoyed to know she would trust him to work out their situation. Julie ... Julie ... Her name sang in his mind, and he could still taste her willing lips and feel the velvety texture of her skin on the tips of his fingers.

One day soon the mornings would start, waking to Julie warm and soft in his bed. Fantasies swirled in his head. Just the thought of the future filled him with intense pleasure.

His parents had already had breakfast, so he sat down to eat, planning after the meal to go into town and buy Julie a ring, then later going on to Amilee's to proceed with his plan. The ring was to be so very special that he had to choose it carefully.

As he ate, he sent for his saddled horse so it would be waiting outside when he was ready to go.

Finished with his meal, he tossed his napkin aside and left Wind Haven.

Chapter Nine

Successful in his search for the perfect ring, Craig returned from town two hours later. He rode across the newly plowed fields of Wind Haven and thought of the wonderful legacy he and Julie could leave their children.

He had to bring her here soon and let her see it through his eyes. Despite his waywardness and his proclivity for wine, women, and song, he was still buried heart-deep at Wind Haven. The frivolous days were over. He would bring Wind Haven the right woman to rule over it, and together they could make it the most magnificent plantation in the whole of Virginia.

He would settle his ways, knowing already he'd forgotten every other woman that had come before Julie. He also knew there would be none after.

He was deeply in love and this amused him. He'd played at love before, but nothing could have prepared him for this. Excitement filled him at the thought of somehow persuading her to meet him somewhere again tonight. Time was growing short, he knew that, and if it came down to finalities, he would force Julie to elope with him and devil take the scandal that would follow. He was certain in his heart that Phillip would be able to compensate Amilee for any emotional injuries she imagined.

Once he had taken care of estate business, he started out for Wide Oaks. He didn't take the road but the shorter way, across the field and the woods until the massive trees of Wide Oaks came into view.

But when he asked to see Amilee he was told she wasn't at home. Questions were followed by answers that satisfied him immensely. Amilee and Phillip had taken a carriage and gone for a ride.

"Wonderful," he said to himself. It seems Phillip was falling in with his plans very well. Now all he prayed for was for Phillip to acquire enough aggressiveness to convince Amilee of his undying love. He was well-prepared to accept their proclamation with dignified approval and pretend resignation.

More than satisfied he rode slowly toward home. He'd not really expected Julie to be at Wide Oaks, but he had hoped to see her. Well, he could send around a note, but that seemed very ungallant to him. No, he would find a way, as a need to hold her already gnawed at his vitals.

He was surprised when he crested a ridge not far from Wind Haven to see in the distance the Sheridan carriage sitting in his drive.

"Amilee," he smiled, "and Phillip, I hope. Come to present me with the news of your sudden and enlightening discovery. Well," he nudged his horse into motion, "let's not keep them waiting. This is one piece of bad news I can't wait to hear."

If he considered Amos' financial trouble, he pushed it from his mind. He would force Amos to accept a loan that would tide him over while his problems were settled. As for his father—Craig sighed deeply—he could either choose to welcome Julie as the future mistress of Wind Haven or Craig would buy land and build them a home of their own. His love for the plantation ran second to his love for Julie.

When he saw to his horse and started across the lawn toward the house, he could see Amilee and Phillip standing inside close together. Pausing, he stood very still so he would not draw their attention.

He watched with a slowly growing smile as Phillip took Amilee in his arms. They spoke to each other for a minute, then the Frenchman kissed her, and Craig felt he enjoyed the kiss nearly as much as Phillip did.

Controlling his features and forcing his face into a look of cool nonchalance, he continued his walk across the lawn to the French doors. When he opened them, the couple was standing apart, and he almost laughed. "Good afternoon, my dear," he sad to Amilee as he crossed the room toward her.

Her eyes were wide and her face a bit pale from nerves, but Craig decided to quickly bring the situation to a head. He put his arm about her and kissed her hard enough to make her sound of reluctance pierce Phillip, who had built up enough indignation to explode.

"Take your hands off of her!"

"Phillip!"

"Why should I?" Craig said arrogantly. "She's to be my wife, not yours. You're not harboring any ideas are you, old boy? If so, forget it. What's mine remains mine."

"You—" Phillip began.

"Phillip, no, let me explain." Amilee was torn between panic and pride as she gazed at Phillip, and Craig had no difficulty reading it. "Craig, please. I—I must talk to you."

"Of course. What is it you want?"

"I . . ."

She wrung her hands. Craig wished to ease her difficulty, but she had to say the words first before he could do a thing. Still, his face gentled and his eyes warmed, and he reached to put a reassuring hand on hers.

"What is it, Amilee? Don't be afraid. I'm sure I'll understand."

"Craig, you are a truly wonderful person and you know I would never do anything in the world to hurt you, but . . ."

He wanted to grab her by the shoulders and shake the words from her, but he resisted with what he considered monumental patience.

"Yes?" he prodded.

"I . . ." Resolutely Amilee inhaled a deep breath, locked her eyes on his, and spoke. "I want to break our engagement. I no longer want to marry you."

"I see," he said calmly. So calmly that he frightened her without meaning to.

"Please understand. I truly believe that my decision is the best one for you as well. I would not be the kind of wife you want, and . . . and I'm afraid of you."

Craig was stunned into temporary amazement. He'd expected a lot of things to be said but definitely not this. He didn't relish the idea of any woman being afraid of him. "Afraid of me? Amilee, for God's sake, what have I ever done to make you afraid of me?"

"It's not what you've done, it's—it's what you are."

"You are talking about gossip. You should know better than that."

"No, it's not gossip I mean. Craig, you and I are so very different. We do not like any of the same things and we have nothing to talk about. I know you would be bored with me in no time at all. We live in two different worlds and I do not think I would be happy in yours, anymore than you'd be in mine."

Craig pierced her with a look of deep curiosity. "This is not all the story, is it?"

"No, it isn't."

"What more is there?"

At this point she held out a hand to Phillip who came quickly to her side. His face was rigid with emotion, and ... he was a bit afraid of Craig as well.

"Let me speak for us both. Amilee and I are in love with each other and we want to marry. I hope you will be gentleman enough to let her go without causing trouble, but I shall fight you if necessary, any way you choose."

Bravo! Craig thought. A little pushing brought the man to the surface. Craig could not resist, though, a bit of teasing. "Even pistols?"

Amilee gasped, but Phillip continued to hold Craig's gaze with his. "Even pistols."

"Phillip! No! You could never hope to beat him. He is a crack shot."

Craig had had enough fun at their expense. Besides, he wanted the news to be spread and to see his beloved Julie. Desiring for the look of fierce resolution to leave Phillip's eyes, he said, "I have no intention of fighting you with pistols or by any other means." The Virginian's lips twitched at Phillip's obvious relief. "This has come as quite a shock to me as it most likely will to both our parents. Not to mention all the other people who will make another field day out of my reputation."

"Perhaps," Phillip said coldly, "this is a just reward for all the gossip you have caused."

"Now you're going a bit far, old boy," Craig laughed. "Don't force your luck. I think I'm being very good about the whole thing. After all, you have stolen my future bride right out from under my nose. I'm afraid I may be forced to take a prolonged trip." A honeymoon, he decided, a long and perfect one. "Just to protect myself from the nasty whispers."

"Craig, really, you have never worried so about gossip before," Amilee said innocently, and Craig fought his laughter. She was right; the gossips had never bothered him and they never would.

"Well," he seemed suddenly resigned to his fate, "I suppose it will do me no good to do battle. I can see that fate has already sealed the situation. I must give into the better man and wish you both as much happiness as you can find."

Their relief was palpable.

"Am I the first person to be told, or is the news a raging fire by now?"

"You're the first," Amilee said. "I wanted you to know, for when I tell my parents, Phillip and I will need an ally. Perhaps if you spoke to your parents first, it might make it easier."

Oh no, Craig thought, the first person to hear this from my lips will be Julie. I'm free! Craig walked to a nearby sideboard and lifted a decanter of brandy. As he poured three glasses, he kept his face turned from them as he asked, "And what will Julie think of this?"

"I don't know. She went into town with Father today, and when he returned, she wasn't with him. When I asked, he said she wanted to stay in town and do some shopping. But he didn't say she was staying with cousin Sara, and that's the only relative we have in town."

Craig spun around as she spoke, the brandy decanter in his hand forgotten. A dark and ugly suspicion entered his mind. "In town? But she knows no one in town."

"I know. Perhaps she is staying with cousin Sara. She went to town to buy me a wedding present. In fact, she told me it was a special gift she wanted me to have. I don't think we need to worry. After all, Julie is quite capable of taking care of herself. She has so much courage; I guess that's one of the reasons I admire her so much." Craig tossed down his brandy, trying to convince himself that the insidious voice inside him was wrong. "I'm grateful to you for being so understanding,

Craig. I know this must have come as quite a shock, and I do regret that. My one consolation is that I know now I would have made you a frightful wife. At least this way we can still be friends."

Amilee continued, but all Craig could see or hear were the last hours he had spent with Julie. He had taken it all for granted. That she knew he meant to break his plans with Amilee, that she knew he meant them to marry, that she knew he loved her. Her last words rang in his ears. "The next time you see me, you can explain." Had she meant there to be a next time?

He shook his head, trying to push these thoughts aside. I'm jumping to conclusions, he thought. Just because it all went smoothly, I'm seeing a problem when there isn't one.

"Amilee, it might be best if we tell our parents together," Craig said. "That should make it easier on everyone concerned. Can you keep this confidential until my family and I come to your home tonight?"

"Of course, that is very little to ask in return for how civilized you're being about all of this."

"I'll take Amilee home," Phillip said. Tentatively he extended his hand to Craig, who took it in a grip powerful enough to make Phillip wince. "We shall expect you later. I appreciate this, Craig."

"Take good care of her," he smiled, "or I might resort to pistols, after all."

Amilee came to Craig and put her hand on his arm. She rose on tiptoe and kissed his cheek, the first sign of genuine affection ever displayed between them. "Thank you."

Craig watched them go, then poured another brandy. He was wrong—he had to be wrong. Surely Julie would be there to celebrate Amilee and Phillip's future. Surely they could share a look across the room and she would know it was his plan that had brought them together. Surely her trust would have been enough.

But the little voice began to suggest maliciously that he might just be wrong.

Amilee and Phillip rode home, both deliriously happy for the first time in a long while. They knew that the barrier of her parents still lay before them, but both felt the most difficult of all problems had been surmounted. Amilee was free, and come what may, she meant to make her own choices from now on.

When they arrived home, neither Amos or Barbara were around. The couple took this precious time to talk and make plans for the future. Amid kisses and subdued laughter, they spoke of the life that lay before them. Amilee was completely happy, but Phillip was a bit worried. "Amilee, if your parents insist I leave—"

"Then I shall go with you," she said positively. "This can't frighten me anymore. Now that I know what happiness is, I don't intend to lose it."

"Love is blind," Phillip smiled. "You know that our circumstances will be much less grand than this."

"Yes, I know. But we'll manage. Mother used to tell me how it was when she and Father first came here. Did you know they lived in a log cabin for a while, and Mother had to fetch her water from the river to wash? Look what they've done . . . together."

Phillip gazed at his delicate and refined Amilee with a new regard. "There is so much we do not know about each other."

"Then," she said softly, "it's time we learned."

He took her in his arms, and their lips blended in a promising kiss. Tomorrow was theirs, and they would not let anyone or anything destroy their newfound happiness.

* * *

Craig opened the door of his father's study without knocking, something he'd never done. Joseph looked up in surprise. He smiled when he first saw his son, but in a moment the smile faded before Craig's steady gaze.

"Craig, is there something important you wanted to say? The way you burst in I—"

"Yes, there is something we have to talk about. Relax, pour yourself a drink, Father. I think you're going to need it."

Chapter Ten

Amos sat at the head of the table with Barbara at the foot. Amilee and Phillip sat on one side, and all four were well-aware of the empty plate and empty chair on the other.

"I don't understand you, Amos. As Amilee has said, it's very hard to believe you would just leave Julie in town like that. Why, she doesn't even have clean clothes with her."

"No, Mother," Amilee said thoughtfully, "I noticed some of her clothes were gone. Maybe she planned on staying. Did she mention it to you, Father, that she planned on staying?"

Amos had never been questioned by his daughter on

any subject before, and especially not with the direct and penetrating stare she was giving him now.

"She may have mentioned it," he said gruffly. "I pay little heed to women's clothes. She wanted to stay and I let her. Why am I subject to so many questions?"

"It just seems strange." Amilee watched her father closely. "And I miss her not being here. Julie is really very sweet. Since she's been here, it's like having an older sister."

"Well, girl, she's not your sister, so if she has plans of her own, I don't consider it any of our business."

Barbara's attention centered on Amos, too, and he was more than uncomfortable under her scrutiny. After all, Julie was Barbara's niece, and he didn't want her asking questions, not yet. Later, when they were alone, he would tell her of Julie and Craig's rendezvous and why he had let Julie leave with no word.

"Amos, really. Julie and Amilee are not sisters, but they have grown very close. I cannot understand your sudden lack of sympathy."

"It is not a lack of sympathy." His voice rose defensively. "And why in God's name would the woman need sympathy?"

Before Barbara could answer him bitingly, the family was informed that guests had arrived.

"Guests?" Amos said in surprise. He looked quickly at Barbara, who was as surprised as he. Then he saw Amilee's face and a tingle of apprehension went through him. "Who is it?" he asked the servant.

"Mr. Miles and his father, sir. I've shown them to the library."

"Thank you." Amos didn't like it. Something was wrong. "Tell them I'll join them in a few minutes."

"Yes, sir."

Amos looked closely at his daughter and realized she knew why the Mileses were here. What surprised him even more was Phillip, who seemed calm—yet changed. Sometime between last night's dinner and tonight's there seemed to be a lot of changes in the people around him. People over which he had always had complete control. It was a damned uncomfortable feeling, and he didn't like it one bit. He couldn't swallow another bite. Angrily he stood and tossed down his napkin. "Well, I guess I may as well see them now. Go on with your dinner."

"If you don't mind, Father," Amilee rose to her feet, "I will go with you. Since Craig is my fiancé, this might concern me—and I might have a few things to say."

If Amos was shocked before, he was flabbergasted now. Amilee had never been this self-assured. He didn't like this turn of events, not at all. To make matters worse, Barbara rose, too. "And I would like to hear what they have to say. This time, I believe it concerns me as well as you, Amos."

With a grimly clenched jaw, Amos led the way to the library.

As the family entered, both Craig and Joseph rose to their feet.

"Amos, I'm sorry for this unannounced intrusion," Joseph said. "But I'm afraid we have an ... unusual problem on our hands."

"Just what kind of a problem?" he said gruffly. He didn't like the look in Craig's eyes.

"A problem of two scheming men who decided their joined properties would be a good reason to unite two people without caring about anyone's happiness but their own," Craig said furiously. "You are not in financial difficulties, are you, Amos?"

The demand in Craig's voice was so intimidating that Amos was shaken. He cast a quick and very guilty look at Barbara, who quickly understood the real bargain that had been made between the two men.

Two spots of bright color appeared on her cheeks and her eyes began to glow with an emotion Amos had not seen since they had been married—anger.

"Craig, we are not in financial difficulties," Barbara said. This accusation cast a shadow on her ability to run Amos' household, and she didn't like it at all.

"No, we're not," Amos reluctantly admitted.

"Do you know that you would have forced your daughter into a marriage just for the sake of profit! Do you care?" Craig snarled.

"Young man, I won't—"

"Yes, you will," Craig said in cold fury. He turned to Amilee and for the first time he smiled. "Amilee, I believe you have something to say."

"Yes, I do." Her voice was surprisingly calm. "Father, Mother, I have no intention of marrying Craig. I love someone else and intend to be his wife."

"Someone else," Barbara repeated softly. Her eyes flew at once to Phillip.

"Someone else!" Amos cried. "Both of you are insane! What will people say? This scandal cannot be tolerated." Amos glared at Craig. "This is your doing, young man, and you and I both know why."

"Yes, we do," Craig said quietly.

"Craig?" Amilee questioned.

"Amilee, you do love Phillip, don't you?"

"Yes, I do, with all my heart."

"And you mean to marry him no matter what?"

"I forbid it! I forbid it, I tell you!" Amos' anger boiled within him. "My daughter will not marry a . . . a nobody!"

"Yes," Amilee answered Craig with a smile, "I do."

"You would have let her marry me," Craig said, "even though you thought I was wild and disloyal. Even though you thought I was having an affair right under Amilee's nose. You would have let her marry me and not marry a man who loves her and would be faithful to his dying breath. You are an intelligent man, but I think your values are misplaced."

Craig went to Amilee and took her hands in his. "Amilee, let me tell you the truth so that no other lies can interfere. I'm in love with Julie. I have been since the day I met her. But I don't want to deceive you." He went on to tell her all he had done. "I knew you two are meant to be together, just as Julie and I are. Are you angry with me?"

"Because you wanted to protect my reputation? Because you've shown me the way to find love? Because you love Julie? No, Craig, I'm not angry. I'm happy. The four of us will have exactly what we want. I think I owe both you and Julie a great deal of thanks."

"You are not of age," Amos roared. "And you will marry who I say."

"No, I won't," she replied. "I love Phillip. If you can't accept that, then I will go. But think about it, Father. If you send us away, I may never come back."

"Amilee!" Amos cried. Despite his machinations, he loved his daughter; he could not let her leave him forever.

"Don't be a fool, Amos," Barbara broke in, her voice chilled. "I will not lose my daughter because of your nefarious plans."

Amos' shoulders sagged. He knew when he was beaten. Amos nodded. He knew his love for Amilee was larger than any wealth, and he knew he had to face the truth. He did not want to lose Amilee and in a way Barbara, too. He could see it in her eyes. "All right. I love you, daughter. If you choose to marry Phillip, I'll welcome him to the family."

"Thank you, Father," Amilee cried. "You will never regret it." She ran to Amos and threw her arms about his neck.

"Now," Craig said firmly. "Would someone send for Julie?"

"Julie has not been here since this morning," Barbara said. "I believe she is staying in town to do some shopping."

"Craig," Amilee said in growing concern. "Julie took some of her clothes with her."

"Is this true?" Craig asked Amos. "It should not be too difficult to bring her home. Just tell me where she is."

"I . . . I'm afraid I can't do that," Amos replied.

"Can't or won't?" Craig said angrily. "Never mind, I'll find her if I have to tear the town apart with my bare hands."

"I'm afraid she isn't in town."

"Tell him where she is, Amos," Barbara said. "There is no point in making this more difficult than it already is."

Amos looked as if he would weep. "It is true I saw the two of you together and I was angry. You were spoiling all my plans. That evening Julie and I talked, and we agreed it was better she go."

"Damn," Craig muttered. Julie had said he could explain the next time he saw her, knowing there never would be a next time. Their coming together had not been a beginning, it had been a goodbye.

"I bought her a train ticket to Philadephia. But when we got to the station, she exchanged it for another. She told me she felt it wiser that I didn't know where she was going."

Craig's face had gone from high color to pale gray. "My God, somebody must know where she has gone. Has she no other family but you?"

"No, Craig," Barbara said. She explained about the other relatives for whom Julie had requested addresses. "If she exchanged her ticket, she probably has gone to

South Carolina to Claude. He would welcome her in his home. But we have to find out for certain."

"Don't worry," Craig said coldly. "I'll find out."

"She took all the money she had with her," Amos admitted. "And I gave her a thousand dollars."

"A thousand dollars," Craig said scathingly. "How cheaply you buy other people's happiness. I'm going to the train station and you should pray to God I find her, because if any harm comes to her, I shall never let you forget it as long as I live."

Craig stormed from the house and those within exchanged worried glances, for none of them had any doubts that he meant exactly what he said.

But on the ride to town Craig was less angry than frightened. What if he couldn't find her? What would he do the rest of his life with nothing but the memory of one magical night to sustain him? He didn't want to dwell on it or it would torment him beyond reason.

When he came into the train station, it was deserted save for the man behind the counter whom Craig vaguely remembered. But the ticket agent knew him. "Evenin'. Young Craig Miles, isn't it?"

"Yes." Craig reached for his warmest smile. "I've come to ask you a question, if I may."

"Ask away. I'll answer it if I can."

"I'm looking for a lady."

"Who ain't?" The man chuckled at his own wit, and Craig had to restrain the urge to do physical violence.

"A very special lady. The one I'm going to marry. She exchanged a train ticket this morning for some reason. I need to know her destination."

"Can't do that."

"What?"

"Can't do that. Company policy. The ticket is the

lady's personal business. I ain't allowed to reveal anything about 'em."

Craig looked at him for a moment, stunned. Then his patience ran out. The ticket agent gave a gasp of shock as huge hands gripped the front of his shirt, jerked him from the floor, and shook him until his teeth rattled. Craig pulled him close. "Now, I'll repeat my question once more. If I don't get a satisfactory answer, I just may get violent."

"Sir, you can't—"

Craig gave him another bone-rattling shake, rage etched across his features, and the agent reconsidered his position.

"South Carolina! She got a ticket for South Carolina."

"Where in South Carolina?"

"Florence," the man squeaked out, breathing a sigh of relief when Craig let him go.

"When's the next train that can get me there?"

"There's an express due about midnight, but it don't stop here."

"But you can make it stop. I want you to flag it down and get me on it."

"But I—" He saw the gleam in Craig's eyes and decided quickly that resistance was foolhardy. "Yes ... yes, I'll flag it down."

"Good. I'll be back with some luggage. Remember, if you don't flag that train down, I may just ride you all the way to Florence."

Julie had been exhausted by the time she reached South Carolina, exhausted and feeling grimy. She was more than grateful that Claude Sommerville was waiting for her at the station. She hadn't thought her telegraph would get there in time.

As she stepped down from the train, her breath caught. He and her father had been cousins, but she had not expected him to look so much like her father that it brought tears to her eyes.

He approached her with a warm smile. "You have to be Julie. You look so much like your dear mother. Welcome to Florence."

"Thank you."

"You must be tired. Let me get your bags, then we can get along home. My wife has a warm bath and a hot meal to rejuvenate you."

"I'm afraid these two are all I have right now. Uncle Amos will send along my trunks later." She tried to smile, but Claude was quick to recognize the glazed and frightened look in her eyes.

"Let me take those." He picked up the two light pieces, and they walked to his buggy. Once he had secured them and helped her inside, he climbed in and they were on their way. They rode in silence for some time. Claude sensed Julie's distress, but he had no intention of asking questions now.

"Your father and I were close as children, and I was very distressed to hear of his death. I want you to know, Julie, that you must consider my home yours. If there is anything we can do for you, please don't hesitate to ask."

This kindness was the last straw for Julie's battered emotions. She began to cry and could not seem to stop. Claude pulled the buggy to a stop and put his arm about her. Then he let her cry until there seemed to be no tears left.

"Suppose you tell me what is wrong," he said quietly.

Haltingly Julie began to talk, and she poured out the entire story. Claude listened with sympathy, and the strong urge to beat Craig Miles into insensibility with a buggy whip overtook him.

"It's all right, child. You've made the right decision. It is utterly dishonorable to take advantage of a young woman. You need not worry; you're safe here."

Claude picked up the reins and they continued on in silence.

Chapter Eleven

When they arrived home, Julie was smothered in warm welcome, hustled to her room, treated to a warm and welcome bath, and a few hours later was seated in the parlor with a cup of hot tea in hand.

Claude's wife, Deborah, had been informed by her husband of the entire story and her ire was up. Had she a chance to cross paths with Craig Miles, she would have boxed his ears. She had also told Julie, in no uncertain terms, that they were very proud of her. "I'm quite sure a woman of weaker character might have fallen victim to this man. You must start a new life here with us, and forget about him."

Forget about him, Julie thought miserably, as if that were possible. Every time she closed her eyes she could see him as if he were standing before her. Worse, he plagued her dreams. She could not seem to tear him out of her mind as she desperately wanted to do. Even now her body felt empty and overheated, and cried out for his. God forgive her, she loved him and always would.

She hated her weakness and still knew she would have only their one night together to keep in her heart.

She truly wished Craig would find happiness with Amilee and that Amilee would do the same. Surely other marriages that had been arranged had worked out satisfactorily. And there would be children. Children, she thought, as she laid her hand against the flat plane of her belly. Could she be carrying his child now? The thought both pleased and panicked her. If it were true, it severed any tie she might have had with Amilee, for Amilee must never know.

The train ride, combined with a hot bath and tea, made Julie's exhaustion more obvious.

"We must get you to bed, my dear," Deborah said. "You look as though you are ready to drop in your tracks. There will be plenty of time for us to talk. Let me get you comfortable."

Julie rose unsteadily to her feet. Deborah was right, she had never felt so bone tired in her life. She was grateful that at least for tonight there was to be no more conversation.

She followed Deborah upstairs, and a half-hour later she blew out her lamp and crawled wearily between the sheets. For some time she slept the sleep of drugged exhaustion, but her body was healthy and recuperated quickly. She wakened in the wee hours of the morning, caught again in poignant memories that brought new tears.

The express train moved a bit faster than the one Julie had taken, but Craig was still a good day behind her. As Craig sat on the train, he wondered about the relatives to whom Julie had run. Most likely, they would do what they thought necessary to protect her. He would cross that bridge when he got to it.

He had a vague idea there might be a lot of barriers to break through just from Julie. If she had left with the misapprehension that he had wanted her for nothing more than a casual mistress, God only knew what she had told them.

It was suffocatingly painful to realize how Julie must be feeling now, but the more he had time to think about it, the more a new and different idea came to him. Julie had thought he meant to marry Amilee and keep her as a mistress, one he could casually take when the mood suited him. One who would live on the fringe of life and never know her own home and family. She had thought all these things and still she had come to him. She had shared that night with him for one reason and one reason only—she loved him. She loved him!

Why else would she have given herself so freely? Why else would the danger of carrying his child prove no obstacle. Because she loved him!

Julie had run away because she cared so deeply for others ... because she cared for Amilee and him. She had accepted the weight of it all, actually believing he could find some kind of happiness without her. But now his heart filled with joy. She loved him ... and nothing else mattered.

When he arrived in Florence, it was midafternoon. He walked from the station into town to work out the stiffness from the prolonged ride and to think.

Before Craig went to find Julie, he considered himself. He was dusty and tired, and he didn't want to look like a desperado or he'd never gain entrance to the Sommervilles' home. Besides, it might be a long siege getting Julie back.

He found a hotel, took a room, then had a bath and a shave. This taken care of, he started out for the news office. When he was introduced to Joseph Wainright, he was more than overjoyed to find the editor knew of

Wind Haven and knew the Miles name. It made this part of the situation a bit easier. Now he had to tell a few white lies to get what he wanted.

Deborah Sommerville had realized, by watching Julie's face and listening to her, that the young woman loved Craig Miles completely. Mrs. Sommerville began to wonder if Julie had truly recognized his motives. She wished she knew the real truth.

As they ate supper together, Deborah found Julie to be a considerate and enjoyable guest. Since her four children were grown and married, she missed having someone else ... another woman around the house.

She noticed at once that Julie struggled to smile and had a feeling it would be a long time before Julie would forget him—if she ever could.

Supper over, Deborah asked Julie to accompany her upstairs so she could show her some embroidery pieces she had just finished. Actually she thought if she got Julie alone for a woman-to-woman talk, she might find what her true feelings were.

"Julie, my dear, I know how difficult this must be for you. Is it possible you misunderstood his motives?"

"No, Cousin Deborah, he made it quite clear that the marriage was important to bring their wealth and properties together—and that he had no intention of hurting Amilee. I didn't want to hurt her either, so ... it was best that I left." She looked at Deborah, begging her to understand her next statement. "If I had stayed," she said quietly, "I would have gone to him whenever he wanted me. I would have stolen any part of him I could. I would have betrayed Amilee and myself. Eventually I would not have been able to live that way."

"No, of course you couldn't. Well, you need not worry. We'll do everything in our power to help you."

"I'll try not to be a burden to you, and I'm very grateful."

"Hush, child. We must not discuss gratitude. You are more than welcome here."

Before Julie could reply, the sound of voices came from below. Deborah stood up at once. "Good heavens, what's going on?"

Both ran to the top of the steps to look over the bannister. Below them Claude and two servants were having a near-violent confrontation with a more-than-angry Craig. At Julie's gasp, Deborah knew the very handsome and very enraged man below to be Craig Miles.

"If you put one foot on those stairs, sir," Claude said in cold fury, "I shall have you shot for forcing your way into my home. Julie is here, and she will remain here—out of your reach, you cur. If I had my way, I'd horsewhip you all the way back to Virginia!"

"If you'll let me talk to her, all this can be resolved," Craig stormed.

Claude had adamantly refused to let him see Julie and the young man seemed just as determined not to leave. But Deborah knew her husband too well. He never said anything he didn't mean or couldn't accomplish. "Julie, stay here," Deborah said. "I'll see what I can do to calm them before something drastic happens."

As she started down the steps, Craig seeing motion, looking up. Then he saw Julie. "Julie!" He started toward her, but his way was blocked. "Come down and talk to me! Julie, we can settle this between us if you'll only listen."

Julie knew her biggest weakness—being too close to Craig Miles. She backed away, then turned and ran to her room. Deborah, who watched Craig closely, saw a look of painful despair. She came to him and put a hand on his arm. "Mr. Miles?"

"Yes?"

"It is obvious Julie is not going to see you now. If you will leave peacefully, I shall talk to her and see if I can arrange a meeting."

She saw the first sign of relief in his eyes. "Julie's mistaken about me, Mrs. Sommerville. Tell her . . . tell her I love her and that there will be no marriage to Amilee. Tell her to let me explain."

Deborah stood very close to Craig, so close that a whispered word could not be heard by the others. "Mr. Miles," she said very softly. "Julie is not prepared to listen to anyone right now . . . even us. If what you say is true, will you swear to it?"

"Deborah," Claude said in a firm voice. "This conversation is at an end. I want this scoundrel out of my house."

"Oh, Claude," Deborah smiled tolerantly, "do be quiet while we hear the young man. I'm sure he'll commit no violence." She turned back to Craig, her eyes sparkling. "You won't, will you?"

"No. I just want you to understand, I'd lay down my life for Julie. She ran from me because she misunderstood. I could not marry anyone but her. Tell her to please let me explain."

Deborah read the truth in his eyes and smiled. "Perhaps," she said conspiratorially, "but Claude is too worried about her to listen, and you will never convince him. He thinks you're a true villain. If you were to leave—"

"No!"

"Let me finish. If you were to leave so everyone can settle down, I can tell you which room is Julie's. I imagine you could solve any problems from there."

"You are an angel." Craig smiled for the first time. Then Deborah told him what he wanted to know.

Craig apologized to a still-wary and ruffled Claude

and the two servants, then to Claude's relief, left the house.

Deborah crossed her fingers and prayed she had done the right thing. But right or wrong, it was better he and Julie talked the problem out.

Julie had cried until she could cry no more. How she had wanted to run to Craig's arms. But she knew she could not accept his terms. Why had he not just let her go? Why had he come all this distance when he knew it was wrong? But her answer came as quickly as her questions. Because he remembered their one night together as vibrantly as she did.

She changed into her nightgown and crawled beneath the covers. No matter what, she meant to put him behind her.

She must have heard the sound several minutes before she realized what it was—stones being thrown at her window. She rose and walked to the window and flung it open to look out. Below, in the garden, Craig stood looking up.

"Come down and talk to me, Julie. I'm not going to go away until you do."

"It's useless, Craig. Please just go away." She started to close the window.

"Julie!" She paused. "If you don't come down, I'm coming up."

Knowing herself safe, Julie smiled wickedly. "You can't. Cousin Claude will kill you. Just go away. Go back to what you love."

"What I love is here. Are you coming down?"

"Absolutely not!"

"All right."

Julie watched as Craig walked to the rose trellis

which clung to the walls. He tested it, then decided it would hold his weight, and he began to climb.

Her eyes grew wide with surprise. Somewhere, deep inside her, hysterical laughter began to bubble up. She couldn't dare laugh—he might think she was encouraging him. She grasped the frame, intending to close and lock it, when a sharp crack rent the night air. The trellis shook, then snapped beneath him, and Julie watched with a silent cry of fear as it gave way. Craig tumbled to the ground, flat on his back, and did not move.

"Craig! Oh my God." She spun from the window, disregarding the fact that she had nothing on but a thin nightgown, and raced barefoot down the steps and out the back door. When she came to him, he still lay immobile, and she fell to her knees beside him. "Craig! Oh my love, don't be dead. Please open your eyes."

She was half atop him, her eyes swimming in tears when two hard arms closed about her and she was crushed against him. She looked down into his smiling eyes.

"Now, you'll have to listen, because I'm going to hold you like this until you do."

"Oh! You scoundrel! You liar!"

"I love you."

"Let me go," she struggled, but he was enjoying the feel of her in his arms.

"I love you," he repeated. "And I don't mind lying here all night."

"You wouldn't!" Her eyes flew to his and saw the devil's laughter there.

"Wouldn't I?" He grinned.

"Craig, please."

"If you lie still and listen, then I'll let you go."

"I won't!"

"Then," he said mildly, "I'll just lie here and hold you until we attract a great deal of attention."

Julie could see he meant exactly what he said, and she had not the strength to stop him ... nor the inclination. His presence, the strong feel of his arms, were too much a barrier, and besides, she was beginning to see the impossible humor of the situation.

"I'll scream," she said, but her eyes had begun to smile before her lips.

"Oh, there are ways to stop that." He held her with one arm, tangled his other hand in her hair, and drew her to him. He kissed her deeply, over and over, until she began to tremble.

"Julie," he whispered. "Listen to me, please. I don't want to lose you." Holding her tight, he began the story, and despite her will not to, she could not help but hear the words he said.

"You ... you're not going to marry Amilee?"

"She doesn't want to marry me either. She's going to marry Phillip Gallierd. Julie, come home. Come back to Wind Haven and be my wife. I love you, you stubborn woman, and I can't think of a life without you."

Slowly Julie smiled down into his warm eyes. Then she bent her head and kissed him with the most welcome kiss he'd ever known ... then it began to rain.

They ignored the fact that they were getting soaked as they clung to each other and laughed between kisses.

Deborah and Claude stood at the window and watched the couple.

"I told you it would be all right, Claude," Deborah smiled.

"Scandalous! Just scandalous," he said, but he could not stop the smile as he drew his wife close to him.

Epilogue
Three months later

Craig and Julie stood together on the veranda at Wind Haven and looked out over the rolling, moon-touched land. Night sounds filled the air and a sense of peace pervaded the atmosphere.

Craig stood behind Julie with his arms about her, and she rested against his hard-muscled body with the confidence of a woman who trusted completely.

He bent his head and pressed a gentle kiss on the soft flesh of her shoulder, and for a moment she closed her eyes, savoring the pleasure his touch could elicit.

"I never believed this dream would ever come true," Julie said.

"I did," Craig chuckled. "I looked once into those beautiful green eyes of yours and I knew from then on it couldn't be any other way."

Julie turned and looped her arms about his neck. He took the opportunity to kiss her leisurely.

"Why didn't you tell me?"

"When did you let me?" he countered. "I was afraid if you thought I was lying to Amilee, you might believe all the things I had said to you were lies, too. When you came to me that perfect night in the meadow, I wanted to explain. Again, you refused to let me. Actually I began to convince myself that you understood." He pulled her closer and tasted her lips again. "I love you so much, Julie. When you left it was like part of me was gone."

"When I think of it now," she admitted, "I wonder how long I would have been able to stay away. I wanted you so much, I think that after a while I would have come back under any terms you wanted."

"Even as my mistress?" His warm gaze held hers.

"Even as your mistress," she replied softly.

"No, that would never have been. A few months ago I was chafing under the knowledge that I had been so jaded and bored that I had allowed the most important part of my life be chosen for me. I'd accepted the wrong bride."

"Amilee is beautiful."

"Yes, she is."

"She's educated."

"Yes, she is."

"She's rich."

"Do you think I should have reconsidered after all? You would make the most enticing mistress." Craig's smile was growing broader with every word Julie said, and his eyes had begun to smolder with a familiar look.

"Your second thoughts are too late," Julie smiled. "You're caught."

"Then I must accept my fate."

"Scoundrel," she laughed.

"My love," he kissed her again, "as I told you, I'm a man who knows perfection when he sees it. There is only one answer," he added as he swung her up in his arms. "No matter what else happens, I'm clever enough to recognize what I have."

"And that is?"

"The right bride," he laughed softly and carried her back to his bed. There they molded their promise to each other into one dream, one life . . . one love.

Ransom My Heart

by

Linda Windsor

"A groom for none, a bride for all
 In treachery's dark sting . . .
'Til Cupid's conquering arrow fall
And wedding bells of joy may ring."

Chapter One

The castle of Sir Randolf Bedford showed little evidence, aside from the unusual bustle of activity in the inner bailey, that a wedding was afoot. So well-liked was the widowed lord, that the knights and noble guests should have spilled over into the early spring fields surrounding the fortress, their banners colorfully denoting their heraldry against the backdrop of new greenery. Instead, the lord was mounted on stalwart steed, readied for a journey to the south coast while the bride, his daughter, watched from her tower room solemnly.

"Godspeed," Jocelyn whispered, hastily crossing herself.

Eyes the color of moss misted as she watched the entourage move out, passing through the gate of the outer wall, It felt as if her breath were being squeezed from her chest, crushed by the wicked turn of fate which had led to this. She was alone now. The rest would be up to her. Much as she'd wanted her father to be present at this, of all occasions, they had both agreed to trust no one to the task ahead but himself.

Nothing was as it should have been, she thought, flinging herself away from the window seat in such haste that she nearly tripped over the white damask train of her wedding dress. There were no guests, no family

... not even the groom was her betrothed! Therein lay the root of all her distress. The irony of her situation twisted an already overwrought heart.

She was supposed to have wed Phillip of Inglenook, the heir to the neighboring estate of Bedford. The arrangement had been made at her birth. Phillip even served as page and squire in her father's house until Sir Randolf himself knighted the lad at the farewell feast which sent him off to the Holy Land. He'd been eighteen and she but seven. Even then she'd felt nothing short of adoration for her intended.

His letters, all too infrequent in the earlier years of their separation, continued to court her heart. Of late, they had had her looking forward to his return eagerly, for he had matured into a most chivalrous and romantic man. His poetic declarations of his love for her were enough to inflame her cheeks and send her beating heart aflutter. She would do anything for him ... anything!

When she and her father learned of Phillip's capture by the Saracens, they immediately set about raising the ransom money. The recent conflict with the Welsh, however, had drained their coffers. The church had agreed to contribute a portion, as did their neighbors, but the largest portion of the sum they needed was her dowry; the royal dowry provided by King Edward as a reward for her father's service in the war; the dowry which was entrusted to His Majesty's March overlord to bestow upon her wedding day.

Never did either of them dream, when they approached Lord Rhys, that he would propose such a dastardly solution. His greed was known far and wide, but to stoop to stealing the betrothed of one of his own underlords was unthinkable, even for him. Yet that was exactly the ultimatum he issued them. Yes, he would give the dowry toward Phillip's ransom ... on the day of Jocelyn's *wedding*.

The idea was so absurd that both father and daughter had thought it a poor attempt at jest. How could Jocelyn wed when her betrothed was in the hands of heathens holding him for ransom? Was he suggesting a marriage by proxy?

There was nothing humorous or suggestive in his answer. Jocelyn was to marry *him*, not Phillip, uniting Bedford and Atworth as one fiefdom. Sir Randolf had instantly appealed to the king, but there was no time to meet the deadline set by the kidnappers. To free her one true love, Jocelyn would have to marry a man who made her skin crawl each time she suffered his lascivious appraisal.

And him not a full year widowed, she thought in disgust. It was hard to say what had really happened to the late Lady Atworth. A malady of the digestion had been offered as the cause, but Jocelyn would not have put it past Lord Rhys to resort to poison to broaden his horizons and produce the heir the poor woman had failed to bear. Therefore it was only just that he should reap a portion of what he sowed, she thought, justifying the desperate plan she and Lord Randolf had spent the better part of the night formulating.

"Milady, his lordship is waitin'."

Jocelyn fairly jumped at the sound of the maid's voice invading her cynical musings. Her cheeks flooded with a guilty color, for deceit was not natural to her.

"There's no need to be nervous, milady. Women become brides every day."

"*I* don't, Gwenith," Jocelyn snapped irritably. "And when I do, I prefer it to be the man of my choice."

"Now, luv, it's a woman's duty to do what she must and do it grateful like." The older woman who had raised Jocelyn since birth heaved a helpless shrug. "'Tis the way of it, I fear."

Her maid had quoted the same advice only that morning when the prospective bride had suffered the humiliation of examination by Lord Rhys' sisters to see if she was fit to bear children. She'd hoped they would find fault of some kind, as she stood nude before their leering eyes. That might have been the end of it.

"And that is exactly what I intend to do, Gwenith," Jocelyn agreed, finding an affectionate smile for her companion to hide her wary anticipation.

"Pretty as a spring mornin', you are, lass. I'm thinkin' his lordship might crack that stone face of his with an outright grin at the sight of you. Now let me help you with your headdress."

Jocelyn waited patiently while Gwenith straightened her cornet and veil. Nervous as she was, she was in no hurry to reach the chapel. Not only did she wish to give the man her father had hired plenty of time to take his place, but anything to vex Lord Rhys was appealing.

"You look like an angel!" Gwenith pronounced proudly as she fussed with her charge's honey brown tresses, which lay in natural waves down her back.

Again the corners of Jocelyn's mouth twitched, for her thoughts were anything but angelic. With any luck at all, she would be quit of Lord Rhys' overbearing company and off to rescue her own true love within the hour.

The chapel was off to the right of the donjon containing the living quarters, requiring Jocelyn and the attendants she'd forbidden from her room to take the stone-canopied corridor connecting it. The sun shone through the arched openings where those servants and townsfolk who were not engaged in preparing the wedding feast gathered to watch what they could see of the impromptu affair.

Her morale boosted by echoes of "God bless you, Lady Jocelyn" and heartfelt wishes for good fortune and happiness, Jocelyn proceeded, head erect, her veil fluttering about an oval face with delicate but set features. She foundered, however, when she reached the steps of the chapel. Through the open door, she could see Father Timothy looking at her expectantly.

The good priest had baptized her in the very same place shortly before her mother died. Although he'd often fondly stated that he looked forward to marrying her off, his eyes reflected his concern for her situation. He knew of her avowed love for Phillip. She'd confessed it to him on numerous occasions.

Next to the robed Timothy stood Lord Rhys and four of his knights, garbed in fine cloth embroidered and trimmed in gold and silver, which sparkled in the light filtering through the narrow stained-glass windows over the altar. They were the only ones who had had adequate time to prepare for the wedding. Even Jocelyn had had to content herself with her mother's gown, exactly as it had been taken from its chest. But for her good fortune that she was much the same size as the Lady Rosalind, she might have appeared a ragmuffin rather than the lady of the manor.

Lord Rhys' expression revealed his distinct triumph at the result of his manipulation. As Jocelyn entered the chapel, he leaned over and whispered something to his companions, giving rise to a low rumble of humor, no doubt at Jocelyn's expense. The only thing genteel about Lord Rhys of Atworth was his title, indiscreetly granted by Edward's predecessor. Without leave, he met Jocelyn halfway and took her arm.

"You grow more ravishing each time I see you, milady."

"And you more detestable, milord."

"I received a king's messenger but moments after your father set out for the channel."

Jocelyn paused and looked up at her companion. Could it be the requested order to give her the dowry in advance of her wedding day? Her heart stumbled to a regular beat again as reason prevailed. If that were so, Lord Rhys would not be wearing that catlike smile of his, which showed none of his uneven and yellowed teeth, but great satisfaction.

"His majesty regrets he is unable to attend our wedding but will honor us with a visit in a few weeks to wish us well."

How was it that Lord Rhys' messenger had gotten to the king with an invitation to the impromptu marriage and hers, with her plea, had not? Jocelyn shuddered as she considered the possibilities and offered another silent prayer for her father's safe journey as she was ushered to a halt before the priest. Was there no level to which the overlord would stoop? Had he added murder to blackmail?

"Children of God, we are gathered . . ."

Cedric was one of her father's most trusted servants. What would his wife and three children do if . . . Jocelyn's hand grew damp, sandwiched between those of her prospective husband. The very idea of his touching her was so repugnant she could not help her impulse to pull away. Yet, as she did so, his hold tightened. Raising shock-glazed eyes to his face, she saw there the confirmation of her thoughts and it sickened her.

"Milady!"

Gwenith's stout arms were about her as she swayed unsteadily.

"Jocelyn?" Father Timothy's concerned inquiry was drowned out by shouts, echoing in the rafters of the ceiling.

Lord Rhys' disclaimer that she suffered naught but the vapors erupted into a startled curse which set things in motion all around her. Jocelyn struggled to right the spinning room and blinked as her would-be husband left her side with drawn sword. The cold clash of metal cut through the fog that seemed to swirl around her, clearing it with the resulting alarm.

"Sweet Mary, we've been invaded!" Gwenith wailed, dragging Jocelyn bodily out of the fray, so that the girl could not regain her footing.

Suddenly they were both down. The earthly chill of the stone floor served to be just what Jocelyn needed to shake her from the swoon that had nearly claimed her. This was it, she thought, crawling away from the floundering Gwenith. This was her rescue and she'd nearly ruined it by fainting. She scanned the motley group of men who had violated the chapel. Huntsmen, by the green and brown coloring of their clothes, she thought, but handy with the sword. At least they were holding off Rhys' knights.

As she debated which of her rescuers to attach herself to, a loud clopping sound drew her attention to the door, where a single rider burst through on a snorting silver-gray stallion. Jocelyn's gaze clashed with the piercing blue stare of the man bearing down upon her at a dangerous speed, her feet frozen to the spot. As he reached her, the forequarters of the stallion brushed past her, but as she reeled away, a strong arm grasped her by her belt and hauled her into the air.

Although this was the moment she'd been awaiting, she couldn't help the squeal that emerged from her throat. Her face grazed the horse's neck, damp with sweat, as the man swung the steed around and rushed the knight who was running to her rescue. All Jocelyn heard above her beating heart was the grunt of the knave as the horse knocked him aside.

"Stop him!"

Lord Rhys' furious order barely registered with Jocelyn, for they were approaching the narrow doors at a full gallop. Certain that she was to be hurled into the wall as the steed charged through it, she closed her eyes, only to be hauled up across its neck at the last minute, a sword resting possessively across her buttocks. Once free of the building, the animal broke into full speed, racing for the black alley, the only opening in the buildings which separated the inner bailey from the outer.

A group of villagers attempted to thrust a cart of rushes in their path, but the stallion leapt over it with little effort. Behind, Jocelyn could hear the hoofbeats of other horses, but when she glanced back, she saw that it was not the knights who gave chase, but the apparent accomplices of her kidnapper.

Brilliant, she cheered silently, wondering that her father could hire such accomplished warriors at such short notice. Her moment of triumph, however, was short-lived. A distance behind them, Lord Rhys' men were organizing for pursuit. She opened her mouth to shout a warning to her abductor, when a tree branch slapped the back of her head, knocking her cornet askew and tearing off her veil.

The sunlight was suddenly cut off by the trees which arched over the riding pass cleared through them. "Damn you, you'll see no pay if I'm dead!" she shouted breathlessly.

Without heed, the hulk of a man whose muscled legs she embraced in desperation rose in the stirrups and twisted to shout over his shoulder. "Well met, men! We'll gather at the appointed place this eve."

Jocelyn slung a holly branch away from her as the horse turned abruptly off the path and cut through the forest. "For the love of God, sir, are you mad? You'll kill us all!"

"You've been a good wench thus far, milady. T'would go easier on us all if you remained so."

"If I could but ride upright . . ."

The rest of Jocelyn's sentence faded, for all her attention was needed to keep the low-growing branches from flaying her face. Out of sheer panic, she yanked off the cornet, which had all but shaken loose, and left it hanging on a thorn bush in their wake.

"Don't think to leave a trail, milady, for I've chosen an escape route that would confound the devil himself."

"Then you must indeed be lost, sir!" Jocelyn grated out, one protective arm over her face and the other trying to keep her unbound tresses from catching and pulling off her head.

She wanted to curse the rich bellow of laughter her captor burst forth with, but the effort was too costly. Damn the villain, he'd pay dearly when her father heard of his uncouth manners.

"You've a ready wit for a woman, I'll give you that . . . and as fine a seat as I've been privileged to view at such a keen vantage."

In addition to the questionable compliment, a hearty slap echoed above the incessant beating of their horse's hooves, bringing Jocelyn straight up, so that she teetered precariously over the beast's neck. This time there was no stopping the string of curses she unleashed, most of which were learned from her bedroom window overlooking the squires' training yard. Damn the branches and the laughing oaf!

"Ho, mayhaps I should stop and see if 'twas the lady I snatched or the swineherd's daughter!"

Jocelyn fully expected another punishing swat from the hand which held the broadsword, but instead she suffered a painful yank of her now hopelessly tangled hair in a small holly tree, the branch of which, thankfully, gave way before her tresses. Blinded by tears, she ceased to struggle, collapsing in defeat over the neck of the horse with outraged sobs which shook her as much as the jarring gait of the stallion. She'd never forgive him for this, she vowed, so incensed in her misery that she hardly noticed their emergence into the network of fields beyond the woods which surrounded the neck of a pond, now green with algae from the string of unusually warm days of late.

At that moment, she could have scratched his fetching blue eyes out with her once neatly manicured nails. The thought consumed her, making her indifferent to his sudden and belated show of concern for her well-being. Through tear-blurred eyes, she saw his sword, rested across her buttocks, spear into the loose turf on the other side of the lathered horse, but she refused to move, even when her inconsiderate captor dismounted, the well-formed leg she'd inadvertently used to steady herself pulling away.

"There now, girl, 'twas just tug of the hair."

As she felt him reach for her waist from behind to help her off, she tensed, drawing up her legs beneath her wedding shift and kicking backward with all her strength. She heard his astonished grunt but had no time to see the result of her calculation, for the stallion began to sidestep, rearing its head and nearly tossing her to the ground.

Sliding to her feet, she seized the reins and fitted her foot in a stirrup as the animal danced away. Let the blackguard find his own miserable way to the predesignated meeting place she and Sir Randolf had settled upon, she thought, hopping wildly after the spooked horse on one foot. She pushed off the ground in a frantic attempt to mount the animal before it yanked her off balance entirely and galloped off, dragging her in the stirrup.

Her effort was rewarded, for now she had sound footing enough to swing her other leg over. The fool was headed in the wrong direction anyway, she thought in triumph, a fact she'd been too distracted to note before now. Yet as she tried to swing onto the horse's back, her skirt seemed caught on something.

"You treacherous little . . ."

Jocelyn kicked at the man who seemed to climb up the train of her mother's wedding dress. All the while she held onto the saddle for dear life, for the stallion broke straight away for the river. The rending sound of material made her wince.

"That's my mother's!" she growled, fingers digging in between the horse's warm skin and the soft oiled leather of the saddle. If the girth gave way, she was indeed lost.

"Let go the cursed saddle!"

"I'll have you boiled alive for . . ."

Jocelyn broke into a scream as the horse plunged into the cold pond. Her shock weakened her hold, so that the man tugging at her dress fell away with her into the deep water. To her horror, they both sank before he let her go. Certain her lungs would burst, she struggled back toward the sun-bathed surface and looked about frantically for her pursuer.

She could barely make out him struggling a few feet beneath the water. What the devil was the matter with him? she thought, fighting her own battle with the lengths of cloth hampering her attempt to swim. In the corner of her eye, she spied the silver stallion turning in an effort to make its way back to the shore, and she reached out for the reins, now floating freely on the green pond scum. The horse veered toward her as she reeled in the reins, until she was able to grasp the edge of the saddle and hang on while the animal dragged her in tow.

Heart beating wildly and coughing from the water she'd inhaled, she glanced back once more. The man was still underwater, fighting his clothing. Mad, she thought as she moved past him. He'd surely drown! Suddenly, as if he had managed to intercept her thoughts, he looked up at her, one arm raised as if in supplication. The word *mad* crossed her mind again, but this time it was self-directed.

Jocelyn reined the horse around in a circle, passing the man closer this time, and tossed out the long train of her dress toward him. Such was the power of his answering grasp that she nearly lost her own hold on the horse. He was an intimidating size, she knew, but she never dreamed the excess of his weight . . . at least from the feel of his stockinged thighs and calves where naught but hard, ridged muscle met her frantic clutches.

In spite of the horse's awkward climb from the cold water and her weakening hold, Jocelyn felt her face grow hot at the direction of her familiar thoughts. Heaven help her, another confession to make!

The moment his feet touched the grassy embankment, her kidnapper fell away, coughing in the worst way. Alarmed that he might die on the spot, Jocelyn rushed to his side and proceeded to beat him soundly on the back. The scrape of her knuckles against what should have been tough but yielding flesh bloodied three fingers, making her withdraw her hand to her chest in disbelief. No wonder he'd sunk like a stone! He wore a hauberk of mail beneath his peasant's shirt!

As he rolled on his back, his breath barely restored, she knelt over him and studied his face. To her surprise, it was a comely one, for a man. His features were well-placed and aristocratic, from his aquiline nose to the dark fringed lashes which fluttered weakly against swarthy cheeks. But it was his lips, well-defined and most intriguing, that demanded her attention.

"I stand . . . corrected. You are . . . of noble heart."

"Which is more than I might say for you, sir!" Jocelyn chastised, her tone not at all as stern as she would have had it. The poor soul had all but ripped open the laces of his shirt in an attempt to escape the metal one beneath. While his manner had been rough, he had plucked her from the hands of Lord Rhys at risk of his life as Lord Rhys' knights were battle-seasoned from the recent conquest of Wales.

"Who are you, sir, and where did you come by this hauberk?"

"Alaric of . . . 'tis milord's shirt of mail, loaned for this very mission."

Somewhere within a keen disappointment registered, but Jocelyn refused to acknowledge it. Knight or knave, she could not have left him to drown. Since he seemed inclined to be civil now, she might reconsider telling her father of her harrowing and uncomfortable rescue. They were safe . . . or would be soon.

"You and your men were most brave, Alaric. I shall commend you to your lord, now that you've learned your place."

Confusion pulled the clear blue eyes fixed on her shoulder, now bared by her torn gown, to her appraising gaze. "As I shall you, milady. You fought not your abduction at all. Had I not known better, I would swear you party to this scheme."

It was Jocelyn's turn to laugh, a lilting sound. "Of course, I was! If you had to wed Lord Rhys, no doubt you would seize the first opportunity to escape as well."

"No doubt."

The empathic nature of his answer set her to laughing again. Perhaps she was suffering from the hysteria spawned by her harrowing escape. Lips still twitching, in spite of her attempt to master her sudden urge to giggle like a schoolgirl, she shifted to her knees and started to wring out the train of her wedding dress. The wary lift of one thick, but admirably tapered brow above the other drew her attention back to her rescuer.

"Father will pay you well," she assured him. "All you have to do is get me to him in one piece . . . upright, if you please. I'm not averse to riding astride under the circumstances."

"Lord Bedford?"

"Aye, who else?"

"Who else indeed!"

Knowing a conjured laugh when she heard one, Jocelyn felt a tingle of alarm at the base of her neck. She rocked back on her heels and rose to her feet as her companion forced himself upright with an agility and strength he'd recouped uncommonly fast.

"I'll fetch the horse, milady, and we'll be on our way."

Her mind working feverishly, she watched as he walked toward the frosty gray stallion grazing a short distance away. He was taller than most, a fact which had escaped her, not having had the time to study him in a standing position.

"Speaking of which, sir, can you refresh my memory as to our meeting place? It's completely escaped me in all the excitement. Was it Athenry Cross or Greenhill?" Jocelyn sought out the location of the sword he'd buried in the turf earlier. It was but a few yards away ... equidistant from both of them.

"Athenry Cross."

Slinging her train over her arm, she bolted for the weapon. "Liar!" she accused, seizing the two-fisted handle and dislodging it from its grassy bed. She tried to lift it as she'd seen the squires do, but was astounded at the weight which refused to rise more than knee level.

"Nay, it's to Athenry Cross that I'm—" Alaric broke off, his face a picture of bemusement. "I'll take that, milady. 'Tis a heavy burden for one so *delicate* as yourself." He dropped the horse's reins and started toward her, undaunted by the drooping point of the blade.

Thinking to gain the advantage of momentum,

Jocelyn charged at him, the blade of the sword skimming the tops of the grass, gaining height with her increasing speed. When the time was right, she swung it with all her might. Alaric leapt backward with incredible speed for the extra weight he carried, so that instead of slashing him open at the juncture of his legs, which was all the height she could muster, the sword point merely grazed the skirt of his hauberk.

"By God, woman, you've gone too far this time!"

Unable to control the momentum carrying her around full circle, Jocelyn pivoted, her feet tangling in the soaked train, and pitched headlong after the plummeting weapon. It struck the ground with a flat thud with her landing atop it with a startled gasp. Yet before her lungs could fill, the air was crushed from them by the heavy body which pinned her to the sun-warmed earth.

It was only natural to scream with what little strength she had left and strike out blindly at her attacker's face with drawn fists. With luck, some herdsman or fieldworker would hear her and come to her aid. There was none who would betray her to Lord Rhys. Indeed, they might help her reach her father at Langley Green before he was forced to go on without her, as they'd agreed, should she not escape Lord Rhys' despicable web of blackmail.

Never did she anticipate the mouth which swooped down to cover hers, blocking her cry for help. Her body went rigid with shock, inadvertently facilitating Alaric's task of positioning her wrists above her head so that he might bind them with the leather laces from his shirt. Tears spilled of their own accord down Jocelyn's cheeks, affirming her reluctant surrender.

With the yielding of her resistance, the silencing kiss ceased to punish and softened in reward. The effect was confounding, warming her despair with an equally overwhelming need to be comforted, to be protected from and by the strong hands which abandoned her bound wrists to cradle her head.

"Don't force me to harm you further, milady," Alaric whispered against her trembling lips. "I would die *for* your hand, but not *by* it."

The voice which had threatened her very life with its bellowing rage, now pledged heart and soul in the tenderest tone she'd ever heard. What manner of man was this and what were his intentions? As if entranced, she nodded in acquiescence, although to what she agreed, she was not certain. All she knew was that she was lost ... truly lost.

Chapter Two

"I saved your unworthy life and you repay me by trussing me up like a market hen!"

"And if you do not cease to cackle like one, I shall be forced to gag you! Be grateful you are upright, as you so demanded."

Jocelyn weighed Alaric's threat heavily, but her ire was too much to bear in thought alone. "Better a filthy rag than your earlier means!" she mumbled under her breath.

She meant it. The episode had been entirely repugnant, even toward the end when he'd softened his muffling punishment into a caress and whispered most distractingly against her lips. The man was a rogue of the worst kind and had forced his attentions upon her. Not even Lord Rhys had dared such familiarity. That would make two knaves Phillip would skewer with his sword upon his release.

The stallion tensed beneath her and a strong arm tightened about her waist as the horse sailed effortlessly over a small stone fence which served to separate two fields. The hard, yet inviting chest which pressed against her back nearly led to another fervent denial, for Jocelyn was uncertain she should be grateful to be riding upright in front of him. It led to unseemly familiarity were she to relax from her stiffened posture, particularly since he'd divested himself of his hauberk, so that manly flesh warmed her back through the thin linen of her shift and the coarser weave of his shirt.

At first she balked when he announced that her dress had to come off. The man had already stripped down to his breeches and stockings, without regard to modesty, baring an impressive width of shoulders, separated by a darkly furred and sinewy chest. She hadn't meant to stare, but his was the first naked male torso she'd seen, barring that of her father's, to which there was no comparison.

Besides, she dared not take her eyes from Alaric, for fear of what he might try next. Thankfully, he pulled his tunic back on, although the missing laces, which bound her wrists, left it open in the front in a blatant display of crude manliness.

When he finished his ministrations and turned to her, however, her reluctant fascination turned to indignation. Regardless that the heavy damask of her gown was soaked and coated in pond slime and that her linen undershift would dry quicker without it, there was a matter of propriety, at least where she was concerned.

She was hard-pressed, however, to be convincing, bound as she was and at the mercy of the hand which slapped her buttocks soundly when she commenced to fight as best she could. One blow was enough warning that his dark mood would tolerate no more. His dagger made short work of her mother's dress—that beautiful gown Jocelyn had treasured in anticipation of her own wedding day. Once white with threads of gold stitched in subtle pattern, it was now covered in mud and slime, shredded beyond recognition, and wadded in the sack which contained Alaric's rusting hauberk.

Her wedding day, she echoed, wallowing in a sudden onslaught of self-pity. What more could go wrong? She'd had the wrong groom. Her father wasn't even there to give her away, having gone to ransom her beloved Phillip. She'd been abducted by the wrong kidnapper, and mother's dress was ruined beyond hope of ever being worn again; that is, should she even survive this new ordeal to marry Phillip.

An impatient curse was hastily garbled at her ear, coming out, "Faith, what is wrong now!"

"I'm cold," Jocelyn accused peevishly. "It's bad enough that you're taking me to God knows what fate, but you've ruined Mother's wedding gown, and I am forced to ride half-naked through the countryside. If I don't catch my death, the humiliation will kill me ... and *you* owe me your life!"

The reminder was less than graciously received. "I owe you naught, milady. 'Twas you that nearly took my life and only fitting that you should grant it back. As for the dress, I recall 'twas you who ran Jack Frost into the water, not I. If you would but act the lady you are reputed to be, you would fare far better."

It was some moments before Jocelyn conjured a suitable reply, for his words did smack of the truth. Yet surely he didn't expect her to submit to his abduction without protest. With instinctive feminine intuition, she pouted. "That does not remedy the fact that I am still chilled and without decent cover. Will you suffer me further to the leering eyes of those churlish companions we hasten to meet?"

"Damnation, I wonder if milord has an inkling of the shrew he's sent for. I've a good mind to abandon this folly altogether."

Jocelyn's spontaneous inquiry as to the identity of this *lord* he referred to was cut off by the sudden forward charge of the noble Jack Frost, spurred on by impatient heels. She fell against Alaric, compelled to submit to his firm hold and grudgingly grateful for it. She was an adequate horsewoman on one of the mares her father had trained for her but had never attempted such a fierce gait as the stallion now assumed. With little alternative, she leaned into her captor, her head cupped beneath a chin now beginning to bristle with shadowed growth. Perhaps, she reconsidered, she'd hold her questions until his humor improved.

When they emerged from the network of fields on a familiar road leading to the village of Millerdale, Jocelyn began to take heart. Someone there would surely know her and come to her aid . . . or would they recognize her in this disheveled state of undress? Her hair was a tangle mat, streaked with dried slime, the stench of which held off any pangs of hunger she might suffer, not having eaten since early morn. Her linen shift was in poor repair, the ribbon which drew the neckline tight having been broken in the struggle at the pond and replaced with a strip of her mother's gown. A swineherd's daughter would seem noble compared to her at the moment, she thought morosely.

Instead of going directly into the village, Alaric circled it and urged Jack Frost into the thick woods beyond. Just as disappointment threatened to overwhelm her, however, he reined in the stallion within the cover of the oaks and elms.

"You'll stay here with the horse until I get back," he announced tersely as he dismounted.

"Where are you going?"

Jocelyn was obliged to go into the arms extended to her, strong ones which lowered her to the ground in a manner far gentler than her companion's tone. Instead of answering, Alaric delved into his sack and withdrew a length of rope, dashing the escape plot that had already started to form in her mind. He was uncouth and rude but no fool. She would do well to keep that in mind.

"Milady," he prompted with a courtly sweep of his hand toward the nearest oak.

Crestfallen, Jocelyn stepped back to the tree and submitted to his task of securing her there. What the devil was he about now? She longed to ask, but the warning blue frost of his gaze was as discouraging as it was cold. She'd lied earlier about being cold in hopes of shaming him for his treatment of her, although her state of undress was enough to chill any gentlewoman.

Still, she hadn't meant for him to abandon her like this. What if Lord Rhys' men found her? Of the two men, Alaric was certainly the lesser of the two evils. But then, while he might abandon her, he wouldn't leave his horse if he were not returning, she reasoned warily.

"When will you be back?" Jocelyn seized her lips between her teeth in punishment for allowing her trepidation to show. He'd made it clear he had no use for hysterical women.

Alaric almost smiled. At least, the corners of his mouth twitched with a degree of satisfaction. He ran the back of his rough hand along the smooth line of her cheek and lifted her chin. There, in the midst of the blue frost of his gaze, danced a thawing light, its source eluding her.

"When my business is done, milady." The perplexing gaze shifted to her lips, as if contemplating to taste them further.

Dismay settled on Jocelyn's face, not from the fact that Alaric was considering kissing her again, but that the resulting rush of blood to her cheeks was warming her to the idea. Dismay, however, turned to indignation with the knowing curl of his mouth as he denied the moment and strode purposefully toward the village. Here was a dangerous man, she realized in the midst of her annoyance, more dangerous than Lord Rhys could ever hope to be.

In what was no more than one hour, yet seemed like thrice to one bound to a tree in the midst of a wooded glade, she heard him returning. Judging from the snapping of dry brush which laid Jack Frost's ears back and caused the stallion to dance sideways as far as his lead line would allow, her captor was in a hurry. The reason became evident with the sound of shouts that followed. Jocelyn's eyes widened as he burst into the glen at full speed, a piece of cloth thrown over his shoulder and his dagger brandished.

He was before her in three bounds, his handsome face flushed and beaded in sweat, so that the dark hair around it was actually wet. The stench which assaulted her nose as he sawed at the ropes frantically with his knife drew her attention to the fact that he was covered in mud and filth.

"By God, you are more trouble than a harem of Saracen wenches," he panted, slinging away the ropes as they fell and nearly dragging her toward his horse.

Jocelyn glanced over her shoulder, wondering at his pursuers. Were they village people, it could be her chance to escape, but if they were Lord Rhys' men . . .

Alaric, even in his haste, seemed to read her thoughts. "Cross me now, woman, and I'll make you rue the day for the remainder of your very *short* life!"

His enunciation of the word *short* was sufficient motive for her to settle obediently in the saddle, her cry for help swallowed as he tossed the material over the horse's back and swung up behind her. In his haste to take up the reins, the tip of the dagger still in his hand nicked the top of her right hand but, again, Jocelyn held back her cry. Her fingers clinging with all their strength to the edge of the saddle, she braced for Jack Frost's surge forward, only to be startled when the stallion reared at his master's beckoning and turned to charge off in the direction from which the man had just come.

Jocelyn could neither help her gasp as the stallion went up, nor the heavy grunt she exhaled as he came down hard and launched forth toward the shouts. She closed her eyes, taking the lashing of the low-hanging tree branches, but the tensing of the body curled over her own brought them open in time to see a crew of villagers armed with staffs entering the forest at its edge. Aside from delving back into the thick wood, there was no alternate route but straight through their midst. With her to the front, it was not difficult to imagine who, besides Jack Frost, would take the brunt of the blows.

"Out of the way, I beg you!" she implored in a voice pitched on the border of hysteria.

Recognition erupted in echoes of "Lady Jocelyn?" and "Milady!" from the group, the shock of which made them fall back, mouths agape.

They passed the group so quickly, the faces were a blur to her, but Jocelyn was certain they would have been familiar. She knew almost everyone in the villages on her father's land, having spent hours with Gwenith visiting with alms and food for the poor, as well as medicine for the sick. Followed in her mother's footsteps, they would say, although the credit for her knowledge belonged to her servant, who had once been her mother's. Poor Gwenith. She hoped the dear wasn't hurt in the wedding chaos.

"You've come to your senses at last," Alaric observed, his voice stronger now that he was on horseback. "Had you resisted, blood might have been spilled."

"Mine, like as not, but *you* needn't have worried," Jocelyn averred passionately. "I call it cowardly, using a woman for a shield." She winced at the oath, hissed between clenched teeth behind her.

"'Twas not your body but that viperish tongue of yours which cleared the way. Were that disposed of, no doubt mankind would be blessed."

Jocelyn twisted to afford him her most condescending glare. "What were you about anyway? You smell like a pigsty!"

Were his hands not occupied with the reins, she'd have sworn he'd have struck her then and there. Green eyes foundered under the fierce assault of blue.

"Fetching you something to wear, milady!" he accused viciously.

"You *stole* it?" She didn't know why that surprised her. He'd already proven himself capable of many despicable acts.

"I left coin enough for two in its place, but the hag who sounded the alarm saw naught but me."

Looking more closely at the coarse material upon which Alaric rode, she wrinkled her nose. "Surely you don't expect me to wear *that!*"

His face pressed against hers, forcing her to look straight ahead to avoid those disarming lips of his. While low and velvet, the words he whispered against her neck were no less threatening. "I do indeed, madam, and you will don it at the next opportune moment or ride naked as Godiva's wench into the camp! Do you understand?"

Jocelyn nodded mutely. Here was a man capable of whispering seductive words while he drove a dagger into one's chest. He possessed the speech of an educated man and the manners of an illiterate oaf. He was half gentleman and half rogue, depending on his humor, which now was all rogue and nothing more. Still, to give him the complete satisfaction of bullying her into submission was more than she could stand. Two could play at this game.

"Indeed, sir, and my thanks. 'Twas most gentlemanly of you to fetch it so *gallantly*," she answered sweetly.

The opportune moment came sooner than she imagined. She suffered the natural demand of her body until it was unbearable. Such was her humiliating urgency upon summoning nerve enough to ask for a few moments of privacy, that, when Alaric helped her down off the horse and untethered her wrists, she all but ran to the closest cover where she might be sheltered from those dastardly blue eyes of his.

She emerged with as much dignity as she could muster, only to find him standing before his horse, the peasant dress held out toward her imperiously in one hand and a ready dagger in the other. Since he'd already cut her mother's wedding gown to shreds, she needed no imagination as to the meaning of the second choice. Teeth grating so that her jaws ached, she took the dress and pulled it over her shift.

It was of rough cloth and prickly to skin accustomed to finer weaves. Nonetheless, it could not be said that it did not make her decent. She literally swam in its voluminous folds, which she drew to her waist with the belt from her wedding dress. Because Jocelyn's slender form could not take it up in its designed width, it was decidedly long, causing her to trip in her regal saunter back to the horse.

Although his gaze was laughing, Alaric was gentleman enough to bear his humor in silence. He caught her easily and lifted her into the saddle without replacing her bonds, eager to be on his way, for she had not missed his concerned glance at the westbound sun. Not that she'd attempt to escape now that darkness would soon be upon them.

Even rogues were uncomfortable in the forest at night. Tree spirits and all manner of supernatural beings lurked there, according to some. While Father Timothy had taught her there was naught to fear but flesh and blood villains, the stories Gwenith passed on to her from past generations had put her to bed for many a sleepless night, surrounded by pillows and buried in blankets.

Had she a proper husband, the servant had told her, she'd have nothing to fear. But since her betrothed had been in the Holy Land, making her nearly a spinster's age compared to her contemporaries, Jocelyn had had to content herself with keeping his letters beneath her pillow and dreaming of him. Since she was but seven when she last saw him, all she could remember of his features were his dark hair and blue eyes. They were always laughing and kind toward her, not fierce and accusing like those of her abductor.

Driven by a wild thought, she glanced over her shoulder at Alaric. No, this man could not be Phillip, no matter that his coloring was the same. The man of her letters was gentle and romantic, not prone to treat a lady as this one had. Besides, Phillip was in the hands of the Saracens, helpless at the moment to save her, if indeed he even knew of her plight. And he was no deceitful knave, she reasoned. He would have revealed himself at the first opportunity.

Jocelyn sighed. Would that Alaric were her ransomed groom, for, aside from his crude manners, he was much as she had imagined the adult Phillip to be. Bold, brave, and handsome, ready to die for her hand. A frown creased her smooth brow as she recalled Alaric's curious declaration. *I would die for your hand, not by it.*

Again, she shook herself. It could not be! What purpose would it serve to keep his identity from her? Nay, she'd fallen victim to some wicked plot, conceived by a lord with more daring than Rhys of Atworth. Perhaps, if she pretended to humor Alaric, she might find out the who and why of it.

It was very late in the day and they had come through yet another crisscross of fields and boundaries when they turned into an isolated woodland. Jocelyn was certain they had left her father's land but was confused as to just which of the neighboring estates Alaric had chosen as a meeting place with his roguish band. For all she knew, they might not be there at all. Lord Rhys' men might have caught up with them. Were that the case, their heads were either hung on the walls of Bedford or they'd been so tortured and beaten that the other fate was preferable.

A hailing shout, reinforced by the scent of woodsmoke, was the first hint that her worry was unfounded. Jocelyn straightened in the confines of Alaric's arms and shook the fatigue which had lured her into dozing off. The manly warmth her kidnapper offered spread to her cheeks as she realized the relaxed state of her defenses. They approached the crude campsite like lovers, not abductor and victim.

"Faith, I hope that's venison I smell. After the race this damsel has put me through, I could devour a hindquarter, well-cooked or nay!"

"Venison and fine ale, good man," one of the men

gathered around the campfire affirmed, rising to take the stallion's reins.

"Courtesy of Lord Rhys' wedding feast!" another quipped, giving rise to a hearty round of amusement.

"Well then, make room for the bride and make it plentiful, lest you suffer the sting of her barbed tongue," Alaric averred, dismounting as though refreshed that he was at last at his destination.

"God's breath, what manner of demon assailed you?" the first exclaimed, eyeing the worn and weary state of the travelers.

"One with pigs, by the stench," the second observed, his bearded face screwed up in distaste.

With an accusing look, Alaric lifted Jocelyn from the saddle. "'Tis a long tale that would take a bard to tell." Upon setting her gently on the ground, he turned her to face his comrades. "Behold the lovely demon and beware."

Jocelyn bristled at his sarcasm and yanked the tresses he'd lifted as example from his hand. It was bad enough to be victim to this plot, but to serve as the source of their ungentlemanly amusement was intolerable. "Will you add ridicule to your growing list of abuse, sir? I know well that I look the bedraggled peasant, but 'tis cruel to be reminded so when the fault lies not with me."

Her chin quivered, undermining her proud approach to the campsite. Damn them all, she swore silently, all five *plus* Alaric. Phillip would indeed have his work laid out for him when he and her father returned for her. Ignoring the blatantly curious looks she drew, she took the cleared place for her on a log pulled close to the fire and tucked her skirts about her as if they were made of the finest silk.

"Will you have some food, milady?"

Moving her fixed gaze from the fire, Jocelyn addressed the man who brandished a knife, ready to serve her. He was younger than the rest, tow-haired, with a fine fur on cheeks which would in time afford him a beard of the same white-gold hue.

"Thank you, no." Jocelyn was hungry and the scent of the roasting meat made her stomach rumble in response. Nonetheless, there was a point to be made. "Though I would appreciate a taste of ale to wash the dust of our journey down," she conceded primly.

"Toss the jug, John."

A big burly sort across from her took a long draft of the liquid, spilling some out the side of his mouth and down his dusty tunic of drab brown. After wiping his lips with the back of his hand, he handed it over to her with a crooked grin.

"Milady."

Jocelyn accepted the jug, her thirst all but dissipating. True, they were in the wilderness, but surely, if no goblet, there was a cup of some crude make about. If not for the grit of the trail in her mouth, she might have declined altogether. Instead, she wiped the lip of the vessel with her skirt thoroughly and took a delicate sip. It was a good ale, one she recognized as brewed in the village where her new garment had come from. Part of their indenture to her father was to supply a percentage of their produce. While honeyed mead or a light wine was her preference of beverages, one sip led to another healthier one before she handed the jug back to the bulky John.

"Thank you, sir. You are more chivalrous than your partner in this heinous crime."

"By all the saints," Alaric grumbled, hacking off a chunk of venison with his knife as if he wished it were Jocelyn herself. "I have stood all this company a man can bear. I leave her to sharpen her tongue on you, gentlemen! Beware, 'tis a most fiendish weapon!"

Carrying his supper and a flagon of ale with him

under one arm and a sack slung over the other, Alaric marched away from the campsite and disappeared into the semidarkness of the trees. The brief victory Jocelyn gloried in, however, faded with his image, for she realized she was now in the company of complete strangers. Some wore chest guards of leather in lieu of the more expensive mail, their thick but sturdy bodies straining at the laces which secured them. Others wore nothing but plain tunics, belted and with little adornment. Most were bearded, and all were well-dusted from their battle and overland escape. Mercenaries no doubt, she decided, not at all comforted by the thought.

"Ho, it appears his lady has fallen short of his expectations," the man who had seen to Alaric's horse snorted, casting a bold look in Jocelyn's direction.

Aware that his was not the only appraising gaze fixed on her, Jocelyn lowered her eyes to the hands she folded in her lap. Of them all, Alaric was by far the most noble. These were men accustomed to fighting and plunder, capable of . . . How dare Alaric leave her alone like this! Taking in a sustaining breath, she rose to her feet once more.

"Here now, where do you think you're going?"

Jocelyn lifted her chin with an imperial tilt. "You have made me see the error of my ways and I would seek your comrade to ask his pardon."

"I wouldn't trust her, Matt."

The one called Matt showed no sign of doing so. "I don't think he's in the humor to receive your ladyship, much less grant pardon." His hand closed around her arm, its size permitting his fingers access to his thumb with no effort. It was callused, no doubt from using one of the heavy swords he'd wielded earlier that day. Jocelyn had little reason to think he couldn't break her arm in half, were he of a mind.

"If you fear my running away, sir, let me put your

mind at ease. These woods are fearsome and I have no wish to founder about in them without escort. Besides," she hesitated, lowering her eyes, "I need a few moments of privacy."

It took a second for her meaning to sink into the slow wit of the man who seemed to be the second in command to Alaric. Then the large brow which rested heavily upon the bridge of a crooked nose lifted in enlightenment. "Oh, I see!" he mumbled awkwardly. "Well, don't wander off the path too far. Snakes are out and full of meanness this time of year."

Snakes! By all that was holy, that was all she needed. Not caring that her hasty steps gave the men at the campsite another source of amusement, she crossed herself and took to the path Alaric had chosen earlier. If she made an escape at all, it would have to be on horseback, not that that was even possible. The horses were in plain sight of the campfire. An unladylike oath exited her lips. What more could possibly go awry?

The sun could disappear altogether, she thought uneasily, now far enough away from the fire that no manmade light was afforded her. Somewhere overhead an owl hooted as if to make the most of her anxiety, and she broke into a full run, skirts gathered in knot at her waist. There was a moon, but it cast ghastly shadows through the trees overhead and failed to light the root that snatched off one of her kid slippers like a wooden claw. Jocelyn never paused, but stumbled on toward the thinning of trees, beyond which she could hear the running hush of water, a small fall perhaps.

"Alaric?"

This time an unseen vine snared her ankle, biting with thorns, and pitched her headlong to the stony bank with a strangled scream. The impact knocked the breath from her chest, so that, in spite of her panic, she lay there stunned. But when she tried to move her leg and discovered that an invisible hand still held the vine around it tightly, she became frantic. Gwenith's tale of the fairy whips which caught victims by the ankle and tugged them into the earth had made its impression all too well. Kicking furiously, she tried to pull away, in spite of the rich masculine voice she'd come to know. "Be still, woman, 'tis just a vine!"

Relief poured through her. "Alaric!"

With the slash of a knife, her foot was free, and Jocelyn threw herself into the arms that lifted her upright. "Damn you, how could you leave me alone with those strangers?" She bit off the addition of *and wood fairies*. She felt fool enough as it was.

"Not strangers, milady, my men."

"But *I* don't know them," she mumbled against him, still drawing from his reassuring strength.

"You don't know me either."

His words were as sobering as the fact that his skin was bare and cold. "But . . . but I've known you longer," she replied lamely, her hand warily traveling over the ridges of his back.

"Long enough to interrupt my bath?"

With a horrified gasp, Jocelyn pulled away, her gaze seeking to confirm her touch, which proclaimed him as naked as his challenge. Sweet Mother, he was as bare as the day he'd been born . . . and as magnificent a man as his stallion was a horse. Masterfully proportioned, she thought, unable to interrupt the journey of her eyes from naked width of his shoulders to the taut narrowness of his hips and . . .

With a snort of amusement, Alaric turned his back to her and waded into the water. Condemning herself for her naive but nonetheless outright and open admiration, Jocelyn spun to face the direction of the camp. To her dismay, the naked man still seemed the lesser of the two evils. At least he showed no inclination to assault her further, and God knew what manner of spirit or beast now awaited her. Not that there really were any, she told herself sternly, able to think more clearly in the soft glow of the moonlight where her eyes might reassure her. There were, however, snakes.

"Since you visited all but the village pigsty with me, you may join me if you wish. 'Tis cold, but refreshing compared to that stagnant pond."

Jocelyn ventured a peek over her shoulder to see Alaric standing waist deep in the running water. His dark hair was wet from washing and slicked back from his face, where a winning smile flashed white at her. "No, but I will have a taste of that ale, if you've some left."

He pointed toward the pile of clothing left on the bank. "Help yourself, milady."

Taking shamefully belated pains not to look at him further, Jocelyn found the flagon, as well as the shank of venison her abductor had cut away. He'd apparently been in such a rush to rid himself of the mud and stench that he hadn't touched it. 'Twould be the sign of a properly raised gentleman, she conceded thoughtfully, uncorking the ale and, after a precautionary wipe with her skirt, taking a drink.

Her mouth had gone dry from her silly fright, and her chest still ached. Gwenith and her overactive imagination! She knew better than to give merit to those tales, but logic had fled her completely. Alaric must think her a witless, hysterical ninny. Not that she cared, she asserted, helping herself to more of the ale.

The venison lying on a hammered tin plate which must have come from Alaric's sack caught her attention, and once again her stomach rumbled threateningly. It had been hours since she'd toyed with the fruitbread Gwenith had served her upon rising. Her appetite had been scant then, cut with worry for her father and

Phillip. If she were not at the predesignated meeting place by morning, Lord Randolf would leave for the Channel without her.

Jocelyn picked a piece of meat off the bone and popped it in her mouth. Except that her plight was somewhat different than they'd anticipated. The wrong villain had her. Washing the succulent piece down with another draft of the brew, she cut her eyes to where Alaric scrubbed himself roughly with his shirt. At least he was decidedly preferable to Lord Rhys.

Licking her fingers, she rose and walked to the edge of the brook. "I don't suppose there would be any harm were I to wear my shift in. It needs laundering as much as I. I could wear the dress until it dries." Perhaps if she were clever, she might find out what fate awaited her with his mysterious lord.

"Here's some soap."

Jocelyn caught the wet soap Alaric tossed her. It smelled of spices, not of flowers like that Gwenith made. From the East, she guessed, wondering how her abductor had come by such a treasure. Then he had made more than one reference to the Saracens.

"What a pleasant smell," she complimented. "Where did you find it?"

"'Twas the gift of a lady friend."

"A Saracen woman?" At his hesitation to answer, she went on. "You did refer to the Saracens earlier in the day, which leads me to think you've been to the Holy Land."

"I have . . . and yes, that is where the soap is from."

"Do you know Phillip of Inglenook? He's been there nearly ten years."

Alaric repeated the name to himself but shook his head in denial. "I have heard of such a man but not met him. He has high repute among the English knights as a valiant warrior. Why do you ask?"

Trying to ignore the shiver running up her spine at the frank appraisal she received when she stepped out of the peasant dress and laid it on a nearby rock to keep it dry, Jocelyn eased into the brook. "Because," she answered with a shudder from the new chill of the water, "he is my betrothed and will skewer you, your men, *and* your high and mighty lord with his lance for kidnapping me."

Alaric laughed. "That will take a considerable lance, milady. Not even a man of Phillip's notoriety could wield such a weapon."

Careful to remain a safe distance from him, Jocelyn dropped to her knees so that the water skimmed her chin. "Laugh all you wish, I should not wish to be in your boots when Phillip returns and discovers your treachery."

She had caught his undivided attention. Good, she thought, leaning back to wet her hair, unaware of the revealing cling of her wet shift to her upthrust breasts. Taking the soap from the bank, she proceeded to work it into her locks with vigor.

"If this Phillip is your betrothed and thinks so highly of you as to take on men the mettle and cunning of mine, why then were you about to marry Lord Rhys?"

"Blackmail!" Jocelyn declared fervently. "But the marriage would not have taken place, even if you had not intervened."

"It seemed well enough underway when I—"

"I was supposed to have been kidnapped—not by you but by my father's man!" She looked up, pleased to see the confusion mounting on Alaric's face. "Now you've made a mess of it all, you and this lord of yours. If you hope to gain ransom, think again, sir. You've risked your lives for naught."

"And why is that, milady? Your keep seemed well-maintained, though the lack of guests was odd for such an occasion."

"Because all the money we could raise, including my dowry from King Edward, for which I had to wed to receive, is on its way to the Holy Land to ransom Phillip. If I am not at Langley by morning, Father will leave without me. Now think, sir! If you were to deliver me there in time, I am certain you would not suffer the loss of life which surely awaits you once Phillip is free."

Jocelyn ducked under the water and swam a distance until she was certain all the soap was gone from her hair. When she emerged, she tossed the long wet tresses over her shoulder. Even with a comb, it would take the remainder of the night to untangle it. But Alaric was right, the water was refreshing. She felt no hint of the weariness that had caused her to doze en route to the campsite. Considering her confounding circumstance, she was quite content and would be even more so if Alaric were to grant her request.

"Ten years is a long time, milady." The softly spoken words were so close to her ear that Jocelyn gasped, spinning in the circle of arms that kept her from losing her balance. "It sounds as if you've prepared to sacrifice yourself for a man who would prefer the life in Holy Land to marriage. In fact, I think your threat a toothless one."

Jocelyn backed against the hands clasped behind her so that they rested at her waist and met Alaric with bold indignation that he should even suggest such a thing. "Phillip loves me!" she argued, unable to ignore the closing distance between them. The water had been cold, but this near to her tormentor, it warmed with the inviting heat of his body. "His letters avow his love for me, as I now avow my love for him."

"Would you not prefer a man of the flesh to this man of parchment?"

There was nothing between them now but the thin linen of her shift. Jocelyn could not deny the man of flesh pressed against her, nor this strange power he wielded that managed to awaken the woman within her. He was going to kiss her. Even as she attempted to arch backward, away from him, she felt a flood of desire weakening her knees.

"I love Phillip with all my heart and soul," she managed against the heat of the mouth which grazed her own.

The body which coiled over hers, crushing her against hard arousal, stiffened as if stricken by her plaintive declaration of love. "Then you had best learn to keep your charms to yourself, lest a man of lesser fiber mistake your wiles as an invitation to sample them."

Alaric left her so abruptly that Jocelyn nearly buckled to her knees. The wash of cold water which rushed to take his place caused her to shiver within and without, and she found herself wondering again, what manner of man was this? Moreover, *who* was he?

Chapter Three

The morning sun hailed another warm day, although the night's chill still lingered in the forest where it was filtered through the trees overhead. Wrapped in a blanket on the bed of leaves Alaric had instructed the men to make for her, Jocelyn stirred to the low conversation of those gathered about the campfire. That was after he'd insisted on carrying her back to the camp, one shoe missing, and seen that the accidental nick from his dagger on the back of her hand, which had begun to bleed once more upon getting wet, had been dressed.

Smothering an unladylike yawn, she shed her blanket and climbed to her feet on unwieldy limbs like those of a newborn foal. The awakening of muscles much abused from her long hours in the saddle served to shake the grogginess from her brain instantly. It was all she could do to will her legs into a proper, if obviously uncomfortable walk, without it appearing that the blasted silver stallion was still between them.

The shifting of attention to her made her stop fussing with arranging her sleep-bedeviled dress. While inside she shrank under the ruffians' gazes, she mustered an unaffected front. "Where is Alaric?" she demanded, as if she cared not one whit whether they answered or not.

Damn the rogue, he had done it again, abandoned her to fend for herself among his men—a fierce-looking lot, save the lad, with their untrimmed beards and unkempt dress. This time, however, Jocelyn was not so certain that he'd left her with the lesser of the evils. It still made her weak to think of her reaction to his naked proposal that she consider him, rather than Phillip. All the more repelling was that he meant no proper wedding to accompany it, of that she was sure.

To add insult, he then proceeded to act as if it were she who had issued such an outrageous invitation. It was not her fault that she'd become frightened and sought him out. He was, after all, the more familiar of the strangers and had, at the right opportunity, tried to be accommodating. He was a puzzlement, like quicksilver, one moment making her fear his taking her life and the next, her soul. Jocelyn felt her skin burn as she recalled how she had almost anticipated his kissing her *and him full naked!*

"Morning devotions," the burly John informed her, drawing her back to the substance of her question.

"Devotions!" she echoed incredulously. "A likely story! He's gone to deliver the ransom letter to Lord Rhys, hasn't he?"

"Now there's a thought! What think you on that, Matt?"

"Only if ye've got a longin' to swing from a rope, would I try that!"

Jocelyn was too caught up in the idea that Alaric even knew the meaning of devotions, much less practiced them. Was he some sort of vagabond priest? The idea seemed too preposterous to consider, particularly the priestly part. He was a kidnapper and accomplished seducer of women, she reaffirmed in stern silence.

She felt the thin linen of the shift she'd tossed over a tree to dry during the night. It was still a trifle damp, but she felt undressed without it. "You do realize," she spoke, in a voice loud enough to gain their attention, "that if you delivered me to my father, a reward would no doubt await you. He's leaving Langley Cross even as we speak, but if we made haste, we might catch him before he reaches the Channel."

"I thought the moneys he carried were to save your beloved Phillip," a cynical voice challenged behind her. "That you were in such desperate circumstance for the ransom that you agreed to marry Atworth in order to meet the sum. Yet now you say there is enough for reward of my men *and* your beloved's ransom. Which is it, milady?" Like a gauntlet, Alaric tossed at her feet the slipper she'd lost in her fright the night before.

Foiled by her own words, Jocelyn shoved her foot vengefully into the shoe and, snatching up the shift from the low-hanging branch, marched with a heartfelt glare past Alaric without granting a reply. No matter what she answered, 'twould be incriminating, despite both statements having merit. Her father would certainly have rewarded them, Phillip too ... after he was set free.

Just as she thought she might carry out her one act of defiance, Alaric grabbed her arm, halting her. "Where do you think you are off to?"

"To dress and perform my toilette as best I may ... *and in privacy,* I hope," Jocelyn added, moving her withering gaze to the hand restraining her, "lest you mistake my ministrations as further invitation to your loathsome advances."

Alaric swore, breaking the vow he'd just made to exercise more patience with his captive. "The night has not dulled your tongue, I see."

"Nor have your *devotions* improved your humor, sir!"

"Ho, she is a prickly rose!" one of the men chirped, adding fuel to an already kindled flame of irritation which sent color from Alaric's throat to the crown of his head.

Looking at his men to decide which he'd send to keep an eye on her, Alaric felt another oath of frustration surging from his chest. As if sensing his indecision, Jocelyn yanked her arm away and strode off with a regal tilt of her chin toward the brook where he'd very nearly broken another vow. It would be so easy to believe her innocence in this tawdry conspiracy which smacked of betrayal ... as easy as it would be to follow his heart's desire and take her for his own. But Jocelyn of Bedford was not his for the taking but for the protecting, a hard fact which left him no alternative other than following her himself to the creek, for, loyal as his men were, the lady presented far too much temptation with her beguiling naiveté.

At the edge of the brook, Jocelyn loosened her belt and pulled her shift up beneath the volume of her stolen dress. As she worked her arms into the tight sleeves within her modest enclosure, she sensed, rather than heard, Alaric's approach. Keeping her back to him, she arranged the shift properly before shoving her arms through the large armholes of the outer garment. Once her belt was cinched about her narrow waist, she turned to challenge the man who now sat on a rock, observing her.

"Truce, milady, and my apologies!" Her surprise at the winning smile which had replaced his earlier scowl was surpassed by the offering he extended to her . . . a comb. "For your hair."

"I know the purpose of a comb," she declared, biting off the *which is more than I can say for your men* which very nearly followed. Suspicion mirrored on her face, Jocelyn took the treasure. "But thank you, sir."

She settled comfortably on the flat bed of rock through which the brook had cut long ago. Its dark surface, warmed by the sun, helped offset the dampness of her shift. Aware that Alaric watched her intently, she hesitated, comb in hand.

"Is there something wrong, milady?"

"Would you turn your back, sir?"

Alaric felt his regained composure faltering once again. "For what purpose?"

"So that I may not be falsely accused again of inviting your attentions."

Grudgingly her captor obliged her. It was an innocent gesture, but one which brought a hint of triumph to the set of Jocelyn's mouth as she put the comb to work. Instinct came into play with the discovery. There was some semblance of conscience amidst his vices. She'd sensed it before but was too frightened to pay it much heed yesterday. If she were careful, very careful, she might make use of it yet.

Taming the front of her hair proved a short task. The

back was another. No matter how she twisted and pulled at it, she risked ruining the comb altogether. Her arms ached and her eyes were as blurred with the painful tugging as they'd been when she was a child, squealing in protest at Gwenith's patient hand.

"'Tis all your fault!" she blurted out, frustration overwhelming her after lodging the teeth in a particularly hurtful snarl which refused to release them. "You'll have to cut the blasted thing out and my hair with it! This abduction will be the death of me yet!"

Alaric's blurred figure appeared before her, hands braced on sturdy hips. "I've never heard of death from baldness, milady, but known the shiny heads to live long lives. Are you sure you'd have me use my knife?"

Realizing the man had taken her exasperated declaration to heart, Jocelyn drew away. "No! I only meant—" she broke off and brushed an irritating tear aside. With a forced sigh, she steadied her voice. "It's not your fault, 'tis that of a most damnable fate. Faith, sir, if you had had the wrong groom, the wrong kidnapper, your whole future shredded like Mother's wedding dress, I vow 'twould exasperate you as well." Of all the degrading things, her chin began to quiver. "Though you've treated me as gallantly as any knave, aside from accusing me of wantonness, my body aches as though it's been beaten and I swear my legs will never straighten again from the force of that stallion between them! To add to my misery, I've had precious little sleep thanks to those snoring oafs you call stout-hearted men, and it seems I shall wear your comb for the rest of my life!" A sob forced its way past her lips. "I've done my best to be as brave as I might, but to cry in front of you is the most degrading of all! Just put the knife to my heart and be done with this wretched life before it worsens!"

Alaric watched as the distraught young lady tugged at her neckline to expose her offered target to his blade, her face streaked with evidence of her misery. As a result of the drama, he wasn't sure if he should laugh or feel remorse. Such was her effect on him. There was always one emotion battling furiously against another. Yet he had to admit that hers had been a trying time, perhaps more than one gentle girl, spoiled by her father's luxury, could bear. So why was it that he felt called to comfort her, rather than offer disdain?

"I've always been a man of challenge, milady. If you will suffer to sit still, I shall promise to put away my blade and do my best to remedy at least one of your trials."

He would have sliced his own throat before he cut away one strand of her silken tresses. Tangled as they were, they were as soft as he'd imagined, still smelling of the scented soap he'd provided her. It was odd that the same spices should smell so differently on her, taking on a gentler, sweeter flavor. Recalling his plea for the strength to fight the desire which welled at the very thought of her, much less when she was so close at hand, Alaric devoted himself to the freeing of the comb.

The girl never complained further, even when he slipped and pulled her head backward with the momentum of his downward stroke. Nor did she object when, of his own accord, he took the liberty of weaving her hair in a single braid. She merely stiffened, her lashes fanned wide in surprise.

"Where did you learn such a tender art, sir? I vow, my maid has no gentler touch."

"I can make the plainest steed shine fair for tourney with ribbons and flowering vines woven in its mane and tail."

Jocelyn glanced over her shoulder to see Alaric wrapping the stem of a wildflower about the end of her braid so that it held as good as any ribbon. "So you're a stable hand?"

The corner of Alaric's mouth lifted in mild amusement. "Of a sort."

"Is Jack Frost your steed?"

"Would a stable hand own such a magnificent beast?" Alaric took her hand and helped her to her feet.

Jocelyn grimaced. "You're going to tell me no more about yourself than your master, are you?"

"Right you are, milady. Now, if you're no other task to perform, we need to be on our way. I've no wish to cross Atworth's men." He extended his arm graciously.

"If I take it, will I be accused of wantonness again?" she asked, "or is that buried with our truce?"

Alaric laughed out loud and took her hand in his own to place it on his arm. "Buried, milady. 'Twas ill bred of me to blame you for my own weakness of the flesh."

Jocelyn fell in with her escort's step, having to hasten to match it, so that when they reached the campsite, her face was flushed and her breath somewhat labored. It never occurred to her how incriminating her demeanor or the act of mopping her brow with her skirt was until she spied the sly exchange of glances among the men who were busy saddling their horses for the journey.

Self-consciously, she withdrew from Alaric's side and walked to where some fire cakes had been left on a flat stone. As she dropped to her knees to make herself comfortable near the now-extinguished fire, Alaric caught her arm.

"You can eat on the road. We must be away from here."

Jocelyn's face fell as she was ushered toward Jack Frost. "Will we go far?" She shoved the cake into a slash in the dress which served as a pocket.

"A half-day's ride to a place where, with luck, a roof will shelter your head tonight."

She turned to grasp the saddle, waiting for Alaric to hoist her up, but to her surprise he turned her back around to face him. Hands firmly about her waist, he lifted her into the leather cradle sideways. "Now see if you can hook your knee over the edge there. I've seen Saracen wenches ride camels in a similar fashion."

"And how many of them have you made off with, sir?" Jocelyn teased, touched once again by the unexpected consideration.

"No more than a dozen, wouldn't you say, Matt?" Alaric quipped, waiting until she was secure in her seat before swinging up behind her.

"Not unless you count them African slave women."

Jocelyn's lilting laugh blended in with the gruffer ones surrounding them as Alaric turned the silver stallion to take the lead. Somehow she no longer felt as threatened in the light of the new day and Alaric's truce, neither by the man holding her protectively in the enclosure of his arms, nor by his rougher companions who surrounded them.

Matt and John were brothers, which explained the difficulty of telling them apart, their like clothing and beards put aside. Matt was the quicker of the two with an ever-ready answer to all who sought to goad him. Such jibes were received in good humor and wittily turned about, affording all a good laugh. His darting brown eyes betrayed the potential for quicker anger than his brother, who, although bigger, was the gentler of the two.

Brian was the youngest and bore the brunt of most of the group's teasing. The callow youth could not seem to keep his eyes off Jocelyn, in spite of the clucking and mooing that went on each time he was caught in a moon-eyed stare.

"I saw a cow once with that look," Matt remarked authoritatively. "Was milk sick an' we had to put it out of its misery."

"'Tis admiration, no more!" Brian challenged, his

belligerence mellowing as he cast a sheepish grin at Jocelyn. "There's no harm in admiring beauty; be it a golden sunset or a honey-haired maiden with cherry-ripe lips."

"Ho, Alaric, we'd best find young Brian a warm and willin' tavern wench or we'll all be lost!"

"Fear not, milady," her abductor rumbled huskily in her ear. "We'll hog-tie the young buck if he becomes bothersome."

Jocelyn smiled at Brian, the result turning his white skin a bright scarlet which clashed with his pale hair. "The young man has given me no reason to fear him, sir. If anything, I am flattered by his attentions."

"One would think it was attention enough to have two noble grooms plying for your hand, much less a peach-faced lad." Something in Alaric's tone drew Jocelyn's attention to his face in time to see him master the scowl that had flashed across it. However, like his expression, his voice, too, was quickly altered. "It is unseemly to encourage our good fellow, however innocent your remark was intended to be."

By noon, conversation had dwindled. They had kept more to the fields and forests than the roads to avoid any search parties, for Lord Rhys would have had time to contact his vassals to demand help in the search for his abducted bride. Although they stopped from time to time to drink the water they'd brought along, the ale house which appeared at the intersection of two deeply rutted roads was a welcome sight. It was an unspoken, but unanimous decision that they stop.

Jocelyn stared up at the dried bush tied to the end of a long pole extending from the roof as they approached, realizing for the first time how appropriate the symbol was. Her throat was parched and mouth full of grit from the cross-country travel, so that when the horses were tied at the hitching rail in front of the wattle and mud building, she was as eager as her companions to sample its ale.

Settling in the corner on a rough-hewn bench worn smooth by the establishment's clientele, she waited timidly while Alaric spoke to the owner. She'd never been inside such a place before. When they journeyed, her father was never at a loss for an acquaintance upon which to depend for hospitality. Bedford was so well-known for its own, that its lord and his family were welcome anywhere in Jocelyn's limited sphere of travel.

When they were forced to stop at a roadside tavern, Jocelyn always remained in the shade of the trees outside while a servant fetched their refreshment, for Sir Randolf would not have his daughter exposed to the ne'er-do-wells known to frequent the alehouses.

The very idea had not set well with the spirited girl. After all, she had seen men of the clergy venture in to the alleged dens of iniquity. What was good company for a man of the cloth seemed good enough for a lady of quality. Her argument, however, fell on deaf ears.

She'd seen better looking roadside houses in her day, some two-story. Hence she could only assume that the interior of this particular one was, thankfully, not indicative of all. There was a kitchen attached to the back where the owner and his wife evidently lived, and it was from that that they emerged when the dusty group of travelers entered. Smoke drifted in through the same door, telling of fat burning on a hearth with a poorly crafted vent. Once her eyes were adjusted to the inside lighting, provided by two open windows on either side with deerskin flaps for curtains, she could see the haze which hung in the air and assaulted their noses.

Alaric flipped a handful of coins on the trestled plank which served as their table, igniting a greedy light in the eyes of the woman who slapped down a pitcher of ale with one hand and a stack of wooden cups in the other.

She gathered the coins up and dropped them into an ample bosom so quickly, Jocelyn thought it was some sleight-of-hand trick. The money taken care of, she lingered, staring outright at the girl next to the tall dark wayfarer with the sword.

"Got a name, pretty?"

"Jo . . ."

"Josephine," Alaric put in. He put an arm about Jocelyn and squeezed her tightly. "My wife and to be mother of my son some months from now."

Jocelyn was so startled by the smooth lie, she could only stare at Alaric, mouth agape.

"Now don't blush so, love. We're married right and proper."

The woman grabbed Jocelyn's hand as fast as she had the money and dropped it back on the table. "Seems she's spent more time abed than at work," she snorted, making a piglike sound in the back of her throat that resembled disdain.

"She was hairdresser for the Duchess of Huntingdon," Alaric admitted, taking up the abandoned hand in his own. "Talented fingers, these." He nodded toward the end of the table. "Don't forget my good companions. I promised them a pitcher of ale if they rode with us this far. Can't take too many chances with the villains about on the roads these days, especially in my lady's condition."

"I ain't forgot." The woman lifted a soot-smeared brow. "So ye ain't together, eh?"

"Just for the morning, I fear. We part at this good place."

"Well, keep yer eyes out for the sheriff's men. They'd like as not find yer wife entertainin', babe in the belly or nay."

Jocelyn inadvertently moved closer to Alaric, grateful for the reassurance of the arm about her. With both hands she grasped the cup of ale he poured and took a swallow. It was wet, but that was all that could be said for it. A more bitter fermentation had never passed her lips. Good manners forbade her from spitting it out, but she could not help the shuddering grimace that overtook her. Somewhere between her throat and her stomach, it began to tickle, resulting in a rebellious sneeze. Her eyes watering, she hurriedly dabbed her nose and mouth where the ale had somehow escaped.

"Faith, that sickness of the morning has spread till noon!" Alaric declared, shaking her in feigned concerned. "Are you all right, love?"

Jocelyn's only answer was a stout stomp of her slippered foot on his booted instep. A flicker of a wince was all the response she got, masked by a wide smile. "I've tasted sweeter vinegar!" she managed in a strangled voice.

"'Twill cost more, but my wife's got fresh bread in the back. It might settle the little woman's stomach." The round shouldered husband came around the single board which served to divide the room from the kegs, carrying a worn chair of solid oak with a rush seat. "But this won't cost a pence more and will no doubt be more comfortable for the lady." He placed it at the end of the table. "Made it meself."

"I don't think I could stomach any food right now, but thank you kindly for the chair."

If the ale was so vile, it was hard to tell what manner of vermin she might find baked, or worse yet, still crawling in the bread. She pushed her aside and took the offered seat, so as not to insult the tavern keeper altogether. "I'll have water when we leave," she whispered to Alaric after the man returned to his station near the door.

The men proved to have sturdier dispositions than Jocelyn and finished three pitchers between them. Thus restored, they began to poke fun at Brian, in whom the proprietess had taken a motherly interest. "I've a girl that works 'ere with all her teeth," she told him, brandishing a smile quite the contrary. "Pickin' wild berries she is now, but she'll be back soon. She's got a likin' for fair lads, she does. Like as not, she'd show you an afternoon you'd never forget."

"S'long as his coin won't bend, ye mean," her husband pointed out.

"Or anythin' else for that matter." The woman laughed coarsely.

It wasn't decent to even acknowledge she understood the undercurrents of what was being suggested, but Jocelyn could feel her embarrassment burning from head to toe. She turned to look out the window, where a scrawny dog roused from its afternoon nap and trotted out, tail wagging to greet an obvious acquaintance. Wondering if it was the girl with more teeth than morals, she peeked around the rough casing to see who the newcomer was.

It was a girl all right, and following in her wake, like toms after a female cat, were soldiers, a dozen bearing the markings of Huntingdon. Jocelyn's breath caught in her throat. The Duke was a vassal to Rhys of Atworth and wed to the overlord's sister. A warning was on the tip of her tongue when Alaric seized her arm and literally lifted her off her chair.

"It's them!" the heavyset proprietess shouted at the top of her voice, planting herself in the doorway. "It's the missin' bride!"

"To your horses!"

Alaric's command clashed with the sound of drawing swords, metal against studded leather. One hand still locked about Jocelyn's arm, he pushed the screaming woman out of the way with the hilt of his blade and stepped into the sunlight. The sound of galloping horses and rattling mail was upon them before they'd taken a step toward the rail where Jack Frost and the other steeds awaited them. She barely caught a glimpse of the barricade of men before she was shoved back inside.

"If they'll take us," Alaric growled, hurling her into the corner, "then they'll have to come in and get us."

Come in they did and two at a time. It reminded Jocelyn of a bizarre dance, for each of Alaric's men waited his turn to pair off before engaging his sword. The angry clanging of metal filled the room, driving the man who had stood near the kegs into the back. When she had been abducted, Jocelyn had had little opportunity to judge the merit of Alaric's men. Huddled in the corner as she was this time, however, she could well guess the reason for the ease of their earlier escape.

They were more than a match for Huntingdon's men, but the latter outnumbered them two to one. As the last of the previously mounted men stormed into the room, the fray increased to a bloodcurdling echo of shouts, clashes of metal, and breaking wood. Taking four at one time, Alaric and John charged the mail-clad men with a table, mowing them down with it before tossing it aside and making quick work of their enemies.

The blood that stained the flawless steel of their swords brought home the fierceness of their situation. This was no tourney played by rules, but a blood battle between mercenaries. No quarter would be granted the losers. Yet there was a raw excitement about it that made her heart pound, more so than her fear, and forced adrenaline into her racing blood. Damn them all, she'd not be taken by Atworth, no matter what fate awaited her with Alaric's lord!

In the corner of her eye, she spied the shriveled innkeeper making his way along the wall, a large kitchen knife brandished as he approached Alaric's back. The young warrior, his sword locked hilt to hilt with his opponent's, struggled, unaware of the danger behind him. Jocelyn seized the sturdy chair the man had given her earlier and, with a shrill yell, charged him with it, its rough-hewn legs first. So startled was the deceitful soul that he stood transfixed by the sight of the delicate figure wielding a chair at him until he found himself pinned against the wall.

"Drop it or I'll run you through!" Jocelyn pushed the leg of the chair harder into the man's thin ribs, and the knife clattered to the floor. "Now flee before I change my mind!" she shouted, easing it away until he had enough room to slither past and stumble out through the back kitchen.

Intoxicated with her first victory, she turned to where Alaric, his face beaded with perspiration, went down to his knees on the earthen floor at the same time as his well-matched adversary. Without thought to the danger of the crossed swords slipping, Jocelyn rushed in and brought the chair down over the soldier's head, lodging it, cagelike, between the spindles.

"Damn it, woman, get back!" Alaric barked at her hoarsely, slinging her aside as he lunged forward to drive the blade into the neck of the man.

Jocelyn caught herself against the wall, her eyes glued to the spurt of blood which burst forth as he withdrew his sword and charged on to help a weaponless Brian, who was now using a bench to thwart the malevolent blows of steel from cutting his slender form in half. God in heaven, how could one body spill so much, she thought, swallowing the nausea which rose from her chest.

"Get her to the horses!"

The words were no sooner spoken than Jocelyn looked up to see John shoving her ahead of him toward the door. But for his strong arm, she would have tripped over the body of a fallen soldier. Instead, John all but lifted her off the ground and propelled her outside into the blinding sunlight.

Jocelyn blinked in an effort to focus when the crack of wood against flesh resounded behind her. She glanced over her shoulder in time to see John reach for the back of his head where the tavern keeper's wife had struck him with a chunk of wood, then turn on the woman with a wounded roar. However, the loud whinnying of the horses drew her attention from the brawl to the post, where the tavern girl was untying the reins in an attempt to scatter the animals.

"Oh no you don't!"

It seemed a natural thing to do, this running leap which carried Jocelyn into the girl full tilt. She'd never fought a day in her life, but the painful tug of her braid told her a like handful of hair was as good a place to start as any.

"Let go or I'll knock your bloody teeth out!" she shrieked, her bold threat losing its bite as the wiry wench threw her over with a knee to her abdomen, knocking the wind from her soundly. Jocelyn saw the fist coming at her face and, helpless to move away, raised her arm to take the blow.

"I ain't kept 'em this long, takin' nothing from the likes of you, bitch!"

In desperation, Jocelyn swung her other hand, landing her palm against her opponent's cheek with a loud slap.

"Ooh, ain't we a priss!"

To her dismay, instead of being daunted, the tavern wench was only angered further. Ragged nails dug into the flesh of her chest as they latched onto her bodice. Arms failing, Jocelyn was lifted off the ground and slammed back, her head striking the hard, dried ground with a heavy thud. Certain her skull had split, she reached behind her as she was lifted again. The sound of her dress tearing cut through the thunder of her pain as she discovered the hard object she had hit. The second time she struck the ground, she seized the stone, so that when the full display of stained and yellow teeth above her face curled into a snarl and she was snatched up again, she slammed the stone against the girl's face with her fist.

Her adversary fell away, screaming like one of Gwenith's legendary banshees. Clutching hand to her mouth, she wailed, "My teeth! The bitch is knocked my teeth loose! Gawd, I'm bleedin' to death!"

Jocelyn crawled to her feet and staggered back, catching herself on the hitching post. "I . . . told you!" she admonished breathlessly.

"Ho, we've a scrapper amongst us!" one of the men running for the loose horses shouted.

Jocelyn looked up, a victorious smile on her lips, when she was startled by the arm which hooked around her waist and hauled her up effortlessly. Thinking the wailing tavern girl was out to avenge her broken teeth, she let go, swinging ferociously in the air.

"Mercy, milady, 'tis none but your sworn protector!"

"Where were you a few moments ago, you braying ass!" Jocelyn spat, too spent to protest further as she was hastily swung up into the saddle.

"It seemed John needed me more than you," Alaric chuckled in her ear as he settled in behind her.

Jocelyn slammed against Alaric when Jack Frost leapt forward at his command, and lay there, eyes shut, drawing courage and strength from his closeness. They'd made it! she thought gratefully. She hurriedly looked about them, counting the heads of the riders with them. *Four, five, six . . .* all of them. She leaned back into her companion in relief.

"Did you kill them all?"

How could it feel so safe in the arms of a man who

had just freely spilled blood with his fierce blade? Somehow Jocelyn could not find it in herself to be repulsed, in spite of what she'd seen. It was a case of them or the soldiers winning. There had been no choice, she reasoned in Alaric's defense. For whatever reason, he was her protector, and the idea was becoming more tolerable all the time.

It was so light, she never felt the sympathetic brush of Alaric's lips on the top of her head, but she heard the wry answer which set the others to laughing and hooting like drunkards with more ale than sense.

"Only those who would not take nay for an answer, milady."

Chapter Four

Sir Randolph of Bedford was dead; robbed and murdered in his sleep at Langley Cross, if the account was to be believed. The news arrived the following morning after a night of celebrating their narrow escape from Huntingdon's men, in which Jocelyn had participated. All were stunned at first, then shock began to thaw into a lust for revenge, as they'd travel on to safer, private lodgings of an old comrade from the Holy War.

Alaric was entranced by the small figure which turned in a swirl of skirts and proceeded to pace back and forth at the foot of the pallet in a small chamber provided by Jacob Emry, a brewer and generous friend to the errant band. Alaric feared she'd collapse in tears, but the last two days should have told him otherwise. Her anger he could deal with. Tears and hurt were harder to ignore, especially those spilling from eyes the hue of which fell between the rich color of wood moss and the bright fire of emeralds. To think how she'd belittled her looks in her letters as having simple green eyes and plain brown hair, when regal gold highlighted them both like sunfire.

"Langley Cross is much closer to Bedford than Atworth, as you now well know, sir. Hence, the dowry is likely at Bedford, waiting for Lord Rhys to flaunt in my face upon my surrender," she fumed, stopping before the window and staring out as if to seek more light on the matter. Angrily she kicked the wall. "Well, damn his odious soul to hell, where he can wait until it freezes, it will not happen! Two can play at this game of treachery!"

"He is a dangerous man to cross, as you and your father have already been sad witness to, milady," Alaric cautioned.

"Every Wednesday, our baker sends a cart to the mill to have our flour ground fresh for the week ... claims it keeps the vermin down in the bread." Jocelyn brushed the inconsequential comment aside with a wave of her hand. "It's brought back on a cart along with fresh rushes for the floors and straw for the beds. If we were at the miller's tomorrow morning, we could steal into the bailey in the cart. I vow our driver Ham is bone loyal and would deliver us unseen into the tower where the private rooms are. The dowry must be in one of those, my own chamber perhaps."

"And how will we get out, milady?" Alaric inquired skeptically. On second thought, perhaps if he encouraged her to come out with her daring plan, which he had no intention of following, it might prove balming to the wounds which now were masked behind a mad hunger for revenge.

"We take Rhys hostage!" Jocelyn informed him, as though it meant no more risk than walking up to a lady to ask her for the pleasure of a dance about the Maypole.

"Aye, he's likely to warm to that right off!"

Jocelyn's gaze flashed fiery at his dour comment. "Make fun of me, if you wish, sir, but I've seen you and your men fight. They are amply able to take the few men at arms that remain at his lordship's disposal. You heard yourself yesterday: the main of his troops is out combing the hillsides for us. We can seize Rhys *and* Bedford," she declared with certainty, "and seal it up within its walls until the King arrives to hear of Rhys' treachery. We've a dungeon that is too good for his likes, but 'twill suffice, and all my father's servants will heel to me."

"And what will you tell the King of the overlord? That he handed over your dowry to you per the letter of royal instruction and insisted you marry him in return for ransoming your betrothed in order to meet the terms?" Alaric laughed humorlessly. "The King's already on a journey to Bedford to endorse your marriage, not punish his overlord. 'Tis well-known a widow or unwed heiress is a bane to His Majesty to find husband for. He will likely thank Atworth for saving him the quandary."

"He blackmailed me and killed my father!" Jocelyn averred hotly. "Besides, I was promised to wed Phillip."

"*Thieves* killed your father, milady. There are no witnesses to the contrary," he reminded her. "Your betrothed, as far as His Majesty is concerned, could be dead, for all Edward knows . . . and who is to say the King will lend an ear to a lady turned outlaw? There is no one to testify to the truth of things except yourself."

"Gwenith and some of the servants knew!"

"I am certain His Royal Majesty will heed the word of your nanny and servants!"

Alaric didn't want to be cruel, but he had to make her see the absolutely folly of her plans. Wrong would be righted, just as soon as his lord was able to reach them. He expected him any day, for the stalwart warrior was not about to let a wounded leg keep him from Jocelyn and her dire straits for long.

Somehow, though, he was far from feeling good about the quandary his words evoked on Jocelyn's face. Such emotions as he'd never seen battled fiercely for supremacy, more than a gentle maid should have to bear. Anger was losing, its fire doused by the tears of despair that spilled over cheeks kissed by the sun of the last two days' journey. Inside, he knew the same in sympathy, although his anger at his helplessness to assuage her nearly left him trembling in frustration over what now was a foolish, but nonetheless binding, oath.

"Oh, Alaric," she sniffed, her proud manner crumbling under the weight of the overwhelming odds pitted against her. "What am I to do?"

"Trust in me, milady."

The irony of his plea left a bitter taste in his mouth. He would not move toward her, not trusting himself to offer his comfort, when he wanted so much to do just that. Instead, it was she who came to him, her steps hastening so that he had to brace for the impact as she threw herself into his arms, clinging desperately.

"I have no one to turn to but you and your men. Surely you must see that!" Her cheeks were hot and wet against the flesh revealed by the opening in his shirt. She nuzzled the lightly furred surface with her nose, distorting her speech as much as her cries. "Oh would that I were dead, too, to be spared this agony!"

"Shush, milady, do not say such things."

Alaric ran his fingers through her hair to move away

that which had fallen in her face, but as he did so, she raised her plaintive gaze to him. That alone, he might have withstood, but when she spoke, his last lingering reserve melted with her tears.

"Hold me, Alaric. Make this go away with sweet words and your tender touch."

"Milady . . ." His protest as she pulled away and unfastened her belt grew hoarse with the desire that surged through him. "I don't . . ."

"You deny me your identity and that of your lord. You deny me your help. Will you deny me this also, Alaric?"

The surcoat, or gown, seemed to lift over her head and slip to the floor as if unseen hands had removed it for him. His eyes were drawn to the delicate fingers that gently tugged at the bow securing the gathered neckline above her kirtle. There was some sort of bordering embroidery, yet it was only the fullness of unbound breasts, peaks straining against the thin linen, that he saw. As the ribbon unraveled, he felt himself suffering the same fate.

Suddenly Jocelyn looked at him. With hesitant step, she approached him, her bewildered and bewitching gaze fixed on his. "I would feel your comforting warmth, Alaric," she whispered shakily, "without this."

She will stop, he thought, knowing better than to help her with the troublesome belt at his waist and the shirt which finally gave way from his shoulders to hang about his neck. Too short to lift it over his head, she drew him down with it, his face to hers until the task was made easier. Were fire set to his feet, Alaric could not have moved but to her will. The garment took him to the edge of the pallet and there brought him to his knees along with its mistress.

Then it was gone, tossed aside by the same hands which now plowed their fingers through his chest hair and attempted to cover the padded muscle surrounding nipples which had grown taut with passion. A practiced courtesan could work no stronger spell, he thought above the clamor of sensations assaulting his brain from her instinctive exploration.

"Jocelyn!" He'd meant it as a reprimand, but her name came out as a plea.

"Here, my lord," she answered breathlessly, "and much in need of your embrace." The searing touch of her soft and yielding body pressed against his was beyond denial. "Hold me, my heart, and soothe me with a kiss, for there is no tomorrow for us."

The truth had never been more plainly declared. There was no tomorrow for them, which made the urgency of the night more desperate than ever. Alaric knew there should not even be that, but there was no longer place for reason within him. There was only a gnawing, aching hunger which had been seeded with innocent letters and gone unappeased too long these last days.

"Faith, but you are an enchantress!" he whispered in surrender, easing her against the mattress.

The soft rustling of the fluffed straw blended with her sigh as he covered her mouth and body with his own. Careful to spare her his weight, Alaric fitted himself into the instinctive bed she made for him with her lower body, his hand pulling urgently at the frayed hem of her only remaining garment. Her slender legs, sculpted to perfection, were as satiny as the rest of her and quivered beneath his masterful caresses until they embraced him to seek respite.

He ground his manhood hard against the tufted mound at the apex of her thighs and sought her lips with his in equal fervor. It was only the thickness of his trousers that saved him as he backed away to make her ready for that which she now so desperately craved. He could no more refuse her than he could the ragged breaths which tortured his chest . . . but he would give her more pleasure first.

His lips wet from the plunder of the kiss she'd begged for, he shifted his attention to the breasts which were now displayed in all their glory above the loosened neckline of her shift. As he seized one of the shadowed peaks in his teeth and flayed it mercilessly with his tongue, he felt her shudder beneath him and heard her ecstatic gasp, both fueling the fire in his loins which threatened to break free at any moment.

Here was female to fill the wildest imaginings of any man, with harlot's blood in a chaste and beauteous body capable of meeting fire with fire. To know her completely, to feel her tremulous responses from within . . .

"My heart, I can not stand this hunger much longer!" Tears and grief filled her imploring voice no more, supplanted by hot and unadulterated desire.

Alaric tore away from her, spurred by his own urgency, and made quick work of the laces of his trousers. With one fluid movement, he shoved them down about his sturdy thighs, freeing the throbbing member which instantly hailed her attention. Her gaze widened, not with fright, but with admiration. With a lingering caress which took amazing temperance on his part, he traced the insides of her bare thighs to their down-furred juncture, discovering the moist invitation which confirmed her plea.

"Now, Alaric, or I shall die!"

Alaric caught the hands that reached for that alone which would appease her and wrestled them gently but firmly over her head, forcing them against the coarse linen as he poised, trembling at the brink of paradise. With a swift and sure thrust, he lanced her innocence and claimed her with his all. Much as he needed to bombard her again and again, like a battering ram to a gate, he remained still so that unaccustomed muscles might adjust to this new possession. He gazed down at her and was troubled to see a glaze had returned to the eyes that looked up at him.

"I've hurt you!"

Jocelyn grasped his naked buttocks, her fingers digging into the hard flesh. "Nay, milord. I am overwhelmed by your tenderness. You are all I have dreamed of and more! I beg your patience with this girlish sentimentality."

"Then dream on, milady, and I shall do my utmost to fulfill your musings."

Yet Jocelyn could imagine no more. Her lover's ministrations resumed with a renewed vigor. If the letter to the king she'd found last night after Alaric had fallen asleep under the influence of their host's ale—the letter bearing Inglenook's seal—was not enough to convince her that Alaric was really Phillip, his lovemaking was. He worshipped her body as he had worshipped her heart before. Her body shook as if it might come apart, so much that she was forced to cling tightly with her limbs to the lean one so thoroughly occupying it to avoid such a calamity.

She thought she knew the meaning of the word until the teasing gave way to outright assault, robbing her of breath and jarring her with carnal pleasure. Though Alaric possessed her, he acted possessed, his eyes no longer feasting on her face, her breasts, but closed tightly, as if he too were struggling to keep from losing himself to the wild currents carrying them away. When he finally lost the fight, however, he did not suffer the convulsing, rapturous surrender alone. So consuming was the tumultous tide that Jocelyn had to cover her mouth with the back of her wrist to keep from crying out for help and, at the same time, in wanton bliss.

The stillness of the room was broken only by the sound of their combined breathing as some semblance of normalcy was gradually assembled. Jocelyn still held

Alaric, reveling in the contented union of their bodies, her mind still reeling in passion's sweet aftermath. If she drew her last breath tomorrow, which was likely, she at least had known love's fulfillment in its most spiritual and physical sense. She combed back Alaric's dark, damp hair with her fingers, lifting his head to reveal his handsome features.

"I love you, milord, with all my body and soul."

A scowl knitted the noble brow above her face. "I am not your lord, milady," he ground out through clenched teeth. "May God forgive me, for I can not forgive myself this treachery."

The icy contempt which assailed her was as chilling as the sudden withdrawal he made from her. As if it insulted his gaze to rest upon her, he concentrated on the fastenings of his breeches, which covered him once again. Feeling as though she too were shamefully exposed, Jocelyn hastily rearranged her shift in confusion.

"Alaric . . ."

Alaric stepped away from the bed. "Don't try to tempt me further, Jocelyn. My need is well met. 'Tis only a wife who deserves the affection you women seek after bedding. I myself am in need of a good drink and a night's rest, which this room is not likely to afford."

"You wanted me, Alaric!" Jocelyn argued, her cheeks flaming with the cruel slap his cynical speech delivered. "The blame is not solely mine as you try to make it."

"Aye, milady, I did, but you will have to find one of the others who are stirred by your beauty to satisfy you hence, for I will not wallow in shame further to aid you in betraying your betrothed."

Jocelyn inhaled sharply at the spiteful blow. She would have had her voice hurl her denouncement with more force, but his had robbed her of it. "Damn you, sir! How . . . how could you?"

"Milady, I ask myself that very question." He fastened his belt in a rough jerking motion that betrayed the bitter anger simmering within, and leveled his accusing gaze at her. "You've had your sport. I trust you will sleep well." With a mocking nod, he pivoted and made for the door. "Good night, milady."

Her earlier certainty that this had been the man she loved disintegrated with the cold click of the latch. Humiliation and disbelief gradually thawed into hurt and rage as Jocelyn stared at the closed door, outlined by the light from the outer room. How dare he! It was he who first suggested she take a man of the flesh, rather than the one of her letters, not she. He could have walked away from her, but he didn't. He'd wanted her as much as she wanted him . . . *needed him,* not just for the physical love but for the affection and comfort he so coldly disdained afterward.

If he were Phillip, she'd not forgive him this. Anyone who would deny his evident attraction to her would deny his identity with just as little conscience. Perhaps he took advantage of her weakness to test her, she thought, to see if she would betray him for another. Jocelyn closed her eyes in despair. If that were the case, she had failed miserably.

But she would have sworn Alaric had written those letters! His expressions, his devotion, even his lovemaking smacked of the same man. And there was the sealed letter to the King in his sack, she thought, confounded to the point of tears. If Alaric was indeed the vassal of some unknown lord, rather than her betrothed, then she was truly alone and vulnerable to God knew what fate. Phillip had gotten himself kidnapped, her father had been murdered by Atworth, and now Alaric had turned against her.

Jocelyn threw herself against the mattress to muffle the tortured sob which escaped her chest. She'd sooner die of suffocation than have her brutal lover hear her.

Damn men all to hell, there was nothing else to do but cry . . . and that made her furious!

The straw from the mattress was scattered about the room by the time she'd taken out her grief and despair on it. Although her eyes were red and swollen, a glitter of new resolve reflected in them in the pale moonlight that flooded the room as Jocelyn, now fully dressed, opened the shutters fully. She'd exhausted all but one of her emotions, and that one had opened her mind to the only other alternative left her. She'd carry out her plan alone. Of all people, she could get close enough to Rhys to bury a dagger in his heart and avenge her father's murder.

Shoving thoughts of Lord Randolf aside before her grief swelled again, Jocelyn dressed, then pulled herself up onto the high window ledge and swung her legs through it. Upon dropping to the ground on the other side, she glanced back once more, her courage wavering. No, she chided herself sternly. If Alaric was Phillip, then the note she cut into the floor with his shaving blade would force him out of his disguise to come to her aid, for he surely would not leave her to fight his battle against Rhys alone, no matter what personal contempt she'd earned. 'Twould be an insult to his chivalrous nature to let a woman right his wrong for him. And if he truly was not her betrothed, then better she die and be done with all her problems.

Chapter Five

It was a good day for grinding. The breeze from the west caught the patched canvas blades of the windmill and turned them laboriously while the inner works squeaked and groaned in protest. The miller and his help, dusted white, went about their individual tasks in the tall narrow building supported on raised legs in order to use nature's power to its fullest advantage. Shrubs which had been allowed to grow wild in the shelter beneath were a grayish green, resulting from the residue which sifted down through the plank floors above them. There Jocelyn huddled behind the narrow ladder leading to the open door of the first level, where sacks of ground flour waited to be carried down to wagons bound for the different parts of Bedford's land.

She was exhausted from her journey, in spite of the horse she'd stolen from Jacob Emry's barn. It was the smallest of the lot, a nondescript brown mare belonging to Brian, and the only one which she could hoist herself up on. But for its sound training, she'd have had to chase it half the way to her destination. As it was, the beast stood patiently while she tugged unmercifully on its mane and crawled up on its back clumsily with the added boost from a fallen tree some distance from the brewer's home.

Hair tucked in the back of her dress so that it would appear short, at least at a distance, Jocelyn wandered in what she thought was the general direction of Bedford, keeping to the crisscross of fields instead of intimidating forests, for fear of coming upon worse brigands than she had left behind. In the first light of day, she happened upon some peasants beginning their day's work. With her best mimicry of Gwenith's speech, she conjured a story about her parents' death, which required her to seek out relatives on Lord Randolf's estate with the only animal she'd kept from their farmstead.

It wasn't hard to convince them. Her eyes were still red from her crying and sunken from lack of sleep, and her clothing was plain enough for a commoner. Hence, the charade gathered sufficient sympathy for a half a loaf of bread and adequate instructions to her father's lands on lesser traveled roads. Peasants in all fiefs understood the danger of a comely wench alone on roads frequented by his lordship's soldiers.

Her stomach no longer growled in hunger, and she was too tired to even feel the pain of her father's loss or the indelibly etched sting of Alaric's harsh rejection of her. She'd confessed her plight in brief to the miller, a longtime and faithful servant of Lord Randolf, as well as her plan. Although he tried to dissuade her, neither he, nor any of his men, rose to her challenge to accompany her, much less go in her stead. Instead, he hid her below to wait for the wagon from Bedford's hall and gave her a blanket with which to fend off the chill she'd taken during her nocturnal travel.

Eventually the grinding of the millwheels, the creaking of the works, and the flutter of the canvas blades became as soothing to her frayed nerves as the warm blanket. Feeling more lost and alone than ever, she drifted into a troubled sleep that was interrupted with the first cart that approached with wheat to be ground for the miller. Head nodding as she eavesdropped on the bright morning conversation, she slipped away again into slumber until another disturbance not in keeping with the general noise of the mill pulled her back.

When the two-wheeled cart from the lord's manor pulled up, Jocelyn had to shake the dullness imposed by her catnapping to convince the driver to help her. Like the miller and his men, Ham was reluctant, but he at least agreed to steal her into the inner bailey after hearing of Lord Randolf's brutal murder.

"I tell ye, m'lady, ye'd best hightail it to London fast as that nag can carry ye and pray ye meet the King 'imself. I'd sooner face a cornered wolf than Lord Atworth. E's mean-livered, I tell ye. Ain't 'ardly a wench in the castle, upstairs or down, he or his men ain't took their pleasure with, with or without the laidees consent, if ye get me meanin'. Half is fled into the fields, sooner then face 'im."

Jocelyn's stomach turned at the sickening news. "Gwenith too?"

The man looked away, his face wrinkled as he observed the rising sun. "Old Gwenith's a story in 'erself! Onlyest thing he's done to her is locked her in your chamber and held back her food till she tells 'im who made off with ye." He glanced back at Jocelyn curiously. "Who *did* make off with ye, milady, if ye don't mind me askin'."

To her dismay, pain welled fresh in her eyes and voice. "A scoundrel with no heart!" she averred, wiping tears away with her sleeve with a silent oath.

" 'Tis not so, milady."

Jocelyn paled at the sound of Alaric's voice. She'd been gone so long, she thought certain he'd no longer cared what she did. From his face, she still was not certain she had gained anything but more annoyance.

"That's him, Ham! For the love of God, keep him

away!" Jocelyn backed to the ladder, which offered the only retreat, but stopped at Alaric's challenge.

"Would you have me harm this innocent man first, Jocelyn, or hear my apology now?"

Her gaze flew to the young man whose hand rested on the hilt of his sword. In truth, it appeared as though the night had robbed him of sleep after all, for he looked no better than she felt. Yet his eyes were very much alive and filled, not with anger, but appeal. Her heart tripped in her chest. Dare she believe the man who had so cruelly rejected her had come about to ask her pardon?

"I would prefer to confess to you in private, but if you'd have this good fellow's ears hear me out as well, so be it."

"No!" Jocelyn felt color return to her cheeks in more profusion than she thought possible. "That is . . ."

"If ye wish, m'lady, ye can step up in here. If 'e means ye harm, I can promise 'e'll not leave this spot," the miller declared from the doorway at the top of the ladder. "Me 'n' the lads'll see to that."

Eyes that rivaled the bright azure of the sky moved to her expectantly. "Well, milady? Your knights have rallied admirably to insure your safety," he pointed out wryly. "We are all at your disposal."

With a stiff nod, Jocelyn turned and started up the narrow ladder. The climb was steep, complicated by the skirts which became entangled in her feet. Once she gasped as she nearly lost her balance, only to feel Alaric press reassuringly against her.

"I'm here, milady. I'll not let you fall after chasing you all night across the shire."

Jocelyn nearly missed the next step as she felt his warm breath at the small of her back in the lightest pressure, as if he had kissed her there. Damn him and his silvered words and actions! Much as she yearned to hear them, she had good cause to remain aloof. Never had she suffered at anyone's treatment of her as she had his. And never did she want to forgive them as much, either, she realized as the miller grabbed her hand in his calloused one and hauled her into the shelter of the first floor of the mill.

Making her way to the other side, as if seeking support from the bags of fresh-ground grain stacked there, she turned to see Alaric step inside. They waited in silence, eyes locked, as the miller and his helpers obligingly made their exit. When they were out of earshot, Alaric reached behind him to close the door, but Jocelyn objected. "Leave it open!"

With reluctance, he heeded her demand. "I vow you've nothing to fear from me, milady."

"But your wounding scorn."

"God's breath, would that I could take that back—nay, swallow it with my dying breath rather than see you smitten with it!"

"You deny your anger?" she challenged skeptically.

"Nay, milady, but 'twas at myself, *not you*. At my own weakness of flesh, not yours, which was born of just despair." Alaric stepped toward her and, taking her hand in his, dropped to his knees. "I took my anger out on an innocent who knew not the danger of the fire she kindled, and now I must beg her forgiveness." He brushed the back of her hand with his lips. "You, Jocelyn of Bedford, are the light of mine eyes and I can not suffer to see it dimmed by my own unworthiness."

Jocelyn never understood the folly of her like way of showing happiness and despair. Yet they were tears of joy which spilled on her cheeks as she, too, dropped to her knees. If she had not known before, she knew now that this *was* Phillip of Inglenook, without doubt. He referred to her often in writing as the *light of mine eyes*.

"You are my betrothed as I have believed all along, sir, even last night when you took me as your own."

Instead of the sweet kiss of mutual forgiveness she closed her eyes to exchange, Jocelyn was shocked as the hands which rested on her shoulders bit into her flesh and shook her roughly.

"For the love of God, Jocelyn, will you bury this notion in the past with all that has happened between us!" Alaric pleaded. He hardened the haze which blurred the bewildered face he adored before him. "You are sworn to another. You are not, *and never will be*, mine! Are you so thick-witted that you can not understand this? I am not Phillip of Inglenook! I am Alaric of Snowdonia, the second son of a noble struck down for fighting against His Majesty in the Welsh wars."

"Welsh?" Jocelyn echoed.

"Aye, *Welsh,*" he derided bitterly. "Unfit to spread the rush beneath the feet of an English gentlewoman, much less take her to wife. I am a heathen, a warrior without armor, of a nobility disdained by those of your blue blood."

"But . . . but you're so well . . ."

"Educated?" Alaric finished cryptically for her. "My years in the Holy Land gave me ample time to study and to lose the accent which earned only condescending looks among my English peers, save a few as noble of heart as of blood."

"But your name . . ."

"My mother was an English captive from earlier raids during Henry's reign. I am named for her father, a borderlord of little consequence. She loved my father, nonetheless."

"If he was but half the nobleman you are, sir, I can well see why," Jocelyn swore earnestly. Her eyes suddenly widened. "Is that it? Are you on a border raid, like your father? Is that why you've taken me?"

Alaric could not bear to see the hope springing into her eyes crushed, as his already was. He pulled her to him, hugging her tightly. "Nay, light of mine eyes, I have never lifted my sword against Edward or any English king. Contrary to what my late father and elder brother thought, 'twas not because I lacked in courage and skill, but that I could think beyond my Welsh temper."

He inhaled the scent of her hair, now lightly dusted with flour from her rest beneath the mill, rather than risk the affection of a chaste kiss at the crown of her head. With Jocelyn it was hard to think at all, beyond her sweetness and softness. "I know a losing battle when I see one, sweet Jocelyn. Like the success of Cymry independence, the winning of your hand is just as beyond my reach."

"So I am betrothed to another."

Jocelyn heard her words, but they were not as convincing as the declaration she had just heard . . . nor did she want them to be. How could she be so misled? It was possible that Phillip used the same term of endearment as Alaric, but it would not give her peace to accept it.

Peace, she reflected bitterly. Would she ever know it but in death? Death was all that would erase the memory of what had happened between her and her contrite and devoted Welshman. She wanted to tell him to fling her over his silver stallion and retreat to the high mountains with her as his captive, just as his father had his mother. It would absolve her conscience of her duty to continue to try to save Phillip of Inglenook . . . and then marry her promised lord, if she was successful.

Her father had died to carry out the agreement between the two houses, making it all the harder to disregard the responsibility for which she'd been groomed since birth: to become Sir Phillip's wife and mistress of their combined estates and bear his heirs. Much as it pained her, much as it tore her heart in two, Alaric was right. There was no future for them, not in this heartless world.

Jocelyn summoned her strength and hesitantly withdrew from Alaric's embrace. Her chin steeled against the rebellious emotions that welled within, she addressed him in a stilted voice. "Then we must right this wrong, Alaric of Snowdonia. Go with me to Bedford and help me strike down Lord Rhys. Give me at least that satisfaction."

She was mad—and so was he, Alaric thought as he nodded in agreement. Their infidelity had brought them to this. "I will go alone, milady. I can carry on with a clearer head without worrying for your safety," he insisted, overruling her objection with a raised tone before she could voice it. "Your presence could be my undoing." As if it had not been already, he mused despondently. "And success is our goal, is it not?"

Again, Jocelyn had to admit to the merit of Alaric's opinion. A well-seasoned soldier could do more harm to Rhys if not distracted by his concern for a woman. "Ham will have the cart ready for your escape with my dowry," she conceded flatly, fearing to let emotion of any sort infect her words lest it run away with her.

Alaric's mouth curled at her logical approach to her goal. She still believed he could execute it with little effort. Along with last night, that faithful look she gave him now would forever be ingrained in his memory. And for it, he would give his life, if need be. At least that would end the misery of facing life with her as Inglenook's bride, instead of his. He rose to his feet, lifting her with him.

"My men are in the wood beyond the clearing, waiting should there be trouble. I want you to return with them to Emry's house and wait for me there."

"Why don't you take John ... or Matt?"

"Because one man will draw less attention than two, especially if recognized as strangers."

Again he made sense, Jocelyn conceded grudgingly. She waited while he called to the men below from the open door, and she struggled to keep from running into his arms and abandoning all but him. But Alaric was too noble of heart to indulge her weakness again, and so she must be, she tried to convince herself.

The miller rushed up the ladder to assist her as Alaric handed her gently out to him. She dared not look up, for her control was slipping and her eyes burned with her heartbreak so that she could barely make out the worn rungs in front of her face. By the time she reached the bottom of the steep ladder, she'd blinked them away and masked her telltale sniffle with a cough as Alaric, skipping the last few rungs, dropped lightly down beside her.

He took her hand to his lips and made a courtly bow. "Your servant, milady." Intense blue held over bright green for a moment in time before he released her hand and climbed onto the wagon. "Toss me down your wares, miller. I've a dragon to slay for the lady as soon as this good man gets me on my way!"

"We've got to get the rushes, too," Ham reminded him, a skeptical appraisal narrowing eyes enfolded with the drooping flesh of old age.

"Then you'll have help for that as well, sir!"

All too quickly the bags of flour were exchanged for those of unground wheat to save waiting. Jocelyn rocked imperceptively on her feet, tugged by an overwhelming desire to leap into the cart with Alaric and tell Ham to ride west as far as the horse would take them. Yet she remained glued to the spot and watched as the cart stirred the dust on the road leading toward

Bedford's keep. With it went her heart, leaving in its place a void filled with unbearable pain.

It had to be, she told herself again as the cart disappeared over a gentle knoll. She owed it to Phillip to pursue his ransom, especially after betraying him. And she owed it to Alaric to be as brave as he in the face of fate's cruel twist.

"Milady, ye'd best take your horse and be gone before soldiers happen along. They've been thick about as fleas of late."

"God's speed," she whispered to Alaric before accepting the reins and the cupped hands offered to help her mount.

Jocelyn was too distracted to guide her horse, but it moved toward the glen as though it sensed its master's presence there. Brian hailed the animal as they broke into the cover of the trees and it snickered in answer. In a single bound the boy sprang to the horse's back and reached around Jocelyn for the reins.

"Excuse me, milady."

Jocelyn's lips quivered in an attempt at a smile but failed miserably. With a forlorn look, she met the gaze of each of the solemn men, accepting their silent reproval as her due and then focused straight ahead, where her tears no longer mattered. Brian was doing well enough, seeing them safely through the low-hanging branches.

Hardly a word was spoken as they took a route similar to the one Alaric had taken before. They stopped neither for food, nor drink, but took what little sustenance they'd hastily brought with them during brief pauses when nature demanded relief, for theirs was a long journey that had taken the bulk of two days before.

This time, it was not her legs and derriere which plagued her sore, but thoughts of Alaric. When they circled the pond where she had discovered he was not her appointed kidnapper, but another rogue, it had been all she could do to hold back the sobs which made her throat ache. She could still see him, his piercing blue eyes looking up at her, his arm extended for help. Even then she had not been able to leave him. Now that she had, she knew a wretchedness the likes of which she could not have imagined then.

Thankfully, from the edge of Bedford's land, they took a less circuitous route, avoiding the forest and brook where the bond between her and her handsome abductor had somehow formed without her even knowing it. Until then she had not known what it was like to long for a man as a woman. Flights of girlish fancy were more her experience. It was as though destiny had introduced them in another time and her body had suddenly remembered and come to life with the recollection.

Jack Frost awaited impatiently in the confines of the stable when they finally arrived at the brewer's late that night, for Alaric had wisely refused to take the easily identified stallion in his pursuit of her.

"Look at him stomping! I'll wager he's fit to run off, if Alaric hadn't taught him better," Brian commented as he slid off his plainer mount to help Jocelyn down. "I think I'll take him out for a few rounds about the cottage to calm him down, since he don't take to ale."

"Can I help?" She knew she was being foolish, but here was something tangible of Alaric, something he cared for, which made the stallion a treasure to her as well.

Brian grinned sheepishly. "Sure, milady. The walk'll probably loosen up your— That is, you'll not be as sore if you walk around a bit after a long ride."

While the others stabled and fed their mounts, Brian led Jack Frost out of the shed and into the moonlight. It was a beautiful horse, as noble as its owner. "What manner of breed is this, Brian?" Jocelyn asked, running her hand along the silken smoothness of the thick-muscled neck.

"An Arabian. Sir Phillip has its sire, though his is a darker—"

"Phillip?" Jocelyn exclaimed, her heart thudding to a halt within her bosom.

"Damn you lovestruck fool!" Matt bellowed behind her. "Ye've done it now!"

Jocelyn pivoted abruptly. "Phillip is your lord?" she demanded.

"Ye heard the loose-tongued idiot!"

"Then why in heaven's name are you not trying to help Alaric get his ransom?"

"Because he don't need it!" Matt's quick eyes touched on the face of every man who stood by. "Damn it, I ain't the one that let it out!"

"Well it's out, so you might as well tell me the rest of your story. I *am* to be Phillip's bride," Jocelyn reminded them tartly.

"Why don't we go in and have some ale—"

"Now, sir, if you please."

"Alaric and us rescued his lordship, but Phillip caught a sword in his thigh and wasn't able to ride with us to stop the weddin'."

"So he sent Alaric in his stead." By all that was holy, was all this for naught—her father's death, her sacrifice . . .

"We've been expectin' him any day now to catch up with us," Brian tried to console her.

"Why didn't he tell me?" Jocelyn cried out in frustration. "Why is he going into the lion's den for nothing?"

"Because Phillip gave strict orders not to let ye know anything, in case ye was part of the treachery."

"But I am not and you well know it! My father is

dead from trying to save a man who does not need salvation, and now Alaric—"

"Don't care about the risk no more, s'long as your ladyship is safe."

Jocelyn let the answer sink in, its implication chilling her indignation like an icy dagger plunged into her soul. He'd told her he knew a losing battle when he saw one, and yet had gone for no cause into Bedford except one . . . to die.

"You let him go, knowing the folly of it?" she cried, turning an accusing glare on the men.

"We follow orders, milady. We don't have to like 'em. Ours is to keep you here until your betrothed comes. We tried to talk him out of it, but Alaric made his own choice."

"He was going to Bedford *before* I spoke to him?"

"Whatever it took to get you back here, milady."

Jocelyn thought her knees would buckle with the weakness that swept through her. "We must go back! We can't let him walk into Rhys' hands!"

His patience expended, Matt shook his head. "No, ye're goin' inside and stayin' there till Sir Phillip comes."

"An' knowin' Alaric," John spoke up encouragingly, "he'll like as not make off with your dowry and Rhys' drawers before his lordship knows what's happened!"

The laughter John's comment generated relieved the tension in the air but fell short of offering Jocelyn reprieve. Alaric might make it, true, but if he didn't . . . With one of the brothers on either side of her, she went grudgingly into the cottage.

To her dismay, the plan forming in her mind to escape and go to Alaric's side was anticipated. Dew and Jeremy barricaded the window from the outside with some planks they found in the shed, so that, short of rousing the whole household, Jocelyn could not force her way out. She was not defeated yet, she mused stubbornly, as she took the place they left for her at the table later and ate cold stew and bread. There had to be another way out, and it was just a matter of time before she found it.

Chapter Six

Jocelyn was grateful that the brown mare she'd once again made off with had had a chance to rest and finish her grain before the opportunity of escape finally came. The idea struck the girl as she swept up the straw from the mattress she'd destroyed in anger the previous evening and stuffed it back into the linen sack. It was as thick as her body, when sufficiently fluffed, and would hide her beneath the linens if she hollowed out a place big enough.

It was a trick she'd played on Gwenith so many times, sending the poor woman into a tizzy when she discovered the child missing and the bed seemingly untouched. Of course, once fooled, the maid had gone along with Jocelyn's prank and pretended to fall for it again and again, causing the little girl beneath the covers to erupt in giggles that gave her away. It was a desperate act, true, but the time was right for just such.

Feigning a headache, she asked Brian to prepare her a cup of chamomile tea while she lay down to favor the malady. Then, taking the utmost care, she climbed into the hollow she made and pulled the straw around her, so that the linens lay flat on the plump mattress. She had to fool these men into thinking she'd somehow escaped so that they would leave the cottage to search for her. Then she could be on her way.

While it took forever for Brian to make her tea, and she had to endure the discomfort of the itchy straw, which pricked at her skin through the material of her dress and threatened to make her sneeze, the ordeal proved worth the wait. Upon returning, the poor boy had gone into a panic. Far from giggling, Jocelyn lay motionless and listened to the drum of footsteps as the men crowded into the room to search for her in disbelief. Then they were gone in an equal rush. She waited what seemed an eternity before she dared move, waiting for any sound which would betray a watchman who may have been left behind.

They were all out looking for her, however, and, certain that she could not have gotten far, were all on foot. After they left the barn—the first place searched—they spread out into the fields, calling her name alternately with swearing in frustration. When her blood thawed enough that her legs would serve her, she hastened to the shed and saddled the brown mare again. Perhaps her mission this time proved more motivating or her experience of the last few days had left her more limber. At any rate, she was able to vault into the saddle on the second try.

She had one chance of getting sufficient lead on Alaric's men, and that was to rob them of their horses. Borrowing from the tavern's wench's bag of tricks, she had untethered them before mounting her mare, but instead of running off, the damnable beasts stood contentedly as if still bound. Leaning over as far as she dared, she slapped Jack Frost soundly on his hindquarters and the spirited stallion did the rest. So desperate was the timid mare to escape his rearing and kicking, that she nearly unseated Jocelyn as she bolted off.

With only the thought of escape in mind, she turned the mare toward Bedford, the way familiar now, and gave the horse full rein, clinging to the saddle for her life with the leather reins woven in her white-knuckled fingers. Behind her, the outrage of the men filled the quiet country hush with the beating hoofs of their spooked mounts.

She had not let the mare rest since, until now. Lathered and frothing at the mouth, the poor beast stumbled toward the pond at the edge of Bedford to drink. Jocelyn let out the reins to allow it access to the water and petted its neck in sympathy.

"You've done well, old girl. But for the urgency of circumstances, I would never have pushed you so hard."

The urgency and the fact that she was frightened half out of her wits, especially after taking the wooded route which cut across Inglenook's land to Bedford. Even with the extra width of the road, which by design of the King's engineers afforded ample moonlight and lessened the likelihood of ambush from the ditches banking each side, the most unholy noises had chilled her to the bone.

Knowing better than to let the animal drink its fill, she tugged hard at the reins and drew it away from the pond. This time she hardly gave the location a second thought as she left it in her wake in the morning sunlight. Her thoughts were only of Alaric and what was now and in the future. There was no leeway for past recollections to cloud her thinking. There was only room for one emotion: love, a love that would not die until her last breath. If that were the fate she hastened toward, then so be it.

With luck, however, Alaric's skill would save him. That being the case, she had but to check at the miller's to hear of it, for whatever had happened would surely spread over the estate like the wind itself. Secrets were few on Bedford, despite its grand size. Jocelyn was distracted from her thoughts by the distant sound of running horses.

Her jailers, she wondered, kicking the mare's sides with her heels to increase its gait. It had to be. The sound was coming from the direction from which she'd just ridden. Taking to the same wooded path that Alaric had used to escape Bedford before, she did her best to parry the branches which lashed at her face and concentrated on keeping her seat. To her chagrin, her mare slowed to a jarring trot in fatigue, its nostrils flaring wildly with its heaving breaths.

"Please, girl, I cannot be taken now!"

She kicked the horse again, to no avail. The poor beast had run its course and would go no faster. Jocelyn slid off its back to the ground and broke off a switch. "If you cannot carry me away, then you can at least distract our pursuers," she averred, laying the switch to the horse and shooing it. It trotted off, unhurried to the east, while Jocelyn plunged into the undergrowth. She could walk to the mill from here.

When it appeared as though her plan had worked, she set out just inside the forest edge, for she knew now this was the same wood which bordered the miller's strip of land. Her face was scratched and her hair a frightful sight by the time she reached the glen where Alaric's men had awaited her the day before. Her appearance, however, could not daunt her elation at seeing the canvas sails of the mill churning dutifully against the spring sky. And then it plummeted just as quickly, for there was a mounted patrol of soldiers speaking to the miller.

Behind her, the loud snap of a branch brought home the fact that Alaric's men were close on her heels, in spite of her trick. The pitiful mare had probably stopped the moment she turned her back, Jocelyn thought dourly. She couldn't blame the horse. Even though she rode, her legs felt as if they would give way any moment from exhaustion.

"There! There she is!"

Jocelyn recognized Brian's high-pitched yell. Adrenaline surged through her veins as she considered her quandary. If she let Alaric's men take her and he had not escaped, all that mattered to her was lost. If her beloved had escaped and she was taken by Rhys' men, then he would not leave her to the overlord's mercy.

Her decision made, Jocelyn burst from the glen, shouting to the top of her voice, "Help! Help me!" She stumbled over her skirt, the green grass staining it as her knees skidded on the ground, but she recovered with surprising strength toward the soldiers who had now turned their horses in her direction.

"What is it, wench?"

Jocelyn hesitated, not wanting to set the soldiers on Alaric's men. "Demons!" she wailed hysterically. "Demons from hell!" The trained fighters burst into snickers of amusement as she met the first and seized the reins of his horse. "Help me, sir!"

"Damn you, wench, there's no such thing as demons!" The man fought to bring the startled animal under control and kicked her away.

"I'm lost, lost!" Jocelyn cried, her legs melting beneath her as she dropped to the ground. "Kidnapped from my wedding, chased by demons, and now assaulted by my lord's own men!"

"It can't be!" the captain of the guard derided, taking in her disheveled state. "If you're the Lady Jocelyn, then I'm Lord Rhys!"

Jocelyn pulled a straight face. "You don't look like him, sir," she replied uncertainly, hoping they'd think her afflicted by her ordeal. She very nearly felt so and justly, considering what she'd been through. "But if you doubt my word, ask the miller. He'll vouch for me!"

"We'll do just that, *milady*, if that's who you really are," the man added skeptically as he dismounted.

Yanked unceremoniously to her feet, Jocelyn was lifted up on the horse of the leader and carried back to the mill where its proprietor looked on. She mustered as much dignity as her circumstances would allow and matched the captain's disdain with her own.

"Ho, sir, tell these *hirelings* whom they treat like some common wench!"

Having been privy to her prior situation, the miller was obviously disconcerted, uncertain as to which answer the lady really wished. "Well, I'm not sure . . . I mean, in them clothes . . ."

"Tell them I am Lady Jocelyn of Bedford, kidnapped from her own wedding by hoodlums and held hostage until last eve, when I at last escaped!"

"Well, man, what say you?"

"There is yer missing bride, Captain, and a lot worse for the wear, I'd say, judgin' by the looks of her. What happened to ye, milady?"

Jocelyn ignored the man's question to deliver a smug look at the surprised officer. "And I shall tell Lord Rhys how gallant his men are, leaving me to escape on my own and then treating me like some tavern slut!"

"But, milady, you must admit you do not look yourself."

"Nor would you, sir, had you been through the hell I've lived these last two days. I long now with all my heart for a warm bath, a decent meal, and a soft bed."

"I imagine his lordship will hear your story before you see any," the captain told her, joining her on the horse. "He's been most vexed, although the capture of that Welsh thief has distracted him a whit."

"Atworth is not alone in that estate, sir!" Jocelyn

quipped sharply over her shoulder. The dreaded news of Alaric, however, undermined her show of aloofness. She leaned against the soldier defeatedly. Let them think what they will, she would need all her strength and reserve to face Rhys of Atworth without expending it beforehand sitting spine stiff and proper. She needed to buy time for Alaric until Phillip could intervene. Were he to remain the missing lord, then, when the time presented itself, she would fight like a tigress to free her handsome kidnapper ... or die trying.

Shouts of recognition greeted her as the entourage entered through the black alley into the inner bailey. Servants and villagers alike followed them to hear of the circumstances that left Lady Jocelyn the bedraggled sight that she was. Speculation as to who had actually abducted her had piqued everyone's curiosity from the smallest child to the most shriveled crone. The fact that she was back somehow instilled hope that the repression under which Bedford had suffered the last few days would end, for surely the overlord would lighten his hand now that his bride was returned.

Having stopped in the midst of the throng at the foot of the main gate which led into the storage rooms and cells of the lower floor, Jocelyn was helped off her horse with the respect demanded of her position. She straightened her weary shoulders, assuming as regal a stance as Lord Rhys of Atworth, who, surrounded by his stewards, emerged from the winding steps of the turret to meet them. His fair hair curled about his face, crowned with a rolled scarf of filigree which she was certain he compared as much as he dared to Edward's own royal headdress.

Lips curling in obvious distaste, he addressed her. "So, it seems my lost bride had found her way home."

"No thanks to your men, milord," Jocelyn retorted in kind. "I escaped on my own and the demons nearly took me back whilst I begged these *alleged men* at arms to come to my aid."

"*Demons?*"

"The lady was most *distracted* when we came upon her, milord. She was wailing like a banshee and dressed common as you see her now. We didn't know her at first and thought her daft when she said demons were on her heels."

Jocelyn nodded. She didn't miss the dubious look the captain at her side gave his lordship. "Aye, sir, wood demons! They screeched like owls and looked like dwarfs!" She turned and pointed at the soldiers. "*They couldn't see them, but I could.*"

Lord Rhys narrowed his gaze at her in suspicion. "It seems she's overwrought from her abduction. Perhaps once she is restored to her office and accustomed appearance, she will be less so." He snapped his fingers at the man closest him. "See the lady has a hot bath drawn for her in her chamber and let that simpering nurse of hers attend her. Then close off the inner bailey and fetch the priest! By God, I'll wed her this time with no interruption. What say you to that, milady?"

"*Another wedding?*" Jocelyn exclaimed with a blank look. "I would think one sufficient, milord, plain as it was." She brightened her face. "I would see my father now. It's strange he didn't come to greet me, but his aching joints do so plague him from time to time. Is he in the hall?"

Were circumstances different, Jocelyn might have giggled at the bemused expression on Rhys' face. At it was, she had to be satisfied that she had convinced him of her loss of wit. She stretched out her hand to the man. "Take me to my father, milord! I would have word with him."

The great hall at the top of the winding steps had been built in Norman times by Jocelyn's ancestors.

Beautiful stone arches ran its length, supporting the solar above where the women of the manor did their stitchery. The walls were hung with rich tapestries from the East, most sent as presents by Phillip during his ten-year sojourn there. Light came in through the overhead gallery which surrounded the room, from tall windows at the end of wall-deep barrel vaults decoratively outlined in a different color stone than the rest of the thick castle walls. The sole purpose being lighting and providing a masterful view of the hall below, it covered the smaller rooms accessed by similar arches on the first floor, the private quarters for family members.

"Well, where is he, sir?" Jocelyn demanded upon emerging from the turret. "I see no lord on the dais, only his hounds."

"He is resting, milady, as I suggest that you do . . . after your bath."

"Jocelyn child!"

Gwenith's delighted cry distracted Jocelyn from her charade. She turned in time to fall victim to a generous embrace which threatened to smother her.

"But you're a sight, dearest! What has happened to you?"

Jocelyn looked about, as if someone might overhear her, and whispered audibly in her nurse's ear. *"Demons!"*

Delight swiftly transformed into horror on the older woman's face. "Don't be talkin' like that, child. It ain't good to tempt what we don't understand."

" 'Twas not I that tempted them, woman. *They* came after me!"

"Dwarfs, she says," Rhys explained dryly.

Much as the servant was loath to believe Jocelyn's statement, she was even more so to acknowledge that of the man who had kept her locked in the tower room. Instead of either, she put her arm around Jocelyn's shoulder. "There now, dear, what you need is fresh clothing and some rest. You'll feel like a new woman then."

"What think you, sir?" the captain of the guard asked as Gwenith closed the door to Jocelyn's private chamber behind them.

His gaze still affixed to the planked passage, Lord Rhys scratched his chin thoughtfully. "I do not know, good knight, but I shall find out if she seeks to make me the fool or is one herself ere this day is out. Either way, she's to be my bride."

Jocelyn slept out of sheer fatigue while her bath was being drawn. Gwenith hovered over her like a mother hen, clucking and scolding if one of the servants made too much noise while they dumped warmed water into the wooden tub near the wall containing the hall's fireplace. When it was sufficiently deep enough to suit the matron, she gently shook her charge from her sleep on the soft comfortable bed to take advantage of it before the water cooled.

Answering only the most direct of questions, Jocelyn pretended to be distracted. She hated to worry Gwenith so, for it was clear the woman was convinced the abduction had robbed her of her wit. However, she had no intention of endangering anyone else she cared for, for she'd discovered in Gwenith's prattle that Ham also had been put in prison with the rogue who sought to steal her dowry. The dampness of the lower floor would play the devil with his aging frame, the servant went on, though few who remained in the castle had escaped some sort of persecution.

"Tried to make me tell what I couldn't," Gwenith snorted in disgust. She patted her ample girth and laughed. " 'Well, I don't know, milord,' I tells him, 'but if ye're set on bein' mean to old Gwenith, well I've enough store to go more than a few days without food.'

That's exactly what I said," she added at the surprised lift of Jocelyn's brow.

The tub required the girl to draw up her knees in order to sit in it and take advantage of the full height of the water. After remaining in it until the water cooled uncomfortably, Jocelyn reluctantly abandoned it for the brisk drying her servant gave her. Over her pink scrubbed skin, she donned one of her fine gowns of a cloth her father had chosen to match her eyes. She closed them and sighed, fingering the material which brought back fond memories.

"My dining dagger, Gwenith," she spoke up suddenly, turning to the woman brushing her hair expectantly. "Where is it?"

"In your chest, luv. I'll fetch it for ye as soon as I'm done untanglin' this wild mane of yours. I vow, ye look as if ye've tangled with a witch."

"Nay, demons I told you," Jocelyn insisted, keeping up her charade.

Gwenith heaved a resigned sigh. "All the same, I guess. Anyways, when Lord Rhys sees ye, he won't know it's the same girl that came ridin' in all bedraggled and dirty."

"As if I care."

Jocelyn drew back as the maid shook the silver brush that Phillip had sent his betrothed last year, along with his apology for postponing his return for a few more months. "You're a lady and all should know it, child. If there's any hope a'tall for this keep, it lies with you temperin' his lordship's heavy hand. You've the looks and the power to do it, don't ever let me hear it said that ye don't."

The dining dagger with its jeweled handle and case were also from Phillip. It had come for her sixteenth birthday, along with the tapestry behind the dais in the great hall with a beautiful picture of a white unicorn being hunted by princes. What wonderful stories she'd made up in her mind about that scene, as wonderful as the fantasies she had conjured of the man who sent it.

Her betrothed had showered her with expensive gifts since she came of age, as if to make up for his not returning for the arranged wedding. Yet how could she hold his noble pursuits against him? It only added to the glorious picture she had of him—handsome and dashing on a prancing steed. Now when she conjured her love's image, however, it was not the Lord of Inglenook, but Alaric, a Welsh lesser lord of Snowdonia.

She fastened the sheath which was also jeweled at her waist while on her shoulder Gwenith adjusted the gold broach Jocelyn had inherited from her mother's family. With little heed to the lovely woman who appeared before her in the huge gilded mirror mounted on a freestanding frame, Jocelyn suffered the last of Gwenith's ministrations, her mind already turning with ploys she might use to gain entrance to the dungeon to see the prisoner.

As it was, she needed none of them. Lord Rhys rose from her father's chair on the dais and met her in the center of the large room. There was a glimmer in his eyes, but Jocelyn was uncertain whether it was admiration or calculation. She extended him her hand as his due, which he lifted to lips that lingered on it. Oblivious to the noise of the servants setting up the tables for the noon meal, she met his gaze squarely, refusing to be intimidated as all others around him were.

"I've ordered a light repast to restore your strength until the main meal as your rest and bath have restored your beauty, *beloved,* after which I would have you accompany me to the dungeon."

Jocelyn cocked a single golden brown brow at him. "The *dungeon,* milord? Faith, is that how you expect to keep me?" She laughed, as if the idea were ludicrous.

"Do you think chains can keep the demons away?" She shook her head vigorously, her hair shimmering in the sunlight which flooded the room from the gallery above. "Nay, milord, 'tis the chapel where I shall sleep tonight. It's the only place safe, I fear."

" 'Tis a demon of the flesh, I would have you see, milady, one caught stealing within the keep."

"A thief in my father's house?" Twisting the slender hand still in Rhys' grasp, Jocelyn wove her fingers through his. "Show him to me, milord, that I may spit in his face for his audacity."

"But your food . . ."

"Can wait, sir. How could I eat without redressing a rat that would steal from its own nest? Is he one of ours?"

"He is Welsh, milady," the overlord answered, obliging his lady by leading her to the round corner stairwell.

"Welsh?" she scorned. "Well, show me any Welshman and I'll show you a thief. They're born to it, so I've heard. It's in their blood, from noblest to the lowest."

One hand in her escort's and the other clutching her skirts on the wedge-shaped steps leading down to the dungeon, Jocelyn braced herself for the meeting with Alaric. With only torches of rush dipped in pitch for light, it took a while for her eyes to adjust to the darker level and the smoke that filled it. Like walking into hell on Satan's own arm, she thought acidly, blinking away the stinging assault.

There were two men chained to the wall in the chamber the guard opened, but until Rhys moved a torch inside the room, it was hard to tell which was Alaric. Marching straight to the younger man, Rhys seized his dark hair and yanked his head up so that the flames revealed his bruised and bloodied features. Jocelyn's cry of horror strangled in her throat, and she coughed into the hand that went belatedly to smother it. Suddenly Rhys shoved the torch at the guard and yanked her closer.

"The lady seems to know you, sir."

Alaric forced the lesser of his swollen eyes open a crack. "Such a beauty, I'd remember," he slurred, as if his tongue too was swollen as well as parched. "She is mistaken."

Realizing her cough had not disguised anything, Jocelyn spat at the battered man. "Liar!" she accused, her voice rising to a hysterical pitch. "He is the man who carried me off, sir! No thief, but a kidnapper of the meanest nature!"

"But you said 'twas demons and dwarfs," Rhys reminded her, unimpressed by her theatrics.

"His accomplices were!" She should have slapped Alaric, but could not bring herself to inflict further abuse than he'd already suffered. "By God, I would drive this dagger into his black heart!"

Jocelyn whipped out the dining dagger and raised it at Alaric, but at the last moment whirled about and stabbed at Atworth's chest with all her might. At the same time Alaric kicked out from the wall, sending the startled guard sprawling backward, the torch rolling on the earthen floor away from him. He strained mightily at the confining chains to help the girl who had risked her life to free him, but Lord Rhys had dragged her out of his reach, wrenching the jeweled dagger from her hand cruelly and twisting her arm behind her so that she cried out in anguish and fell to her knees.

"I thought that fate had favored me overmuch with the capture of my wife's abductor and her miraculous escape, all within the span of the clock passing the same hour twice!"

"You killed my father, you bastard!" Jocelyn ground

out, refusing to give voice to the pain in an arm which felt as though it were being wrenched from its socket. "You betrayed us!"

"And you are lily white of the same, milady?"

"Let her be, Atworth. She knew nothing of our plot to kidnap her."

"But she would risk her life to save yours, Welshman? I find that hard to believe," Atworth growled. "Nay, I sense there is more here than is at first apparent."

"Phillip will come skewer your black soul with his sword, milord. He has escaped your hoodlums and makes his way here this very moment!"

"Silence, woman!"

Jocelyn felt the heat of Alaric's outrage before she even met his penetrating gaze.

"Your Phillip is dead . . . or so says the abbess at Dover. The wound he received in the escape would not cease to bleed, it seems."

"Damn you, is the abbess in your employ as well, Atworth?" Alaric challenged hoarsely.

Phillip dead? Jocelyn hardly noticed Atworth releasing her arm from behind her back to haul her upright. Then it was over, she despaired. There was no hope of rescue now that she had bungled her attempt so miserably.

"Alaric!" she whispered, her voice breaking. She tried to go to him, but Rhys held her back.

"What's this? Could it be you've cuckolded not one, but two prospective grooms?"

"Yes!" Jocelyn averred passionately. "So chain me to the wall as well, sir, for I would rather die with Alaric than live with you."

"Slut!" Rhys struck her cheek, sending her reeling against the wall in a daze.

Jocelyn dragged herself up, trying to focus on Alaric.

"My brave love." She cried out as she was seized by the shoulders and spun around. Her head struck the wall with the force of Atworth's forearm against her throat.

"Since you've as much as admitted you are no longer the innocent virgin, I see no need to await the priest's arrival to sample your obvious charms."

Unable to scream for the arm cutting off her breath, Jocelyn flinched at the rending sounds which bared her breasts to cruel fingers.

"Atworr..rth!" Alaric bellowed, pulling helplessly against the chains so that they cut into his skin without conscience.

The room whirled around, and she was slowly being sucked into a black whirlpool, haunted by a floating torch, her assailant's twisted face, and Alaric's fierce cries. Just as she felt herself giving into the senseless melee, she was shaken from it. Her lungs filled with a startled gasp that burned her throat, and she opened her eyes to see Lord Rhys staring down at her.

"You needn't think I would deprive either of you this sweet revenge, do you, milady?"

The floor had somehow replaced the wall, smoother, but just as cold at her back. The dagger she'd wielded against Atworth, flashed in the torchlight, and again she felt her gown surrendering to the superior strength of its steel. The cool damp air of the dungeon was suddenly smothered with the heavy weight of the overlord, which held her helpless to his loathsome fondling.

"Milord! Milord!" A voice that didn't belong penetrated the sickness that washed over Jocelyn and threatened to deny Rhys after all. "Milord, it's the King's messenger! His Majesty approaches even as we ..." The excited steward broke off in shock as his master shoved away from the dazed girl sprawled beneath him. *"Milord!"*

"Make her decent and lock her in her room!" Rhys

growled, rearranging the trousers he'd been tugging down in his fevered assault.

Jocelyn seemed to float upward, carried by unseen arms. As the dizzy fog took shape before her face, she saw Alaric and whispered his name. Then the room spun again, and this time, total darkness became the victor after all.

Chapter Seven

The fields beyond Bedford's walls were littered with tents belonging to the knights accompanying His Majesty King Edward. Their squires and stewards, however, occupied them the night before, for Lord Rhys of Atworth provided private chambers inside for his noble guests. Filled with a succulent feast which the overlord declared paltry to that planned for his wedding, the boisterous company had kept the minstrels and dancers at their best until the wee hours of the morning. Hence, preparations for the tourney the King requested between his knights in attendance and Lord Rhys' knights were off to a late start.

Nonetheless, Atworth was determined to give His Majesty a blood-stirring contest, even if it was on short notice. Servants had worked the better part of the night while the ale-and-wine-addled noblemen slept off their overindulgence in bed ... or wherever they had happened to pass out. So far, all had gone exactly as he'd planned, even where his future bride was concerned.

Rhys had found her weakness in the Welshman, the key to bending her to his will. His simple threat to execute Alaric of Snowdonia not only kept her in line but engaged her grudging company and help in the preparations, as well as solicited her concurrence with the story he told the King to explain the delay of the wedding to which His Majesty had earlier been invited. Her bruised cheek further collaborated the part about her abuse by the knaves, who had kidnapped her from the chapel on her wedding day, and her despondent demeanor was easily explained by the added tragedy of her father's murder by brigands in the night.

"The poor dear is so overwrought, I fear for her sanity, my liege," Atworth had confided after Jocelyn retired early the previous evening. "First her betrothed's death en route from the Holy Land, then her kidnapping, and now her father's brutal murder."

He was a good deal more convincing than his future bride had been in her earlier charade, but then, he'd had a lifetime of experience in deceit. Little ever came to one who waited for it, and he'd become impatient at an early age.

As he was now, he thought irritably, wondering what was taking the ladies so long to ready his bride for the tournament. He could hardly wait to see her reaction when she saw her precious Alaric dragged into the banner-bound arena. If she attempted to tell His Majesty the truth, no one would believe her. Even her devoted Gwenith questioned her sanity, Rhys thought smugly as the door to her chamber opened to admit the girl to the hall.

"Milady, His Majesty has already gone to the viewing box, and I fear you've kept him waiting."

"It takes time to cover bruises, milord," Jocelyn

whispered, her voice not having regained its volume since Atworth's vicious attack.

It pleased him, but she no longer cared. As long as he was pleased, Alaric lived. And as long as the King was their guest, the overlord had no time to torment his prisoner. That was all that mattered. There would be a chance to find another dagger, one which would keep well beneath her pillow until her husband came to her tomorrow night. She prayed it would be Atworth that died, but if not, it would be she. Once she married him, the overlord would have no further use of the influence of Alaric's safety on her.

Her kirtle of golden braided cord glistened in the sunlight, gathering a gown of broched cloth highlighted to match. Its pale green hue was contrasted by the tawny color of an undershift with sleeves tapered to corded laces at the wrists. A large cross of gold and silver lay upon her chest, strung from a chain about her neck. Jocelyn constantly fingered it with her free hand as she accompanied her future husband and his retinue to the stand beyond the outer bailey where villagers and noblemen alike gathered to watch the show.

With downcast eyes, she mounted the platform and knelt in homage to the King of all England and Britain. At his beckoning, Jocelyn took the chair to his right while Lord Rhys took the seat to his left. At the raising of the royal hand, the sound of trumpets filled the air and the pageant began. The lesser nobles paraded before the dais first, bearing their colors as proudly as the greater ones who followed. Yet for all the gaiety, Jocelyn's spirit could not be lifted. There was nothing to cheer, in spite of the crowd that roared at the spectacle.

The first of the matches, like the pageant, was carried on by the lesser knights whose wealth was in keeping with their skill. No amount of inherited moneys could win acknowledgment on the tournament field without the skill to accompany it. Money could not buy knighthood. It was earned for the most part on the battlefield in war or in the tournament arenas of Europe in times of peace, although, in some cases, it was granted by royal favor. Those foolish enough to meet a man beyond their experience rarely lived long enough to regret their error.

There being no fools among this gathering, however, there was more wounded pride than flesh after the first lots had been played out, and the winners prepared to battle the next level of warriors. The third rounds came with a roar of anticipation, for it was these for which everyone waited. That was when the champions of the earlier sorties would battle each other for the purse put up by Lord Rhys and the King. Gambling, both rich and poor, was rampant around the arena as the lots were drawn for the final matches. The king and his overlord no exception, they made their wagers freely.

One by one, the knights met, clashing in mid field, falling or leaping from their mounts to continue the meet with swords, and slashing it out until one yielded against the cheering of the winning speculators and the booing of the losers. There was nothing gallant or noble about it, Jocelyn derided, for the first time seeing it that way. While she had not been enthralled by such a spectacle before, it sickened her now. Seeing two men beat themselves bloody with the broadside of a blunted sword or knocking themselves off a running horse with an equally dull lance for sport had no appeal. But then, neither had life itself at present.

At last the champion and winner of the purse was determined: it was Lord Rhys' man, Derrick of Gascony. Unlike some of the earlier losers, who forfeited armor, steed and weapons to their victors, the King's man only lost the purse and earned the cost of repairing his armor. Gascony approached the dais to receive his prize from Edward, who congratulated him heartily.

"Well done, sir! It was a fine a meet as we've seen! My word, what entertainment! A tourney one day and a wedding the next! Milord, you do us great honor!"

" 'Tis you that does my future bride and I the honor, Your Majesty," Rhys conceded graciously. "But I would stay your attention for one more meet, granted, not as well put on as that which we've just seen, but guaranteed to be entertaining, nonetheless."

Edward was known for his love of the fight and it showed in his enthusiastic, "Then by all means, the feast will wait! Let us see it!"

Jocelyn, however, rose. "If you will excuse me, milords, I shall see to the setting of the supper."

"Nay, milady. I've planned this combat in your honor. What better way to punish the knave who kidnapped you from the chapel and enjoy good sport at the same time?"

"What?"

Against her will, Jocelyn followed the direction of Atworth's sweeping gesture to see Alaric brought into the dusty arena now cut like a freshly plowed field by the beating hoofs of the prancing charges. Her gaze returned to the overlord with slashing contempt. "You gave me your word!"

"Of course, beloved, and he will be punished ... here, before all." Atworth snapped his fingers. "Bring the prisoner forward!"

"He lies, Your Majesty!" Jocelyn declared, seizing the royal hand in her own. "He has practiced naught but treachery and murder from the start! It was by the hands of his men that my betrothed was kidnapped and murdered. If that was not enough, he has added my father's blood to his conscience and even now blackmails me into this marriage!"

"Those are harsh charges you make, milady." Edward

indulged her with royal patience. "Have you proof of them?"

Jocelyn looked to Alaric, but the young man held his tongue. Crushed by the overwhelming odds against her that he had predicted at the mill, she shook her head. "Nay, milord, none but my word."

"And mine, such as it is, Your Majesty," Alaric spoke up at last.

"The word of a madwoman and that of the man who made her that way!" Rhys scoffed. "What say, you Your Majesty? Shall we pursue our entertainment and carriage of justice or nay? The man is of sound build and skill, despite his bruises. How long will you give him before he falls to Gascony's sword?"

"I will make you an even more challenging wager, Atworth!" Alaric charged. "I will bet my life against the choice of the lady to choose her own husband!"

"Well, well, this does add teeth to the wager," Edward exclaimed excitedly. "Go on Atworth, take the bet!"

"Your Majesty, Alaric is in no shape to fight a trained knight!" Jocelyn pleaded, certain that the insanity of which she stood accused had infected them all.

"I challenge you, sir!" Alaric taunted the disconcerted overlord, squaring rebellious shoulders bared by his torn tunic.

Rhys laughed nervously. "He can't *challenge* me! He's a lowborn Welshman. A wager, yes, but a challenge can only be made by another knight."

"Then make better sport of the wager and knight me, Your Majesty. I have fought with the best of your warriors in the Holy Land these last ten years."

"Your boldness speaks well of you, sir," Edward agreed. "But tell us, who are you? What is your family name?"

"I am the son of Rowen ap Griffyn, cousin to the Prince of Wales himself."

"Traitors, Your Majesty! Let us do away with this nonsense and get on with the fight."

"You act as if you fear I might win, Atworth!" Edward lifted an equally challenging brow to the fidgeting Lord Rhys. " 'Twould make the wager more tasty."

"Then knight the thieving bastard!" Atworth hissed through teeth clenched tight as his fists. "If God himself were to back him, he'll not live long enough to know the honor much."

Edward rose and snapped his fingers. "A sword!" Instantly one of the men at arms produced a weapon and placed it in the royal hand. "Have I your word, sir, on the honor I am about to bestow upon you, that you will behave as your coming station will demand?"

"Aye, Your Majesty."

"Then unchain the man! I'll not knight him in bondage."

As the chains fell away, Alaric approached the dais and knelt low at the King's feet. Raising the sword, Edward lifted his voice to the heavens. "We bless this sword to the use of righteousness, from this hour on!" Solemnly the weapon was lowered to Alaric's shoulders with a light blow. "In the name of Saint George," the man announced, striking one, "and in the name of Saint Michael," he added, doing the same to the other. "Oh, Lord, who didst institute the order of knighthood for the safeguard of Thy people, may this man never commit unjust harm to anyone with this sword, or any other. I dub thee, Sir Alaric of Snowdonia, son of Rowen ap Griffyn and knight errant. Rise, sir and take thy weapon."

Jocelyn caught her breath as Alaric rose unsteadily, the fatigue and torment of his imprisonment telling in spite of his brave front. In the background, mixed roars of approval and disapproval rose from the onlookers as, gripping the rail of the dais, the prisoner straightened before the King. Upon kissing the sword, Edward handed it over to him, whereupon Alaric imitated his act reverently. The brief ceremony was sealed with a royal embrace.

"Now that this nonsense is out of the way, shall we begin?"

"By all means, Lord Rhys," Edward condescended, his dancing eyes betraying his enjoyment of the occasion. "We are ready." He turned to Jocelyn. "Will the lady grant a favor while the squires find outfitting for Sir Alaric and the heralds announce the joust?"

"I would, Your Majesty!" Ignoring Atworth's searing look, Jocelyn leaned over the rail and placed her cross pendant over Alaric's head. "God be with you, sir."

"And you, milady," he replied, bowing courteously.

With Jocelyn's endorsement, the onlookers cheered again, this time with little opposition, for they were beginning to understand the unusual turn of events. Upon the heralds further elaborating, they could not be quieted.

"Prepare yourselves for combat, good knights," the King shouted above the melee.

Jocelyn watched Alaric walk proudly to the steed brought about for his use, her heart fluttering and beating like the banners waving in the breeze. He was a seasoned warrior, but he was weak from his imprisonment . . . and while he'd fought with knights, that did not mean he was accustomed to battle armor. It took young men weeks to acquire adequate mobility in the heavy gear! She seized her bottom lip in her teeth as Alaric's knees nearly buckled under the weight of the hauberk slipped over his head. His ruddy complexion was frighteningly white, even at this distance away, she fretted.

No matter how they dressed this up, it was murder, and Edward was as guilty as Rhys in the plot!

So fervent were her prayers for the man now weighted down with the armor, that she barely heard the approaching horseman who rode through the crowd and approached the stand in full battle raiment. It was only when the dust he stirred threatened to make her sneeze that she looked up to see the source of it and heard the deep, booming voice which echoed from within the red-plumed helmet.

"Your Majesty, Lord Atworth, have I arrived too late to try my hand at the games?" The man was a fearsome creature, encapsulated in polished armor devoid of markings. His horse was no less so, appearing monstrous with peering eyes behind armor plate which served it well against the jab of a lance or a shower of arrows.

"And who are you, sir?" the overlord demanded in annoyance.

"A gamecock eager to test my mettle against any man . . . your champion, if you wish."

"My word, Atworth, is this ingenious turn of events part of your plan?" Edward marveled in delight. "A mystery knight, the knighting of a knave and novice . . ."

"The matches are over, save the one between yon novice and my champion," Rhys grumbled. "Now get off the field so that we may commence, sir!"

The knight twisted in the saddle in time to see Alaric drop to his knees in his attempt to mount the horse fully armed. "Will you have a match of skill or a bloodletting? The man is so weak, he looks about to faint."

The overload's temper snapped at the impudence in the stranger's remark. "Get off the damned field or I shall personally—"

"Your Majesty!" Jocelyn intervened, tugging at the

royal cloak in a wild renewal of hope. "If Atworth can choose a champion, why can't Sir Alaric? It would not speak well of your reputed fairness to favor one lord over another so. Good knight, will you fight as Sir Alaric's and my champion?"

" 'Twould be an honor, milady."

"Well, Your Majesty?" Jocelyn beseeched earnestly.

"I'll not stand for it!" Lord Rhys declared vehemently. "You go too far, milady!"

Edward rose from his chair and eased the outraged overlord down into his with a firm hand. "It is not for you to decide, milord. We are intrigued and would see the outcome. Give us a bet," he cajoled good-naturedly. "The Welshman dies regardless, and who is there for this girl to marry, save you? What say you?"

"Fifty pounds and the head of the knave on the front gate till the crows pluck his eyes out!" Rhys growled lowly.

"Done!" the King averred. "And if the mystery knight wins, we shall dispose of the man's head as we see fit. Fair enough, milady?"

Jocelyn could have sworn Edward winked at her but was too caught up in her concern for Alaric to pay it heed. The bet was not exactly what she wanted. Either way, she lost. She nodded mutely and watched as her newly appointed champion tried to make it clear to Alaric to clear the field above the clamor of the crowd. For a moment, she thought the brave Welshman was going to object but breathed in relief when he submitted to the squires to remove the armor he'd just donned. If this stranger were to win, at least she might plead royal mercy for Alaric.

Lances were first. Jocelyn tore her gaze from Alaric to the opposite end of the field where her champion, now wearing the necklace she'd given Alaric, sat astride his pawing gray stallion in a formidable stance. Gray!

she thought, her face brightening with the dawning of recognition. Like the sire to Jack Frost and the charger of Sir Phillip of Inglenook! She closed her eyes and offered a hasty prayer that this time she was not fooled, that Rhys had lied of Phillip's death, for Inglenook could convince the King of the merit of her story and vouch for Alaric ... *if he won.*

The chargers raced toward each other, their riders leveling their lances at the coming opponent as if they weighed nothing. Jocelyn flinched as the ring of armor filled the air. The Red Knight, whom she dubbed so because of his plume, twisted in the saddle from the blow of Gascony's lance, his own going wild in his attempt to keep from losing it.

The common spectators booed Gascony, apparently having tired of his consistent victories on the field. Besides, the hint of mystery surrounding the other knight, added to Jocelyn's favor of him, had earned him their support. Those of nobler blood watched in great interest with more restraint, lest the overlord take note of whom they offered visible favor.

The horses circled gracefully, nostrils flaring with their excited breath, and squared off again for another charge. At an imperceptible signal, they lunged forward into a full gallop. Gascony, confident from the near success of his last blow, leaned forward to drive the point of his lance into the armored plate covering his adversary's broad chest.

Dear God! she prayed in the deafening silence which muted the crowd and held it spellbound. Jocelyn wanted to close her eyes but could not. Just as it seemed Gascony would be successful, however, the Red Knight lifted his lance and parried the blow with such force that his opponent, holding on to his weapon tightly, was carried off his seat by the momentum of his moving horse and the opposite slam of the fierce parry. Again the people erupted in deafening enthusiasm.

The knight recovered his feet quickly by the time the gray stallion had circled for another charge and drew his sword to meet it. Lance dropped low, the Red Knight bore down on the footed one. Gascony hacked at the lance, which to his horror, was driven between his braced legs. As the gray galloped past, its rider carried the weapon upward like a vaulting pole. His opponent took to the air, tossed like a rag doll up and backward, before crashing to the ground, where he balled into a knot. The gray returned to him in a masterful pivot, stopping just short of trampling the fallen man. Its owner shoved tip of his lance at his victim's throat, pinning him soundly to the dirt, once again silencing the mad spectators.

His triumphant challenge echoed across the field. "Do you yield, sir?"

Gascony's raspy surrender gave rise to more than Jocelyn could bear to hold back. Leaping to her feet in delight, she joined the wild cheering. Whether the Red Knight was Phillip or some mercenary for hire mattered not. Her prayers had been answered, at least in part. Alaric's challenge had won her her choice of husbands and the chance to plead his cause with the king.

"I knew you would come, sir!" she called out to the knight as he waited for Alaric to approach the dais at his side.

"You know this man?" Rhys demanded.

Jocelyn beamed as she face her tormentor. "He is Phillip of Inglenook, my betrothed come to my rescue, sir!"

Rhys leapt to his feet to tower over her. "Inglenook is dead, you daft woman!"

"The lady is not daft, Atworth!" the Red Knight challenged, lifting off his helmet and handing it to Alaric.

"See for yourself that I am very much alive, no thanks to the men you hired to kill me while you stole my bride."

"And had my father murdered," Jocelyn gloated victoriously.

"You have no proof, neither of you!"

Phillip laughed and shook out his long beard, as dark and thick as his equally long hair. "But I do, sir! I spared a few scoundrels who would testify to your hiring them. My men are bringing them along in short time, but I hurried to the aid of my squire and betrothed, lest you spill more blood in your greedy quest for wealth and power."

"Seize this man!" the King shouted, pointing at Rhys.

Before the men at arms could draw their swords at Edward's command, however, much less use them, a dagger flashed from Rhys' belt and flew straight to Jocelyn's throat. She gasped as his other arm hooked her by the waist to pull her close to him. "Order them to back away, sire, or I will lay open the lady's white throat like a hog at slaughter."

"You may escape this fief, Atworth, but you'll not escape my kingdom," Edward warned him.

"Perhaps not, but I will take the lady's life before I go." He dragged her to the edge of the dais to get down when Alaric's voice rang out in challenge.

"Hold, Rhys, or I will put this arrow through your throat before you even think of using the blade!"

She glanced wildly to where Alaric now stood, an arrow mounted and drawn on a bow as tall as he. Where it had come from, she didn't know, much less could she account for the speed with which he'd brandished it while Rhys was distracted by the men at arms.

"Are you that good, *Sir* Alaric, that you would risk Lady Jocelyn's life, perhaps take it yourself?" Rhys snarled contemptuously at Jocelyn's ear, putting her squarely between them.

"Stay your hand, sir!" Edward cautioned. " 'Tis not worth the risk."

"Take the shot, Alaric," Phillip advised calmly from his horse, "before the lady *swoons.*"

Jocelyn hardly dared to breathe, so frozen was she by fear, but Phillip's hint did not pass her by. Expelling a groan, she let her head loll to the side, her knees buckling at the same time. The knife followed her as her captor tried to hold her up, and she felt the sting of its blade against her throat. Her strangled scream was punctuated by the hissing thud that echoed behind her ear and suddenly the body at her back went stiff. Jocelyn saw the knife as it hit the planked floor of the dais and raised her hand to her throat, fully expecting to find her life's blood covering it when she withdrew it for examination.

The crash of Rhys' body behind her released the pent-up terror that finally escaped her chest, taking with it her strength. As she collapsed, Edward caught her and shouted for the steward to send for her maid. Then, hoisting her in his arms gallantly, he stepped over Atworth's body without a second glance. His eyes glowed with the exhilaration of the contest of nerves.

"Excellent shot, sir! I would speak with you at your leisure, once the lady is attended."

"She's hurt?"

The alarm in Alaric's voice drew Jocelyn out of the sickening swoon, and she reached for him assuringly. "Nay, sir. I am but weak with relief."

Alaric's fingers were warm as he tested her neck. "God's breath, but that was close!" he swore to no one in particular, ending in a nervous laugh pitched uncharacteristically high for his deep baritone voice. "The blade but scratched her."

"Here, sir!"

Jocelyn raised up groggily as Alaric sunk briefly from her line of vision to be uprighted by the men at arms who caught him as he stumbled. "Alaric?"

Regaining his feet, her white-faced knight managed a sheepish grin. "I am but weak with relief, milady."

Chapter Eight

The day looked like a wedding day at Bedford. All those whom the imprisoned Lord Rhys had invited were there in their finest splendor. Gossip abounded in every corner, from within and without the embanked walls, of the events which had supplanted the overlord as groom with the rightful one. There were none who seemed in the least displeased. Indeed, it was as if a heavy cloud had lifted, allowing the bright sunshine to infect both noble and commoner to their very souls with joy. Even the Duke of Huntingdon had personally conveyed his deepest regret over the death of Jocelyn's father and his understanding of the incident which had led to the demise of twelve of his soldiers.

" 'Twas misfortune spawned by treachery all round!" he'd declared fervently at the feast following the tourney of the day before. "Who would have guessed Atworth had led so many astray?" To Jocelyn's astonishment, even his lady, sister to Rhys, agreed to the extent that she insisted assuming the role of the lady of the house, so that the bride might rest after the trials of the last few days.

Not that, nor her fatigue would permit Jocelyn more than a few hours' sleep at a time, even when she'd seen that Alaric had had all the care that was proper to give him. His front was as bold as his heart, but each time their gazes met, she sensed he shared the same guilt and frustration which made it difficult to address their rescuer in clear conscience—guilt over their betrayal of Phillip's trust and frustration over the hopelessness of their situation. Even with Alaric's knighthood, Inglenook was her promised. It was expected by all, from king to peasant, that she would marry him and honor her late father's arrangement.

After tossing and turning in her bed, having excused herself earlier after the evening repast to rest, Jocelyn had finally donned a silk-lined cloak and intruded on the boisterous celebration the groom shared with royal company by asking for a private audience with the newly arrived knight. Phillip's face had born a ruddy glow from the ale, and his temperament was just as bright when she opened the door to her chamber to receive him.

"I have sworn my maid to silence, milord, so that we might speak frankly to each other, yet maintain propriety. Gwenith would have her tongue cut out, ere it repeat a word we say."

" 'Tis great compliment your mistress gives you," Phillip addressed the woman sitting unobtrusively in the window seat under the barrel-vaulted arch. "Tho' the need for such secrecy, now that all is out, bewilders me."

"Not all, milord," Jocelyn whispered nervously. 'I cannot marry you in good faith until I confess the rest."

Then and there, she told him how, against their mutual wills, she and Alaric had fallen in love; how, in spite of his fervent denial, she had believed him to be her betrothed, the writer of the wonderfully romantic letters she'd received over the last few years since she'd come of age and sought his arms for comfort upon hearing of her father's brutal murder.

" 'Twas as much like seduction as my inexperience would afford, sir, but his tenderness of heart reminded me much of you. Even that which he called me after our moment of weakness was the same. So upset was he, when it was done, that he marched to his own death out of guilt. Even when he had the chance to win his pardon, he asked naught to save himself, but that I be free to choose my own husband . . . which, of course, is you, milord," she said humbly, "if you will still have me in the light of my confession. Such is my gratitude for your saving Alaric's life that I would do my utmost to be a good wife to you without complaint."

Phillip's answer should have lightened her heart, but all it lifted was her guilt. "Milady," he said, taking her hand to his lips to brush her knuckles reverently. "Your purity of heart does you credit, for that which a person is lies in the spirit, not in the physical which can deceive. What I have heard makes me anticipate the morrow all the more." And then he was gone, the closing of the door behind him sealing her pardon and her fate.

The memorial mass, held for her father before the wedding, was sufficient explanation for her eyes, which were swollen with crying rather than with the brightness expected of a bride as she approached the altar of the small chapel on the royal arm of King Edward. The entourage at the altar reminded Jocelyn of the last time she walked up the stone aisle between the scant rows of plain benches, but this time, the right groom, for all intent and purpose, stood at Father Timothy's left with his fellow knights in attendance.

No kidnapper could force a horse into the chapel this time to keep her from avoiding her duty, for there was a thick cluster of people, who afforded just enough room for the bride to pass, gathered within to watch the affair. The one man she would gladly have stood now at Phillip's side, bedecked in a rich and vibrant blue cloak over lighter velvet breeches and a white tunic. He stood solemn, his face not nearly as gruesome as it had been when she first saw him in the dungeon, but handsome in spite of the healing red cuts and yellowing bruises.

Grateful for the thin filigree veil, which one of the neighboring ladies had loaned her, Jocelyn stepped up to the altar and stared straight ahead at the icons beyond the priest. She didn't want Alaric, who was so brave, to see her cowardly tears . . . not just yet.

"Children of God," Father Timothy began after clearing his throat, "we are gathered on this blessed day to unite two people in love and in the sacred bond of holy matrimony. What say you to this end, sir?"

At the priest's prompt, Edward stepped forth with Jocelyn still on his arm. "So I give thee, this our daughter, to honor and wife . . . and to half of thy bed, of locks and keys, of every third penny and all the right which is hers after the law."

Jocelyn could not help the trembling of her hand as the King gave it over to Phillip, nor could she see beyond her veil. She inhaled deeply to contain the threatening explosion of emotion of which the tears were only the surface.

"And I, Alaric of Snowdonia, accept her to honor and wife and accept all obligation that comes with this pledge for as long as God sees fit to give me breath."

Jocelyn raised her startled gaze to the man who had somehow taken Phillip's place amidst the sudden outburst of whispers which filled the tiny church. Not daring to trust her ears, she lifted up the edge of her veil to peek in disbelief at Alaric's smiling face.

"So I give thee, milady, *my* wedding gift," she heard Phillip declare loudly above the joyous beating of her soaring, winged heart.

"But—"

"Milady," Inglenook explained patiently, "I leave at the end of the week to return to the Holy Land, where I shall pledge my life to the Order of the Knights Templar. I was on my way to tell you in person when Atworth launched his treachery. It was my full intention to knight this smitten squire, who, at my request, had too well carried on my suit by letter, and propose him to take my place."

"You did write those letters!" Jocelyn exclaimed, glaring out from under the thin material half-cocked over her face. "Why . . .?"

Alaric silenced her indignant outburst with a brush of his lips. "Will you stay the ceremony with your questions, *light of mine eyes,* or shall we get on with it?"

Jocelyn's half-laughed and half-cried, *"On,* milord!" giving rise to titters of amusement behind them, but she didn't care in the least. She let the veil drop properly into place. Let them think her the overenthusiastic and wanton bride, for that was exactly what she was! She would have this ceremony done and over, lest fate rob her of this promise of paradise.

"Wilt thou, Alaric of Snowdonia, take this woman as wife in the eyes of God and these people?"

"Aye, I will."

"Then place thy ring upon her finger and claim her so."

Again Jocelyn was plagued by tears, but she felt the confirmation of the ring slip over her finger and the tender kiss that accompanied its presentation.

"And you, Lady Jocelyn of Bedford, will you accept

Alaric's claim to you, to half your bed, your lands, and buildings with all locks and keys, and pledge your faith to him till death shall part you?"

"Aye, I will!" With shaking fingers, Jocelyn withdrew the ring which had belonged to her grandfather from her right middle finger and slipped it onto Alaric's left hand.

Father Timothy's dour and belated, "Then place the ring on his finger in token of your acceptance and submission," flushed her cheeks with a becoming blush which burned beneath the veil as the undaunted priest proceeded to wrap his stole over their joined hands for the closing prayer. "Let the yoke she is to bear be a yoke of love and peace . . ."

Yoke? Jocelyn echoed incredulously as the holy man went on. If the happiness she felt in her heart was a yoke, then it was a light one which she could bear forever. Now all was right and fitting, save the absence of Lord Randolf. Yet, as the light above the altar filtered in through the small bits of patterned and colored glass filling the narrow window, Jocelyn felt deep in her heart that her father was indeed there and smiling over the scene as only he could do.

She smiled back, unaware that the prayer had ended until Alaric turned her toward him and lifted her veil to reveal the sparkling green eyes he vowed to treasure forever. With the permission of the priest, he leaned down and tenderly kissed the diamond droplets spilling from them, praying none but those born of joy would ever touch her blushing cheeks again. While it was unseemly for a man to express his emotions in the same way, he nonetheless conveyed all that abounded within his chest when he claimed her lips as her husband, her lord, but more than all, her love for a lifetime.

FEEL THE FIRE IN CAROL FINCH'S ROMANCES!

BELOVED BETRAYAL (2346, $3.95)
Sabrina Spencer donned a gray wig and veiled hat before blackmailing rugged Ridge Tanner into guiding her to Fort Canby. But the costume soon became her prison—the beauty had fallen head over heels in love!

LOVE'S HIDDEN TREASURE (2980, $4.50)
Shandra d'Evereux felt her heart throb beneath the stolen map she'd hidden in her bodice when Nolan Elliot swept her out onto the veranda. It was hard to concentrate on her mission with that wily rogue around!

MONTANA MOONFIRE (3263, $4.95)
Just as debutante Victoria Flemming-Cassidy was about to marry an oh-so-suitable mate, the towering preacher, Dru Sullivan flung her over his shoulder and headed West! Suddenly, Tori realized she had been given the best present for a bride: a night of passion with a real man!

THUNDER'S TENDER TOUCH (2809, $4.50)
Refined Piper Malone needed bounty-hunter, Vince Logan to recover her swindled inheritance. She thought she could coolly dismiss him after he did the job, but she never counted on the hot flood of desire she felt whenever he was near!

Available wherever paperbacks are sold, or order direct from the Publisher. Send cover price plus 50¢ per copy for mailing and handling to Zebra Books, Dept. 4198, 475 Park Avenue South, New York, N.Y. 10016. Residents of New York and Tennessee must include sales tax. DO NOT SEND CASH. For a free Zebra/Pinnacle catalog please write to the above address.